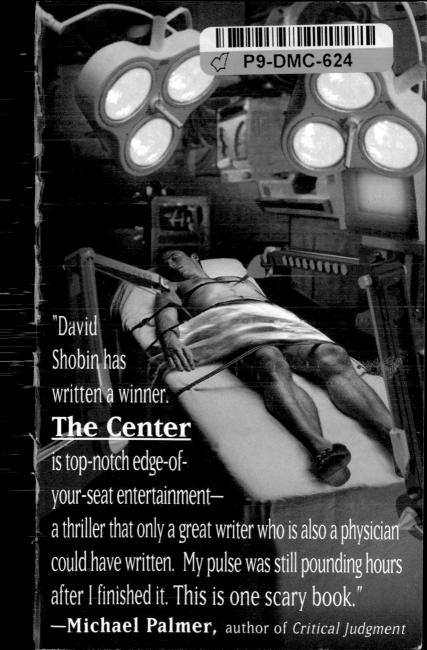

P9-DMC-624

"David Shobin has written a winner. **The Center** is top-notch edge-of-your-seat entertainment— a thriller that only a great writer who is also a physician could have written. My pulse was still pounding hours after I finished it. This is one scary book."

—Michael Palmer, author of *Critical Judgment*

The little girl was emerging from stupor when the autobot reached the incinerator room. Her heavy lids struggled to open as her body metabolized the anesthetic. Pulling up in front of the incinerator aperture the autobot inserted its adapter into the receptacle and relayed digital instructions. The heavy door slid open.

The incinerator had a metal specimen cradle not dissimilar to a fireplace grating. She remained unaware of her surroundings as the autobot slowly moved her into the oven. She did, however, perceive something cold against her back. Her vision gleamed weakly through the fog of her consciousness. She feebly pursed her lips, trying to force sounds that would not come. On the oven wall beside her head, a small pilot light flickered ominously . . .

THE
CENTER

DAVID SHOBIN

OUACHITA TECHNICAL COLLEGE

St. Martin's Paperbacks

NOTE: If you purchased this book without a cover you should be aware that this book is stolen property. It was reported as "unsold and destroyed" to the publisher, and neither the author nor the publisher has received any payment for this "stripped book."

For Rick, Jon, and Jill.
May your ordeals bear no resemblance to those
depicted here.
Love, Dad

ACKNOWLEDGMENTS

The author would like to thank Donna Henry and Deanna Gebhart for their help and technical assistance.

For advice and support with personal dilemmas, the author is grateful to Jim Byrne, Bob Kaplan, Jerry Levin, Bob Riley, and Jerry Garguilo.

Thanks also to Henry Morrison for sticking with me through lean times.

THE CENTER

Copyright © 1997 by David Shobin.

All rights reserved. No part of this book may be used or reproduced in any manner whatsoever without written permission except in the case of brief quotations embodied in critical articles or reviews. For information address St. Martin's Press, 175 Fifth Avenue, New York, NY 10010.

ISBN: 0-312-96167-7

Printed in the United States of America

St. Martin's Paperbacks edition/September 1997

St. Martin's Paperbacks are published by St. Martin's Press, 175 Fifth Avenue, New York, NY 10010.

10 9 8 7 6 5 4 3 2 1

PS
3569
H567
C46
1997

Prologue

THE CENTER WAS a world unto itself. Innovation was the watchword of the day. If there were a breakthrough, a technological advancement, or a new medical concept, it would be found at the remarkable edifice known as the Center.

Patient charts, for example, were unknown at the Center. Information and data were transmitted electronically from the computer mainframe to peripheral terminals, which executed the digitalized instructions. That day, the order for patient transport was routed to a relay junction on the sixth floor, which replaced the traditional nursing station. A service robot was dispatched and motored silently down the corridor to the patient's room.

From her bed, the four-year-old girl peered listlessly at the approaching autobot. Stealthy in appearance, the ominous black rectangle would ordinarily terrify a young child. But this little girl, like all patients under the age of fifteen, had been sedated from the moment of her admission. Her pale blue eyes, dull and glassy, reflected a peculiar apathy in an otherwise haunted expression.

Soon, after the child had been transferred to the cool, green sheet of the OR table, the autobot returned to its station. In spite of all the mechanical activity occurring within, the gleaming operatory was largely silent, save for a faint whirring as robotic arms raised and lowered. Like human eyes, the optical sensors were dependent on light. A large overhead spotlight clicked on, outlining the child in its beam.

She squinted in the harsh glare. Spots danced before her eyes, and the shimmering subliminal image of real people floated upward from her retina, allaying her fear, prompting a singsong verbalization.

"I'm having my tonsils out," she said, the words hoarse and imprecise. "I can have ice cream tonight." She lifted her arm toward a softly flickering apparition. "Are you . . . are you . . ." For several seconds her hand wavered there before slowly falling back to the mattress.

Beside her head, a small nozzle with a two-millimeter aperture silently began to emit a jet of colorless gas. The volatile anesthetic, which customarily had an odor like cleaning fluid, was cloaked in the fruity disguise of cherries. Within fifteen seconds, the last opaque glimmer had left the child's eyes, replaced by a leaden, obtunded stare. In short order, an IV was begun and a pediatric endotracheal tube inserted.

The traditional pre-surgical routine consisted of prepping and draping the operative field to reduce the risk of bacterial contamination. In a tonsillectomy, the operative field—the throat—could not be made antiseptic, since it normally teemed with bacteria. Each of the Center's OR's had a technically sophisticated prepping robot equipped with scrubbers and spraying devices. As the little girl's level of anesthesia deepened, the autobot neared the operating table and briefly hesitated. Then its automatic arm lifted the pediatric gown and dowsed the child's abdomen with antiseptic.

When it had finished, the gleaming artificial surgeon motored into position. Resembling some multi-armed Hydra, its numerous mechanical limbs could perform many functions simultaneously, eliminating the need for assistants.

The surgical instruments had been delivered before the patient arrived. All of a sudden the waiting tonsillectomy instruments were replaced by a different tray. Each of the stainless steel sets had an unusual bar code, which the surgical robot scanned. Yet the tray still bore the manufacturer's logo, which read: ENDOSCOPY, GYN, BASIC. To all appearances, the last-minute substitution seemed a completely random act. But there was nothing haphazard about it.

Everything that occurred in the Center followed a precise choreography. The final results were still produced by machines that complied with fundamental principles of physics and electromagnetism. Yet however straightforward the outcome, there was nothing direct about the reasons that now lay behind it. For understanding, whether of method or motive, was a human quality, a characteristic that still eluded the most sophisticated machines. And so a grand but incomprehensible design unfolded from the very heart of the Center, where a powerful computer obeyed the software of its silicon soul.

In the operating room, the overhead spotlight switched off. The room seemed irretrievably black, heavy and mutinous, dark as death. On the operating room table, the girl remained quiet, in steely anesthetic torpor. Her endotracheal tube had been removed. In the darkness, the sound of her ponderous inhalations reverberated through the air in coarse and jagged breaths.

The main video terminal came to life in shades of dazzling blue. There was something soothing in the rich, organic tones that lent the room an undersea quality. Cast in its bluish glow, the girl's partially gowned torso seemed pale and dreamlike, trapped between life and death. Three small Band-Aids on her abdomen were the only evidence of her surgery.

The sudden lettering on the monitor was incandescent, lengthening into a scintillant word-string that spelled out a frightening message. PROVISIONAL ANATOMIC DIAGNOSIS, it began. MALFORMATION, MYOCARDIAL, ATRIO-VENTRICULAR CONDUCTION SYSTEM. It was an unequivocal postmortem description of a congenital cardiac abnormality for an autopsy not yet performed. There was no one in the room to appreciate the fact that the description bore no relation to the young patient on the operating table.

DISPOSITION, the wording continued: CREMATION.

The OR doors opened. An autobot silently wheeled into the room, coming to rest parallel with the operating table. Hydraulic transport arms extended. In incremental up-and-down adjustments, they slid under the girl's still body, preparing to lift. Obeying an internal signal, the autobot slowly swung the obtunded child up and over, until she lay atop its transport mattress. The autobot paused, awaiting further instructions.

Someone was watching.

In a distant location, hidden eyes observed a remote monitor, taking in everything that occurred. All was proceeding as planned. The figure's arms were clothed in a white lab coat. Beyond its starched sleeves, carefully manicured hands were poised over a computer keyboard. After a momentary pause, the fingers typed the word "execute," then hit the ENTER key. On the monitor, the autobot motored away in silence.

The Center had no true crematorium. What it did have, in a small room between the lab and the morgue, was a medium-size incinerator for disposal of the larger human body parts. The Karlson Model 12 was a four-foot-high rectangle resting on a slab base. When properly sealed, its gas-powered furnace could generate 1,700 degrees Fahrenheit.

The Karlson was a necessary concession to the past, utilizing technology that was eighty years old. In state-of-the-art hospital pathology labs, there was rarely the need for disposal by burning. Rather, when the pathological exam of a spleen or a lung had been completed, what was left of the organ was quickly decomposed in an industrial microwave oven. The residual debris was funneled to a high-speed garbage disposal, where it was rapidly pulverized and flushed down the drain.

But on rare occasions, when a specimen was exceptionally large, such as an entire leg, the incinerator was used. Its intense heat could reduce the largest specimen to fine, powdery ashes in less than an hour. The Karlson's physical dimensions made it ideal for a four-year-old child.

When installed in the Center, the incinerator had been modified and upgraded with computerized controls. It could be remotely operated from the computer center or externally activated by a service robot. A receptacle located beside the traditional manual controls housed an RX-32 cable interface for inputting commands.

The little girl was emerging from stupor when the autobot reached the incinerator room. Her heavy lids struggled to open as her body metabolized the anesthetic. When the autobot entered the room, the door closed behind it. Pulling up in front of the incinerator aperture, the autobot inserted its adapter into the receptacle and relayed digital instructions. The Karlson's heavy door slid open.

The incinerator had a metal specimen cradle not dissimilar to a fireplace grating. She remained unaware of her surroundings as the autobot slowly moved her into the oven. She did, however, perceive something cold against her back. Her vision gleamed weakly through the fog of her consciousness. She feebly pursed her lips, trying to force sounds that would not come. On the oven wall beside her head, a small pilot light flickered ominously.

The autobot withdrew its adapter, triggering the incinerator's digital starting clock. It showed fifty-nine seconds, then fifty-eight. The autobot swiveled one hundred eighty degrees on its wheeled axis before silently leaving the room.

Growing more alert, the little girl stirred. The darkness was thick about her. "Maks?" she slurred. "Maks!"

Outside, the timer had reached forty-two seconds.

She rolled heavily onto her side. Banging her head on the incinerator sidewall, she began to whimper. She was cold and frightened, and her stomach hurt. Her sister told her she would be there when she woke up, and she wasn't there. Chin quivering, the little girl groggily sat up.

She reached out and touched unyielding walls all about her. She thought she was trapped in some sort of box. It was cold and claustrophobic, enclosed on all sides but one. A dull, grayish light outlined the open end. The dark confinement was scaring her, and her lips turned down in a frightened child's grimace.

The clock was down to nineteen seconds and counting.

In her mounting anxiety, the light was a familiar ally. She moved with awkward, leaden clumsiness toward what little she could see, crawling toward the opening on knees and elbows. Her progress was painfully slow and unsteady. Finally she was drawing abreast of the boxy perimeter when there was a click, immediately followed by the hum of an electric motor. Ten seconds remained. The door of her would-be tomb automatically began to close.

She was panic-stricken. The idea of being sealed up in a blackened, hostile chamber was overwhelming. She began to scream uncontrollably. But as her terror increased, so too did her inner spark and drive. An instant before the door closed entirely, she alertly grabbed its rubber-rimmed leading edge. The door's progress abruptly stopped. A laser safety sensor, designed to detect impeding foreign objects, had caught her small fingers in its beam. It signalled the electric motor to shut down.

She quickly drew her fingers back. The incinerator door remained not more than a quarter inch ajar, barely enough to admit the faintest light. But it was sufficient to indicate the freedom denied her. In the icy grip of fear, the child-turned-captive shrieked heartbreakingly and began to flail helplessly at the door to her prison. She was convinced that if she could only make someone hear her, she would be rescued. But it was not to be. Her juvenile tantrum, charged with fright and fury, lasted ten minutes. When it subsided, the little girl sank onto her haunches—breathless, sobbing, and spent.

Hours later, in the immutable darkness, she lay on her side, cheeks wet with tears of neglect and lament. Exhausted, wavering between sorrow and slumber, she alternated whimpering with sucking her thumb. She was numb, beyond terror. Every so often she was roused by a faint breeze which wafted through the slender opening to her cell.

She desperately had to go to the bathroom. Her underpants were gone, and all she wore was the thin hospital gown. While she lay there yearning for her sister, she was startled by a sudden humming sound. Stale air began rushing past her. Craning her neck in the near-darkness, she could make out a vague light from what had been the blackest reaches of her confinement. Curious, she rolled onto her stomach.

Twice a day, whether the incinerator had been used or not, it automatically vented itself for ten minutes. Fine, accumulated debris and floating particulate matter were forcibly egressed through a twelve-inch-wide galvanized pipe built into the oven's rear wall. The ductwork twisted for thirty feet before reaching the building exterior. Despite its serpentine course, when the vent was opened to the outside world, enough light streamed back through the conduit to be detected by the human eye.

The little girl grew curious. Right behind her was something she hadn't noticed before—a sort of hole in the wall that resembled a narrow tunnel. Air was rushing into it, and an impossibly dim light came from somewhere in the distance. She extended her neck turtlelike and peered into the recess. She couldn't make out a thing. Yet the light remained, attracting her like a barely perceptible beacon.

Repressing her cries, she wriggled head-first into the aperture. It was a surprisingly gutsy act for a four-year-old, but she was no ordinary child. She had courage and tenacity far beyond her years. And she was desperate. Behind her lay nothing but fear and abandonment.

She had gone only a few feet when she came to a bend in the ductwork. After a moment's hesitation, she rounded the corner and was rewarded with measurably brighter light. Her eyes widened with hope. As her anticipation increased, so did her speed. Knee-to-elbow, her lizardlike movements clattered noisily through the narrow pipe. In her eagerness to escape, she couldn't detect the mounting strain her weight was causing in the thin ductwork.

If evenly distributed to all fours, her forty pounds could easily have been absorbed by the galvanized sheeting. But as she lumbered headlong, it was more often dispersed to two limbs, rather than four. The slender ductwork support brackets, designed to sustain little more than the weight of air and dust, began to bulge at their attachments.

The weakest point in a ventilation system are the joints beyond a right-angle turn. Plunging forward with abandon, the little girl raced wildly past another corner toward the tantalizing illumination. The heel of her palm struck the meager sheetmetal beyond the seam. With a sudden rip, the ductwork unexpectedly gave way beneath her weight.

She screamed, plunging headlong through the opening. Her small torso did a midair somersault before she landed heavily on her back. The wind was knocked out of her. In that moment between clarity and unconsciousness, all her senses became alive for one last instant. She was in a lighted room, and she thought she smelled food. And then her consciousness receded; but in the twilight before total darkness, Christine Lassiter knew she was safe.

Chapter One

"DR. DUNSTON, THIS is service. I have Porthaven ER on the phone. Can I patch?"

"What time is it?"

"Five after two."

"In the morning?"

"Yeah."

"Sure. Patch away."

"Go ahead, Porthaven."

"Dr. Dunston? This is O'Reilly in Porthaven ER. We've got a really bad four-year-old MVA, and we wonder if you could come in and take a look."

"How bad?"

"Shocky. She's got about forty percent third-degree burns, a compound fracture of the right tibia, and some sort of abdominal or thoracic trauma. Dr. Pardanani thinks it's a flail chest. They've done films and labs, and the kid's going right to the OR once she's stabilized."

"Do they have anesthesia and a team?"

"On their way."

"Give me fifteen minutes."

With an emergency of that severity, there was no time to shower. Dunston was quickly out of bed and into his clothes. Less than five minutes after he awakened, he was

in his car, heading west. At that time of night, with little
or no traffic, the hospital was a scant nine minutes away.
Soon his car careened into the ER lot, coming to rest next
to an ambulance whose red-and-white lights still blinked
ominously.

He caught up with the gurney as it was being wheeled
to the elevator. Dunston grasped the raised metal siderail
and joined the procession whisking the child away. As they
hurried down the corridor, he made a careful visual assessment. The child was pre-comatose, barely conscious. Staring blankly past sunken lids, her clouded gaze was fixed
on nothing. Most of her hair was singed off, leaving random islands of short brown tufts. Her arms and legs appeared to have suffered most in the fire: hurriedly covered
with a pasty smear of Silvadene cream, they were crusted
with a blackish eschar interspersed with patches of denuded
blisters, wet with weeping serum. Her lower left leg was
encased in a transparent vinyl cast, through which jagged
shards of white bone were clearly visible. An IV dripped
into her right arm, and an endotracheal tube was already in
place, attached to a portable respirator.

As the entourage paused at the elevator, the staff greeted
Dunston with strained hellos. Dunston lifted the thin gown
and took in the splotchy, raspberry-colored welt covering
the child's skin from sternum to umbilicus. Each time the
respirator cycled, the thorax expanded asynchronously,
with the right side rising while the ribs on the left remained
flat.

"Seat belt injury?" he asked, pointing to the ecchymosis.

"Probably," said O'Reilly. "It looks like it wasn't put
on right. Must have hit the seat's cross-bar, too."

"What's with the burns, gasoline?"

"We think so. A gas tank explosion."

"Christ, what a nightmare. Any family, parents?"

"Don't know."

"Terrific. These her films?"

"Yep. All yours."

As they reached the OR, he took the x-rays to a nearby viewbox while the transport team moved the child to a ready operating table. The OR nurses had recently arrived and were busily opening and counting sterile instruments. In the background, the anesthesiologist questioned the ER physician about IV fluids and lab data.

"Jesus," said Dunston of the films. "What a mess."

"How's it look, Chad?" asked the anesthesiologist. "A pneumo?"

"Yeah, on the left. But she's also got a chestful of guts. Must have an eventration of the diaphragm, plus a half-dozen busted ribs. I wouldn't be surprised if her spleen took a hit, too. We're going to need blood, lots of blood."

"Four units are on the way," said the OR circulating nurse.

"Who's the orthopod on call?"

"Nichols. His service is beeping him."

"How're her reflexes, Rich?" he asked the anesthesiologist.

"Basically good. No sign of cranial trauma."

"They didn't do a CT, by any chance?"

"No time. What're you going to start with, Chad?"

Dunston was now at the child's side, helping remove the spattered gown. The small girl looked pathetically frail. Dunston's trained fingers walked gingerly across the injured abdomen and trunk, searching for telltale diagnostic clues. He didn't like the doughy bulge in the upper abdomen. "There could be a liter of blood in her belly. And that bowel's got to come out of her chest. I'll do a quick laparotomy, stick the guts back where they belong, and sew up the diaphragm. Run the bowel, check the spleen, that sort of thing. See if anything else is ruptured."

"How about a chest tube?"

"First I've got to stop the bleeding. Then I'll place the tube and debride the burns. All you have to do, Richie," he said to the anesthesiologist, "is keep the kid alive."

A bare bones trauma team was comprised of four people—surgeon, anesthesiologist, scrub nurse, and circulating nurse. Aware of the urgency, each of them worked furiously as several ER personnel lingered in the background, paralyzed by ghoulish curiosity. With the anesthesiologist drawing up injectable drugs and placing EKG leads, the circulator gently prepped the child's abdomen with brownish iodinated antiseptic. The scrub nurse, already gowned, was finishing her sponge and instrument count as a capped and masked Dunston vigorously lathered at the scrub sink. After an abbreviated three-minute scrub, he walked into the OR, his uplifted forearms shedding bubbles of soap.

The scrub nurse handed him a towel and then helped him gown and glove. Together, they applied sterile drapes to the operating field, effectively covering their young patient, leaving only a small portal of skin.

"Up and down, Dr. Dunston, or subcostal?"

"Vertical midline. I'll need all the exposure I can get. How's she doing, Richie?"

"She could use a little help. She's taching like crazy, and it's all I can do to keep her pressure over sixty."

"You giving her plenty of fluids?"

"Any more and she'll drown. They gave her half-crystalloid, half-colloid in the ER, and I'm pouring in Ringer's until the blood gets here."

"How's her oh-two sat?"

"It's all I can do to get it to ninety." He eyed an ominous blip on the cardiac monitor. "Can you get started, Chad? This could turn cruddy any second."

Dunston's practiced hand made a vertical incision from sternum to umbilicus, slicing through skin and subcutaneous tissue. Opening the fascia, he exposed the peritoneum, whose purplish hue hinted at internal bleeding.

"Hemoperitoneum," he said flatly. "I'll need a Poole sucker."

His meticulous opening of the peritoneum was greeted by a gush of plum-colored hemorrhage. Dunston quickly inserted the suction tip and aspirated a copious amount of blood and clots. As he widened his peritoneal incision, the already rapid beeping on the cardioscope accelerated, a staccato warble. Dunston hesitated, his startled eyes immediately diverted to the waveforms on the oscilloscope.

"V-tach," said the anesthesiologist, a tense edge in his voice. "She's got no hemoglobin. Christ, we need *blood*."

"Does she have a pulse?"

"Barely."

"You going to give her lidocaine?"

"What do you think I'm drawing up? I just hope it'll do the trick until those red cells arrive. Do your surgeon stuff, Chad. Please, buy me some time!"

As Dunston started operating, a shrill alarm sounded on the cardioscope. The new pattern had degenerated into menacing, up-and-down complexes.

"Jesus," muttered the anesthesiologist. "She's in fib! Get me the defibrillator!" he screamed to the circulator. "And I've got to have that blood *now!*"

The child's heart had ceased beating effectively. The severely damaged organs were no longer being perfused. The team's previous hurried deliberation became a rushed frenzy as what had been an urgent situation now bordered on catastrophe. The once-salvageable situation was complicated by severe loss of blood and its components, as red blood cells accumulated in the traumatized abdomen and serum oozed through burned capillaries. Unless they could get blood into the child quickly, their success at resuscitation would require a miracle.

Dunston placed a moist towel over the incision and helped rip off the drapes, exposing the fragile chest. The defibrillator paddles had to be applied to bare skin. The nurse ran in with the crash cart and quickly plugged the defibrillator into the wall socket.

"How much do you suppose she weighs?" shouted the anesthesiologist.

"Twenty kilos, maybe."

"Okay," he said, adjusting the energy level. "I'll start with fifty joules. I really need that blood, people. Clear!"

The small body went rigid, rising slightly as the current surged through it. All eyes instantly fixed on the monitor, where the morbid pattern persisted. Until the blood circulation was restored, no amount of transfusions would help. The anesthesiologist turned the dial to seventy-five joules and shocked the girl twice more, to no effect. He threw down the paddles disgustedly and yanked open his drug drawer. Dunston looked on helplessly.

"What can I do, Rich?"

"You can get her damn heart beating!" he said, drawing medication into a syringe. He located the rubber hub on the IV tubing and quickly injected. "See if you can find a vial of bretyllium on my cart!"

In short order he administered lidocaine, bretyllium, and procaineamide, interspersed with more electroshock. Nothing worked. On the cardioscope, the feeble waveforms were a taunting testimony to their ineffectiveness. Dunston was impossibly frustrated. He felt that the gift of life had been almost within his grasp, but he'd been denied the opportunity to salvage it. The blood arrived. The circulating nurse perforated the first unit with plastic tubing, whose needle she inserted into the main line, waiting only for the restoration of blood flow.

Three minutes into the arrest, Dunston's sense of powerlessness was total. He had a mental image of the fibrillating heart twitching ineffectually, like a mass of writhing worms. But the image was distorted by the cold reality of the child's injuries. He pictured the depleted cardiac muscle, straddled by intestine invading its domain. . . .

"Knife!" he snapped, to no one in particular. Quickly

throwing aside the sterile towel, he retrieved his scalpel from the Mayo stand. Dunston quickly widened his incision, deftly slashing through the xiphisternum.

"Chad, what in God's name are you *doing?*"

"Anything I can. Maybe there's a damned good reason this kid's so screwed up."

Within seconds his hand was immersed in the abdomen, reaching upward toward the chest. To his dismay, he found the traumatic rent in the diaphragm much larger than he'd suspected: the entire stomach, part of the transverse colon, and loops of small intestine had herniated into the left thorax. He quickly reduced the hernia, pulling the bowels down and out like lengths of glistening sausage, which came to lie in moist, pink coils atop the child's pale skin.

Dunston was fully aware that open cardiac massage had long since been abandoned. Rather, what he was performing was a last-ditch search for answers, for reasons the heart had stopped—a sheared aorta, perhaps, or an unseen, penetrating cardiac injury. But as his hand encircled the small mass of fibrillating muscle, he was unimaginably saddened to find the heart encased by a rubbery envelope of semiclotted blood. He shook his head.

"Cardiac tamponade," he managed. "Shearing trauma from the damn car seat!"

Although demoralized, he was not out of the fray. He nicked the pericardium, the heart's outer sheath, and liberated the blood which was smothering the underlying muscle. The myocardium fasciculated uselessly in his palm. But he massaged it nonetheless, squeezing the ventricles rhythmically between thumb and fingers, trying to urge the weary heart back into vitality. He persevered for the next ten minutes, slowly acknowledging his futility, realizing that he had acted just minutes too late—nevertheless hoping that, through expertise and sheer determination, he could coax the small and wounded organ to life. Finally, he stopped. Dr. Chad Dunston hung his head and closed his eyes, the silent ache in his heart every bit as great as the pain in his soul.

It was 2:52 A.M.

Chapter Two

"WHAT THE HELL is this?" thundered the bureaucrat. He stormed across the room and threw the document on his assistant's desk as if it were jettisoned waste.

Picking up the pages, the assistant briefly studied them before returning to work. "Some kinda legal crap."

"Now, ain't you brilliant."

"Look, we've been through this already. Same old happy horsecrap."

"Yeah? This time it could be our ass."

"Says who? I told you, we've got nothing to give them."

"Run it through again, all right?"

"But—"

"Just run it through, for Chrissake!"

"You got it," the assistant acquiesced. He swiveled in his chair, turning to the computer console. "Waste of time, if you ask me. Not even our department." He punched the buttons to access the Medical Information Network, typing in the code for Brookhaven National Laboratories. Then he hit a series of special function keys linking him to Brookhaven's nearby Center for Human Potential. CHP was the nation's premier hospital and medical research facility.

The bureaucrat watched the screen. "Think it's a bluff?"

"Who's gonna sue us, a couple of peons in the Bureau

of Vital Statistics? All we do is collate the data and send
it to Albany. Period. We got nothin' to do with death cer-
tificates.''

"I don't know. It still might be listed."

"Wasn't before." The assistant watched the flickering
screen. "When was this supposed to have happened?"

"March thirty-first."

"Coming up."

The Bureau of Vital Statistics of the New York State
Department of Health kept detailed records of all births and
deaths in the state. Once the data was on computer, the
Bureau organized it by county, date, ethnic characteristics,
hospital or nursing home, contributing medical factors, age,
and other demographic information. The data was a statis-
tician's delight and a clerk's nightmare. When called upon,
the computer was designed to regurgitate the most insig-
nificant epidemiological detail.

"Okay, here we go. Thirty-one March. County, Suf-
folk." He punched another button. "Hospital, CHP.
Deaths," he said, pointing to the zero on the screen,
"none."

"How about the thirtieth? And April first?"

"Whatever you say." The assistant repeated the process,
but the outcome was identical. "Zippo."

"Try it by the town."

"Brookhaven Township, right?"

"Yeah."

"What was the name again?"

"Lassiter. Christine."

"Sweet little Christine." He watched the screen change,
then read aloud. "Nearest we got is an old lady Larrabee,
who croaked at home. No Lassiter."

"Try the hospital computer itself."

"What'll it tell me I don't already know?"

"Just do it, huh?"

The assistant shrugged, typing away. "Okay, we're in. What should I ask for?"

"Well, the kid was admitted. Start there, I suppose."

"Admissions, alphabetical," he said, hunched over his keyboard. "CHP, Brookhaven, month of March." Soon finished, he looked up. "Oh, momma."

His boss grew agitated. "What's that mean?"

"I don't know. Let me give it another shot." He repeated the process and got the same result. "They jerkin' us around?"

"Cut the bullcrap!"

"Swear to God, I never saw that before! Hold on. Let me try through Brookhaven's classified network." He worked feverishly, beads of sweat breaking out on his forehead as he accessed the Department of Defense linkup for Brookhaven National Laboratory. Once on-line, he plugged in the parameters for CHP.

Flickering horizontal lines appeared on the screen. Then, with crystal clarity, came the message: ACCESS DENIED.

"Jesus son of God."

All at once, the monitor went totally blank.

One hundred fifty miles south of Albany, in a twenty-acre enclosure that had once been pine barrens adjacent the Brookhaven National Laboratories, the Center for Human Potential stood as a multi-tiered monument to architecture and medical science All was now quiet in the computer center, where scores of desktop computers were arranged in neat rows, a mechanical phalanx linked in parallel with two enormous supercomputers at room center. At terminal forty-seven, a cursor blinked as the monitor sprang to life. The lettering which appeared on the screen seemed to scintillate.

CHRISTINE LASSITER, it read. INQUIRY ABORTED.

Chapter Th

22

long, blond hair a sha...

ning, my wheels."

"You, Miss...

year-old f...

that s...

CHERYL DIDN'T HAVE to watch the door to know when Maks arrived. In fact, she didn't even have to look up. All she had to do was tune in to the level of conversation in the room: its ebb and flow was a barometer. Her chopsticks were barely moist when the customary lunchtime din diminished with the rapidity of Moses parting the Red Sea. Cheryl peered over the rim of her sunglasses toward the businessmen lunching at the next table. Trained ferrets, she thought, as they all simultaneously looked in the same direction. She sighed and looked up to catch the last few strides of Maks' eye-turning approach.

"Now that's a dress with a serious attitude," she said of the cool, white slip-on. "God, you always manage to look so incredibly hot."

"Thanks, Cher. Waiting long?"

"Nah. Just got here. One of those Mondays for you too, huh?"

"Oh, brother. Ever feel like you're playing pool with a rope? I can't believe how much work can pile up in three days. As if I didn't have enough to worry about."

"How'd your meeting go Friday afternoon?"

"I didn't get much accomplished." she said, giving her

e. "Sometimes I think I'm just spin-

Efficiency?" Cheryl said. Her twenty-seven-
iend had a deliberation of action and movement
poke of no wasted effort. Maks now wore an expres-
on of an intensity that Cheryl had rarely seen. "That's
hard to believe. What'd the guy say?"

"Typical lawyer-speak. Long on adjectives and hypoth-
eticals. Did you already order?"

"Yep. The eel for me, a California roll for you. So what
was the bottom line?"

Maks shrugged. "His bag of legal tricks is empty. At
least he's honest enough to admit he's out of his league.
He wound up referring me to a specialist."

"You have a bad Pap smear or something?"

"Right field, wrong area. The guy he referred me to is
some sort of expert in hospital cases."

"Malpractice?"

"No, health laws and regulations, that sort of thing. I
don't know. Ever have days when you feel like you're
bashing your head against a brick wall?"

Cheryl sipped her tea. "Story of my life."

"This business with Chrissie is like that. It's like I'm
going around in circles. Talk about bureaucracy, I thought
dealing with the Center was bad enough. Remember, after
Chrissie died, I spent entire days there getting the runaround?"

"Vaguely."

"She died in March, and here it is the middle of the
freaking summer; and I don't have any more answers now
than I did five months ago! What does it take to get a copy
of a measly death certificate, anyway? The registrar in town
hall tells me they never received a worksheet thingamajig
from the hospital, something they need to generate the official paperwork. Fine. So I go back to the hospital, and for

God's sake—have you ever tried dealing with a place that has no humans?"

"Sure. Everyone I work with is in that category."

"That Center's filled with robots, video screens, and computerized menus. You know how maddening it is to get one of those 'if you're calling about your available balance, press one' recordings on the phone? This was a thousand times worse. After a whole week of working their computer, the only thing I got was cross-eyed. I couldn't get those damn machines to admit I *had* a sister who was a patient there, much less that she'd died! Believe me, I'm not finished with them yet."

"Pretty frustrating."

Maks shook her head. "That's not the half of it. After I struck out at the hospital, I had to do battle with the insurance company. Or rather, some company clerk. You know how it is. They won't even begin to consider a claim, much less issue benefits, without a bona fide death certificate, which the Center won't provide. Just incredible."

"What's really incredible is your worthless attorney. What are you paying him for?"

"Sometimes I wonder. Anyway, after getting nowhere with the insurance company, I went back to town hall to plead my case. They dumped me like a hot potato, giving me the number of some office in the State Health Department that oversees births and deaths."

"You won't get anywhere with the State."

"Tell me about it. They looked at me like I had two heads. After about a month of their Mickey Mouse nonsense, my attorney finally did something—"

"Besides going to the bank?"

Maks allowed a halfhearted smile. "He had a writ issued to the Bureau of Vital Statistics. I guess he thought that, in some convoluted way, threatening a lawsuit would make them force the Center to come up with the death certificate.

But,'' she said, taking a sip of her tea, ''it didn't work out that way.''

''Naturally. Why should they be any different?''

''A lot of times everything seems so futile, I just want to give up. And then I think about Chrissie, and how she wouldn't have wanted me to.''

''So who's this new character your attorney referred you to?'' Cheryl asked, taking out a cigarette.

''Lester something-or-other. I have an appointment with him tomorrow.''

''I hate to sound like a pessimist, but do you have a fallback plan if this lawyer doesn't work out either?''

''Like what?''

''That's what I'm asking. But, government employee that I am, it seems to me you might be barking up the wrong tree.''

''Meaning what?''

''If I wanted to get information out of a bureaucracy, I wouldn't waste time with the people who regulated it. I'd go right to the top, to the people who designed it.''

''And who might that be? I don't recall seeing a list of them anywhere.''

''Let me see what I can find out. Maybe there's something on Brookhaven's classified network.''

A waiter brought their orders on two wooden serving blocks. As Maks watched Cheryl anoint a saucer with soy sauce and wasabi, she wondered just how far she was prepared to go in pursuit of her goal. One thing was certain: her will and resolve were stronger than ever, and her determination grew hot and fierce inside her.

The day proved exhausting. Her backlog of work kept Maks at the office until dusk. Returning home, she contented herself with iced tea and a small salad from a local diner. Once in her bedroom, she turned the air conditioning on high, slipped into a long, loose T-shirt, and checked her e-mail. There was a message from Cheryl.

Maks yawned, too fatigued to check out the two names Cheryl had unearthed. She printed the screen and set the hard copy aside for future reference in the event she got nowhere with the legal specialist, dimly wondering if one of the names had, in fact, helped design the Center. She certainly had her share of questions to ask, if it came to that.

Maks had a daily ritual without which she was unable to sleep. A month after her sister's death, she began making electronic inquiries of the various online computer services to which she belonged. Posting messages on computer bulletin boards and subscriber forums, she hoped to elicit the assistance of a fellow networker in solving the riddle of Christine's death. Once online, she generated the unvarying message simply by pressing a function key: reward for confidential information about the death of Christine Lassiter on 31 March at the Center for Human Potential. Allowing for the occasional salacious response, no one had showed the slightest interest. Nonetheless, bone weary though she was, Maks went through the motions of fulfilling her debt of family honor.

There was nothing on Compuserve or America Online. Accessing the Internet, she routed her message and hesitated, overcome by a headache, which had been growing all day. She interrupted her search for a brief detour to the bathroom, passing Chrissie's vacant bedroom en route. She took two Tylenols from a bottle in the medicine cabinet and downed them with a swig of tap water. Coming back, she momentarily entered her sister's darkened room. She sat on the edge of the bed, pinched the bridge of her nose, and massaged her sinuses.

Just for a moment, she told herself.

Maks stretched out on the twin bed's satiny, pressed quilt

and rolled onto her side. She closed her eyes, her mind vibrant with bygone images of shared hours and kindred dreams. Without intending to, she quickly fell asleep.

She was awakened by a click. There followed a faint electronic buzzing, the familiar motorized changing of gears as her computer switched drives. Maks opened her eyes. The lighted bedroom wall clock read three A.M. She arose in lazy self-criticism when she remembered that her computer was still online. Gliding back to her room, she squinted in its brightness.

Her eyes widened at the sight of the image changing on her computer monitor. The screen displayed not the Internet forum she recalled, but the DOS main menu on her hard drive. Could she have changed . . . no, she distinctly remembered logging onto the Internet, something which, for six hours of uninterrupted use, would cost her dearly. Maks frowned, eyes fixed on the monitor.

Earlier in the year, her security-conscious employer had given all workers a software package called Filesecure, for use at home. As the name implied, it had special features to guard against electronic espionage, in addition to enabling modem access. One of those features, the "Watering Hole," was a small window in the screen's upper right-hand corner that displayed the remaining megabytes of memory and the time of last user access, denoting when the operator last "drank" from the files. Watering Hole's digital clock read 02:55, little more than five minutes previously.

Maks narrowed her eyes, perplexed. The only person who could have logged onto her computer was her—period. The Filesecure program required multiple passwords, none of which she had given out. Moreover she was at home by herself, and the computer couldn't have logged on by itself.

She gazed at the modem, suppressing a chill. Was it remotely possible that some adolescent hacker could have rummaged through her internal files by accessing them over the Internet? She knew that the Internet had a myriad of features, such as the World Wide Web and the File Transfer Protocol, which facilitated sharing of information. Still, such digital tools were intended for communications, not pilfering. And even if it were possible, Filesecure's safeguards were specifically designed to thwart access.

No, Maks concluded, it simply was not possible. But she was shaken. Unnerved, she hit a series of keys to exit the menu and to reveal exactly which file had been reviewed. After a transient delay, the screen reilluminated, revealing, to her absolute astonishment, the words CHRISTINE.DOC, her file name for all the information she'd collected which pertained to her sister.

Maks was dumbstruck. Her fair complexion grew pale as her mind struggled to come to grips with the unseen intruder. Why should anyone concern himself with her confidential investigation? And if someone were interested, why not simply confront her or ask her directly?

A fear clouded by confusion descended upon her, leaving her cold and uncertain. Something was happening that she didn't understand, and it was beginning to scare her to death.

Chapter Four

THE OBLONG PENINSULA of northeastern Long Island is a predominantly rural community with a sound agricultural base. A patchwork of farms and farmstands dots the land quiltlike, and the North and South shores offer easy access to prime fishing grounds in the Atlantic and Long Island Sound. But aside from the eye-catching beaches of the Hamptons, nothing so typifies the Island's topography as its spectacular flatness.

The road most representative of such horizontality was the Island's ribbonlike interstate, the Long Island Expressway. With neither mountains to cross nor rivers to ford, the traveler might just as easily have been on the Great Plains. It was that same lack of natural barriers that led to flourishing trade between the Island's indigenous Indian tribes— the seafaring Shinnecocks, the Mattitucks, the agrarian Massapequas. Tribal boundaries were more a matter of general agreement than geological division. Long before the area provided a foothold for Dutch expansionism, and generations thereafter for potato farming, vast, unplanted stretches were smothered in thickets of robust black pine, through which deer and raccoon moved unmolested.

Dr. Chad Dunston often reflected on the Island's board-like evenness as he drove on the Expressway. This morn-

OUACHITA TECHNICAL COLLEGE

ing, however, he was still too emotionally numb from the night's disaster to think about much of anything. He'd learned long ago that obsessing over circumstances he couldn't control was to be avoided. When Ann left him, his detached, psychological withdrawal nearly killed him. Thus, he forced himself into mental diversion, to think, to act, to do anything that removed him from the pain of obsessional thinking—for to be alone with himself in his mind was to be behind enemy lines.

He keyed the lapel mike to his pocket voice recorder. Admitting to a poor memory, he had long made it a habit to dictate his thoughts and recollections while he drove. Knowing that his secretary would transcribe his dictation, he tried to keep his recitations to medical matters; but the limitless highway often caused his mind to wander, leading to rambling, personal monologues, that were not quite as embarrassing to him as delightful to his secretary.

"Wednesday the fourteenth, ten-thirty in the A.M., a lovely morning following a disastrous night. Passing exit 66 and the Yaphank yahoos. Man, I could definitely use some relaxation. I'd give my left arm to be on my boat right now. Well, not quite. But business is business, and duty calls . . . Ceil, look up the CPT code for a cecopexy on that patient for tomorrow, Robert what's-his-face. I haven't the faintest what to charge. Make up a number. Better yet, call Singh's office. They've got prices for procedures I've never heard of. Sometimes I wonder if they make 'em up. Think so? Nah.''

He paused, looking to his left, where a forest once stood. Not long before, a clearing had been hewn for an astonishing medical facility, eventually named the Center for Human Potential. When construction was begun in 1996, CHP was a logical extension of medical technology's most remarkable advancement: the evolution of completely computerized medicine. The stimuli for such computerization had been mounting for decades, as increasingly greater aspects of medical performance were relegated from man to machine. There was little sense having a technician perform blood counts, for example, when a computer could do them more quickly, more comprehensively, and far more economically. And as sophistication of computers increased, so too did their impact on general medicine.

"Lord, I pray this meeting'll be quick. Arthur'll show. He's no sweat. But if Merlin comes, I might have to push back office hours. The guy's a genius, but he's also a marathon mouth, especially if he's brought along one of his weird new gadgets. Roger and ten-four."

Computer advancements made steady and expected inroads into fields once dominated by human endeavor. By the late 1980's, a Harvard-designed software program led to the highly accurate differential diagnosis of various diseases, simply by providing the computer with relevant signs, symptoms, and lab data. By the early nineties, computerized x-ray diagnosis had supplanted human interpretation at several leading medical schools across the country. Many soon held the view that not only was physician participation superfluous, but it was too often flawed by human error, to the point of becoming dangerous.

By 1994, the stage was set for the computerized takeover of many facets of medicine. The most significant breakthroughs were in the fields of ophthalmology and neurology, where laser optics and holography provided precise mapping of virtually any lesion. Once localized, the cataract—or tumor, or cyst—could be stereoscopically excised by a robotic surgical manipulator, whose astounding precision exceeded the skill of the most accomplished physician. The phenomenal accomplishments prompted development of a new generation of artificial surgeon.

"Ceil, remind me to call Sudo over at Hitachi about the cable guide for the fiberoptic arterial threader. You want sushi? The Pfizer rep's coming today, and I know he'd spring for some carryout."

The expected stampede of venture capital into the field was overwhelming. A glut of investment excess led to keen competition, and inferior products soon fell by the medical wayside. What resulted was a series of sophisticated machines that shared several common characteristics, all computer-driven: optical precision, for exacting dissection and excision; laser photocoagulability, for virtually bloodless surgery; and a stepwise, mathematical reasoning, a kind of artificial computer intelligence, that passed for surgical judgment. The spectacular success of these surgical devices was unprecedented. Inevitably, the fallibility of the human surgeon was repeatedly called into question, such that by the mid-nineties, medicine's greatest historical bastion had been breached.

That the artificial surgeon prevailed was not unnoticed by political decision-makers. Indeed, it was considered the stepping stone of total medical computerization, for surgical robotics was viewed as the most formidable obstacle to realization of the concept. Once achieved, everything else followed suit. There were two stimuli for the giant strides in surgical robotics. One was the increasing use and sophistication of endoscopic surgical instruments, many of which relied on ancillary computerization, in fields such as gynecology and general surgery. The other was refinements in virtual reality. The two, which often followed parallel paths in development, inevitably merged; and once they did, most other things fell into place. As it became second nature for a computerized laparoscope to excise a gallbladder or remove an inflamed appendix, tasks such as mechanical venipuncture and robotic physical examination became virtual child's play.

Not everyone shared the medical establishment's general enthusiasm. Several critics were quite vocal in their opposition to relinquishing control of the human body to machines. Dunston called them "flamers," and as he neared his destination, he wondered if any of the ardent anal types would be there with confrontation in mind.

He glanced at the cloudless sky. "Lord, I'd rather be fishin'."

There was no such opposition in Washington, however. The debates in the Department of Health and Human Services, and shortly thereafter in Congress, were short-lived and bipartisan. Within a matter of months, and despite the Administration's disinclination toward social spending, grants were forthcoming for models of entirely computerized medical wards. Their unparalleled success led to an outpouring of funds the Executive Branch considered its crowning glory: creation of the Center for Human Potential. Ironically, the project's most controversial aspect proved to be finding a name for the technically dazzling institution.

One by one, suggested names were rejected because they sounded mechanically imposing (Institute for Medical Robotics), because they were too political (Republican National Disease Center), or because their acronyms were ludicrous (Computerized Research and Prognostication, or CRAP). It was ultimately decided that what was needed was an apolitical logo which imbued hope instead of fear in prospective patients. Thus was born the Center for Human Potential, whose only drawback was that its initials were the same as the California Highway Patrol.

Dunston turned off the expressway at exit 68A, a newly constructed ramp built especially for the Center. It was a warm summer day, and he drove with the top of his Mustang convertible down. The breeze sent his wavy hair riffling, and brown strands danced spiderlike across his tanned forehead. He considered his own appearance, if anything, more rugged than handsome. But there was a bronzed outdoorsiness to the thirty-five-year-old physician's features most women found quite appealing. Soon he pulled the car into the Center's parking lot.

Given the size of the eight hundred-bed institution, the single fifty-car parking garage seemed incongruously small.

But that was before recalling that the Center had no employees whatsoever. Every aspect of its daily functioning was mechanical, from the automated parking facility to the digitally run food service to the twelve gleaming robotic operatories. There were normally only four occasions when people entered the Center: as patients, as visitors, as supply vendors, or—as in the case of Dunston—what was called the "human interface."

Dunston pulled into the parking lane marked "permit holders only" and braked to a stop. He took his ID from his wallet and inserted it into the designated slot outside the driver's window. There were several seconds of audible whirring and clicking as the machine validated the information on the card's magnetic stripe. Simultaneously, a video surveillance camera rotated slightly to frame the driver's face. Dunston looked up and said, "Cheese." Shortly, the card was returned to him.

"Good morning, Dr. Dunston," said the computerized male voice.

" 'Morning to you."

"Please proceed to space number three. Have a nice day."

"You bet."

The gate went up and Dunston drove forward, unclipping the lapel mike and stowing the recorder in his glove compartment. He laughed to himself and inhaled deeply—conscious acts intended to calm the peculiar nervousness he sometimes felt upon entering the Center. Despite the fact that he had been instrumental in the Center's development and construction, it had an otherworldly remoteness, a kind of cold and distant personality that he sometimes found disturbing.

"But not today, pal," he said in forced self-assurance.

He left his car in the garage and began strolling across a carefully masoned bluestone walkway that would lead to the hospital's main entrance. Head down in daydream, eyes

fixed on the stone, he'd gone no more than ten yards when
he heard a noise like chanting. He stopped, looking in its
direction. Some fifty feet from the hospital entrance were
perhaps two dozen marchers who appeared to be picketing.
Three police cars stood between them and the hospital, one
with dome lights flashing, behind an aligned row of wooden
horses marked, POLICE LINE—DO NOT CROSS.

"Not again," Dunston moaned. It was the flamers.

Trying to remain inconspicuous, Dunston hastily made a
wide detour of the assemblage. Out of the corner of his
eye, he saw two placards, one reading, REAL DOCTORS FOR
REAL PEOPLE, and the other, EXPERIMENT ON DOGS, NOT
HUMANS. He wondered what the animal rights activists
would have to say about the matter. Another few strides
and he'd be past them.

"Dr. Dunston!" called one of those being interviewed.

"Oh Christ," he mumbled, his pace slowing, torn between politeness and the desire to make a single-finger gesture. He was no stranger to journalistic inquisition.

He was approached by a well-coiffed, white-haired man
in a pinstripe suit. Smiling broadly, the man extended his
hand as he grew nearer. The newsmen were close on their
heels.

"Howard Sapperstein," the man said, loudly enough to
be heard on tape. The journalists formed a loose circle,
camcorders rolling.

Dunston shook hands unenthusiastically. "What do you
want, Howard?" His reply was modulated, and his lips
scarcely moved. Sapperstein, a general surgeon, was a local
delegate to the American Medical Association's Hospital
Medical Staff Section, and a man Dunston had known for
five years. The AMA was in a bind. Although it had gone
on record as supporting the Center and its technology, some
of its members complained of being economically disen-
franchised. "Whose bandwagon are you on this time?"

Sapperstein squeezed the handshake and laughed warmly

as he turned to the press. "Dr. Dunston wants to know whose bandwagon I'm on. For those who may be unaware, Dr. Dunston has been instrumental in creation of the Center." There was a chorus of boos from behind him. When the jeers subsided, he looked back at Dunston. "My 'bandwagon,' Doctor, is the same that carries ninety-five percent of this country's physicians. Not to mention untold thousands of nurses and trained hospital personnel. A posture endorsed by the Joint Commission for Accreditation of Hospitals, I might add."

"Ah. The wrath of the JCAH."

"Hardly wrath. Sound judgment would be a better term. To those of us in the AMA, it doesn't make sense to throw out the baby with the bathwater. For centuries there's been an ethical, professional relationship between doctors and hospitals, all for the welfare of the patient. It's a tried-and-true union, proven beyond doubt. This new hospital," he said, pausing to point an accusatory finger, "is risky business, Doctor. I shudder to think what would happen if this experimental venture caught on statewide. Then what—nationwide, worldwide? It could blow up in everyone's face. Take the human out of the equation and you're courting disaster, mark my words."

"If it ain't broke, don't fix it?"

"My point exactly."

"Golly, you wouldn't by any chance happen to think there might be an economic motive to your position?"

Sapperstein's expression of outrage was transparent. He made a point of wagging his finger in Dunston's face. "If I thought for one minute that these robots of yours could provide better medical care than a trained physician with decades of experience, I'd be the first to support this . . ." he waved in the direction of the building. ". . . this monstrosity. But the facts prove otherwise."

"How do you respond to that, Doctor?" asked the *Newsday* reporter.

Dunston forced a smile, trying to ignore the camcorder but distracted by the clicking of a camera's autowinder. "I don't know what facts my colleague's referring to, but the ones I'm most familiar with are the monthly quality assurance reports we send to the State Health Department. They're a matter of public record. Look 'em up. They speak for themselves."

"Karen Kessler from News 12 Long Island," said a young woman who thrust a microphone his way. "For the benefit of our viewers, can you explain what you mean by quality assurance?"

"We call it QA. Basically, it's a summary of mortality and morbidity statistics, complication rates, or medical screwups. In a nutshell, Miss . . ."

"Kessler."

"—Kessler, the Center has never had a blunder and probably never will. You might ask Dr. Sapperstein whether physician-manned hospitals make occasional mistakes, known as 'state-reportable incidents,' though I doubt you'll get a straight answer. But I guarantee you, they do. To err is human, as they say. The Center has no humans. It makes no errors. And if you check with the Health Department, you'll find that the Center's complications are so minor and so rare that they're considered trifling, the lowest in the world. Now if you'll excuse me—"

"But, Doctor, surely you can understand the fears of those people who are, well, simply frightened by the idea of being a patient in a hospital that has no human contact?"

"I'm afraid your facts are wrong. There's plenty of opportunity for staying in touch with family or friends. Each patient has his own phone, as well as a TV-type monitor through which he can communicate with whomever he pleases."

"Then you don't consider this to be experimenting on people?"

Dunston chose his words carefully. "If by experimentation you mean progress, all progress is experimentation. Advances have to begin somewhere. And in medicine, that somewhere is here and now. None of the Center's patients is experimented upon, in the sense of a research project. Everything performed here has been thoroughly tested and never found wanting. This place is not only good, hell—it's the best there is.''

"How would you feel about being a patient here yourself?"

He was rapidly losing patience. ''I wouldn't give it a second thought.''

At the hospital's main entrance, the sliding doors parted at his approach. Escaping the newspeople, he sauntered into the lobby at a brisk pace. To Dunston's eye, the lobby never varied: a square, compact room, forty feet on a side, with off-white, sterile-appearing walls. The color scheme of the furnishings was pink and light brown, and framed prints in matching hues embellished the walls. Maintenance-free potted plants softened the angularity of the room's corners, and seating was provided by chrome-and-black naugahyde couches. At that hour, three "visitors" were present.

The word was a misnomer, for friends and family did not, in fact, "visit." Rather, they met with patients electronically, by means of closed-circuit TV monitors. Several privacy-assuring booths were provided for that purpose. True bedside visiting was not only discouraged, but downright impossible. No one was allowed to freely roam the Center's corridors—including Dunston.

Two of those visiting were seated, while a third stood before a chromed rectangular wall unit marked CASHIER. The unit consisted of a recessed microphone/amplifier, a red LED screen for message display, and a funneled credit card receptacle similar to a bank's automated teller machine. Out of the corner of his eye, Dunston noticed the LED screen enumerate a running readout of a patient's billable costs. The words drifted across the screen from right to left, looking very much like stock market quotations.

There were several tastefully hidden doors in the lobby. One, bearing the label PATIENTS ONLY, was a drop-off point for inpatients, who were conveyed to and from the building's interior by mechanized wheelchair. But the door Dunston approached had no identification. Its only feature was a bronzed card receptacle, into which he inserted his ID. The door slid soundlessly open.

Stepping inside, he felt the barest rustling of air as the door automatically closed beside him. He was in another squarish room, starkly empty except for a conference table at room center. At Dunston's approach, a man arose from the table and held out his hand.

"Good morning, Chad. How was your long weekend?"

"Hello, Arthur. It was super." He eyed the man's paunch. "I see we've skipped the weigh-in?"

Arthur Weiman, a heavyset man of fifty, reddened. He released the handshake to pat his girth. "That bad, huh? The Italians have landed. I swear, with my in-laws over, it's been two straight weeks of pasta and pesto." He appraised Dunston's somewhat haggard appearance and grinned. "Crowd got you outside, huh?"

"Yeah. That and a rough case last night. How'd you escape?"

"I got here just before they set up. I take it you were your usual diplomatic self?"

Chad smiled. "What's on the agenda today?"

"The usual. Admissions and procedure review. The pharmacy and therapeutics figures. Quarterly morbidity stats, then the Interface. And the memo requested we save some time at the end of rounds."

"For what?"

"I don't know. I suppose they want to surprise us."

"Terrific," Dunston said, shaking his head. "Randy coming?"

"No. Couldn't make it. The same goes for Merlin."

"All right. You and I make a cozy little group. Let's get on with it."

"Rounds" were a bimonthly meeting of the Interface Group, professionals selected to interact with the Center via the main computer. Weiman, an internist, was one such professional, as was general surgeon Dunston. Merlin, whose real name was Marlon Adams, was a PhD in electrical engineering assigned to Brookhaven National Labs. Merlin was an ingenious tinkerer and computer wizard, while Randall McKenna, who had boards in psychiatry and neurology, was the fourth member of their team. Other human staffers, including psychologists, laboratory managers, and pharmacists, met less frequently, usually at quarterly intervals. In addition to being medical professionals, they all shared one thing in common: an intricate knowledge of, and an interest in, computers.

Working quietly, the two physicians methodically sifted through the paperwork atop the desk, making checkmarks and notations as they went. Soon Dunston put down the surgical morbidity summary. He slowly shook his head as he eyed the totals.

"Unbelievable. A thousand cases a month, and the results never change. A couple of wound infections, a few pneumonias, hardly any urinary problems. Any other place, you're talking at least a fifteen percent complication rate. How the hell's this place do it?"

"By keeping us out," Weiman said. "You said so yourself. No human contamination, and strict antisepsis."

"I said that?"

"Every month."

"Score one for me. But did you ever get the impression," he said, a faraway look on his face, "that the results are, well, *too* perfect?"

Weiman's response was an unnerving, silent stare.

"Forget it," Chad said after an uncomfortable pause.

Swiveling to his right, he picked up a helmet from the seat beside him.

It looked like an ordinary motorcycle helmet, but its edges were angular, giving it a squarish appearance. Instead of having a clear visor, it sported an opaque, retractable facepiece. A cable dangled from the back. Weiman plugged it into a nearby jack.

"Got anything for the Interface?"

"A little," Dunston said. "There's a new crazy glue for heart prostheses, a synthetic polymer. Saves time and sutures in open hearts."

"Cut and paste, huh?

"Sort of." Dunston snugged on the helmet, connected the adapter, and donned a pair of gloves. They were bulky, a hybrid of those worn by hockey players and railroad engineers. They were, in fact, electronic, and their wiring transmitted each of Dunston's finger movements to the computer, where they could be simulated. A tracking device in the helmet used low frequency visual fields to monitor both the position of the gloves and the direction of the operator's gaze. Finally, Dunston flipped down the visor. For a moment, everything went blank. But then his vision was filled with a whiteness like dazzling snow. The visor's inner surface lit up with digital lettering.

VIEWS INTERFACE, VERSION 4.0, it read, followed by the date. Dunston's name was next, surname first. Then came the message.

DO YOU WISH TO MAKE AN ENTRY?

There was no keyboard to type responses. Instead, Dunston gave his reply via the newly refined technique of psychotranscription, in which he visualized lettering in proper sequence. Sensors in his helmet picked up his brain's electrical impulses and correctly deciphered what he "said." First he thought of a Y, then concentrated on an E and S.

SPECIFY CATEGORY, his helmet read.

Database update, he thought. There followed a series of

questions and answers until he successfully linked up with the Interface. Once online, the communication between man and computer was comparatively easy.

He simply had to relax and visualize what he wished to impart, much like daydreaming. Optically enhanced electrodes built into the helmet collected the images from his cerebral cortex and transmitted them to the visor's interior pixels. Its surface illuminated with a hazy but distinct image that corresponded exactly to what he was thinking. Only his hands moved; and when they did, the motion of his fingers seemed to scintillate inside his visor.

Soon, instructions for the psychotranscription were complete. The computer understood that Dunston wished to "teach" it the mechanics of the cardiac development he'd mentioned to Weiman.

LOWER OCULO-ADAPTER AND PROCEED.

Dunston pressed a button, and a faint whirring came from the helmet. A rectangle, the thinness of a computer floppy diskette, lowered itself in front of his face, millimeters from his eyes. Inside were two tiny video screens, one for each eye. Special optics in the rectangle provided a wraparound, stereoscopic view of the simulated reality—in this case, the actual cardiothoracic operating field.

Within seconds, the sight before Dunston's eyes became that of what surgeons called a "cracked chest": the thorax of a patient, split down the sternum to bare the heart and lungs. He lifted his right hand, opening it palm up. On the screen, a simulation of his hand appeared. He thought the word "knife," and a gleaming scalpel appeared in his fingers. The operation began.

The beauty of the psychotranscription interface was that it enabled Dunston to skip parts of an operation the computer already knew. Thus, inasmuch as the computer was familiar with things such as incising the rib cage, opening the pericardium, and placing the patient on a heart-lung machine, Dunston sped ahead to the crucial operative developments unknown to the computer. Within minutes, he was done. The update finished, he left an imaginary assistant to finish the case. With simulation, he'd accomplished in a short while what in reality would have taken hours to complete.

But the process was taxing. When the Interface was over and Dunston removed his helmet, droplets of sweat were on his upper lip. His neck muscles ached. He took slow, deep breaths, willing himself to relax. Weiman was staring at him.

"You look like you got hit by a truck."

"Wipes me out, it does." He looked at his watch. "God, it's almost eleven. Are we done?"

"Not quite. We're supposed to hang around awhile, remember?"

This was unexpected. The computer had never made a similar request before. "I'm supposed to be in the office by twelve."

"You and me both. I'm—"

Weiman was interrupted by a hum from the desktop. An almost-invisible surface panel retracted. Slowly, a small video monitor rose and clicked into place when it reached eye level. A cursor on its screen blinked on and off, and several seconds went by before lettering appeared.

SELF-TEST COMPLETE, it began. AUTHORIZATION REQUIRED TO INITIATE ALPHA INTERCEPT.

"I give up," Dunston shrugged. "Mean anything to you?"

"Alpha . . ." Weiman pursed his lips, thinking. Then his eyes widened. "Right. That's when it's supposed to have completed internal processing. We thought it'd take another five years, not ten months. God, this thing's advanced."

Dunston remembered. He and the team that helped create CHP had allowed for a period of mechanical growth and development. The computer was self-adaptive, meaning that it learned from its mistakes—from errors in internal

processing, not patient care. They estimated that ironing out
the kinks would require five years of painstaking self-
analysis, after which the computer would be completely
autonomous, requiring little, if any, human intervention.
And, perhaps, eliminating the need for the Interface.

Dunston suppressed a shiver. Ever since he was a medical student, he'd been completely absorbed in the computerization of medicine, looking forward to the day when
computer science would be sufficiently advanced to remove
the human element from the equation. Yet now that it was
here, he didn't feel quite ready. It wasn't that the concept
was wrong. It was simply that the power of the Center was
so awesome that it sometimes seemed spooky, to the point
of being frightening. He forced a smile.

You're being ridiculous, he told himself.

The monitor's message continued. PROCEED TO LEVEL
THREE.

"Level three?" he asked.

"Below ground, third level," Weiman said. "Heart of
the computer center. Remember the nickel tour just before
the place went online?"

"Some. We weren't supposed to come back until . . .
Well, I guess the time has arrived. How do we get there?"

As if in reply, there came a low hydraulic hiss and a
rustling of air. Behind them, a concealed door slid open.
Beyond it was the upper landing of a stairwell.

"I guess that answers my question," said Dunston.

They proceeded together into the darkness. Infrared sensors detected their presence and abruptly bathed the area in
the pale orange glow of halogen lamps. The stairway was
poured concrete slab, with an iron railing painted nautical
gray. Dunston held out his arm.

"After you."

"Thank you, Doctor."

They started down the steps. There was a whir above
and behind them as the door closed. They momentarily

stopped, looking one another in the eye before continuing. The concrete walls had a honeycomb texture, cool and stark. Otherwise, the wall was featureless.

"How can you get used to a building without signs or numbers?" asked Weiman.

"Who's here to read them?"

"True. But how can we tell when we're on the right floor?"

Again, a door opened as if on command. Dunston smiled. "How's that for service?"

Going through it, they came to a long, dark corridor. They paused, peering into the blackness before faint red lamps began to glow overhead. Dunston felt as if he were in a darkroom. Weiman hesitated.

"This is truly weird."

"Come on, Arthur. I've got patients to see."

"I was on a submarine once that had lighting like this. During an alert."

"If I hear any depth charges, I'll let you know."

They slowly walked down the corridor, Dunston in the lead. Rounding a corner, they came to a series of retractable doors, all unmarked.

"Is this it?" Weiman asked.

"No, I think it's farther on. If I'm not mistaken, this is the lab. You know, one of these days I've got to review the plans."

"As long as we're here, why don't we take a quick peek?"

"You know as well as I do that we can't go anywhere without authorization."

"Hey, who's gonna know? We helped *design* this place, right?"

Dunston sighed and nodded his acquiescence. The doors had no knobs. Beside each partition was a large button, ostensibly for servicing or emergency access. Dunston approached the middle door and pressed its button. The door slid open.

Weiman entered first. The lab was a large square, roughly a hundred feet on a side. Unlike the corridor, it was nearly totally dark, without overhead lights. Yet there was enough illumination radiating from lighted switches and digital readouts to enable sight, once one had acclimated to the darkness. Weiman took small steps forward.

Dozens of machines lay side by side on slate countertops, arrayed in long rows. They were auto-analyzers, devices designed to evaluate or measure the constituents of a lab specimen. Each was different, having a special function and unique gadgetry consisting of tubing, suction, siphons, and glassware. Together they emitted a medley of primarily liquid sounds, a plumbers' convention gone berserk. Dunston followed in Weiman's footsteps, listening to the faint bubbling and squishing.

"Incredible," Weiman whispered. "I never dreamed it'd turn out like this."

"How do they get the specimens down here?"

"Autobots. Those little service robots that General Dynamics developed, remember?"

"Vaguely. Now, can we get going—" He stopped, his eyes drawn to an inconstant flickering at the rear of the lab. "Did you see that?"

"What?"

"Over there," Dunston said, walking in the direction he was pointing. "Little flashes, sort of like twinkling." His pace quickened, and his heart began to beat more rapidly. He heard an indistinct hum, as if something were closing. He traversed the room in a dozen long strides. Yet when he reached what he thought he'd seen, he found nothing but a cool, dark wall. He ran his hands uncertainly across its surface. His voice was flat. "I swear I saw something."

Weiman was a few steps behind. "Like what?"

Dunston shook his head. "I . . . Well, something. I don't know."

"The room ends here. Nothing but a wall."

"What's behind it?"

"Damned if I remember. But it's got nothing to do with the lab. Your eyes are playing tricks."

Dunston slowly exhaled. "Yeah, probably. Let's get out of here."

They wound their way into the hall, walking quietly, purposefully. Dunston had a resolute air about him, all business.

"Arthur, ever wonder if we bit off more than we could chew with this project?"

"It's a little late to be philosophical."

"It's just all so . . . *fantastic.*"

"There's no fantasy involved, Chad. This hospital might be advanced math, but it's still a simple equation. A leads to B leads to C. Period. Don't look for something that isn't there."

Around another corner, a hundred feet down, they came to a room that was unmistakably the computer center. Though it had no lettering or designation, there was a perceptible aura about it, a vibrancy that seemed to convey the rich fullness of life. Dunston entered first, Weiman close on his heels.

Inside, the air itself seemed to throb. Dunston held his breath and surveyed the panorama before him. The room was vast, the size of an airplane hangar. Spread out with mathematical precision were row upon row of what appeared to be personal computers, each lying on its own desktop. Dunston estimated there were hundreds of them. They were all tethered together, umbilically linked with insulated, heavy gauge coaxial cable. An armada, he thought. Troops massed for battle.

Weiman gawked. "This someone's idea of an IBM commercial?"

Dunston was in awe. "Most of the stuff's Japanese," he said. His vision was drawn to room center. "Jesus. Take a look at that."

In the middle of the huge chamber were two massive rectangles, fifteen feet high and nearly half as thick. These, he knew, were the supercomputers. Feeling strangely drawn to them, he slowly began to walk in their direction.

"Incredible," he said in a modulated tone, not really caring if Weiman heard. "It's one thing to imagine them or see them on the drawing board. But up close? Positively awesome."

The room had a heavy background noise, a low hum that was throaty and rumbling. The atmosphere felt charged, tense and electric like the moments before a thunderstorm, smelling faintly of ozone. Dunston held up his hands, waving them slowly, as if in a fog.

"Their power . . . Can you feel it?"

The floor beneath them had an earth-tremor unsteadiness. "Like vibrations. What is it?"

"Magnetic fields. Superconductors, remember? The world's first and only superconducting supercomputers."

"Some sort of hybrid, isn't it?" asked Weiman.

"Right. Josephson logic circuits and semiconductor memory, all running at seventy-seven degrees K. Parallel processing, high-speed interfaces, you name it. The works."

"This stuff always fascinated you more than me."

"Why shouldn't it? I mean, these machines can do what no computer has done before. Their speed alone is close to the human brain's. There's nothing like it anywhere. It's what makes the Center the place it is."

As they neared the middle of the room, the temperature dropped precipitously. Their breath became a frosty vapor. Weiman rubbed his palms briskly together.

"What gives with the thermostat? It's like an icebox in here," Arthur said.

"That's the coolant. Liquid nitrogen or liquid helium, I can't remember which. Superconductivity works at very low temperatures. But some of the coolant's going to escape no matter how well the place is insulated."

They were suddenly startled by the unexpected voice of the computer, which resonated in their ears.

"Good morning, gentlemen," it began. It was the same synthesized male voice Dunston had heard before, but now it seemed deeper, richer. Still, it retained an oddly mechanical quality, less than human. The two men stopped in their tracks and shared a glance. The mist of their breath hung about them wreathlike. They waited, but the computer was silent. There was apprehension in Weiman's voice.

"If this is Oz and that thing calls me Dorothy, I'm outta here."

"Take it easy, Arthur. Don't twist this into something supernatural. We're in charge here. We came down to finalize authorization, and that's it. It must be waiting for us to do something." He studied the huge machines that towered before him, now only feet away. In the room's dim light, they seemed to pulsate. Finally, he spotted one of the ubiquitous video cameras on top of the console. The lens of its mechanical eye constricted, focusing on them. "Well, well. Hi, guys. What's the magic word?"

Two segments of the floor retracted, leaving gaping open squares between man and machine. Almost immediately two chairs rose from below floor level, snapping into place with a mechanical click. They resembled sleek dental recliners. Simultaneously, two sliding doors hidden on the computers' paneled surfaces opened. Mechanical arms extended, to the ends of which were attached bulky helmets, replete with wiring that linked the mainframe with the recliners. Weiman was puzzled.

"Another VIEWS Interface?"

Dunston's brow wrinkled, then he brightened. "No, I think these are the new NMR's we heard about. Portable magnetic resonance helmets for imaging the brain.''

"We're supposed to give authorization by getting scanned?''

"Well, it does make sense. The first big commercial use of superconductivity was magnetic resonance imaging in medicine." He motioned toward Weiman's chair. "Ready when you are, *amigo.*"

As if sensing hesitation, the computer spoke again. "Please don helmets to initiate Alpha Intercept."

"Here goes nothing," Weiman sighed.

In tandem, the two physicians sat down, leaned back, and put on the helmets. Dunston knew that magnetic resonance imaging, or MRI, used a superconductivity magnet to align the body's hydrogen nuclei. Radio impulses jostled the nuclei, which, when they wobbled back into alignment, emitted weak but detectable radio signals. These, in turn, could be converted to a visual image. But as far as he was aware, magnetic resonance was used only in imaging—creation of a picture which revealed potential abnormalities within the body. Yet doubtless the technology had other applications of which he was unaware.

Dunston was in good health, only once being on the receiving end of medicine when he'd torn knee ligaments in college. He therefore felt the same anticipatory anxiety as any other patient about to undergo a diagnostic procedure. He tried to relax, breathing deeply, aware that his heart was beating more rapidly than usual—but nonetheless supremely confident in the technology.

You can read my mind, can't you? he thought.

He closed his eyes and stared at the dark images which flickered behind his eyelids. Suddenly a blinding whiteness exploded in his brain, brighter than the sun's full glare. He involuntarily winced, and his helmeted head snapped back against the cushion. Then the brilliance receded, and with it, his consciousness, as the whiteness dulled to gray, and then to black.

Chapter Five

"ARE YOU ALL right, Dr. Dunston?"

"What?"

"You haven't heard a word I've said," said his receptionist.

"Forget it, Ceil. Mind was elsewhere, that's all."

"Should I bring the patients in?"

He nodded. "Let's get started."

The middle-aged woman lingered, a concerned look on her face. She was tempted to say something but thought better of it. Walking to the waiting room door, she showed the first two patients into examining rooms. It was a familiar routine—the signing in, the weighing, pulling the charts. And even when one of the elements was out of sync, it functioned smoothly enough. She concluded there was no reason to press him if he was intent on remaining silent.

In truth, there was precious little he could have told her. Dunston's memory of what happened at the Center was hazy, a poorly remembered dream. He recalled standing in the hospital lobby at twelve-thirty and looking at his watch. The marchers were gone. Everything that happened after he donned his helmet was a blur.

He felt annoyed and more than a little embarrassed. But he was also concerned. He'd never had a blackout before.

Could it have been a seizure? He had no history of cerebral trauma, and he didn't do drugs. Well, not since college. It had to be some sort of syncope—fainting. He'd wanted to ask Weiman about it, but when he came to his senses, Weiman was gone. He presumed the Intercept had gone smoothly, although he lacked the courage to call his friend to find out. Clearly if anything even remotely like a blackout happened again, he'd have to undergo a complete neurologic workup.

His fuguelike state lasted most of the afternoon. He worked mechanically, changing dressings and examining incisions in near silence, speaking only when spoken to, largely ignoring the hushed murmuring around him. Neither patient nor staff could recall his ever being so reticent. Sensing he was preoccupied, they left him alone. It wasn't until his hours were nearly over that he snapped out of it. He was sitting at his desk, going over paperwork, when his receptionist interrupted. She handed him a business card.

"Can you spare five minutes to see someone?"

"What's it, a drug rep? The guy from Pfizer?"

"No, she says it's personal."

"That usually means trouble. Like getting a certified letter." He glanced at the card. It was inscribed with the name Maxine Lassiter, along with an address and phone number. The expected company name wasn't there. He thought that either very bold or very foolish. "Bet she sells insurance."

"I don't think so. And she *does* look like someone who might brighten your day."

He put the card on his desk, crisply snapping its corners. "Now that you've whetted my appetite, how can I refuse?"

Ceil smiled and left the room. She returned moments later, accompanied by a young woman. Dunston rose and shook her hand. The grip was firm and the body language direct, suggesting a no-nonsense straightforwardness.

"Maks Lassiter, Doctor. Thanks for seeing me."

"You've given up on Maxine?"

"Only my parents called me that. To everyone else, it's just Maks."

"Just as well. You don't look like a Maxine."

In fact, she looked like something out of the *Sports Illustrated* swimsuit edition. Maks Lassiter was an absolutely stunning woman with poise that matched her good looks. Dunston estimated her height at five-seven, six inches shorter than he. She had sparkling blue eyes and shimmering blond hair that tumbled over her shoulders in enticing disarray. He motioned toward a chair. She sat down with casual elegance, leaning forward with directness. She brushed back her hair and immediately came to the point before he could ask what brought her there.

"I hope you can help me, Dr. Dunston. It's about my sister."

What was it, he thought, about her hair? Was it the way she touched it, banishing a wayward strand from her forehead? Even when she sat still, her hair appeared to be moving, a restless motion like the sea.

"Is she one of my patients?"

"No, she was a patient at the Center for Human Potential. Almost six months ago."

He pursed his lips and nodded, saying nothing.

"Christine died, Doctor. She was four years old."

He hesitated, making a steeple of his fingers. "I'm sorry about that, Miss Lassiter. Or is it Mrs.?"

"Miss."

"What happened?"

"I . . . I really don't know. She went in to have her tonsils out, but something went wrong. Or so they said."

"When was this?"

"March thirty-first."

Dunston looked away, frowning as he jotted down notes. His memory for statistics was good, and he didn't recall any pediatric deaths at that time. "Are you sure?"

She bristled. "Am I sure of what?"

"Don't misunderstand me, Miss Lassiter. But I'm pretty familiar with that place, and it's not the sort of thing I'd have forgotten."

She reached into her purse. "Maybe this will help."

The telegram was dated April first. Dunston read it quickly, astonished. Then he carefully reread each of the terse lines. It was exactly as she'd claimed. Christine Lassiter, it explained, died from unexpected intra-operative complications. In accordance with institutional policy, an autopsy was performed; the results would be forwarded when available. Dunston put the notice down.

"My apologies, Miss Lassiter."

Her upturned lips hinted at a smile. "Call me Maks?"

He smiled back. "Sure. So: how can I help you?"

"I don't know that you can. Trying to get information out of that hospital is like pulling teeth."

"Everything's on computer."

"So I've heard. But I can't seem to get any answers. That place is worse than the phone company. I was hoping to talk with someone who works there, someone with clout. A real flesh-and-blood person, like with a pulse? Apparently there is no such animal. But the more I looked into it, the more your name kept popping up. Which is why I'm here."

Again, her captivating smile. To Dunston, Maks conveyed a sense of drive and purpose that matched her beauty. He looked into her eyes, and at her flawless complexion. She had great skin. "I do head over there every so often. But back up a minute. What did the autopsy results show?"

"I never found out."

He was confused. "But—"

"No letter, no telegram. Nothing."

Dunston rubbed his chin in thought. "Miss Lassiter . . . I'm sorry. Maks. That's it? Everything?"

"The whole kettle of fish."

"All right. Let's say I can find out the autopsy results. What then?"

She breathed deeply, composing herself. "This is much more complicated than it should be. It's like this. Except for the telegram, I have no way of proving Christine is dead. And the insurance company insists on it."

"Health insurance?"

"No, life insurance. You see, Chrissie had a hundred thousand dollar policy. And before you accuse me of being mercenary—"

"I'm not accusing you of anything."

"—let me explain that it's for a scholarship fund. I want to set one up in her name."

"Okay. But why don't you just show them the death certificate?"

She looked exasperated. "That's the whole point. Apparently, the hospital is supposed to fill out some sort of worksheet listing the cause of death before the town, or Board of Health, or whoever, issues a formal death certificate. I've been to the town I don't know how many times, and they insist they never *got* anything from the hospital. It's a runaround."

"Sounds like you need an attorney, not me."

"God, it's a mess. I did hire a lawyer, supposedly an expert. He yelled and screamed, threatened to sue, the whole nine yards. He had a show-cause order issued to the State Health Department, but . . . well, it just didn't work out." She leaned forward, intent. "Dr. Dunston, is there any way you can help me?"

Something about her fascinated him. "No promises. But I'll do my best."

"That's all anyone can ask."

They rose and shook hands. He picked up her card. "This your office number?"

"No, that's home. Leave a message on the machine if

I'm out." She lifted an eyebrow. "Or are you shy when it comes to machines?"

"Oh no, no. Machines and I get on famously. I'll let you know as soon as I find anything out."

She turned and was gone. Dunston stared at the empty doorway long after she'd gone, lapsing into a wry grin. He was nobody's gofer, but this had all the makings of a job he couldn't refuse. And once he discovered what she was looking for, he'd have the opportunity to see her again. A pleasing prospect indeed.

He sat down, swiveling in his chair to face his personal computer. The PC was seven years old—an IBM clone— but it suited his needs, accessing databases and opening up networks. On the monitor, the prompt was idly blinking on and off. Finding what Maks Lassiter needed should be child's play. With any luck, he'd have the hard copy in ten minutes. He leaned forward and began to type.

Forty minutes later, he was still sitting there. His brows were contracted in a sullen, determined scowl. There had to be a glitch in the system. Finding an autopsy result should have been simple enough, especially since he was one of the few people privileged to log onto HEALTHNET, the statewide conduit for confidential information that also served as the Center's in-house communications grid. Yet each time he typed in the name of Christine Lassiter, his monitor unaccountably went blank, as if interrupted by a power surge. Frustrated, he tried a more roundabout approach, going through the back door by searching CLEAR, RETRIEVE, EMSCOPES, and MEDLINE. Each time the results were disappointingly similar.

This is nonsense, he thought. First you faint during the Interface, then your computer goes haywire. Helluva day.

His thoughts strayed to Maks Lassiter, and he brightened. Eventually, he knew, he'd find what he was looking for, if for no other reason than as an excuse to see her again. If electronic sleuthing failed, he'd ferret out the information on his next visit to the Center. There hadn't been many deaths in the hospital, and what autopsies there were should be readily retrievable.

At the same time in the Center's lab, the clatter died. The analyzers shut down in unison, and the room was filled with a heavy, expectant silence. A nearby wall slid open, revealing a dark and hidden chamber whose air was lush, teeming, fragrant with vitality. A chill mist flowed noiselessly inside. It drifted eerily across the floor, a gray and heavy vapor that rose like cemetery fog. The glass receptacles were etched with what seemed to be frost. But despite the cold, from the room came a steady, inexorable beat.

Chapter Six

QUITE SEPARATE FROM the development of the Center for Human Potential—but occurring at roughly the same time—was establishment of the Human Genome Project. Ever since the days of Gregor Mendel, a nineteenth-century Austrian monk considered to be the father of genetics, scientists had been fascinated by the prospect of deciphering the complete human genetic message stored on the DNA molecule.

"The message on the genome—"

"The entire set of instructions for making a human being?"

Merlin stopped walking to look at the young man beside him. Seth Bertone, a PhD candidate in bioengineering, was one of the few students Merlin had ever taken under his wing. Merlin, a tinkerer and inventor of ingenious gadgetry, was a practical man who had little use for theory. But Bertone's mind was so sharp that Merlin thought the student had real possibilities. Introducing the young man to the staff at Brookhaven National Laboratories would pay off down the road and would add one more to the list of Merlin's large net of connections.

"Everyone likes a cute ass," said Merlin. "But nobody likes a smartass. Let me do the lecturing, okay?"

"Yes, sir."

"And cut out that 'sir' crap. Anyway, the idea of unraveling the genome was first proposed about 1985, even though individual genes, which are small fractions of the actual genome, had been studied for years."

"How many genes are there?"

Merlin resumed their walk, knowing full well Bertone already knew the answer. "The best estimate is that about one hundred thousand genes populate the genome. By 'ninety-six, only seven thousand had been identified, or seven percent of the total. There are those who suggest that the technology to do the job in a reasonable time just isn't there. Then you have guys who freak at the total cost of the project. The initial estimate, back in the eighties, was three billion bucks."

"Lot of money."

"Better believe it. But despite the naysayers and budget cutbacks, a couple of government agencies had real interest in gene research. One was the Department of Energy, which is where we're headed now."

"Why them?"

"The DOE is responsible for investigating radiation-induced DNA damage. As an offshoot of that work, they launched their own independent genome program in 1987. Then others jumped on the bandwagon. What really turned the tide was a 1988 report by the National Research Council that endorsed a coordinated genome study. Congress took the bait and rushed to hold committee hearings. The results made them drool. So, by eighty-nine, financial constraints notwithstanding, Congress allocated fifty million dollars to the DOE, the National Library of Medicine, and the National Institutes of Health."

"All three?"

"Yep. Medical breakthroughs fascinate the boys on the

Hill. They voted for more gene research the same year they appropriated funding for CHP."

"It's a twofold process, isn't it? Understanding the message on the DNA molecule?"

"Right. The DNA molecule is a twisted ladder with connecting rungs called base pairs. Humans have three billion of 'em. First came proper identification of all base pairs. The second part of this twofold process, as you call it—and even more formidable for geneticists—was listing the precise order of the base pairs. It's that order which constitutes the letters of the genetic message."

"Isn't that called sequencing?"

Merlin paused, rubbing his thin mustache. Bertone probably knew most of this already. But it was precisely such insight which led him to invite the student to a DOE brainstorming session.

"Exactly. The problem was, sequencing base pairs had always been a tedious, time-consuming process. The NIH formed a Human Genome Advisory Committee. At its inaugural 'eighty-nine meeting, the Committee suggested the solution lay in automation. Their reasoning was, sequencing is largely an engineering project, our field. If they could develop a computerized, assembly-line approach, it might be possible to sequence up to a million base pairs a day."

"Even at that rate it'd take years."

"You want me to explain this, or what?"

"Sorry."

"What the HGAC did was to collate and coordinate data from various groups and projects across the country. Theoretically, each group was answerable to its own department. By sharing common goals, they worked in pretty much the same direction. Still, no matter how much the data piled up, the overall progress was a snail's pace."

"They needed to build a better mousetrap."

"That's why I invited you, my friend."

* * *

They had nearly reached their destination, the Department of Energy's Brookhaven Area Office in Upton, Long Island. As work on the Genome Project progressed, Upton became one of the three regional genome centers for the DOE, largely due to its access to the sprawling scientific campus at the nearby Brookhaven National Laboratories. The Upton group's genome researchers conferenced every other Monday. Merlin made his way to the conference room and introduced his protégé to those assembled. After an exchange of formalities, everyone took his seat and deferred to the group leader, geneticist Victor Sawyer.

Summer was drawing to a close, and attention turned to how the change in weather might affect outdoor studies in progress. "Suggestions, anyone?" asked Sawyer.

"Just a second," interjected Cheryl McKitrick. "Before we get to that, I have an update on a report that's a little freaky."

"Namely?"

"The one I mentioned ten months ago. About missing data, remember?"

Sawyer frowned. "Vaguely. Go on."

McKitrick took a deep breath. She had a reputation for refreshing, almost brazen insouciance. The twenty-eight-year-old computer scientist turned bioengineer had intensified her studies a year before, when she first detected hints of duplicated data. After a preliminary report to the group, during which she'd downplayed the finding, she began months of checking, tracking, and cross-checking. She was now convinced that data had not only been copied, but diverted.

"Most of us are working on sequencer and computer hardware projects," she resumed. "We've emphasized speed and decreased cost. One of my pet goals has been to develop databases and computer programs to scan the data."

"What's your point, Cheryl?"

"Just this. That in scanning the data, I've come to the conclusion that some data is, well, missing."

"What do you mean 'missing'?"

"I mean gone. Blotto. Disappeared."

"How's that possible? What data? And how much?"

"Good question. First, as to what. That came up during last year's research on molecular magnification. Some of the files on experimental microscopy, files I'd designed myself, were simply gone. I thought it was a glitch, because it only involved a few files. But it wasn't. Then I thought it might be a computer virus, like maybe someone was breaking and entering our programs. So I showed it to Jim," she said, nodding to a colleague. "He convinced me."

Sawyer lit his pipe and began puffing furiously, lost in thought, looking at everyone in turn. He eyed Seth, wondering if the grad student Merlin touted as a genius might have useful suggestions. He doubted it; the problem was too complex. Then he gazed at Merlin. The man looked nothing like his namesake wizard. When they first met, years ago, Sawyer had expected someone with that moniker to have the wild-eyed stare of the institutionalized, with electrified hair that stood on end. Instead, bespeckled and balding, and with a considerable paunch that rendered his pencil-thin mustache incongruous, the middle-aged Merlin was more like a hybrid of grease monkey and accountant. No matter, Sawyer concluded, this wasn't up Merlin's alley. His eyes fixed on the man next to Cheryl. "James?"

"No virus, for sure. When a virus gets into a computer, it's usually through a communications network. But all of Cheryl's files were in-house, off network. When a virus does sneak through, most files are deleted. Sometimes whole software programs. But it didn't happen here. It took me months to double-check everything, but it looks like certain files, selected files, were missing. In other words, it looked like they'd been copied rather than nabbed.''

"What files?''

"Mainly ones related to how microscopy might help crack the genetic code.''

"Can they be replaced?'' he asked Cheryl.

"Oh sure. I've replaced most of them already. But that's not the point. The important question is who did it. And why.''

"And?''

She shrugged. "Got no answers there, boss. I have some thoughts, but they're wild guesses. Now, the second part of your question, about how much data. I had a hunch that if some of my files were copied or missing or whatever, then maybe some other people's were, too. So I asked around, and guess what? There must be a dozen guys who thought that some data was gone. They all thought they'd just made an error.''

From around the conference table, there was a hushed murmur, and several heads nodded slowly.

"But they hadn't,'' she went on. "So I went back to Jim. We came up with a program that had the ability to sift through all our combined in-house computer memory and find out if other files were missing.'' She held up a ream of computer print-outs. "I won't bore you with what we learned, other than to say it's pretty impressive. Somebody's got us.''

"Jesus,'' said Sawyer. He read the concern in everyone's eyes, but the room was silent. "I'd put my money on the Japanese.''

"Possible,'' said Jim. "We know the Japanese have a consortium of high-tech companies that compete with us in gene research. But this? Not their style.''

"I somehow doubt it's MITI,'' said Cheryl. "They've said hands off to industrial espionage ever since State slapped their wrist in that Soviet fiasco in the eighties.''

"That's not to say they're beyond doing it again."

"True. In fact, now that you mention it, I have a contact who might know just what they're up to."

"See to it."

Chapter Seven

"LET ME LOOK it up on my screen," Maks said into the phone as she eyed her monitor. "Yes, I have it. No problem. I'm going to put on my receptionist. Tell her what you want, and she'll fax it to you." She put the caller on hold and pressed the intercom button. "Dottie, pick up on three-four. Fax some junk to this guy in the city, okay?"

"Sure." Dottie pressed the blinking button. "Hi, this is Dottie, junk faxer."

Overhearing the light exchange, Maks smiled. Dottie was as pleasant and logical as they came, an invaluable assistant. But even more than being her right hand, Dottie was a friend, a confidant to whom she could tell anything. Well, almost anything. What was happening with Dunston was as yet too formless to discuss.

"Cancel my three o'clock, Dottie," she said over the intercom. "See if you can put it on for next week."

"You going for cocktails, or what?"

Maks smiled. "That'll be all, Dottie. Thank you." Cocktails? She wouldn't mind. But Dunston hadn't mentioned it when he called to ask if she could meet him that afternoon at the Vanderbilt Museum.

All he said was that it concerned Christine. Why he couldn't discuss it over the phone, or why he didn't want

her to come to his office, he didn't say. She simply knew
that in the two weeks since she'd met him, he'd been constantly on her mind, surfacing in her thoughts at the oddest
times; and if he hadn't called her first, she darn well might
have called him within a couple of days herself. The museum? Maybe he was a history buff.

She straightened up her desk and removed her work coat,
a beige smock that was the signature of Kashiwahara Electronics. Though she was well up in the company hierarchy
as East Coast sales director, the uniform was *de rigeur* of
all Kashiwahara employees. She wielded a modest amount
of power in her position, and that alone made her somewhat
unusual, for women were rarely accorded preferential treatment in Japanese concerns. But it wasn't dumb luck that
landed her the job. She earned it. A computer major in
college, Maks's brilliant thesis on optical computers had
AT&T nearly knocking down the employment door before
she graduated. She was on the verge of signing when Kashiwahara's lucrative offer and promise of free departmental
reign steered her their way.

The digital wall clock read 2:45. She estimated she had
just enough time to leave her Hauppauge office and return
home for a quick do-over before the short trip to the museum. Outside, it was a brilliant late summer day with a
high sky of dazzling clarity. She felt exhilarated, as much
by the weather as the prospect that her elusive search might
finally be nearing an end. She got into her Acura coupe
and followed the highways and the winding length of Route
25A until she reached the narrow back roads to her home.
Turning into her driveway, her tires kicked up stray bits of
dirt and gravel until she pulled to a halt.

Going inside, she dashed upstairs and shed her garments
in a way that was at once haphazard yet punctilious, leaving
a concise, tidy trail. She turbaned her hair in a thick bath
towel and stepped into the shower. She was out in less than

two minutes, wrapping herself in a terry robe as she sat down to her makeup mirror.

There was little she needed except blush and eyeliner and some color to enhance her lips. She didn't wear perfume. A few strokes of a brush were sufficient for her fine hair. Then it was on to her wardrobe. She had a general idea of what might constitute museum wear, although she somehow had a feeling she wouldn't be spending much time indoors. She took a hint from the weather and decided on rich knit separates, whose soft textures, properly coordinated, were as much at home on the beach as in front of a Van Gogh. After an indecisive moment for color selection, she opted for the simplicity of black and white: a small-dotted tee, pull-on pants and a striped bandeau, very Arabian. She put everything on and cocked her head, satisfied. Then she locked up and returned to her car.

Living close to the museum, she was there after a ten-minute drive. It was well before rush hour, and her upbeat mood left her looking and feeling good. She spotted Dunston as soon as she pulled into the museum's nearly empty lot. He was leaning against the door of his Mustang, arms folded across his chest and one foot tucked around the other. When she saw him, her first thought was that she was overdressed. All he wore was a V-neck tennis sweater, shorts, and Nikes. Yet her second thought banished any thought of being out of place. He looked somewhere between fabulous and gorgeous, but with a masculine rather than pretty manner, with a well-muscled physique, tousled wavy hair that looked as if he were plucked from a volleyball match, and an even tan suggesting a lot of time spent outdoors. Best of all, he was smiling at her.

"Right on time," he said, without looking at his watch.

"Did I miss something? If we're playing tennis, my Reeboks are light-years away."

He laughed. "I haven't played in years. No, I thought we might take in a little cruise."

"On what?"

"My boat. Spend some time on the water, get a little fresh air. Talk about your sister along the way. Come on, get in."

She walked around the front of his car. "You mean we're not going to compare the merits of nineteenth-century impressionists?"

"Hell no. This was just a convenient place to meet."

"Convenient to what?"

"Centerport Harbor. My boat's tied up there. It's not very far, but the directions are kind of confusing. Do you mind?"

Maks just smiled. Mind? She was thrilled. And provided they weren't planning a cruise on the Trump yacht, her outfit was fine. She opened the passenger door and got in.

In the convertible, the swiftly rustling air precluded conversation. As they drove toward the harbor, she was content to lean against the headrest and soak up the waning rays of afternoon sun. They arrived moments later. Dunston parked the car and walked around to her door.

"You didn't ask if I get seasick," she said.

"Should I have brought along one of those patches?"

She gave her head a shake. "Actually, we used to sail a lot when I was a kid. My dad had an endless succession of these little boats, like Sunfish."

"No kidding? Does he still sail?

"My parents died not long after Christine was born."

He seemed to stiffen. "Christ, I'm sorry." He smacked himself apologetically in the head. "I had no idea."

She followed him as they started down the dock. "No apology necessary. How could you have known?"

"Well, I might have guessed it from the computer. Christine's hospital admission form listed you as next of kin. With a kid her age, that's kind of unusual. Pretty stupid of me."

"What else did you find out?"

"Not much. In fact, I'm hoping some nautical relaxation can make up for what I *didn't* find."

"Did you track down the autopsy?"

"That much, yes. At least on one of the hospital's video monitors. For some reason I'm having a helluva time generating hard copy, but I'm sure it's only a question of time."

They reached his boat, but she was too wound up to look it over. "And?"

"Your sister had a congenital anomaly."

"A what?"

"Birth defect. A pretty unusual one, at that. It's got an unpronounceable name I won't bore you with. Basically, it was a heart problem."

"Heart problem? Her pediatrician said she was in perfect health, except for her tonsils."

"And so she was, if it weren't for this little bit of heart muscle called the sinus node. I'll explain it in a sec. Can you untie that line in the back?"

Maks unlashed the stern rope while Dunston removed the bow line. When she straightened, she paused to glance at the craft. It was magnificent—a sleek, white launch that was a powerboat in every sense of the word, where speed was paramount and how fast you went was as important as where you went. Gracefully tapered to a point at the bow, it rode low in the water, neat and compact, a statement of simplicity of design and function. She knew he must be very proud of it.

"She's beautiful. What's it, about thirty feet?"

"Twenty-eight."

"How long have you had it?"

"Oh, two weeks tomorrow."

"Two weeks! No wonder you're so anxious to get out here."

He nodded. "I've become addicted to it."

"I don't suppose you can just say no." She eyed the spotless foredeck. "Nary a scratch on 'er."

"And destined to stay that way. Allah willing." He offered his arm. "Now, can I interest milady in a new level of cruising fun?"

She fluttered her eyelids, liking the feel of the sinew below his elbow. "Depends what you've got in mind."

"How about seventy miles an hour against a flat horizon?"

She gave a nervous cough and thumped her chest. "My, we live dangerously. You do carry life jackets, I hope?"

"What's a life jacket?" Then he laughed, helping her over the gunwale and gesturing toward one of the contoured bucket seats, snatching aside a wayward snorkel, stowing it along with diving gear. "I don't suppose you dive, do you?"

"Is this one of those times I'm supposed to say I'll try anything once? No. I don't dive." She sat down and propped her arms on the soft, cushioned bolsters. "Full speed ahead, scuba man."

The lowering sun cast a strong glare, and she put on a pair of Carrera's while he puttered in the back. Shortly, he was beside her, leaning over and pushing the boat away from the slip, putting distance between them and the dock. Then he broke the spell, resuming his medical explanation.

"This sinus node," he went on. "It's sort of an electrical junction box, the heart's natural pacemaker. In your sister, it wasn't developed normally. In lay terms, I guess you could say there was something wrong with the heart's wiring."

"But don't people with heart trouble get short of breath, or have chest pain?"

He shook his head. "Not in her case. She probably had no symptoms whatsoever. Until she was under stress."

"You mean like tension?"

"No." He worked the ignition, and the boat shuddered

as the twin MerCruisers throbbed to life. Together, they developed over seven hundred horsepower, and although the engines were idling, Maks could feel the raw power of a thinly restrained beast. Dunston barely throttled forward, and the craft seemed to lurch. Despite doing barely five knots, the engines' throaty rumble was the voice of raw brutality. Something told her that "picking up speed" would be euphemistic understatement for this boat. Dunston had to shout to be heard.

"Are you still with me?"

"I reckon for about a minute, before deafness sets in."

"Good. Now when I say stress, I mean physical stress. Like pumping adrenaline, and raised blood pressure. In surgery, even elective surgery like Christine's, one of the greatest stresses is the anesthesia. The body doesn't like being put to sleep. All sorts of reflexes kick in, and the cardiovascular system's under a tremendous burden for a few minutes. Most people weather the storm fine."

"But not my sister."

"I'm afraid not. Her sinus node couldn't handle it. She developed a fatal arrhythmia. Her heart sort of short-circuited. It wasn't built to handle it."

She fought back the tears. "I see."

They both fell silent, not speaking for the next few minutes as they slowly cruised past Eaton's Neck. Finally, the land was behind them. Well out into the Sound, with no other vessels in sight, Dunston leaned toward her.

"Shall I put her through her paces?"

"She's all yours, Cap'n."

He throttled up. The inboards roared, and the bow angled skyward as the props churned water into froth. Maks was thrust sharply back and had to grip her seat tightly. The boat seemed to have an appetite for speed.

They raced relentlessly toward the horizon, hurtling forward, kissing the crest of each wave with the grace and power of a rocket. Maks' gaze was locked straight ahead in a kind of tunnel vision as she learned the meaning of acceleration firsthand. Although her toes seemed glued to the deck, there was something immensely pleasing about the marriage of speed and gut-wrenching power, and about the arrowlike smoothness of their watery trajectory. But there was no way she could express that to him. The wind and sea have ways of thwarting communication; and anyway, she could barely move her head, although she did manage a glimpse at the gauges.

Somewhere below seventy miles per hour, and with the needle off the tach at 5,300 rpm, their surroundings became a tunnel of wind and water. The rest of the world seemed to disappear, and she entered a vortex of suspended reality. Tears streamed from the corners of her eyes, and her sunglasses pressed flush against her sockets. Her cheeks wanted to wrap around her ears, and she felt force-fed on rushing air. Finally, when she was beginning to suspect that at any minute she might need resuscitation, it was over. The engine roar lessened to a throaty growl.

"My God," she murmured.

"Say what?"

"Do you do this often?"

"Only before brain surgery."

"How long have we been out here?"

He looked at his watch. "Forty-three minutes."

Her jaw dropped. "You're joking!"

He smiled. "Kind of does that to you, doesn't it? When the engines are at max, sucking on vapor, and when you're planing along, voom! You think, it's been what—five minutes? Ten? Next thing you know, you check out the time, and the day's slipped by."

The boat slowed as he throttled back even more, aiming the bow toward the harbor. "Some tension reliever, huh? Beats having a drink."

"You might say that. You must have a lot of tension in your line of work. What kind of doctor are you, anyway?"

"Trauma surgeon."

"What's a trauma surgeon?"

"Car crashes, stab wounds. That sort of stuff. Humpty Dumpty work."

"Out at the Center?"

"Nah. There aren't any human surgeons at the Center. Just computers and robots. I work out of a couple of hospitals in the Port Jeff area."

"You must have a top-of-the-line beeper to hear it over this racket."

"Lady, I'm off until tomorrow morning."

"Who's minding the store?"

"I'm in a coverage system with two other guys. Solo practice'd be impossible in my line of work."

Soon, he pulled up at the moorings and tied up the boat. After Maks helped stow a few things below deck, they walked back to the parking lot, slowing when they neared his car. She extended her hand.

"Thanks for finding out about Christine."

"No sweat. As soon as I get that hard copy, I'll send one off to you."

They lingered, holding the handshake, at a temporary loss for words.

"If you're off call," she suggested, "maybe I can repay the favor. There's a little Mexican place near here that makes a mean Margarita. Or does medicine have any of those airline rules about not drinking before duty?"

He laughed. "Nah." He checked his watch. "But it's almost five, and my in-laws are coming over for supper pretty soon. Thanks anyway."

She turned beet red. In-laws? Somehow, she'd assumed that . . . Her eyes darted toward his ring finger: no band, no white circle of flesh sheltered from the sun. Still, what an idiot she'd been! She momentarily considered storming away, except she was flustered into near paralysis.

He held up a conciliatory palm. "Before you jump to

conclusions, you ought to know that I've been pretty tight with my in-laws since my divorce. I'm off again on Saturday. Is that place open weekends?"

Maks just smiled.

"This is great guacamole," he said, scooping some onto a tortilla chip. "And here I always hated avocados. In surgery, anything that's green and runny is bad news."

She made a face. "I'm supposed to put up with this for the rest of the meal?"

"Oops, there I go, talking shop."

"How was dinner with your in-laws?"

"Great. It's always great. Fantastic people. I mean, Sid practically furnished my whole office for free. And Lorraine? A real straight shooter. How many prospective mothers-in-law tell you you'd be an idiot to marry their daughter?"

"But you did anyway."

He sighed. "Admittedly, the handwriting was on the wall."

"Which wall?"

"In Ann's case, the bathroom wall. It got to the point where I was afraid to go into the men's room so I wouldn't find her name scribbled inside some toilet stall."

"Get out."

"I kid you not. My wife was an anachronism, a free-love flower child of the sixties who grew up in the nineties."

"How long were you married?"

"Not long. Eighteen months. I'll be divorced two years this January."

"Two years can be an eternity."

His expression turned glum and distant. "It sure can."

Watching him toy with the silverware, Maks was nonplussed by his sudden reticence. It didn't fit the wearer. Here was a man who seemed supremely confident both at work and at play—but pursuit of a harmless inquiry into the ruins of his romantic past made him turn turtle, withdrawing into an emotional shell. He reminded her of the outgoing little boy who becomes pouting and uncommunicative when distressed, something she'd seen before in bright schoolmates. There was something quintessentially nerdy about his reaction, but it was an endearing nerdiness when packaged in sullen silence.

"Was it a drug thing?"

He shrugged. "I suppose you might say she was a party girl. Whatever it was that Ann wanted, I just wasn't able to give it to her."

Maks felt a desperate need to comfort him. "I know what it's like to be hurt. Not the same as you were, but I have scars too. There are times it seems like such a struggle."

"I'll tell you something. In a weird way, the struggle is a gift. I'm a different person because of it. Struggle can lead to change, and if you're lucky, change can lead to growth. I'm able to handle things now that I never could have before this happened."

"Very philosophical. Also very convenient If you had it to do all over again, would you go through all that hurt for the sake of some personal growth?"

"That's a tough choice. All I know is, Ann never bothered being choosy. Maybe she was just a free spirit, who knows?"

Maks tried a consoling smile. "Does the word slut mean anything to you?"

She had tried the uncertain comfort of humor—but from his quickly averted eyes, his intensely wounded look, she knew she'd said the wrong thing. Levity was not her strong suit, and now she felt horrible. She placed her palm atop his, a soft apology.

"I'm sorry. That was terrible of me. You really loved her, didn't you?"

"Yeah. Anyway, she didn't love me, which is more to the point."

"No loose ends, like.kids?"

He took a sip of his Margarita. "No . . . But enough about me. I realize you're paying for drinks, but dinner's on me. If you can stand plain American food."

She had a deadpan expression. "I don't know. I'm expecting my in-laws."

Dunston laughed, and little crow's feet crinkled the corners of his eyes. "Touché. Tell you what. Let's blow this joint and boldly go where no man has ever gone before: my place."

"Golly, Captain Kirk. Why would I want to do that?"

"Because I make the greatest spinach salad this side of Rome."

He had repositioned his hand atop hers, and he lightly pressed her wrist. She liked the gentleness of his touch, but she wasn't quite ready for it.

"Well, I'd really like this to be my treat. It took me forever to get an answer about Chrissie, and I owe you at least a meal. I've got a couple of great steaks that are crying out for charbroiling and a quick béarnaise sauce. What do you say?"

He shook his head. "I don't know. I'm usually not this easy, but . . . what the hell. You win."

Maks threw a twenty on the table, took Chad's arm, and led the way out. They had come in separate cars, and now, ten minutes later, Chad was following her tail lights as they turned onto a long, gravel driveway. Stately ash trees lined the path, forming a green canopy overhead. In the twilight, between the tree trunks, Dunston could make out a vast expanse of sprawling neighboring properties. Maks' property encompassed a long, slender rectangle, flanked by baronial estates on either side.

The two-story frame house was set against the backdrop of Cold Spring Harbor. Dunston pulled into a spot behind her at the end of a circular turn-around, watching the distant play of moonbeam on water. He stepped out of his car and glanced toward the properties to either side.

"This is quite the location. How did you manage to find a house wedged between playgrounds for the rich and famous?"

She led him toward the door. "It's a long story. The property has been in my family for about a hundred years. Around the time of the First World War, a lot of this area was turned into summer homes for the Gatsby crowd. But they couldn't get this skinny little acre away from my great-grandfather. Been handed down ever since."

He followed her past the front door into a wide entryway. Beyond it was a comfortable kitchen in French Provincial decor, with an enormous central wooden chopping block and racks for overhead pots and pans. He was duly impressed.

"You could feed an army in here. Or even a shift of hungry nurses."

"My parents used to entertain a lot."

"What happened to them, anyway?"

"Plane crash. It was supposed to be a weekend trip—" She sighed. "Christine wasn't even two." She opened the refrigerator. "Want another drink?"

"If you're having." He shifted gears, sensing her discomfort with the subject of her parents' death. He was also aware that he'd monopolized the conversation until now, talking about what happened to Christine, his work, and his past with Ann. He really knew very little about her, other than that she had a gritty determination he very much admired.

As she spoke, every so often Maks would twirl a wayward strand of her hair between thumb and forefinger before putting the ends to her lips, as if she were moistening the tip of a watercolor brush. Dunston watched in fascination as the interplay between tongue, hair, and fingers threatened his concentration. "So. When you're not playing lady of the house," he said, with a wave of his hand, "what do you do in real life?"

"I work for Kashiwahara Electronics."

"Yeah? What department?"

"I'm in sales. Optical computers."

"Fascinating stuff, cutting edge," he said, with an approving nod. "Still in the research stage when I was in school."

She went to the liquor cabinet for the tequila. "Actually, they've been around since 1960. But the technology was too primitive, and it guzzled energy, about half a megawatt for power and cooling."

"Enough to light five thousand hundred-watt bulbs."

"Just about."

"They use lasers, don't they?"

"Right, instead of wires. The number-crunching guys could never get the chips tight enough. The closer they packed 'em, the more the electromagnetic interference scrambled their data. That really restricted their speed. But digital optical processors operate at more than a billion cycles per second."

Dunston did a mental calculation. "That's a thousand times more powerful than a supercomputer."

"And able to leap tall buildings at a single bound. The guys at Cray wanted to die when they found out."

"When did that happen?"

"They solved the energy problem about ten years ago with these low-voltage units. Then, in the late eighties, they developed the hardware—light lenses called Symmetric Self Electro-optic Effect Devices."

"S-SEEDS."

She gazed at him as she shook the margarita. "This is old hat to you."

He shrugged. "Just what I've read. Isn't it like parallel processing?"

"Same principle, different modality. Digital computers think in a serial way, one piece of data at a time. But even with supercomputers, the computations took too long. Optics lets you process a large amount of information simultaneously. Endless possibilities."

"What do you sell for Kashiwahara?"

"Lenses, mostly. But they also let me do some research, which is why I signed with them. Right now, it's still exciting. Even the military's interested, but . . ." She clucked her tongue, then smiled politely. "Sorry, can't talk about that."

"Sounds like a great job." He paused, not wanting to push her. He looked around the room as she poured his drink. "It's very comfy here. Was it just the two of you here, you and your sister?"

"Yes. Mom and Dad always claimed they wanted only one child. I was flabbergasted when my mother told me she was pregnant."

"How old was she?"

"Forty-five."

"Accident, huh?"

"No, I don't think so. More like she was hearing the finality of her reproductive footsteps. She never said it in so many words. It was the way she talked. I'd just finished college by then and was out on my own. Maybe she was lonely, empty-nest syndrome and all that. Here, how's this?"

He tasted the drink. "Hmmm, nice. Can I help with anything?"

She gestured toward a cabinet. "There's a bag of charcoal briquets in there. Maybe you can get them going while I trim the steaks."

In the center of the kitchen area was an ample brazier for indoor grilling, with an overhead exhaust hood for venting fumes. As Dunston spread out the coals, he noted that the grill had an ingenious built-in briquet lighter. When he switched it on, an exhaust fan simultaneously began to purr.

An hour later, they were seated at a small table outdoors. Adjacent to the exterior kitchen wall was a compact veranda that afforded a breathtaking view of the water. On the horizon, there was the distant twinkling of running lights from boats that slipped silently past. They ate by candlelight. The meal was simple yet sumptuous: hot, crusty bread, peas with water chestnuts, a side of rewarmed *frites,* and the steaks, accompanied by a cabernet from a local Long Island vineyard. Nearly finished, Dunston dabbed his lips with a napkin.

"Delicious. Now that we've established you're a gourmet cook, it's full speed ahead and damn the calories. Dessert's on me."

She raised her eyebrows. "The doctor's also a cook?"

"No, just basic bachelor survival. Now, which way to the crepe pan?"

For Maks, dessert was a pleasing as the rest of the meal had been to Dunston. While he cooked, she cleared the table and loaded the dishwasher, allowing him free reign of the kitchen and pantry. He hummed as he went along, something pleasant but unrecognizable. The painful subject of his ex-wife didn't come up again. He followed no instructions, seeming to rely on some recipe in his head. Maks silently marveled at his apparently haphazard way of making do with what was available. The result was anything but "thrown together." He fashioned fresh peaches, cream, marmalade, and Grand Marnier into a concoction that was nothing short of spectacular.

She made coffee, and they followed it up with Courvoisier, sipping the brandy from delicate oversize snifters. They retreated to the veranda and an old but sturdy porch swing. They made small talk, discussing their lives and careers for what seemed like hours, each obviously increasingly interested in discovering the other person than in self-promotion. Yet just as such interest was obvious, it was becoming less and less apparent, for they had nearly emptied the bottle of brandy by midnight.

The porch faced west. Beyond it was a small but well-tended backyard which gradually slipped away into Cold Spring Harbor, which in turn widened as it spilled into Oyster Bay. Maks leaned forward, intent, staring out at the distant, watery panorama.

"What time is it?"

"Ten of twelve."

Somewhat unsteadily, she put down her glass and got up. Kicking off her shoes, she walked barefoot onto the grass—cool at that hour, moist with dew. She wrapped her arms around herself and slowly glided toward the horizon. Although her gait meandered, her gaze was unwavering.

Dunston watched without comment. Her unexpected silence confused him. Up to that point, they had been laughingly outspoken, even boisterous, except for those moments he was distracted when she did her hair thing. She was now clearly concentrating on something, obviously upset. He mulled over his words but couldn't think of what he might have said to offend her. He got up.

"Maks?"

She didn't answer. Dunston stood there, concerned, watching her glide across the slick turf. He had a strange feeling of déjà vu, of helplessly watching Ann spin away like some ill-fated comet, while he was powerless to do anything about it. But then he realized that Maks bore no emotional resemblance to his unstable ex-wife. The doctor in him took over. He slowly followed her footsteps.

She stopped as unexpectedly as she'd started. From behind, Dunston could see that her chin had sunk to her chest, and her shoulders slumped forward. Then those same shoulders began to slowly quake up and down. As he drew closer, he could hear the softness of her crying.

"Maks, what's wrong?"

Still she kept silent, absorbed in her anguish. The phy-

sician in him said to remain impartial—detached, even; to
draw her out with deliberate, open-ended questions. But the
man in him couldn't tolerate her suffering. He drew even
with her and grasped the smooth, cool skin of her bare
shoulders. Her body seemed to relax at his touch, but her
sobbing continued. As he held her, she slowly turned toward him until her lowered forehead rested against his
shoulder.

"It's so damn unfair," she finally managed.

"What is?"

"Life. Everything. Tomorrow would've been Christine's
birthday."

So that's it, he thought. He stroked her hair, pulling her
closer, soothing her as he might an injured child, letting his
arms go around her. "It's not your fault. Don't torture
yourself."

Leaning against him for comfort, she felt her body un-
wind. "She was only a kid, a baby. Life's never like the
movies, is it?"

"No," he said. "It never is."

While she clung to him, her tears slowly ceased. Overhead, the stars glittered. Maks felt safe and warm in his
arms, her face nestled in the crook of his neck. She felt
wonderfully content, absorbed in her thoughts. There
seemed no need to talk. She didn't dare hope that something more might develop between them. Yet as she relaxed
in his gentle embrace, it was plain from the gentleness of
their touch that something was happening to both of them,
but Maks couldn't get Christine out of her mind.

Chapter Eight

"THIS BEING A Monday, Dr. Dunston, I can give you gloves which actually fit."

The nurse widened the latex cuff, allowing him to thrust in his fingers. He smiled at her. "Always such a crowd pleaser?"

Before she could reply, the emergency room physician called him. "I think you better get in here before we lose this guy."

Dunston turned toward the patient, an unconscious man of about thirty whose life was seeping out through three bullet wounds. One was in his right chest just above the nipple; the second, just below his right rib cage, probably pulverizing the liver; and the third, smack in the center of the umbilicus, seemingly less serious than the other two, unless it nicked one of the great vessels or transected the spinal cord. The patient needed to have his hemorrhaging stopped fast. And that meant trauma surgery.

Dunston checked the monitors. There was a good pulse, but the blood pressure was dropping. The endotracheal tube was in place, but the end-tidal CO_2 was pretty dreadful, and the pulse oximeter showed poor oxygenation. While they were waiting for the operating room to get ready, an arterial blood gas might help. He snugged on his gloves. There were five people in the trauma room, all feverishly working on the patient. Dunston spoke to no one in particular.

"This guy a regular?"

"Nah, no tracks. Cop that brought him in says he was dealing."

"Cops shot him?"

"No, it was a bad buy. Over in the mall."

"Can you turn his wrist up a little? Good. Spray it, okay?"

One of the nurses sprayed the exposed wrist with a brownish antiseptic. Dunston removed disposable sterile towels from the radial artery catheterization set and draped them to expose a triangular portal of skin.

"I'll tell ya," he said as he worked, "suburbia's going down the tubes. May as well live in the South Bronx."

"Tell me about it."

Dunston felt for the radial artery, found the pulse, and eased the needle under the skin. The procedure was done by touch. Sensing just the right resistance from the arterial wall, he plunged the needle home. A pitifully watery stream of arterial blood gushed back. He quickly hooked up an anticoagulated syringe, drew off several cc's, and handed it to one of the techs.

"Here's the gas. Must be acidotic as hell. You have any ice for that thing?"

"Just one of those cold packs."

Dunston shrugged. "Port in a storm. It'll do." As he began threading a narrow plastic catheter into the artery, he glanced at the man's blood-streaked chest. "Aren't bullet-proof vests required attire for these characters?"

"Usually. But not at ten in the morning."

Dunston shook his head. "So much for business ethics. Maybe they should unionize. Did you say no exit wounds?"

"Yep."

"The weapon must have a real low muzzle velocity. I'm

sure they used hollowpoints—maximum expansion, minimum penetration. I hope it wasn't Magsafes or Glasers. Entry wounds look like nine mil, don't they?''

''That or thirty-eight. Too small for a forty-five.''

''Must be that subsonic crap. They use a silencer?''

''Beats me. Ask the cop outside. If you ever get out of surgery.''

''You got that right.'' He finished hooking up the arterial pressure transducer and taped everything in place. ''How're we doing for an OR?''

''They just called. The room's ready.''

''Okay, folks. Show time. Keep that IV open wide.''

Working as a team, they unhooked the endotracheal tube from the respirator and steadied the patient on the trauma stretcher. When all was ready, Dunston said, ''Go.'' Then the team wheeled the stretcher toward a waiting elevator.

At eleven in the morning, emergency rooms are generally quiet, having attended to most of the non-emergencies that glutted the waiting room at seven A.M., before the start of work. Maybe it was something in the appearance of the two men, who suddenly positioned themselves in the hall; or perhaps it was the subtle, knowing change in the police officer's expression as the stretcher rolled past. In either case, the hairs on Dunston's neck stood on end. As he turned in the cop's direction, everything seemed to happen in slow motion.

The officer seemed stuck in molasses—pathetically slow to clear his holster of his duty-issue Glock-17. Simultaneously, both intruders drew weapons. Dunston would later recall the vivid clarity with which his eyes immediately fixed on their guns, no doubt the result of a morbid fascination for implements of destruction he'd developed during his training.

One man held a glitzy, chrome-plated CZ-75. From under a long jacket, the other took out a Heckler & Koch MP5, an expensive, German-made submachine gun which, in this case, sported a thirty-round magazine and a long, screw-on silencer. Dunston saw terror in the officer's eyes as the man with the CZ aimed at him. There were four thunderous explosions as the stranger pulled the trigger rapid-fire. At a distance of five feet, it was hard to miss. The first shot struck the officer in the middle of the chest, propelling him backward into a wall.

His partner, meanwhile, descended upon the stretcher. Amidst the screams and shouts of sensible people madly scrambling for cover, Dunston remained peculiarly motionless at the stretcher's side. The second man swung the H-K toward him in a vicious arc. The heavy silencer smashed into Dunston's cheek, making him see stars as he staggered out of the way. The man then aimed at the stretcher and fired.

Despite the silencer, the submachine gun was hardly silent, though it was muted to the loudness of a cap gun. The second intruder fired a continuous, thirty-shot burst, emptying the magazine in less than three seconds. As he raked the dying patient's torso, glittering shell casings went flying. So, too, did bits of skin, muscle, and bone, splattering the wall with a fine, grisly crimson spray.

Assuming the police officer was down, the first man turned to watch the second. What he did not know was that when the cop had fallen backward, the CZ's other three shots were wide of the mark. Nor had he known that, unlike the patient, the officer *was* wearing a vest; and that although stunned by the slug that crashed into his chest, the policeman was hardly out of the fray. He righted himself and was just leveling his Glock when the first man looked his way.

They both fired at the same time. The patrolman was hit again, this time taking a hollowpoint outside of the vest's upper body strap, effectively shattering his right shoulder and sending his pistol skittering across the floor—but not before his Glock had spoken. The officer's single returned shot entered the man's head at the bridge of his nose. The exit wound at the back of the skull was enormous, and a particulate spray of blood, brain and bone was showered twenty feet across the room.

The second man seemed coldly deliberate in what he did next. Seeing that the officer was wounded and unarmed, and perhaps sensing that his accomplice was dead, he reached into his pocket for a spare magazine. Finding it, he ejected the empty clip from the H-K and let it fall to the floor as he clicked its replacement into the magazine well. The policeman, despite his pain, was aware of everything that was happening and frantically began to scamper across the floor toward his gun.

By now, Dunston's vision had cleared. Although those around him were terrified, he felt the opposite. He was positively enraged by the unprovoked assault against him. The killer's calculated, methodical manner infuriated him even more. As he watched, the intruder chambered the fresh magazine's first nine-millimeter round and grinned at the officer. With a sadistic leer, he slowly, tauntingly, pointed the still-smoking silencer in the officer's direction.

Dunston sprang. Lowering his shoulder like a linebacker, he hurtled across the intervening space in two frenzied strides. His shoulder struck the middle of the killer's spine with a jarring impact. Both the man and the submachine gun went flying.

That was all the time the officer needed. He retrieved his Glock and scrambled to one knee, steadying the gun in his uninjured left hand as he aimed it squarely at the now-sprawling killer. Seeing the fury in the cop's eyes, the man froze into motionlessness. At that moment, a hospital security guard arrived. Most of them were off-duty cops anyway. Immediately assessing the situation, he pulled a Seecamp .32 auto from a concealed holster with one hand and used the nearest ER phone to call for back-up with the other. The remainder of the scattered medical team slowly

regained its composure. They took a collective deep breath
and turned to evaluate the carnage.

There was nothing that could be done for the patient,
whose perforated head and torso were largely unrecognizable pulp. Once the security guard took over for the downed
policeman, the latter was helped into the first treatment cu-
bicle available, which happened to be a casting room. This
was fortuitous, both because of its abundance of gauze and
dressings and its proximity to x-ray. There the officer's
bleeding was stanched, a pressure dressing applied, and his
shoulder x-rayed. The films showed that the head of his
humerus, where the upper arm met the shoulder, was frag-
mented. But although his tennis serve was now history,
neither major vessels nor nerves were seriously impaired.
Once he'd had emergency reconstructive surgery—which
would be within the hour—his arm would remain func-
tional. But the intruder with a bullet to the brain was a
different story entirely.

He wasn't dead. The cop's single shot had essentially
liquefied all of his cerebral cortex and cerebellum, but his
brain stem and autonomic nervous system remained intact,
allowing his body's vital functions to continue. Thus his
heart still pumped, his lungs breathed, and his kidneys still
put out urine. Except for the fact that he was now a veg-
etable, his remaining organs were quite normal. This was
something of an unexpected bonus. The medical team
sensed what it had here and directed all its efforts toward
keeping him stable. His bogus New York State driver's
license had a remarkably authentic photo, and most sur-
prising of all was the checked-off box on the back of the
license in which he'd agreed to make an anatomical gift,
"to be effective upon my death, of any needed organ
parts." Alas, a man of integrity.

Half an hour later, he was in the Intensive Care Unit,
hooked up to the appropriate monitors, IVs, and other life-
support gadgetry. Blood was sent for screening, hepatitis

antigen and HIV testing, and tissue typing was begun. The national organ bank computer was notified. With any luck, and with help from the courts, they would be able to harvest the man's heart, lungs, pancreas, liver, and kidneys. In this instance, at least, drug dealing became society's blessing.

The frenzied activity made time pass quickly. Then began the inevitable police questioning once the homicide unit arrived on the scene. It was two P.M. by the time everything finally wound down, save for the housekeeping department's locating a high enough extension ladder to remove small remnants of grisly human debris from the ER ceiling. Dunston's cheek had been x-rayed. There was no fracture. But despite constantly applying an ice pack, a purplish bruise crept upward from his eye, leading to a remarkable resemblance to a raccoon. He turned his attention to his groin.

He'd felt a sort of pop when he knocked over the gunman. Years before, in college, a team physician had diagnosed an "incipient hernia" and admonished him to avoid undue stress to his inguinal region. More of a bookworm than dedicated athlete, that wasn't terribly difficult for Dunston to do. Yet over the years, more from dumb luck than conscious avoidance of certain activities, nothing had occurred to aggravate his latent problem. Until now. The increasing tenderness where his lower abdomen met his hip would have made the diagnosis obvious to a first-year med student.

Still, he was mindful of the dictum about doctors not treating themselves, and he didn't want to jump to conclusions. Besides, he'd arranged to meet Maks that night, and he was looking forward to it. He grudgingly pulled aside a surgical colleague, went into an empty examining room, and pulled down his pants. When his friend told Dunston to turn his head and cough, a golfball-size bulge appeared in his groin.

"Yessiree," said his colleague, "that is truly lovely. Just

waiting all these years to show itself.''

''Terrific.''

''Since the OR's not tied up any more, we could probably get you prepped for surgery now. Do the whole thing under local. Throw in a few sutures, half hour, tops. Have you home in time for cocktails.''

''Now that's a dynamite offer, but I have hours at four. Not to mention, well, another obligation tonight.''

''Doctors and nurses,'' said his friend, shaking his head. ''World's worst patients. You wouldn't happen to have something in mind for tonight that might make this thing worse?''

''Me?''

Maks heard about the day's events on her car radio while driving home from work. Although the news report suggested Dunston wasn't seriously injured, she worried nonetheless. No sooner had she returned home than she called his office, only to find he'd just left. She spent most of the next hour fretting instead of getting ready for his arrival.

After the tender concern he'd showed her on the eve of Christine's birthday, Maks knew she had to see him again. Her motives confused her. She didn't know if she was simply interested in more information about her sister, companionship, or something that might evolve into a relationship. Perhaps it was a little of everything. Dunston seemed a compassionate and caring man; and after months of self-neglect, Maks felt she'd earned the pleasure of a man's company. When she'd invited him over, ostensibly to discuss Christine, he'd readily agreed.

When he finally arrived, Maks was appalled by the condition of his eye and its vivid purple color. She cautiously touched his cheek with her fingertips the way one might hesitantly reach out to a frightened animal. She mixed him a drink and tried to get him to talk about what happened, but he was still too stressed out to discuss it. All he mentioned was that it had probably earned him a hernia.

As a diversion, they took in an early movie. Afterward, he suggested a bite to eat at a coffee house near the university. But when she saw how noticeably he was limping, she insisted that he get some rest instead. He'd be in no condition to take care of anyone, she said, if he didn't first take care of himself. Dunston wondered what he'd done to appeal to her maternal instincts.

"What time do you have to be at work tomorrow?" she asked.

"Late. I don't have any cases. Nine, nine-thirty."

"I have an eight o'clock breakfast meeting not far from your condo."

"Yeah? With who?"

She was flattered by his interest. "It's strictly business. Why don't I just drop you off tonight and bring your car back tomorrow, before you leave?"

"Whatever you say, doctor."

The rest proved helpful indeed. He'd been unable to admit how emotionally draining the day had been. For the first time in months, he had eight full hours of uninterrupted rest. The next morning, while he was showering, he noticed that the swelling had gone down considerably. It was 7:45, and he had just put on a bathrobe when the doorbell rang.

It was Maks, arms laden with packages of croissants and cheese. He thought she looked fantastic in her black leather mini—not too short, but lots of leg, upscale without being trendy. She returned his car keys.

"Didn't you have a breakfast meeting?" he asked.

"God, that eye looks gruesome. Does it hurt?"

"Only when I wink." He helped her with the packages. "All this for me?"

"Depends how hungry you are. My meeting was cancelled. Message on my machine—you know how those things go. I guess I figured that you could use a few calories while convalescing. So, here you are. Sorry I'm so early, but there was absolutely no traffic."

She set everything on the table and let her arms fall to her sides, suddenly at a loss for words, staring at him. He had a fresh-scrubbed look, his hair still wet, and she found him incredibly appealing as he moved about in his open-chested bathrobe. For the moment, she did nothing but stand there in artless silence.

The strained hiatus was proving as awkward for Dunston as for Maks, and he found himself slipping toward inarticulateness, on the verge of saying something foolish. In her eyes, he saw an interest tempered by uncertainty, a feeling that mirrored his own. He was relieved when she finally began untying the string around the packages.

"No woman's made me breakfast since Ann left."

"Everyone should get pampered sometime. Especially if you're under the weather."

"I suppose. And as much as I enjoy cooking, eating by myself is never the same as eating with my family."

"Is that what it was like when you were growing up?"

"More or less. Meal time was family time. It's pretty much what I expected when I got married."

"What stopped you?"

"Ann. She was hardly ever around. Even when we were together, she seemed to be someplace else."

Maks helped herself to coffee. "Hardly the stuff the family unit's made of."

"No, it wasn't. I realize now that Ann was a very lonely person. And she had this ability to make everyone around her feel lonely, too. In fact, it was beyond loneliness."

"Loneliness in a crowd?"

He shook his head. "More like the ultimate in isolation, isolation cubed. It was uncanny how she could be there, and yet be absent, you know?"

"Maybe she was shy."

"Ann? Ann was about as shy as Madonna. She could get a ten for exhibitionism."

Sensing his uneasiness, Maks tried shifting the conversation elsewhere. "You're still young, Chad. There's plenty of time to make up for what you missed."

"I still want a family, if that's what you mean. Like Ozzie and Harriet. But not where I'm Harriet."

She was struck by how much his ex-wife was still alive for him, playing with his mind, renting space in his head. Maks knew it was still too early in their embryonic relationship for her to become so absorbed in someone else's problems. Yet she *did* care, perhaps too much, too soon, a deep concern that was the measure of her own vulnerability.

She smiled reassuringly and held out a wedge of Jarlsberg as if it were a peace offering. He accepted with a gracious nod, understanding the healing that was her intention, willing to drop Ann from further consideration, at least temporarily. The cheese was good. They both sat down to eat and launched into a discussion of breakfast breads in general, and focaccia in particular. When he got up to clear the table, she noticed his lingering limp.

"It bothers you, doesn't it?"

"Hmmm?"

"The hernia."

"It's more annoying than anything else. Kind of like a dull toothache."

"What's it look like?"

"You really want to see it?"

Maks reddened. She hadn't meant her question to emerge as boldly provocative as it sounded. She'd intended a generic inquiry, a fuel for conversation, along the lines of wondering what makes the stars shine. Instead, it sounded as if she were questioning the origin of the universe. Yet she didn't feel as if she could diplomatically back out now. She summoned up her courage.

"Only if you want to show me."

The ball was now back in his court. He hadn't expected that. He was grateful he'd put on Calvins under his robe. Without missing a beat, he swept the blue velour off his hip. He wondered whether she'd want to touch it, as she'd touched his cheek the night before. He pointed out the bulge.

"So that's a hernia?"

"Yep."

"Not very impressive."

"I beg your pardon?" he deadpanned, closing his robe.

"I'm referring to the hernia."

"Oh. Well, it doesn't have to be gegunda to incarcerate."

"What's that?"

"In lay terms, they call it 'strangulated.' It's when a loop of intestine gets twisted in this bulge here, cuts off its own blood supply, and bingo: off to the OR. And yes, we take Blue Shield."

"God. That could happen at a very awkward time."

"Yes, it could."

"So you really have to have this done, huh?"

"I'm afraid so."

"It won't harm your—well, anything in that area?"

He looked her way in mock alarm. "Jesus, I hope not."

"You can still have that family with children?"

"Oodles."

"When are you going to have it done?"

"It's same-day surgery. Any time I pick."

"Who's your doctor?"

"More like what. I'm going to schedule myself at the Center."

"You're *what*?"

"Why so surprised?"

She propped herself up on an elbow. "I . . . I don't know. Somehow, I just figured that . . . what am I trying to say?"

He refilled her coffee. "You're trying to say that something that happened at the Center created a nightmare for you, so why would anyone in his right mind admit himself to the place?"

"It's not that."

He sat next to her. "Look, Maks. There's no denying that what happened to Christine was a tragedy. I won't try to minimize it or pretend it didn't happen. You're still living through the pain. All I'm saying is, it wasn't because of the Center. There's no way it could have been detected or predicted. It would have happened anywhere."

She had a chastened, glum expression. "If you say so."

"I say so."

Still, something didn't sit right with her. "Are you sure?"

"I'm positive," he nodded. "Look. This is a very personal, selfish decision I'm making. And no doubt there are lots of very capable surgeons out there, including friends of mine, who consider this a piece of cake and wouldn't mind getting an extra set of golf clubs from me. But this body's got a few more years left in it," he said, tapping his chest, "and I don't want anything—*anything*—to mess it up. That means choosing the place with the lowest complication rate and the most state-of-the-art techniques. As far as surgery goes, there's simply no comparison. That place is the Center. It's the best the world has to offer."

She sighed, unconvinced. "I guess you're right. I just wish I felt the same way you do."

"Trust me. The place is absolutely infallible. Everything'll work out fine."

Chapter Nine

THE TRANSITION FROM healer to patient is an experience most physicians find immensely humbling. Gone is the capacity to issue orders in a crisp, decisive way and with it, the not unpleasant feeling of power. As a patient, one becomes controlled, rather than being a controller. It's common for the physician-patient to develop a sudden insight into, and empathy with, the mind-set of those about to go under the knife.

Beneficial though this newfound insight might be, it is not without its down side. A mild depression might result, especially when the doctor-patient had been imbued with the panache of a surgeon—that breed of practitioner most smitten by boldness. Thus, on the morning of his admission to the Center, Dr. Chad Dunston's ego was slowly whittled away. After being poked and prodded and having his blood robotically drawn, he felt like crap. This worsened when he had to undergo a mandatory pre-op physical.

In the late 1960's, the Annie mannequin had been developed, a life-size doll used to teach cardiopulmonary resuscitation. Now, more than three decades later, the experimental prototype Annie IV turned the tables, having gone from a literal dummy to something akin to a robotic house physician. Although not even remotely human in appearance, the fact that the robot had a female voice was making Dunston progressively more uneasy.

"Please remain standing," said the pleasantly synthesized voice, "and kindly remove your underwear."

"Come on, is this necessary?"

"I am not programmed to reply to that question. Please recall the consent form on which you authorized the pre-surgical physical examination. Without it, your surgery will be cancelled.

"Hey, lighten up. Remember what happened to the Tin Man."

"Kindly remove your underwear."

"That was a joke. Little humor, y'know?"

"Kindly remove your underwear," came the monotonous reply.

"Jesus," he sighed, his smile now gone. "And I helped set up this place?" He paused, hands on hips, clad only in his shorts, glaring at the machine in front of him. Then, shaking his head, he stepped out of his underpants, gaining some small satisfaction from the fact that his taste ran to plain Calvins rather than tiger-stripe bikinis.

"Thank you," said the robot. The machine was, in fact, nothing like the public's conception of an android. Rather, it resembled a four-foot rectangle on wheels. Its "eyes" were top-mounted optical lenses which fed high-resolution color video cameras, and its "arms"—three in number— were mechanical manipulators that were refinements of the technology developed to handle radioactive substances or manipulate cargo in the space shuttle. The arms had tactile, thermal, and auditory sensors that replaced the stethoscope, thermometer, and digital palpation. Still in development was an olfactory sensor which could detect odor changes.

Swallowing his pride, Dunston stood still in meek humility as the machine inched closer. The optical sensors swiveled in the direction of his hips, and he saw the lenses constrict as the cameras focused on his groin. He prayed that, standing there cold and naked, he didn't have a reflex erection. And he didn't. But he'd forgotten about the bulbocavernosus reflex; and when the tip of the manipulator arm ran up his inner thigh, he felt the involuntary muscles of his scrotum constrict.

"Good Lord."

If the machine heard him, it didn't respond. Instead, guided by its optics, the three fingerlike tactile sensors rose to where hip met groin. The spongy pads at the tip of each finger were actually highly refined microprocessors that could detect subtle differences in contour, firmness, and texture; and by comparing them to the "norms" in its databank, could diagnose alterations in human anatomy. The pads stopped precisely on the almost imperceptible bulge of his hernia.

There was a subtle shifting as the pads pressed and retracted. It was without a doubt the most gentle exam he'd ever undergone. But rather than being relieved, he felt annoyed. The process gave him the creepy sensation of being touched by a tarantula.

"Please turn your head and cough," said the robot.

"Really, isn't it pretty obvious?"

"Kindly turn your head and cough."

So he did, covering his mouth, out of habit. With the cough, he felt the hernial bulge expand. There was the slightest twinge of pain as the pads maintained their pressure. But just as quickly the mechanical fingers withdrew, and the arms fell back to a neutral position on the machine. Dunston prayed it wasn't about to ask him to bend over for a rectal.

"Thank you," said the robot, rolling back on its wheels several feet. "The examination is completed. Please put on your gown and lie on the bed."

"What for?"

"You will be given further instructions. Your core temperature is 36.5 degrees centigrade. That is below normal.

If you are cold, you may cover yourself with the bed sheet. Is there anything further you wish?''

"Yeah, a double Glenlivet. And I'd like to get this over with.''

"Your ten A.M. procedure should begin on time. Have a nice day,'' said the female voice. A wall panel slid open, and the machine motored off into a service passage.

Dunston stood there for thirty seconds, trying to control his indignation. He found the experience dehumanizing. Did everyone feel the same, or was it because he was a doctor? Kids were probably terrified. And then he remembered that patients under sixteen were routinely sedated immediately upon entering the Center, to minimize the emotional trauma of being separated from their parents. Also, if he remembered correctly, someone—was it Randy McKenna, in the Interface Group?—had insisted on giving every patient a potent neurolept sedative, one with amnesiac properties, to enhance the positive aspects of their hospital stay while helping them forget things which were upsetting. Certainly, he hadn't been given anything so far. He made a mental note to talk with McKenna as soon as he got home. Assuming he could remember anything.

He looked about the room. It was a compact twelve-foot square, painted an aseptic white, as austere as it was sterile. There was a nightstand beside the bed and a telephone. Each room was private and had its own bathroom, which also served as a specimen repository. There were no windows. The most prominent feature was a forty-eight-inch video screen built flush with the wall, which provided programmed entertainment as well as communication with "visitors.''

Forgetting that a pre-admission form letter had instructed him to keep all valuables at home, Dunston looked toward his wrist for his watch. He guessed it was about 9:15. He sighed, letting his arms fall to his sides. "Pretty smart, coming here. Pretty smart.'' With nothing to do but wait, he lay on the bed and crossed his arms behind his head.

"Are you worried, Dr. Dunston?"

He bolted upright, startled, looking around. No one was there. The voice seemed to come from everywhere, like quadraphonic sound. It was a synthesized male voice: deep, resonant, and authoritative, yet with an avuncular familiarity that was profoundly soothing. His eyes darted from floor to ceiling. "Why should I be worried?"

"You seemed ill at ease before."

"Says who?" He continued to scour the room for hidden speakers. "Whoever you are, you weren't even there."

The laugh which followed was disarmingly gentle, reassuring. "But I was. You know me as Sygmund."

"Sigmund . . . ? Oh, right. Sygmund," he slowly said, recalling the acronym for Symptom Gathering Mechanized Universal Diagnostician. Syggy, as the Interface Group referred to it, was the Center's resident psychoanalyst, a refined interactive software program. But unlike other types of computer-driven psychiatric tools, Sygmund combined information from the entire nation's network of psychological databases into one superanalytic program, which had the unique advantage of also knowing the patient's lab data, diagnosis, and physical exam. This not only allowed it to rule out organic pathology, such as a brain tumor causing psychological symptoms, but also made it virtually intuitive. Where earlier software programs simply replied to key trigger words like "mad" or "mother," Sygmund had a sophisticated capacity to reason.

"Why do you feel uncomfortable?"

"I don't recall saying I was."

"I suppose it's natural to feel that way in this setting."

The damn thing's trying to get me to open up, thought Dunston. "Look, Syggy. I know we programmed you to explore a patient's psyche, but it's not necessary in my case, get it?"

"Why are you angry, Dr. Dunston?"

"Dammit, I'm not . . . I'm not angry in the least," he deflected. "I feel perfectly fine. I'm tickled pink and looking forward to my operation. How long until they come to get me, anyway?"

"About fifteen minutes. Why don't we discuss it while you wait?"

"Thanks all the same, but I think I'll grab a few winks."

"As you wish. But if there's anything you want to talk about, simply say 'Sygmund.' "

"You bet. Appreciate it." The thing was uncanny. It was certainly performing the way they'd planned, as an instrument of verbalization and catharsis for those in a hospital. People in stress-filled situations needed to talk. His own reluctance stemmed from . . . well, he wasn't sure. Perhaps because, having had a hand in its creation, it was a bit like speaking with one's child. And then, as he'd once remarked to Weiman, it was almost *too* perfect. Bordering on human.

And that, he knew, was absurd.

For the next quarter hour, he lay there in silence. He thought mainly of Maks—her long blond hair, her generosity, her vulnerability. She'd wanted to drive him to the hospital, but he refused out of what he thought was independence, but what in reality was a perverse chauvinism. He wished she were there right now. He couldn't wait to see her again. He was having delightfully lewd fantasies about her. He wondered if one of the reasons he'd chosen the Center was because its surgical wizardry would speed his convalescence without unduly limiting his libido.

The sliding doors hissed open to admit a gurney. Most of the updated gurneys were no longer simply flat, padded stretchers, but ones that were mobile, contoured operating tables. The devices would not only transport patients to the operating room, but once there, lock themselves into place without needing to move the patient again. They had built-in conduits for suction and irrigation and tubing for oxygen and nitrous oxide. But in Dunston's case, the old style was used.

"Good morning, Doctor," said a voice only slightly less mellifluous than Sygmund. "It's time to go to the OR."

"I couldn't just walk?"

It ignored the question. "Please lie still." As he lay there, a periscope-like pole arose from a corner of the gurney. Reaching a prescribed height, it clicked into place. From a hole in its top, three tungsten-carbide arms projected downward and outward to the corners of the bed, attaching to fasteners on the bed sheet. The sheet, he knew, was made of a disposable polymer which would be discarded once the operation was over. The purpose of the system was to move the patient, especially the patient in pain, more comfortably. Instead of having to turn or roll the patient, the apparatus transformed the sheet into a textured cradle that lifted the patient in speed and comfort.

He felt a tug, and the sheet rose into the air. It swung effortlessly toward the stretcher, a magic carpet ride that ended when the sheet mated with the corners of the gurney. Without hesitation, they were off. The stretcher had a faint motorized hum and moved at five miles per hour. Unlike the examination robot, it had no optics, being directed by a laser guidance system whose master computer, several floors away, knew the precise location of every object in the hospital, and thus could control their speed and direction to avoid collision.

He heard a muffled "pffft," accompanied by pressure on his right buttock. He knew what it was but asked anyway.

"Your pre-op medication, Doctor."

"And what breakfast cocktail am I getting today?"

"I wouldn't know, sir. Pharmacy section selects all medications."

Probably atropine and a tranquilizer, he thought, likely one with amnesiac effects. Or would that be given separately? He couldn't remember. But the virtually painless intradermal injection was certainly preferable to the traditional needle. Moments later, they arrived.

The operating room was actually twelve separate opera-

tories, served by two wide corridors that branched off the
main transport hall. The ORs were in three rows of four,
standing side by side. They were large by contemporary
standards, thirty feet square, each abutting a hundred and
fifty-foot corridor on one or two sides. Unlike traditional
hospitals, which had separate rooms for separate procedures, each room was multipurpose, with capabilities that
ranged from heart transplantation to trimming bunions.

Another departure was that there was no recovery room,
as such. Patients recovered in the room in which they were
operated upon, then were transported back to their hospital
bed. The upshot was that overcrowding, logjams, and
scheduling backups were unknown. Each room averaged
slightly under four procedures a day, though on any given
day, one room might do a single very lengthy case or seven
shorter ones. The only major concession to the Center's
human designers was that no cases were scheduled on Sun-
day.

With no need to screen prying eyes, the main entrance
to the operating suites were wide, doorless portals. Lying
on his back, Dunston felt the gurney turn and maneuver
down the corridor. The ceiling was a white sea of fire-
resistant acoustical tile. There was another turn fifty feet
further on, and he was wheeled into the OR proper. Dunston had toured the nearly completed OR area two weeks
before the Center opened. He'd been impressed then. Now
he was speechless.

The interior was immaculate, pristine, a marriage of
white ceramic and stainless steel. It was intensely bright.
In place of the traditional mirrorlike overhead spotlight, illumination came from a myriad of recessed high hats, with
dazzling argon or xenon light sources. Dunston's lids narrowed, squinting. Once the surgery started, many of the
instruments had supplemental fiberoptic lighting. As the
gurney motored to room center, the operating table—
which, between cases, lowered below floor level for clean-

ing—rose into receiving position. When they were side by side, Dunston was silently transferred from stretcher to operating table. The gurney wheeled noiselessly away.

Dunston lay on his back and tried to relax. Whatever he had been given was starting to take effect. He felt a soothing mellowness. The very heart of the OR was located where the spotlight once was: a spherical multi-lensed optical sensor, which guided all aspects of the procedure. Dunston stared at it, fascinated. To the best of his diminished recollection, all of the OR spotlights had been replaced by the sensors three months before. In his slightly altered state, it looked like a cross between a greatly magnified fly's eye and a rotating disco mirror. Built into the ceiling on either side of it, and, in some cases, extending upward from the floor, were the neoprene housings of instrument wells. Tubing, instruments, and other devices descended through rubber conduits toward the patient.

"Relax, Dr. Dunston," came a synthesized voice. "We'll be starting the procedure soon." He knew the words by heart. "Please place your arm on the arm board to your right." He did.

Most hospitals used two arm boards, which imparted a crucified look. The Center needed only one. But it was unusual: thicker than most, containing the vital signs monitoring equipment. As Dunston somewhat dully stared at his extended arm, one of the arm board's panels opened and a blood pressure cuff appeared. It extended on malleable support wiring that allowed it to move in any direction, much like a cherry-picker. Guided by the overhead optics, the cuff wrapped itself around Dunston's biceps. He felt it inflate and tighten.

From another compartment, a pulse oximeter arose and attached itself to his index finger. The device, which resembled a plastic clothespin, measured his blood's oxygen saturation. Simultaneously, a video monitor lit up on the adjacent wall. The monitor was largely superfluous in a room without humans. In had been installed with an eye toward split-screen video taping for subsequent review or teaching purposes. The digital lettering was white on a blue background. Dunston looked at it through progressively foggier vision.

First his name appeared, followed by his ID number and the date. Next followed his vital signs: blood pressure 132 over 76; pulse 84; temperature (where, he wondered, was the temperature sensor?) 37 degrees centigrade; oxygen saturation, 98%. Beneath it was a line of video blips reflecting his EKG, a normal configuration in regular sinus rhythm. Dunston wore a silly grin. All right, he thought. Never have to kick-start *this* ticker.

His diminished concentration was interrupted by a barely perceptible whir from the ceiling. A robotic arm lowered, containing an intravenous infusion catheter attached to transparent, fluid-filled tubing. At the same time, the blood pressure cuff reinflated, acting as a tourniquet, making the veins in his forearm distend. He watched in fascination as the mechanical arm neared him. It hovered for a moment, then stopped over a prominent vein which crossed his radius, the uppermost of his forearm bones. There was a hiss, and a brief spray of pink antiseptic moistened the area. The arm lowered until nearly touching his skin. There was a final adjustment of the IV needle's inclination, following which it plunged home. As a backflow of blood appeared in the tubing, the cuff's pressure dissipated. Then the blood returned to his vein when the solution began a steady drip.

And away we go, he thought.

Velcro restraining straps wrapped snakelike around his left arm and both thighs, virtually pinning him in place. It was a formality that he, as a surgeon, was familiar with, for patients undergoing anesthesia often involuntarily thrashed about. In his case, they were unnecessary, for all he was scheduled to get was a local. But what the heck: routine was routine. No need to upset the apple cart.

There came another whir, and the surgical manipulator arm descended. He smiled, for he'd played a large part in its creation. To the unknowledgeable, it might appear grotesque. But to Dunston, it was a thing of beauty. Made of black anodized aluminum, it was four inches wide and entirely flexible, containing numerous hinges, levers, and joints, able to maneuver and operate from any angle, changing positions countless times during a procedure.

Technically, it was known as the Telesurgeon. The most remarkable feature of the Telesurgeon was its rotating optical head, the size of a softball, located at the robotic arm's tip. Within its hollow core was a vast array of miniaturized instruments adaptable to almost any surgical procedure: scalpel blades, retractors, and dissectors, guided by a pincerlike grasper; an assortment of lasers, for bloodless incising and photocoagulation; high resolution optics, for microsurgery; spaghetti-thin tubing, for suction and irrigation; and countless spools of fine suture material. It also contained ultra-thin needles for injecting local anesthetics. In complex procedures, like cardiothoracic or brain surgery, two or more telesurgeons might operate in tandem. For a simple hernia repair, only one was necessary.

Dunston watched in fascination, feeling more and more lightheaded. He smiled in what he knew was an inebriate's uncontrollable grin. The Telesurgeon's head lowered into position, stopping just above his scrotum. Dunston felt his pulse quicken.

"Whoa, fella," he slurred. "Back up a bit. Too close to the family jewels."

He heard a click, and a small surgical blade snapped into place on the mechanical grasper. What's with this blade? he thought. His type of hernia incision was supposed to commence with a thin red laser beam. He blinked his eyes. As he looked closer, the smile disappeared from his face. What's going on here? And where the *hell* was the needle that was supposed to inject the local?

His heart was now pounding. He lifted his head, intent, for it was getting harder and harder to focus. More lettering appeared on the monitor and attracted his attention. He squinted at it, feeling beads of sweat break out on his forehead as he forced himself to concentrate.

Anesthesia, it read: GENERAL INHALATION.

"Hold it!" Dunston screamed at the top of his lungs, unaware that his voice had raised an octave. "I'm having a local, not general!"

There was no response. All of his attention was now directed toward the monitor, where more lettering appeared in a digital glow.

Procedure: 1. TESTICULAR BIOPSY 2. CARDIOVERSION.

His eyes opened in stark, abject terror. A biopsy, of the testicles? *His* testicles?

"Wait, dammit!" he shrieked. He tried lifting himself up, but the Velcro restrainers held tight. "There's been a mistake! Stay away from my crotch, for God's sake! All I've got's a hernia! For the love of Christ, stop!"

He struggled uselessly against the restraints. Oh my God, my God . . . There came a gurgling from overhead, from the IV tubing. A whitish solution began to slowly flow into the tubing, an emulsion which he knew, with nightmarish clarity, was the intravenous anesthetic propofal. His jaw began to quiver, and he watched in complete, utter horror as the liquid slowly inched toward his vein.

Chapter Ten

COMPARED TO MAKS, Cheryl had a no-nonsense disposition, avoiding superfluous etiquette and the stumbling blocks of tact or discretion by coming right to the point.

"So are you two getting it on, or what?"

Maks speared an asparagus tip, largely ignoring both the question and the remainder of her lunch. She looked at her watch. "I'm supposed to pick him up from the hospital at three."

"You are, then."

"I am what?"

"And you probably pick up his shirts from the laundry too. Nobody would act *that* domesticated unless she was actually doing it."

"Cheryl, this is the nineties. First, it's none of your business. Second, what difference does it make if I am or not? And finally, I have a feeling he'd pick up *my* dry cleaning if I asked him."

"Oy, vat a prince we have here. An unmarried doctor—"

"Divorced."

"Same difference. He's eligible, right? Probably got a nice credit rating from TRW. A new boat. Making great money, too. This guy's not exactly roadkill. What more could a girl ask for?"

"I don't need his money."

Which was true. Cheryl was aware that although Maks' parents hadn't left much of an inheritance, Maks was earning a comfortable salary. Ever since they'd been sorority sisters eight years before, Maks had impressed Cheryl as being today's woman: independent, carefree, with a mind of her own, and determined to make a mark in what they both perceived to be still a man's world.

Yet for Cheryl, what remained the greater mystery was why Maks had taken the largely unknown Kashiwahara job rather than one with greater name recognition. AT&T and General Motors were both known to have been actively recruiting her in college. Ultimately, Cheryl accepted Maks' explanation about needing job freedom as her motivation for joining the Japanese firm.

"You got a picture of him?"

"Cher, you didn't ask me to lunch to discuss my love life."

"Well . . . true." She toyed with a burrito, ate some of the meat and cheese filling, and pushed the rest aside. "Okay, enough. So long as you promise to introduce me sometime. Next item. What are they up to at Kashiwahara these days?"

"Same as before. Mainly HDTV," she said, referring to high-definition television, on which the Japanese had cornered the market.

"That's all?"

"Why so interested?"

"I'll level with you. They make lenses, right?"

"Some. But that's only a fraction of their inventory."

"Anything experimental? Ultra-high resolution stuff? I'm talking way beyond the electron microscope here."

"No, just for TV screens." She knew Cheryl saw through the lie. Maks' interest in research pertaining to optical computers was common knowledge. Yet in her code of ethics there were some things warranting integrity which made any discussion of them taboo. Cheryl's question confused her. Maks knew full well Cheryl's position in the DOE, but that didn't explain her inquiry. "What are you getting at?"

Never one to beat around the bush, Cheryl's questions became more pointed. "I told you about the Human Genome Project, right?"

"Up to here," Maks said, making a gesture with her hand. "How's that going, anyway?"

"Good. Well, slow. But we expected it to go slow. It'll take years. The thing is, someone's messing with our computer files."

Maks' surprise was genuine. "And they suspect Kashiwahara?"

"Honey, we're talking the U.S. government. They suspect *everybody*. There's a conspiracy behind every door, y'know? The thing is, most of the files dealt with experimental microscopy. Ever hear of the scanning tunneling microscope?"

Maks reflected. "No."

Cheryl accepted Maks' subterfuge. "If you insist. Now, listen up. There are two prototypes in this country. One up at MIT, and other at Lawrence Livermore. Hush-hush, still being refined."

"What's that got to do with me?"

"This STM, as they call it, is one hunk of machinery. It can magnify an image up to a million times, maybe more. You remember when I explained our work on base pair sequencing in DNA?"

"Vaguely."

"Lawrence Livermore—or maybe MIT, I'm not sure— is adapting their STM for satellite surveillance. You know, spot fly droppings from a hundred miles up and all that."

Maks knew full well the essentials Cheryl was referring

to. To map the human genome, scientists had to somehow make sense of the vast amount of genetic information encoded in the three billion DNA base pairs that make up the genome. The process was called sequencing. To sequence a chromosome, biologists first had to make a genetic map that contained known biochemical sequences, or markers. When the map had enough of these markers, it would then be possible to sequence the DNA segments between them to locate each segment on the overall map.

Although some of the technology was similar, Maks' job had nothing to do with genetics. In her still-classified research at Kashiwahara, Maks was instrumental in evaluating computers that performed complex pattern recognition tasks. The optics of such computers could, for example, help a missile identify a target, visually correct itself, and then home in on the target. Despite her knowledge of the essentials Cheryl was referring to, Maks remained silent. She knew nothing of STM particulars, and so she let her friend do the talking.

"Anyway," Cheryl continued, "in genome research, it's got a different use. The STM, if they ever get it to work right, can give a direct image of a strand of DNA. If it can be refined and sharpened, hell, we could literally *see* base pairs, and then read them like a road map. The old methods of sequencing would be out the window. You could crack the genetic code inside of a year, instead of ten. Get the point? We're talking megabucks for whoever irons out the kinks."

"Kashiwahara doesn't build microscopes. Not even in their R and D."

"So far as you know."

Maks stared back, holding her ground. "Right."

"The point is, we're still years ahead of the Japanese in STM development. We think. But we could be wrong. Those guys all work together."

"Maybe, collectively, their scientists have come up with

a breakthrough. If they have, we're up the creek.''

"Let me get this straight. You suspect some Japanese firm of tampering with computer files? And of using that data to build their own STM?''

"All I'm saying is, you work with these people. Do me a favor, and I'll owe you one. I'm not asking for company secrets. If you overhear any STM chitchat, just remember your old friend Cheryl, okay?''

"Sure. Nothing there, if you ask me. But I'll keep you posted.''

"Great. Now, about your doctor friend—Chuck?''

"Chad.''

"Chad, Angelo, whatever. He have any single friends?''

The man hunched over the office desk, studying the computer console. His carefully manicured hands were poised over the keyboard like some bird of prey. He didn't know what to make of the blackout during the alpha intercept, but he'd become obsessed with finding out what happened during the period of unconsciousness. Thus far, despite several weeks of hard work, he'd garnered surprisingly little. At least, about the Intercept. But other, seemingly unrelated facts that surfaced were astonishing. He'd circumvented outside and largely useless computer networks like HEALTHNET by going to the source, CHP itself. Under the guise of updating certain Interface errors, he'd gained access to the private room off the main lobby. After he logged in and accessed the mainframe, the computer turned uncooperative. It should have been a simple enough process: query the database and receive the answers. Yet no matter how he reworded his inquiry about the Intercept, the computer kept replying with "inaccurate entry" or "invalid format." It was clearly a stall, and one that had him perplexed. An inanimate piece of digital hardware was giving him the runaround. What the hell was going on?

Not one to give up lightly, he persisted, the fingers beneath his white-coated sleeves typing in questions about CHP policies and procedures. He already knew the answers, and for the most part, the replies were prompt and straightforward. Yet here and there, bits of unsolicited information appeared, like unexpected meteors in a familiar starscape. There were references to "File C.L.4-1," the repetitive command "locate," and, most surprisingly of all, a name: Christine Lassiter. He'd brought along a portable laptop computer. After plugging it into a jack, he had the mainframe regurgitate the seemingly illogical data onto a floppy diskette. This he labeled C. LASSITER. When he had time, he'd review it further.

Chapter Eleven

CHAD KNEW HE was almost out of time. In the average person, a drug injected intravenously crosses the blood-brain barrier in twenty seconds, and its effects on cerebral receptors begin ten seconds after that. Yet Dunston had no intention of getting any more mellow than he already was. His mind screamed for a response from his sluggish muscles. He grimaced, struggling to pull himself upright, but he managed to rise to no more than a thirty-degree angle. The tendons of his forearms stuck out like bloodless wires that threatened to erupt from his skin. Think, dammit!

He glanced frantically at the IV tubing. The propofal displaced the last of the clear fluid preceding it and flowed into his vein unchecked. Twenty-five seconds—damn! He tried buckling his knees chestward in a sort of massive stomach crunch, but the strap pinioned his thighs. In his receding consciousness, it dimly occurred to him that someone might be playing a monstrous joke on him. Concentrate!

Through the mere blur of his vision, he looked at his left arm. It was still firmly bound at his side. Fifteen seconds! In his heart-pounding agitation, he was now sweating profusely. Without actually thinking it, it somehow registered that the sweat might act as a lubricant. So instead of strain-

ing against the wrist strap, he began to frantically move his
forearm back and forth in seesaw fashion, trying to wriggle
it free. What the hell was holding it down? Your fist, stupid.
Relax your freaking fist!

He did. With a chaffing swipe, he yanked his sweat-
drenched left arm out of the wrist strap. Ten seconds. His
vision was going fast. Individual objects were no longer
discernible, consumed in a fuzzy, white haze. He craned
his body forward, lurching with his freed arm toward the
knee strap. He pawed at it, fumbling with numb fingers
until he found the fastener's seam. With his little remaining
strength, he tore at it savagely, until rewarded with the
sound of ripping Velcro.

His legs now free, he struggled to a semi-sitting position.
His limbs flopped off the operating table, and everything
began to darken. Five seconds. In his last vestige of consciousness, he knew he had to get out of there. Yet his right
arm, IV attached and running, was still secured to the arm
board.

"Yaaah!"

The primordial shriek erupted from his throat as he
ripped at the blood pressure cuff with all he had left. It was
too little, but not too late. His fingers snared the cuff's
inflation tubing with just enough force to dislodge it. There
was a loud hissing noise, and the tubing writhed wildly
through the air until it fell to the floor like an empty bal-
loon. The blood pressure cuff instantly deflated, unwrap-
ping itself from his right arm. The restraints were now
gone.

There was a sudden taste in his mouth, a taste peculiar
to propofal. That's it, he thought. Show's over. As blackness descended, some primitive instinct told him to try to
stand, to escape. But his legs were useless jelly. Instead he
wound up falling forward, and gravity did the rest.

The IV catheter was torn from his vein. His arms flailed,
and a stream of venous blood spewed through the air as if

shot from a water gun. Dunston's torso arched downward in a half roll. His right shoulder and cheek simultaneously struck the floor.

He didn't feel the impact at all. In fact, his body was filled with a warm sensation that was not at all unpleasant. It was a little like . . . dying. That one last, terrifying thought, as he flickered on the verge of unconsciousness, galvanized him into a final movement, borne from desperation. With a spasmodic lunge, his gown-clad body uncurled itself from fetal position, rolling ever so slightly under the operating table. But it was enough. He fell off the edge of the floor into the peculiar well which had been built for cleaning the OR table between cases. His now-unconscious form toppled toward the sub-floor four feet below, striking it with a dull and lifeless thud.

The room fell silent. The EKG's audible beat was gone. The life support systems, now detached, revealed straight lines where there should have been visible readings. It remained that way for several seconds, like a moonscape bathed in an artificial glow. Then, overhead, soft whirring began. The spherical multi-lensed optical sensor started to rotate. It began its search, stopping, turning, scanning the room's nooks and corners for the patient who had disappeared. As a machine, it drew no conclusions, merely conveying its data to the computer center.

Inside, the supercomputers came alive with activity. The room brightened with a dazzling display of flashing lights as the computers sifted through the confusion of incoming signals. Something didn't compute. The entire process that began months ago was now in jeopardy. Analysis of all the data—the thermal sensors, sonography, the infrared detectors—clearly indicated the patient hadn't left the room. And with the overhead optics showing nothing, that suggested only one possibility: the patient must have relocated in the recess under the operating table. In the case of Chad Dunston, MD, CHP #9649037, the gamut of possibilities quickly led to only one conclusion—that his usefulness to the project was now over. His continued existence was, in fact, a liability.

The instructions from the computer center were explicit. In operating room four, all monitors went blank, and the overhead lights dimmed. The OR table, still warm from Dunston's body, retracted into its cleaning well, rose again, and then repeated the process, slowly, at first, and then with trip-hammer speed, slamming up and down to ensure that whatever lay beneath it was totally, methodically crushed.

Chapter Twelve

MAKS SHIFTED HER legs uncomfortably on a bland and tasteless couch as she waited for Dunston in the Center's reception area. It was 3:32 P.M. She'd been sitting there for an hour, intentionally showing up early to make sure she didn't miss him. After lunching with Cheryl, she'd returned to her office, hoping to get some work done before the time came to pick up Chad. But she couldn't concentrate. After an hour of halfheartedly reading interoffice memos, during which she kept constantly looking at her watch, she admitted defeat and gave up. She strolled swiftly from the office, mumbling something incomprehensible to her puzzled secretary.

The weather had gone from sunny to overcast, making it all the more suitable, she thought, for convalescence. She understood why she offered to pick him up. To be sure, she was beholden to him for all the free help he was providing. But her motives went beyond indebtedness. This was something Maks was doing for herself. Chad's vulnerability while recuperating evoked something in her, something she hadn't felt since Christine's death. She needed to be needed.

En route to the hospital, she'd shaken her head with a little sniff of amusement. Waiting on someone hand and foot would be nothing if not unusual. Yet she planned nothing more than to totally dote on him. Although such shepherding was foreign to her, she didn't think it'd be difficult. How much training did one need to fix a stiff drink or two, to turn down the bed and fluff the pillows, to prepare something light to eat—in short, to become someone's modest slave? How ironic that here she was, a successful female executive, playing the contrarian. Yet not once did Maks feel she was forsaking her ideals.

During her hour-long wait, she'd observed the discharge of at least two dozen other patients. The routine varied little. First the patient's bill was paid by whoever had been delegated, everything being transacted electronically at the cashier monitor. After a short wait, the patient himself arrived on a motorized wheelchair, brought through one-way doors that read NO ENTRY. Upon reaching the lobby, and without regard to hugs or kisses, the wheelchair spit out a printout of instructions, proffered vials from the pharmacy for those requiring medication, and, on two occasions, assisted patients with leg casts onto crutches. The patient and his entourage were then prompted toward the exit, beside which was a wide, interactive monitor whose prompt read ANY FINAL QUESTIONS? The process went very smoothly. Its aspects reminded Maks of combining the illuminated maps in the Paris metro with taking a ride through a Disney theme park.

But where in God's name was Chad?

By four o'clock, she was decidedly worried. After what happened to Christine, it had been hard enough to come here, but she suppressed those memories with grit and determination and a liberal dollop of Dunston's carefree reassurance. Now those fears were resurfacing with an increasingly dry-mouthed anxiety. She got up and walked to the monitor marked PATIENT INFORMATION.

At the top of the screen, a single illuminated instruction read PLEASE TYPE IN NAME OF PATIENT, SURNAME FIRST.

She immediately went to work on the console keyboard. After a short but increasingly apprehensive pause, the message lit up in digital lettering.

DUNSTON, CHAD, it began, followed by the date. CHP #9649037. UNDERWENT SUCCESSFUL SURGERY AT 1022 HOURS. OPERATIVE TIME: 17 MINUTES. POSTOPERATIVE CONDITION: STABLE. COMPLICATIONS: NONE.

"So?" Maks asked. "Where the hell is he?" She clucked her tongue, then remembered she had to keep typing. WHERE IS PATIENT NOW?

Another brief pause, followed by DISCHARGED FROM CENTER AT 1417 HOURS.

Two-seventeen? she thought. Oh Christ, just before I got here! "Swell," she said with intended sarcasm, although she felt infinitely relieved. "Sitting on my duff for nearly two hours, while you're probably nursing a drink and catching up on the soaps." She turned, started walking toward the exit, and then stopped. Patients weren't supposed to drive themselves home, and she'd definitely seen his parked Mustang in the garage. On a whim, she turned back to the keyboard and typed in DISCHARGED TO WHERE?

HOME, it replied.

Maks frowned. She supposed he might have taken a cab, but she was certain he knew she was coming to pick him up. Wouldn't he have called?

She looked across the lobby, spotted the bank of pay phones and hurried toward them. She was of many minds: partly annoyed, partly relieved, mainly concerned. She picked up the receiver, inserted her charge card, and dialed his number. She drummed her fingertips while waiting for the clickover. Then came the ring. Soon three rings, then four. When it reached seven, she hung up and dialed again, taking care not to press the wrong buttons. After ten unanswered rings, she replaced the receiver in its cradle, looking thoroughly desperate. Was he all right?

She ran out of the hospital. Getting into her car, she

gunned the engine and screeched out of the parking lot, heading for Chad's place.

The operating room was silent. The OR table returned to the upright position and locked itself in place. The transport gurney motored in, taking up its position beside the OR table. Its arms extended, swung out, and effortlessly transferred the OR mattress onto its frame. It was a perfectly synchronized routine it had performed thousands of times before, except that now, the stretcher was empty. It left the room in the same eerie silence with which it entered. The overhead lights dimmed, and the OR fell into darkness.

Half an hour passed. It began as a buzzing, a faint and high-pitched tone, like ringing in his ears. Dunston groaned. He struggled to open his eyes, but his lids were impossibly heavy. He lay there in the blackness as his consciousness slowly returned. Bit by bit, minute by minute, he became aware of sensations. His mouth was dry, and his head throbbed. Most of all, his right shoulder had an intolerable ache. More than anything, it was that pain which helped counteract the effects of his still-drugged mind.

He wasn't aware that the aching shoulder had also saved his life. The retractable OR table was supported by a pole much like a hydraulic lift in a service station, one which had a sub-floor four feet below the car carrier. But the sub-floor, rather than being solid, was a rectangular frame merely eighteen inches wide. When he'd fallen into the recessed cleaning well, he landed at an oblique angle, taking the full impact on his shoulder. The foot-and-a-half metal frame was far too narrow to support his torso. The torque of his fall carried him off its edge, his unconscious body tumbling another five feet onto one of the many numerous, permanent concrete slabs that separated the building's stories.

Propofal is rapidly metabolized. A fast-acting non-barbiturate, its hypnotic effects wear off in less than fifteen minutes. But propofal, rarely administered alone, is usually given in conjunction with other sedatives. It took another fifteen minutes for their diminishing effects to combine with Dunston's increasing pain to jolt him into consciousness.

He awakened in total disorientation. He could see nothing—well, virtually nothing. Gravity told him that he was lying on his back. He stared upward toward a faint but perceptible lightness whose origin was the corridor beyond the OR above him. He saw what little he did through a haze. He rapidly blinked his eyes, trying to rid himself of double vision. But the filmy sensation remained.

He tried to sit up but groaned and fell back heavily. For several more minutes he lay there without moving, still not fully conscious. His memory was blank. He knew who he was, but where, and for what reason, eluded him. He massaged his right shoulder with his left hand. His shoulder was badly bruised, but he was able to move his arm. And from his ingrained medical training, he realized, albeit subliminally, that nothing was broken. He felt his chest and took in the texture of a patient's gown. What . . . ? He touched the length of his left arm with his right hand, found nothing amiss, and repeated the process in reverse. Something clotted and sticky covered his hand and forearm. He concentrated, growing more and more thoughtful. Blood? Yes, blood. *His* blood. And then, with sickening clarity, reality returned.

He gasped as his heart began to beat wildly. His eyes, now wide and staring, flickered in all directions, searching for an unseen enemy. But he found nothing, save the distant, indistinct illumination from above. It took all of his willpower to impose a degree of self-control. He concentrated, using biofeedback to slow his respiration with deep, cleansing breaths, which in turn helped reduce the nearly uncontrollable pounding in his chest. He counted out each inhalation and exhaled twice as slowly. Within minutes his terror had diminished to the point where he could link mental fragments into something resembling hazy thought.

It was all coming back now. The restraints, the monitors, the propofal . . . what in God's name had gone wrong? He struggled with that for a moment but found the mental process too taxing, for there were no obvious answers, and his brain was still too cloudy. Instead, he tried to figure out where he was.

He rolled onto his left side and winced. Scraped and bruised from the fall, he took a moment to flex his legs, bend his arms, and clench his fists: no serious damage. He discovered an almond-sized lump on his forehead, but it wasn't bleeding. He felt a little nauseated and wondered if he had a concussion. Then again, it could be the drugs. Those goddamn drugs.

Dunston sat up cautiously, inch by inch. He had no recollection of falling and was perplexed by the overhead light, feeling drawn to it. Once he was sitting, he tried to stand. But no sooner did he arise than he was overcome by a wave of vertigo. He reached out to steady himself but found nothing to cling to. With a dizzying spin, he collapsed back onto the floor.

He felt exhausted, in pain, and confused. Once more, his breathing came in spurts. This time he didn't fight it. He let his pulse and respiration wind down slowly, naturally. The near darkness compounded his lack of equilibrium, and his disjointed, fragmentary thoughts were disturbing.

If I just lie here, he told himself, I'll be all right.

Yet in his heart, he knew it wasn't true. He couldn't just lie there forever. Something terribly, sickeningly wrong had occurred, and his only hope lay in figuring out what it was.

I've got to concentrate, he decided. All right. I'm here, somewhere. And I'm alive. Good. First things first. My name is Chad Dunston. I'm a surgeon. A *real* surgeon, not one of those—right, I'm in the Center. I'm a patient, I was going to have surgery. Did . . .

Steady, old son. Hang on. Okay, there was a screwup. A royal, colossal, mind-boggling screwup. They didn't touch my testicles, right? And . . . yep, there it is. They didn't do the hernia either. Okay, now we know where we stand. Or lie. Mistakes happen. Well, almost. Soon as my head clears, once I can see straight, I'm gonna get the hell outta Dodge, right?

Wrong.

To the best of his memory, which was admittedly rather poor at the moment, nothing even remotely resembling a procedural error of this magnitude had ever occurred in the Center. Oh, there had been the occasional instrument failure. Like any machine, instruments had a measurable life span. And there had been the isolated case delay. But never, ever, had there been an anesthetic error once the agent of choice had been pre-selected. And although he was aware of surgical foul-ups in other hospitals—such as amputating the wrong foot—there had never been such an egregious blunder at the Center. If he really let his imagination wander, he supposed he *might* be able to contemplate a worst-case scenario in which, say, the computer programmed a hernia repair for the wrong side, right? Nah! Well, maybe. But an entirely wrong organ system? An appendectomy instead of a hysterectomy? A testicular biopsy instead of a hernia repair? Not a chance in hell!

No, there was something more than simple error here. This was no minor gaffe or silly technical problem. The system had built-in checks and balances, self-tests, and redundant backups, all designed to prevent catastrophe. He and the Center's other designers had challenged the system a million times and never found it wanting. It was simply impossible for a system so well conceived and tested to go berserk. So, for a mistake of this magnitude to occur, that meant one thing, and one thing only: that it wasn't a mistake.

Dunston felt himself grow cold.

If it wasn't a mistake, he concluded, it had to have been planned. Planned, obviously, by someone. Some sick bastard must have tampered with the system. Someone wanted his testicles biopsied. Not someone else's testicles, but *his*. But who, for God's sake? And why?

Even worse, he thought with a sickening chill, was the entire message on the computer monitor. The mistaken indication of general anesthesia was bad enough. That was then compounded by an improper surgical procedure. But there was something else, he suddenly recalled, the final, frightful word on the screen. Cardioversion. Dunston thought about it, and he paled.

In its strictest sense, cardioversion was a medical term for restoring an abnormal heart rhythm to normal by electric shock. It implied an abnormal cardiac rhythm to begin with. But what if the heart's rhythm was already normal, Dunston thought, as mine was? To the linguist, cardioversion might also mean conversion of a normal rhythm to something abnormal, such as tachycardia, fibrillation, or even asystole, when the heart stopped beating entirely.

And heart stoppage meant death.

He shuddered, unwilling and unable to mentally pursue it. One thing, though, was frighteningly certain. If the system had been tampered with to that extent, he couldn't naively presume that he could simply walk out of there. Wherever "there" happened to be.

Come on, he thought. That's paranoid.

But almost immediately, he knew it wasn't. Exhibit A, your honor: I *saw* the propofal flow down the tubing. I *saw* the words on the monitor. I *saw* the manipulator arm position itself. I am not dreaming. I'm a trained observer. I know these to be facts. *I know what I saw*.

He was thinking more clearly now. Deductive reasoning replaced fear and intuition. But what he concluded was terrifying. And it made no sense. He shook his head in confusion, like a fighter trying to clear cobwebs. One thing was certain. If he had any hope of figuring out what happened, he had to get out of there.

This time, he was more careful when he tried to stand. He was still dizzy, and focusing wasn't much easier. He proceeded in increments. From a sitting position, he went to kneeling. Then he went onto hands and knees, inching slowly forward. The light from above didn't reach the floor, and he carefully pawed the area before him like a blind man, searching for something with which to orient himself. He had gone perhaps two feet when his fingers found a pole.

It was thick, about a foot in diameter. His hands went around its circumference, touching, probing. It was metal, cool and slick, with a greased or lubricated coating. It felt vaguely familiar, yet he couldn't place it. But it was a starting place.

He leaned forward and hugged it. Even that slight exertion was tiring, and he clung tight, until his breath slowed. When his strength returned, he got into a squatting position and carefully stood up. His cheek was resting against the pole, and its strange, unctuous grease was like oil against his face. Finally, he was standing. Catching his breath, he looked upward. He was peering through a rectangular hole in the floor of the room above. The room itself was dark, and the dim light came from somewhere beyond. Directly overhead, though, was another flat black rectangle that matched the shape of the hole in the floor. The pole he was holding extended up into it, holding it about three feet above floor level. It all looked so damn familiar . . . His gaze strayed to what he thought was one of the room's walls. Dunston squinted. By concentrating hard, he could finally discern a faint latticework of grout that outlined the room's ceramic tiles. And then it struck him.

Jesus, I'm looking right into the same OR!

He recoiled, nearly losing his balance when he reached the slippery pole. But in stepping backward, his head thud-

ded into something hard and metallic. He winced, more
from fright than pain. He slowly turned, reaching up to see
what he'd struck. His fingers came to rest on a smooth,
cold ledge

Though his nose was virtually touching it, he could
scarcely see it. He ran his hands across its surface. From
below the floor level, it appeared to be some sort of rectangle. He didn't recognize it as the sub-floor in the cleaning well, for he'd never paid much attention to the physical
aspects of the Center's construction. He held his fingers to
his nose and sniffed. The metal was slightly damp and
smelled of disinfectant. He turned to peer up again into the
darkened OR. The room was obviously powered down, and
had been cleaned after his—

His what? His case? Surely the computers knew that his
case hadn't been completed. Or did they? If they did, what
had they done then? Clearly, he wasn't where the computers thought he was. Or was he? Christ, did they know he
was *here?* He quickly ducked down onto his haunches,
feeling the fear and desperation return.

He crouched there until his nerves steadied. He certainly
couldn't go out the way he came in. Powered-up or not,
the OR was alive with sensors. Even if he managed to
slither up the pole, which, in his still-weakened state, was
very doubtful, there was no *way* he could get out of the
OR undetected.

Suddenly the OR lights clicked on, full intensity. Dunston's eyes had grown accustomed to the darkness, and
even below floor level, the brilliance of the lights was dazzling. He scuttled backward, out of the glare. He had no
idea if he'd been spotted, or even if he *could* be seen down
there. His back hit something solid, and he braced himself.
It was a poured concrete slab wall. Sinking as low as possible, he looked around.

The precast walls had the rough, unfinished look of a
parking garage. There were no visible doors or exits. The

floor was wet. Everything seemed to have been just cleaned. That, along with the re-lighting of the OR suggested that another surgical case was being prepared, which meant that all sensors and monitors would be fully operative. He absolutely *had* to get out of there. But how, dammit?

He looked at the damp floor. There were nozzles mounted low on the wall, apparently for spraying some sort of disinfectant solution, another advantage the Center had over manual mopping. He couldn't see any drainage pipe, but the water had to go somewhere. He momentarily studied the shape of the room, the lay of the floor. And then he spotted it.

The floor had a slight tilt. It was the barest inclination, perhaps only four or five degrees, but it was enough for drainage. The concrete sloped toward a corner of the room ten feet away from him. Keeping to a crouch, back pressed against the wall, he sidestepped crablike toward the corner.

He expected it to be covered with some sort of grating, or strainer. Instead, there was just a hole, a two-foot square with beveled sides that made it a sloping trough. About a foot into it began what seemed like the concave piping of a sluice.

Dunston wondered where it led. No doubt all the OR's had a common drainage system which ultimately connected with the main sewage pipe. The pipe, in turn, fed an enormous septic tank buried well beyond the building's perimeter. But between here and there, he thought, there had to be some sort of exit. At the very least, the vapors and methane had to be vented, but probably not through a conduit wide enough for him to escape. Still, a system so vast had to have alternative entry points to let plumbers enter for repairs.

He was counting on it. Without another thought, he crawled headfirst into the drainage portal and the sluice pipe beyond it, slowly wriggling forward. After a slight bend, the pipe leveled off. It was just wide enough for his shoulders. As he proceeded, he was again plunged into darkness.

The pipe was cold and wet against his nearly naked body, which was covered in places by the flimsy, tattered gown. He was venturing into the unknown, motivated by fear. He stretched out flat, arms extended straight in front of him like an underwater swimmer kicking off the side of a pool.

It was no place for the claustrophobic. The going was difficult. Dunston inched along on knees and elbows, crawling on his belly, an army recruit shimmying under barbed wire. The air grew fetid. He inched forward, shoulders and hips in almost constant contact with the pipe walls.

He had only the slightest idea of what he was looking for—some sort of hatch or exitway that he could climb out of. As he wriggled along, he kept feeling the top of the pipe for latches and handles. But the conduit was smooth and seamless, the going slow and arduous. Every few feet he had to pause to catch his breath, for his muscles kept cramping. He tried to ignore the darkness that enveloped him, for this was no time to panic. He simply had to keep going.

He saw light up ahead, a faint glimmer ten or fifteen feet away. He slowly, painfully crawled toward it, hoping that by some miracle it might be a way out. Yet when he finally reached it, he discovered that it was nothing more than the square drainage hole for another OR. Disappointed, he lowered his head and moved on.

He felt a tremor in the pipe, a vibration that rapidly increased to a rumble. From above and behind him, there came the whooshing noise of water under pressure. It was thunderous, like a volley of fire hoses. Amplified by the hollow, cramped pipe, it quickly became a deafening, liquid roar. Dunston closed his eyes and winced, knowing that at any second the water would come gushing through the pipe.

The suddenly advancing front struck him like a tidal

wave. It surged over his ankles and knees, rushing forward, filling the pipe. In a microsecond, Dunston was under water. He held his breath, having the sense not to fight it, letting himself be swept along, instinctively knowing that whether he lived or died was completely up to fate. Like a cork in a torrent, he was briskly hurled through the tube.

The deluge of rinse water lasted a mere ten seconds, although it seemed to take an eternity. Yet it carried him a hundred feet before receding. His body slowed and then stopped as the water drained away. Finally, when he could no longer hold his breath, he exhaled in a wheezing gasp. He lay on his stomach, breathing in fiery spasms.

The dank air smelled putrid. His whole body was wet and sticky and seemed to be covered with slime. He lay there without moving, feeling as if he were going to vomit. When he finally opened his eyes, he found it was still dark. Soon the nausea passed. His lashes felt coated, waxed with something pasty. He wiped away the muck. He was clearly in jeopardy of being embalmed in human waste.

Yet as disgusted as he was, Dunston remained determined. Summoning up his grit, he resumed slithering through the rank slime, desperate to avoid another near asphyxiation. Here I am, he thought, like toothpaste waiting for the next big squeeze.

Muscles trembling, he continued his crawl. He estimated that, propelled by the wave and his own efforts, he'd gone about a hundred and fifty feet. That should put him well beyond the edge of the entire suite of ORs. But try though he did, he couldn't remember what lay beyond the operating theaters. He didn't even know what floor he was on any more. Probably, he was at least one full stair level below where he'd begun—but given the pipe's tilt, he might be two or even three floors lower. His best guess was that he was somewhere in the vicinity of the lab. But that was only a guess, and he couldn't hold out much longer.

If the floodgates opened again, he had no doubt he'd wind up submerged in some toxic vat.

His knees were chafed, his elbows bleeding. The pipe's angle steepened, and he began slipping downhill. It was a gentle, headfirst slide, not more than an inch a second. But with nothing to check his fall, he rapidly gained speed, sliding headlong into God knew what. And then, once more from behind him, came the terrifying tidal roar.

He didn't know what frightened him more, the idea of being drowned in a wave of assorted human excretions, or being submerged into a decomposition vat. Or more likely, both. In desperation he began to reflexely flail about with his outstretched hands as he plunged downward, searching for anything to arrest his accelerating descent. And then, miraculously, he found it.

It was a hand rung—a simple metal outcropping like those on a smokestack's exterior. Why it was on the inside of a pipe never crossed his mind, for in the few precious seconds remaining he concentrated on grasping it in both hands, clinging to it like life itself. This time the wall of water and debris smashed into him with even more ferocity than before. The torrent wrenched at his muck-slickened wrists, bending them nearly backward as the surge swept over him. In an instant he was completely submerged in swirling liquid filth that filled his ears and nostrils. By sheer imposition of will he stifled repeated impulses to gag, knowing that doing so would kill him. He tried desperately to hold on.

Somehow, he did. The full brunt of the noxious tide lasted only seconds, though in his weakened state, it seemed to take forever. He coughed and spluttered as the water ebbed away, not wanting to think about what sort of particles he was spitting from his lips. What in God's name had compelled him to climb into this lethal culvert in the first place? But he knew the answer. Escape. Escape from certain death.

The rungs had to lead somewhere. Since they were on the top half of the pipe, he hadn't felt them when he first began his crawl. After catching his breath, he explored the metal handpieces. They were about a foot apart and seemed to lead upward and backward from his downhill direction. They reminded him of the kind of rungs a chimneysweep might hold onto when cleaning a chimney's interior. On second thought, the drainage pipe might just be surplus conduit some contractor had on hand when submitting the lowest bid. Still . . .

He slid backward, pulling hand over hand. Like a human snake slithering in reverse, he worked fiercely back the way he came. Soon he was sweating profusely. Already lubricated by debris, each handhold became increasingly difficult to maintain. For every two inches he wriggled backward, he fell forward one. There was no way he could keep this up forever. Every so often he would paw between the rungs, along the top of the slickened pipe, searching, seeking. He had no idea if he would find anything, for all he really understood was that going in any direction other than out would doom him. He doubted he could withstand another deluge.

While holding on tight with his left hand, the fingers of his right unexpectedly swiped across a large spinner nut. Its three triangular surfaces, some six inches across, reminded him of the custom spinners that sometimes replaced lug nuts on sports car wheels. Without wasting another second he tried to unscrew it, as if opening a submarine's hatch. But it held fast. Christ, he thought, is this thing welded? Yet it had to be securing something in place—a door, a panel—and that "something" was his road to freedom.

And then he heard the roar again.

Panicked, he pried at the spinner with both hands, fighting exhaustion and frustration and the certainty of doom. The spinner wouldn't budge. Every fraction of a second

was a nightmarish eternity, for the water surged on relentlessly. Its sheer force and velocity made the entire pipe
vibrate. As his body was rattled about, one of his hands
lost its grip. The wave was now only seconds away. He
reached back in desperation. There, in the very center of
the nut, he found what he was looking for.

It was a cotter pin—stout, of heavy gauge steel—but a
cotter pin nonetheless. And it was the pin, not welding or
rust, that secured the spinner and prevented it from working
loose. Dunston grabbed the ring on its round end and pulled
with every ounce of strength he had left. It gave, slowly,
at first, but then more steadily. And yet the roaring water
was headed his way even faster.

"Damn you, bastard!"

With one last, furious pull he yanked the pin from its
retaining hole. He quickly dropped it and resumed work on
the spinner with both hands. This time it rotated easily,
turning counter-clockwise. He slapped at the flanges, swat-
ting them repeatedly until they spun like a top. The wave
was nearly on him, and he could smell the foul air preceding it. At last, the heavy spinner flipped off its bolt and
cartwheeled down the sluice. The section of pipe above him
came free.

He knew what he had to do. With a final, frantic effort
Dunston thrust his palms straight upward, knocking the
molded pipe section aside. Above him the air was fresh,
though he couldn't see a thing. He lunged into the dark
opening. Its metal edges were dry and firm, and his fingers
bit in firmly. He succeeded in pulling his body halfway
through the newly created hole when the wall of water
struck him.

He was like a gymnast, supporting his upper body with
elbows locked while the surging tide sucked at his legs.
But it was nothing compared with the strength of the previous wave. He patiently waited while the onrushing current swirled about his thighs.

The water slowly ebbed away toward its unseen destination at the end of the pipe. Dunston painstakingly lifted one leg, then the other, into the opening. Soon he was squatting on the pipe's outer surface. He carefully maintained balance. For all he knew, there might be nothing on either side of him. He cautiously looked about. Only yards away was a perfectly straight line, pencil-thin. Peering closer, he recognized it as a red laser guidance beam. These, he knew, were only at floor level, which meant that there had to be a floor somewhere nearby. Maintaining his posture, he reached out with his right hand.

Indeed, there it was: a flat concrete slab that felt cool to the touch. He swept his fingers over its surface. Judging from the angle of the concrete to that of the pipe, it looked like the sewage conduit was transecting the slab in a downward direction. He carefully stepped off the drainage pipe onto the welcome footing of the precast flooring. He straightened up, dripping and filthy, taking a moment to savor his victory.

Where the hell was he? Well past the ORs, to be sure, but the laser beam provided insufficient light for vision. After what he'd just been through, he had no desire to go pawing about in the darkness. Yet he had little choice. Holding his hands in front of him, he walked forward with ghostlike caution. He tested his other senses. Despite the filth in his nose, he thought he detected the faint aroma of food. And as he slowly moved ahead, he began to perceive a glimmer of light. Food . . . that meant the hospital kitchen. If he remembered correctly, the kitchen was on the same level as the lab. That probably meant the light was coming from the automated analyzers in the labs. And beyond the lab, he knew, was nothing but the vast, open expanse of the Center's campus.

Okay, I'm in some sort of passage. He sniffed again and smelled dust, suggesting that the passage was little used, perhaps never used. If he weren't so eager to flee, he could probably stay there indefinitely. But he *was* anxious, and so he nervously continued ahead. The light was brighter now, the images more distinct. He thought he could detect gurgling from within the lab, which indicated that he hadn't been completely deafened by the water which had roared over him. At least his hearing still worked.

Perhaps it worked too well. From just above him, he heard a whir. As he looked up, he saw the faint but recognizable outline of a video surveillance camera, which had just rotated in his direction.

He quickly ran back to his starting place and retrieved the section of pipe he'd kicked free. It was useless as a shield; it had now become a weapon. He picked it up in both hands and charged the video camera. Wielding it like an axe, he smashed the monitor repeatedly before it was finally knocked off its hinges and fell to his feet, shattered. Exhausted, he let the piece of metal clatter to the floor.

He felt thoroughly drained, and his breath came in gasps. He didn't know how much stemmed from his ordeal, and how much was a residual effect of the medications he'd received. More important, had he been spotted? The answer came depressingly soon.

There came another whir, louder this time, from inconspicuous sliding glass doors, remarkably well disguised as part of the lab's rear wall. As the doors parted, the interior of the lab became more visible from a perspective previously unknown to Dunston. He knew his priority was to get out of there, but what he saw left him mesmerized. The routine noises of the lab died as all the autoanalyzers shut down in synchrony, following an unheard command. Dunston stood there transfixed, silently gazing through a vapor as eerie as moonlit fog.

He couldn't see clearly, for the room seemed filled with mist. But there, no more than ten yards away, were row upon row of what appeared to be glass receptacles. The mist was fragrant, and the air had a robust vitality. He felt drawn ahead. Against his better judgment he stepped forward, waving his hand to disperse the steam.

He caught a glimpse of sudden movement, off to the left and just his side of the doors. Whatever it was scampered quickly out of sight. But before it disappeared into the darkness, Dunston was left with the distinct notion that it was alive. He wondered if it was some sort of lab animal. Yet it struck him as far too large to be a rat or guinea pig, and Dunston had the faint but unsettling impression that it moved on two legs rather than four. He strained to see better, wanting to reach out to it, to say something.

Without warning an autobot plowed through the fog, coming directly at him. Guided by the floor-mounted lasers, the mechanized robot rolled to a stop and peered at him through its artificial optics. Clearly it wasn't there to do a history and physical. But Dunston wasn't certain what other functions had been programmed in. It was blocking his way, but he thought he could easily get around it. Did it also have some security function? He didn't notice any weapons—at least, not in the traditional sense: no obvious firearms, stun guns, flechettes, or Tasers. As he took his first step around it, wondering what to do next, a little portal opened on the autobot's front panel. The opening was small, about the size of a camera shutter, but big enough for its intended purpose. It all happened in the blink of an eye.

He heard a muted pop, like the sound of an air rifle, immediately followed by a stinging in his abdomen. He looked down and saw a BB-size hole in his tattered gown. It was virtually bloodless, though it left a red mark on his skin. Within seconds, he felt himself growing woozy.

He'd been shot.

Not in the traditional sense, he knew, but with something he'd only read about. He thought that the pneumatic chemical gun, or PCG, was still in the experimental stage, and even then, intended strictly for the military. Yet like many other things in the Center, there were prototypes galore, adapted for medical use.

A refinement of the needleless intradermal syringe that administered his medication, the PCG, used air molecules to "fire" drugs at 4,000 feet per second. Applying a breakthrough in biochemistry, it had the ability to combine ambient air, made up of oxygen and nitrogen, with a variety of chemicals. Its development followed close on the heels of a silicon chip-size gas chromatograph, which separated the oxygen and nitrogen molecules. It then chemically bound the drug or chemical to the oxygen component alone, for the nitrogen was biologically inert.

Using particle beam technology, the PCG literally shot a dose of the oxygen-drug compound through the air, overcoming atmospheric resistance by streamlining flow. Although the compound's microscopic size precluded creation of a deep wound, the rapid velocity was ample to penetrate cloth or skin to a depth of five millimeters. In a human, that was sufficient to place it in the proximity of the bloodstream. The beauty of the PCG lay in the known affinity of oxygen for hemoglobin. Via a physiologic process known as diffusion, the oxygen component rapidly crossed the capillary membrane. There, it was quickly absorbed by red corpuscles and transported throughout the body.

Dunston prayed the compound wasn't some sort of poison or nerve gas. With each passing second he grew somewhat relieved, for if it were, he'd be dead by now. But at the same time, his giddy lightheadedness worsened. It was apparent that someone, or something, wanted him unconscious again. But for what? The answer which suddenly sprang to mind was frightening: to get at his testicles again.

With a drunken vengeance, he tore at the remains of his soiled gown. The autobot simply watched him, awaiting his fall. No doubt the master computers would summon a gurney once he collapsed. But he sure as hell wasn't giving up without a fight. Balling up the gown like wet laundry, he flung it at the laser beam on the floor. His aim was perfect. The cloth fell with a heavy plop, interrupting the thin stream of red light.

The autobot immediately reacted. It began swiveling in place, first this way then that, like a windup Christmas toy whose controls had gone haywire. Dunston had no idea what other tricks it had up its sleeve, but with his vision again starting to blur, he had precious little time to waste. He staggered toward the autobot just as it turned his way. He ran his hand across his chest like a scoop, gathering some of the fecal slime which covered him. Reaching the robot, he smeared the filth onto its top-mounted optical sensors, coating the lenses.

Dunston drunkenly ambled past, heading for the lab. The autobot's disrupted gears made low and rumbling noises, which had an unpleasant resemblance to a growl. He reached the sliding glass doors just as the mainframe calculated his direction. The computers sent a signal to block him with the doors, but too late. He breached the barrier an instant before the doors slammed shut behind him.

He stopped and looked about, gasping again, totally confused. Not only was his vision going fast, but the mist filling the strange chamber was thick and heavy. He found himself surrounded by the receptacles. The containers had an eeriness, an otherworldliness that spoke of forbidden new horizons. He reached out to touch one, as much to steady himself as to feel it. It was smooth as glass. Perhaps it *was* glass, but he couldn't be certain. It was also surprisingly warm, nearly body temperature, and covered with dewlike condensation.

He started to wobble, head spinning. Curious though he was, he couldn't see a damn thing any more. He felt strangely detached, like a man for the first time asking to walk a tightrope, knowing that the next minute could prove fatal, yet wondering what the sensation was like. And Jesus—what *was* that thing he thought he'd seen on the other

side of the doors? A sudden wave of nausea jolted him back
to reality. He had to move fast.

He looked around, straining to see. But by now, he could
only make out light and darkness. Yet as the darkness was
his enemy, so was the light his only hope for survival.
Subconscious instinct took over, and a voice in his inner
soul told him to go for it. He plowed straight ahead, no
longer caring what was in his way. Like a sailor topside on
storm tossed seas, he lurched right and left.

He knocked something over and heard a crash of glass
as it shattered on the floor. Screw it. Let someone else
worry about damage control; his life was on the line. Reach
for the brass ring, man. You live or die by that light!

He was audibly wheezing, on the very edge of consciousness, a boxer on the ropes. One more punch would put him
down for good, and there was no ref to stop the contest.
He knew it had to come from within.

And it did, for Chad Dunston wanted very much to live.
Bent over, racked by pain and exhaustion, he staggered
forward, desperate to be surrounded by brightness. With
one final lunge he leaped ahead, arms and legs churning.

He struck something again, something hard, and dimly
heard an explosive shattering. He had the strangest sensation of falling, of heading ever downward. So this is what
it's like to die, he thought. An instant later consciousness
left him, and he was overcome by darkness.

Chapter Thirteen

IT WAS ALREADY an hour after shift change, late in the afternoon. Thus far the day had been far too bizarre, and Officer Crowley was anxious to leave. Yet here he was, stuck at the captain's desk, going over his report like a schoolboy.

"What the bejesus you want me to do with this?" asked the captain, tossing the handwritten report onto the desk.

"I don't know, sir."

"I got files for DWI, I got files on perverts and bail bondsmen." He scowled. "You takin' some sort of short story course?"

"No, sir."

" 'Cause if you are, I got *no* file called creative writing. You follow what I'm saying?"

"I'm just tellin' it like it was."

Perplexed, the captain stepped back, arms folded across his chest. Crowley was a good kid. He couldn't think of a single reason why the young cop might lie. "Okay. Let's go over it from the top."

"Sir, I already—"

"Not with me you haven't. This guy," he said, glancing at the top page of the report, pausing for effect, giving the impression that he didn't already know the perp. In fact, he'd met the doctor on several occasions. "Dunston. *Doctor* Dunston. Y'know, Crowley, doctors give me the creeps. Haven't been to one in years. Doctors got clout. Guys with clout could make my life miserable. Whadya suppose'd happen if this Dunston makes waves or the commissioner gets holda this report?"

"I'd change it if I could, Captain. But suppose Dunston and the commissioner already know each other?"

Good point. "All right, all right. Just run it through for me."

Crowley shrugged. "It's like I wrote, sir. It was about a quarter of twelve. I was doing the day shift drive around the back of the Center, like we're supposed. Standard patrol, no reports."

"How fast were you going?"

"Real slow, maybe five miles per. And . . . well, that's when it happened."

"You're sayin' he landed right on the hood of your patrol car?"

Crowley shifted uncomfortably. "Yes, sir."

"How'd he hit?"

"Sir?"

"How'd he land on your hood?"

"Damned if I know."

"Crowley, what I'm asking is, which part of his body struck first?"

"Oh. He was stretched out, flat on his back."

"Lucky." He picked up the report. " 'Subject male cauc, unconscious. Appears thirty-five to forty. Impacted patrol car without warning. No ID. Subject naked. No smell of alcohol. Covered with BM.' BM, Officer?"

"Swear to God, sir. I never saw anything like it."

The captain put down the papers and shook his head. "Okay. What'd you do next?"

"Well, I got out of the car. When he hit, I braked hard, and he sorta rolled off the hood onto the ground. So I checked that he was breathing and had a pulse."

"You use those latex gloves?"

"You better believe it. How was I supposed to know he was a doctor? Smelled like he crawled out of a sewer."

"Then what?"

"I radioed in, and they called the paramedics."

"You didn't move him at all?"

"Christ, I didn't want to go *near* him. I thought he must have been some psycho."

"How long before the ambulance got there?"

"Ten minutes, tops."

"And they took him to Brookhaven?"

"Yes, sir. The Center doesn't have an ER."

"You didn't actually see him fall, then?"

"No, not really."

"So how do you figure it?"

"I don't know, sir. I honestly don't know."

"But he did fall out, is that what you're sayin'?"

"Well, I can't swear to that. I suppose he could've been skydiving without a parachute. But there *were* fragments all over the hood, and a helluva hole in one of the Center's glass windows."

"What floor?"

"Second."

"How far was that to your hood?"

"Ten, twelve feet."

"This window. Did it look like something someone might accidentally fall through?"

"No, sir. It was like a picture window, but those fragments were pretty thick. If he went through, it must have been under a full head of steam. That's why I thought he was a nut case."

"Anyone get a look at what's inside that window yet?"

"We're still workin' on that. Kind of hard to get information outta that place. But it ain't the psych ward, like I first thought."

"How do you know that?"

"The paramedics told me the place doesn't have one."

"He still unconscious when they took him away?"

"Out cold. They said it didn't look like anything was broken."

He held up a page. "This is a fax of his ER exam. Just so you know, the paramedics were right. No serious injuries, but he'll probably be sore as hell tomorrow. Assuming he wakes up."

"When did they ID him?"

"As soon as he got admitted. They know him over there. It's one of the places he works."

"What was he doin' at the Center, Captain?"

"I'd like to know that myself, Crowley." He walked to the door and opened it. "Okay, take off. A cop's supposed to see everything sooner or later. But this is sure a new one on me."

The officer left without further prompting. The captain closed the door and paced slowly around his desk. Now that he'd spoken with Crowley, he'd have to return the DA's call. He hoped the feds didn't get involved, although, strictly speaking, the incident did occur on federal property.

He shook his head as he reached for the phone. It just didn't compute. Even if the guy had totally freaked and tried to commit suicide, that didn't explain why he was smeared with what the captain now knew was a trace of disinfectant, bile, blood, saliva, and every other type of human secretion. How could something like that happen?

He remembered when, as an intelligence spook in Vietnam, one of his many jobs had been to debrief POWs who'd escaped NVA camps. They'd come through the jungle, on the run for days or weeks. They were covered with all sorts of filth. Of course, when you're trying to escape certain death, there's not much of a chance to shower and shave. Escape . . .

What were Crowley's words? "Under a full head of

steam''? Was it even remotely possible that . . . no way, he figured. Dumb idea.

And it was scaring the hell out of him.

His eyes opened with infinite slowness, like a spasm ending. He saw bright lights overhead, and an IV dripping into his arm. Most of all, he felt the restraints that bound his wrists. And the singular thought which came to Chad Dunston's mind was that they had somehow gotten him back into the OR. In white-faced panic, he struggled to sit up, letting out a shriek.

"No!"

Heart pounding, nostrils flaring, he stared wide-eyed at his surroundings. Someone was rushing toward him—a nurse? She looked familiar, *was* familiar. Didn't she work at Brookhaven?

"It's all right, Dr. Dunston." Holding him gently by the shoulders, she eased him back onto his pillow. "How're you feeling?"

His throat was dry, his voice raspy. "Julie?"

"Well, at least your memory's not gone."

"What are you doing here?"

"This is where I earn my paycheck. Don't tell me you've forgotten all the hours we spent working here together."

Here? His heart slowed, and he took a moment to check out his surroundings. To his left was some old gomer on a respirator, and on his right, an unconscious teenager, likewise intubated, head swathed in bandages. He was in an ICU, not an OR. And although many ICUs had a cookie-cutter similarity, this one was distinctly Brookhaven's.

"What am I doing here?"

She checked his pulse, examining her stopwatch as she spoke. "This is where they brought you."

"From where?"

"You came in on days, so I didn't get the whole story. But on report, they said the EMTs brought you in from the

Center around lunchtime. Well, from the grounds of the Center, anyway. And that,'' she said, finishing with his pulse, ''is all I'm allowed to say.''

''According to who?''

''Dr. Stingley.''

Chad frowned. ''Not that jerk.''

''I'm afraid so. I'm supposed to notify him the instant you come to.''

''What time is it?''

''A quarter of six.''

''Jesus,'' he said softly.

''And I'm afraid he usually sticks around until seven. Don't make such a yucky face. Sorry, but I've got to call him.'' She turned to go, hesitated, and turned back toward the raised siderails. ''Chad, they told me to keep my trap shut, but I figure I'm entitled. I mean, we've known each other long enough.''

He smiled weakly. ''Through thick and thin.''

''You don't seem like the type. Then again, who is?'' She paused, looking him straight in the eye. ''What I'm saying is, are you on something?''

He vaguely remembered the PCG injection, and his eyes narrowed. ''Good question.''

''They did a toxicology screen.''

''I bet. But I have a hunch that if anything shows up, it won't be your typical stuff.''

''What, then?''

Again, a wan smile. ''Look, Julie. I don't remember much of the past eight hours, but I swear on a stack of Bibles that I'm not on drugs. At least not the self-administered kind.''

''Okay, I had to ask, you know?''

''Sure.''

''Right. Now I'll phone the schmuck.''

''Julie—''

''I can't, Chad. Not until he's spoken with you.'' She

túrned and headed toward the phones at the central nursing station.

Walter Stingley, MD, the hospital's head of psychiatry, was a relatively recent colleague of Dunston's. A peripheral member of the Interface Group, Stingley combined his knowledge of the psyche with an aptitude for computers that led to development of the software program Sygmund. After Sygmund was installed, however, Stingley became an infrequently needed consultant. He had little to do with the more active Group members.

To Dunston, it was just as well. Stingley was one of Dunston's least favorite people. They'd had numerous run-ins in the past, mainly over the management of trauma victims strung out on drugs. Archly conservative, Stingley had little concern for the psychological welfare or rehab of those drug users who survived surgery. Psychiatry, to him, should be reserved for outpatient neurotics or inpatient psychotics. Dunston, on the other hand, felt drug abusers had problems enough without further making them pariahs or merely paying them psychological lip service before they once more hit the streets.

Stingley approached the bedside rather stiffly, wearing a dated double-breasted striped suit. "Returned from the dead, have we?"

"Damn close to it."

"Whatever happened to you, Dunston? Here you are, a well respected surgeon. By some, at least. From what I understand, you went to the Center for a simple hernia repair, and left it by trying to commit suicide."

Dunston looked at him incredulously, then sighed. "You say potato, I say polenta. You say suicide, I say step aside."

"Surely you can do better than attempted levity."

"You really think I tried to kill myself?"

"What would any reasonable person think? If truth be told, I expected something like this long ago. You've been under a great deal of stress since your wife left. Everyone knew it, but you wouldn't accept any help. So there you were, a patient in a hospital, no longer in control. And you snapped. It's not often one exits a hospital through a plate glass window. Unless he's trying to exit life itself.''

So he *had* made it to the window—to the light! He looked at one of this arms and saw only a smattering of fine cuts. Ignoring Stingley, he pulled over the bedside tray table and pushed down a place in its top to swivel up a vanity mirror. He inspected his face closely and found a handful of nicks and abrasions, nothing requiring suturing. He'd been damn lucky. "Thank God for safety glass.''

Stingley turned patronizing. "Care to tell me about it?''

"That'd be just ducky, except I don't remember a thing.''

"Oh come on, Doctor. We're here to help you. You know my feelings about drug use. But if you have a problem, arrangements can be made. You'll get the help you need. In confidence, of course.''

"How uncharacteristically generous.''

"Charity begins at home, Doctor. For better or worse, you're a member of our medical family. So: where would you like to start?''

Losing his patience, Dunston's lids narrowed. "How's your hearing, Stingley?''

"Pardon?''

"I'm gonna say this just once. First, I didn't try to kill myself. Second, the only thing I remember is going to the Center's OR, and getting something through an IV. Next, I woke up here. That's it. End of story. I have plenty of questions myself, but I doubt you're in a position to answer them.''

Stingley glowered. "You're making this hard on yourself.''

"Is that so? The way I see it, *I'm* the one in the hospital bed.''

"Very well,'' he said, lacing his manicured fingers together as if wiping his hands of the matter. "But I suggest you think about it tonight. You're admitted for observation, you know. Suicide precautions and all that. I'll be back tomorrow morning. If you persist in this fantasy of amnesia, you'll probably be suspended from the hospital staff. And if you are, we're under an obligation to report it to the State's Office of Professional Medical Conduct.''

"I'll make it easy for you. Tell you what. Go on and report me, tonight if you want. I'm outta here. Just have one of the nurses bring me a consent form, because I'm signing out against medical advice.''

Stingley seemed to gloat. "AMA? Your decision. Frankly, I didn't think you were man enough.'' Smiling, he headed for the nurses' station.

Dunston lay there, fuming. I saw it coming, he thought, but I let that idiot get to me. Smart, real smart. Nothing more inspirational than a cool, levelheaded surgeon. He looked toward the nursing station. After Stingley sauntered out of the unit, Julie headed toward the bedside.

"Chad, you can't just sign out! If you do, it's like admitting they're right. That jerk could make your life a shambles.''

"That guy should be canned. The way I see it, Julie, considering everything that's happened, 'a shambles' sounds pretty good to me.'' He shifted in bed. "What I want to know is, is there anything physically wrong with me? If there were, I'd consider staying. I feel like I got hit by a truck, but you know what I'm getting at. Any fractures, blood loss?''

"No, your films are negative. Vitals are normal, 'crit's stable, labs are all okay. Of course you haven't had your EEG or CAT scan yet.''

He grinned slyly and pointed a finger at her. "Thanks for the offer. Gonna take you up on that one of these days. Now, take off these damn restraints, take out the IV, and bring me an AMA consent, okay?''

"Chad—''

"Mind's made up, Julie. I'll owe you one, promise."

She sighed. "I'll have to report this to my supervisor."

"Report away. I understand."

"And you're gonna owe me one helluva lot."

He smiled. "With pleasure."

"All right, I'll get the ball rolling. Oh, there are a couple of people here to see you. You up for visitors if they keep it short?"

"Do I have to?"

"No, but one's a cop."

"Then I guess I have to."

Moments later, after Julie had removed the restraints, he was approached by a burly six-footer with receding reddish hair. Dunston knew and respected cops; he often worked with them. Tom Donohue was a captain at what they called "the county," the Yaphank Precinct. Dunston hadn't seen him in over a year, and he knew that Donohue rarely did his own field work unless it was urgent.

"How's it goin', Doc?"

Dunston sat up, still a little woozy, but sufficiently clear-headed. "Off critical, thank you. And about to make tracks to my *hacienda*."

"They told me you'd be staying for a while."

"They told you wrong."

"I got here just in time, then."

"Looks that way." He hated playing cutesy. He knew and liked Donohue and didn't want to give him a hard time. But Dunston had his own agenda, for the day's events had been more frightening than any in his life. "In time for what?"

"Come on, Doc. Level with me. I got things to do, you got things to do. I don't wanna waste your time. So how about it? You wanna tell me what happened at the Center?"

It was too horrifying to think about, much less discuss. Anyway, he'd already committed himself when he'd spoken to Stingley. "I would if I could. But the facts are short and sweet, because I don't remember squat. Not after they put me to sleep. And then bingo, I wake up here and don't even know what the hell I'm doing in this place.''

"Okay. What were you doing in the Center? Everyone knows there're no people there. Except patients. Place is run by robots.''

"First of all, it's not run by robots. It's run by a system of very sophisticated computers. Well,'' he conceded, "maybe some of the machines act like what you'd call robots. And second, it just so happens I *was* a patient there.''

"Yeah?''

"That's right. A simple little hernia, a med student could do it. I went to get it repaired.''

"If it's so simple, why'd you go there?''

Dunston took in Donohue's patient expression. The guy was no dummy; he cut right to the chase. "It's like this,'' he explained, struggling around the cold edges of a nightmarish flashback. "Believe it or not, I helped design the place. For my money, it's the safest hospital there is. And contrary to popular opinion, it's not just for open hearts or brain surgery. You got a hangnail, they can remove it at the Center.''

"If it's that safe, what happened to you?''

Dunston looked away. "I wish to hell I knew.''

Donohue pulled over a chair and sat on it backward, Western style. "Doc, I've got two problems. First, you might not know this, but the Department's got a contract with the government. We send a patrol car around the Center a couple of times a day, and the U.S. Treasury sends us a shitload of taxpayer money in return. Ever since the place opened, we never had a serious problem. Until now.''

"Nobody's told me anything yet.''

"Crowley swears some psycho—read that as you— comes smashing through one of the place's few plate glass windows, just as Crowley was drivin' by. Lands flat on his

back on the patrol car's hood. We're talkin' inches here,
folks. You land a little in front of him, and his tires turn
you into dogfood. Do a little more dive and roll, you hit
your head first, your neck snaps, and you're a paraplegic.''

''Quadriplegic.''

''Whatever. Either way, I know you ain't one of the Flying Wallendas, and since all you got are a few cuts and
scrapes, I'd say you're pretty damn lucky.''

''I can't disagree with that.''

''And you remember none of this?''

''Not a blessed thing.''

The captain searched for more of a response but found
none. ''You like paperwork, Doc?''

''Do you?''

''Hate it. Half a cop's job is paperwork. And the craziest
part of Crowley's paperwork, the report he filed on you,
was that you were, to use his words, 'covered with BM.'
Shit and turds. What his report doesn't say, but what I
happen to know from talkin' with the ER folks who cleaned
you up, was that you were also covered with every other
kind of snot and crap that can come outa the human body.
Like you were batter dipped, but not by Colonel Sanders.
Now, I ask myself. Just how is this possible? A guy comes
crashin' through a hospital window onto a police car, unconscious, slimed worse than in *Ghostbusters*. What I'm
sayin' is, can you help me with any of this, Doc? 'Cause
if you can't, I'm just jerkin' myself off.''

Dunston smiled. ''Don't cops do that all the time?''

''I'm bein' serious.''

''So am I, Captain. I really can't help you. This whole
thing's as much a mystery to me as it is to you. I have no
rational explanation for anything after I went into that OR.''

The policeman gave him a long, hard stare. Then he got
up and turned the chair around. ''I honestly don't know
who's jerkin' who off, Doc. But if you remember anything
else, you'll give me a call?''

"You bet."

"Okay. Lady wants to see you. If the nurse gives thumbs up, I'll send her in."

As the captain walked away, Dunston closed his eyes and made a long, slow exhalation, as if surfacing after holding his breath on a long, underwater journey. He began to shiver all over. He pulled up the covers, eager for the warmth and comfort of his own bed, when he felt the tender softness of lips brushing his cheek.

Maks took his hand. Her chin quivered as she fought back tears of joy and anguish. "How're you feeling, Chad?"

He opened his eyes and simply looked at her standing there, her blond hair and blue eyes the most tantalizing vision anyone in his condition could hope for. He gazed at the luxurious silkiness of her hair. Backlighted by the overheads, each strand seemed to live in harmony with the light, dancing in its shadows. He wondered what lay behind her kiss.

He squeezed her hand in relief. She was such a welcome sight. When trapped in the bowels of the Center, he wondered if he'd ever see her again. Now, he longed for her. Maks waited, staring at him with concern, wanting him to speak. But he seemed reticent. She touched his forehead with cool fingers.

"They have funny rules here," she finally continued. "No more than two visitors per shift, and then only fifteen minutes each."

"How long've you been waiting?"

"Not long."

He held her fingers tight. "I'm glad you came."

She suppressed a tear and summoned the courage to ask. "What happened, Chad? Did the surgery go all right? I came to the Center an hour early to pick you up, but the computer in the lobby said you'd already been discharged home."

He was stunned. *"Home?"*

"That's what the monitor said. I just don't understand. I figured you'd have at least called. Then I called you. I got no answer, and your car was still parked in the lot." She sounded frantic. "I thought maybe you took a taxi, or . . . Chad, talk to me!"

He looked away, still clutching her hand. Grateful to be alive, he felt his own tears well up, knowing that she cared. He forgot that she'd planned to pick him up. But he just regained consciousness, and undoubtedly there were lots of other things he couldn't remember.

What in God's name could he say? That a place he had a hand in designing, a hospital he publicly touted as the world's best, had simply screwed up? No, not screwed up; what had happened was intentional, by design. She believed in him. How could he possibly convey to her what went wrong when he didn't know himself?

His evasive words were muted. "How'd you find me?"

"I went to your apartment looking for you. I was desperate. The police were already there. I mean, they'd just gotten there. They said you'd been brought here. I told them I was supposed to pick you up and . . . Chad, what *happened?"*

Impossible, he thought. There was just no way he could explain it. The images were too fresh, the nightmare too real: the wrong operation listed on the monitor; the propofal instead of the local; his frantic attempt to escape. The memory of his crawling, willy-nilly, through a pipe of God knew what, and his final, one-in-a-million lunge through the lab window . . . Was it the lab? And what in the world had he seen there? Bizarre receptacles and the drugged vision of something on two feet scurrying away? In time, maybe. But right now, how could he explain even a fraction of that?

"Let's get out of here."

"They told me you were admitted." She lowered her gaze. "Attempted suicide."

"Maks, you know me better than that." He squeezed her hand reassuringly. "I'm going to un-admit myself. Find Julie at the nursing station and ask her to come over here, okay?"

Moments later, Julie returned with Maks in tow. Dunston detected a certain friction between them, and for some reason he was secretly pleased. Julie carried alcohol swabs and a clipboard.

"Are you sure you want to go through with this?"

"Paint me gone."

She pressed a moistened swab over his IV site, removed the thin plastic catheter, and put adhesive tape over the swab. "There. Now I'm supposed to read you the consent form."

"Trust me, Jules. I know it by heart."

"Your funeral," she said, handing him the clipboarded piece of paper. He saw an unnecessary *X* indicating the line on which he had to sign. He signed and dated it and printed his name underneath, wondering if he was putting an irrevocable end to his professional career. Then he handed it back to her to co-sign as witness.

That done, she looked up at him. "There's only one hitch."

"I can handle Stingley."

"I'm referring to something more mundane. Like clothes. Unless Miss Lassiter brought some. This hospital frowns on patients leaving bareass."

Maks shook her head apologetically.

"All right," Julie said. "I'll check with the ER. They usually have hand-me-downs. Might not fit, but fashion night's next week. You don't mind a few bullet holes in your jeans, do you?"

She winked at him and departed to make her calls. Dunston somehow doubted that the clothing he'd worn that morning was still in his hospital room at the Center. He contemplated trying out a reasonable story on Maks, but he didn't want it to be an outright lie. Still, he owed her some sort of explanation. He needed time, and lots of it, both for himself, to try to sort things out, and for those like Maks, who were counting on him.

"I don't know where to start. You're not going to believe what I have to tell you."

"I will if you say so."

He hesitated. "I didn't have the operation."

"Why not?"

He ran fingers through his uncombed hair. "I wish to Christ I knew. Something . . . happened."

"What?"

He shrugged. "Nothing. Everything." He frowned. "This is really difficult. It's so damn complicated. It's like . . . there's something very peculiar going on at the Center. I don't know what it is yet, but it has a lot to do with me."

Julie interrupted, and it was just as well, for his explanation already had him confused. She was carrying a large shopping bag containing rumpled brown trousers, a Yale Bulldogs sweatshirt, and an old pair of thongs. She dumped the contents onto his mattress. "Sorry, they're out of designer stuff. There was some underwear, but I don't think you'd like what was crawling in it."

"Appreciate it, Jules."

"Need a hand?"

"I think I can manage, thanks."

"Okay." She motioned for Maks to wait outside and pulled the U-shaped privacy curtain closed.

Dunston stripped his hospital gown off, feeling stiff and achy. He got out of bed somewhat shakily, wondering if he'd been too cavalier in dismissing Julie's assistance. He steadied himself against the side rails and slowly put on the clothing. When he was finished, he pulled open the curtain and painfully made his way to the nursing station.

"How do I look?" he asked Julie.

"Thoroughly scruffy. Vagabond look. Maybe it's in this

week. Give me a call tomorrow, okay? Let me know how you're doin'?''

"Will do. And thanks. Where's—"

"Outside, in the waiting room."

Looking like an undercover narc in a B movie, Dunston slowly ambled through the ICU toward the swinging door exit. Pushing it open, he found Maks standing right there, waiting. She suppressed a smile when she saw him, quickly taking his hand. She reached into her purse and gave him a pair of sunglasses.

"Maybe you should put these on."

"Afraid to be seen with me?"

"Stick around here, and you'll start getting handouts."

"Right. You lead. I'll follow. I promise not to mug you."

Hand in hand, they headed quietly down the corridor. She broke the silence a few moments later.

"I talked with Captain Donohue."

"A good man. What'd he have to say?"

"He didn't volunteer much. Did you really fall through a plate glass window?"

"I'm not sure. I suppose so. At least, I remember heading in that direction."

"Can you remember why?"

He seemed amused. "Funny. That's more than I've told anyone up to now." But his smile quickly faded, replaced by an expression of anguish and fear as the memories resurfaced. He gripped her hand tighter. "I think it might've been trying to kill me."

"*What?*"

"I hope you're ready for this, because this is where the incredible stuff starts. You sure you want to hear this drivel?"

She did. As they slowly left the hospital and headed for her car, Dunston began to recount what he thought happened. It was a painstaking, arduous recollection, for there were many things he didn't know, and he had to guess to fill in the gaps. He would stop and start again, going over little details as he suddenly remembered something, dragging his thoughts through a drug-induced haze. He felt as if he were wading through the Byzantine hedgework of a Victorian garden, always having to mentally retrace his steps.

Maks kept silent on the way home, not wanting to interrupt, understanding his need for catharsis. She drove with one hand and held onto him with the other, every so often glancing his way. He spoke with eyes closed, leaning back against the headrest. She could see an expression of real torment lining his face, mixed with generous measures of uncertainty and ongoing fear. He was just finishing his recitation when she turned the car into her driveway. He finally opened his eyes.

"Your place?"

"Yes. My tub's bigger than yours."

He sniffed an armpit. "It's that bad, huh?"

"Worse."

He tugged at the sweatshirt. "I have no sentimental attachment to these rags."

"Then dump 'em. I still have a lot of my father's old stuff. Something'll fit you."

She parked the car, got out, and walked around to help him out. He made a little groan when he stepped onto the driveway, hunching forward against the increasing stiffness of his muscles. She took his elbow and steered him toward the house.

"How come you haven't said anything?" he asked.

"What's there to say?"

He stopped, a wounded look on his face. "Don't be so patronizing. I didn't make this up, Maks. Do you believe anything I've said?"

She wrinkled her nose. "I certainly believe you were in a sewer."

"No, the other stuff. The parts I said would sound incredible."

It was her turn to be serious. "You're forgetting I had a horrible experience at that place last spring. You gave me very logical explanations about what happened to Christine. You told me the place was infallible. I trusted your sincerity, but I still wasn't sure. And after what you've just told me, I'm less sure than ever. Believe you? Jesus, Chad, I believe every word you said."

"Does it make any sense to you?"

She slowly shook her head. "Not at all. Yet neither did Christine's death. But enough for now. Let's get you properly cleaned up. God, those clothes. Don't move."

He remained in the foyer while she headed inside, walking through the kitchen. She returned moments later with a large plastic garbage bag. "Okay, drop 'em."

"Right here?"

"If those lovely garments go one more inch into this house, the building inspector'll have it condemned. I'll see if I can find you a robe."

After she left, the thongs went first. He wriggled out of the sweatshirt with some difficulty, and he had to hold onto a chair for balance when he stepped out of the trousers. Then he put everything into the garbage bag and doubly knotted it, not quite prepared when Maks waltzed back into the room and found him naked.

His hands went to cover his groin as Maks averted her eyes, handing him a thin robe. She hadn't meant to walk in on him like that. She'd been so intent on assisting him that she'd forgotten he wasn't wearing anything. But in that brief moment before she looked away, her eyes took in his lean, sinewy body. And she liked what she saw.

"I feel naked."

"Cute," she said. "How's that robe?"

"It'll do."

She took him by the hand again and led him through the

house to a staircase that led upstairs. Holding the bannister with one hand and Maks' hand with the other, Dunston carefully navigated the carpeted steps, reaching the second floor only slightly winded. He paused for air and looked around self-consciously.

"Which way to the stables?" he asked.

"Follow me, sire."

Halfway down the hall, she pushed open a door that led to a well-appointed bathroom. He could tell that it had been tastefully remodeled, with recessed high-hats, which gleamed off a floor-to-ceiling mirror. The room's center-piece was an enormous, circular, sunken tub, already filling with water. He nodded approvingly while Maks turned on one of the showers.

"My parents had this redone about ten years ago. My mother was into long baths."

"I'll say," Dunston agreed, gazing at the tub. "About ten feet long. Must have some outrageous parties in here."

She tested the shower water. "That should be about right. After you've rinsed off, relax in the tub. You've earned it. Call me when you're done. I'll be right outside."

"Maks," he ventured, "you've really been helpful, and I don't mean to push things. But at the risk of being way out of line, would you mind staying here? I ache all over, and I might need some help. And I need you to do my back."

She shrugged. "Okay by me. I used to bathe my cousins all the time. Why don't you go into the shower and wash all that junk off."

He sidled into the brisk spray and let the warm stream course through his hair. He turned his face up into the water and let the fine needles rinse out his nose and ears, then opened his mouth and gargled thoroughly. After several minutes he turned off the spigot, feeling he'd done his best. Opening the shower door, Maks held out a bath towel for him. He noticed that she, too, was now wearing a robe.

"Quick change artist?" he asked.

"No sense both of us getting soaked."

"Amen to that. Lead on."

She did. After what he'd recently survived, Dunston didn't mind a little out-of-character docility. The huge tub, which looked like it had a sixteen-inch depth, was half filled with water that gushed from brass fixtures. There were two entry steps, the lower already submerged. Knowing they might prove slippery, Maks let Dunston exchange his towel for a firm grip on her forearm. He held onto her and stepped carefully, watching the water swirl around his shins. Then he slowly squatted until the water lapped at his haunches.

"How is it?" she asked.

"Divine. Like holy water. My tush is in your debt. Ahhh," he sighed, sitting and straightening out his legs, then pushing back until his spine touched tubside. He closed his eyes. "God, this is relaxing. I might fall asleep in here."

"Don't you dare. My CPR's a little rusty. Lean your head back."

On his scalp, he felt the cool flow of liquid shampoo, which had a fragrant almond scent. Her fingers went to work, rubbing up a lather, kneading his skin, massaging in the suds, working out the knots of tension in the muscles of his neck and temples. She rinsed his hair with a spray attachment, and the shampoo drained away into a recessed scupper that rimmed the tub's top. Then he felt more shampoo, and her fingers again. After several minutes of her delightful ministrations, he concluded that he'd died and gone to heaven. Another rinse—then, a slight breeze in the air, and a pleasant sensation upon his chest. Curious, he opened his eyes.

Bending over the edge of the tub, Maks was lathering his chest with two ingenious mittens.

"It's true," he rasped. "An angel."

"Feel good?"

"Indescribable. What are those wonderful paws?"

"Luffa sponges."

"Of course, silly me. What's a luffa sponge?"

"Oh be quiet."

He let his lids close again. My own personal geisha, he thought. Where'd she learn this stuff? Oh, right. She works for that Japanese place.

He heard the flick of a switch, a rush of water, the pleasant liquid jets from the Jacuzzi. She was doing his feet now, fastidiously, one toe at a time. Then she was doing his soles, his ankles, scrubbing, kneading. She slowly worked her way up his calves to his knees. Dunston felt himself growing increasingly languid.

As she bathed him, Maks could not help looking at his body. His skin was a dappled quilt of scrapes and abrasions. She admired his compact musculature. She stole a glance at the tightness of his abdomen and at the way his manhood floated beneath the soapy bubbles. Maks felt herself grow aroused. She knew she was risking the illicit, and she loved it. But she knew that if she continued bathing him much longer, her increasing boldness would lead to places she wasn't yet prepared for. She rinsed him off.

"Up and at 'em, Doctor. I think we should get you to bed."

"Yeah."

She got up first, then helped him out of the tub. He began to shiver all over. She gave him a dry towel and retrieved the robe for him. After he put it on, she used the towel on his wet hair. When it was dry, she led him out of the bathroom and toward a bedroom nearby. Dunston looked inside.

"You sleep in here?"

"No, it was my parents'. I haven't slept in their bed since . . . well, a long time."

"Bad memories?"

She followed him in. "No, just too much hassle." She

pulled back a large quilted bedspread. "They liked a big bed, too big for my taste. A sort of super-king. I still like a bed where I can tuck my toes in the corners."

He lifted a sheet and climbed in. The bedding was smooth and cool. Under the heavy covers, he slowly stopped shivering. Growing warmer, he closed his eyes and took a deep breath, thoroughly relaxed. He was asleep within thirty seconds.

He woke up twice that night, the second time screaming, in the throes of a nightmare, the likes of which he hadn't had since he was a child. He found himself sitting up, shivering again, wide-eyed, chilled by fear. Within seconds Maks was in the room, sitting on the bed beside him, soothing him, calming him, speaking in hushed, reassuring tones. It seemed completely natural when she pulled back the covers and crawled in beside him. He moved close to her, snuggling up for warmth.

The next time he awakened, it was morning. The first beams of dawn filtered past thick, hanging drapes. The memory of the previous day was still vivid in his mind. He slowly sat up and pulled off the covers without waking her. He could not shake the lingering terror he felt from being trapped in the sewage pipe. He suddenly felt filthy again. Walking quietly across the carpet, he returned to the bathroom. He turned on the shower, got in, and scrubbed himself compulsively all over.

He knew that in truth, although he could wash his body quickly and often, it would take days, even weeks, to even begin to cleanse the horror from his mind.

Chapter Fourteen

CHERYL MCKITRICK ADJUSTED her sweater as Jim walked into her office. She straightened up smartly. He wasn't exactly her idea of every woman's fantasy, but he was the correct gender.

"There it is," he said.

"There what is?"

"Operation Wiretap. The computer program I was supposed to work out?"

She perked up. "The one that can help us find out who's accessing our data?"

"The same."

She reached for the printouts. "You already found out!"

"Sheer stroke of luck," he nodded. "Here I was, all geared up for fancy footwork to tiptoe through networks nationwide. It turns out it was right under our noses."

"Here in Upton?"

"More like here on campus. You ready for this? All the files were being pulled by the computers at CHP."

"The Center?" She looked away, astonished. So *that* accounted for the speed of Jim's discovery. All the buildings in the Brookhaven site were on a vast acreage of federally owned property, be they the Upton research center, the hospital, or the National Lab itself. Even though they might be several miles apart, they were all linked by the same in-house computer network. But why in the world would the Center be interested in the Human Genome Project, and more specifically, the experimental microscopy related to it? Nobody even worked there. The place was fully automated, run by computers.

The thought was chilling. Computers accessed other computers all the time to exchange information, or to reference databases. But always under human control. The notion that the Center's supercomputers might be doing it autonomously, listening to no internal dialogue but their own, hinted at a kind of interrogation—or, more frighteningly, artificial intelligence.

"Any idea why?" she asked.

"No, but I can tell you this. It started almost immediately after their computers went on line. And it's not just limited to STM data. They want every shred of info we have on genome research."

"I don't believe this."

"What makes it even spookier is that although we now know what they've been given, we don't know what they've concluded. I mean, their computers are a generation ahead of anyone else's. We could be talking about machines that actually think."

"No way," she scoffed.

"Think about it. Their computers use parallel processing, superconductivity, and advanced neural networks, modeled after how the brain's supposed to function. What does that suggest?"

"It suggests," said Cheryl, feeling increasingly mortified, "that we'd better kick this upstairs to Victor right away." Jesus. Wasn't Maks' doctor friend a patient at the Center?

"Already done. He's expecting us in fifteen minutes."

* * *

It was morning when Dunston woke again. He rolled over and saw that Maks was gone. He slowly sat up and gazed about, taking stock of the tastefully appointed room. The door creaked. It was Maks, entering from the hallway, pushing the door open with her hip, carrying one of those breakfast-in-bed platters that you could order from Hammacher-Schlemmer.

He noted that she was already dressed, wearing black cable leggings beneath an unusual neo-sweater he couldn't quite figure out. God, she had great legs. He truly adored the way she looked. In fact, he was coming to adore everything about her. She placed the tray in front of him.

"How long have you been up?"

"About an hour. How're you feeling?"

He hunched his shoulders and made a face. "Stiff as an ingot."

"I'm not surprised. Maybe breakfast will help." She uncovered a silver serving dish, beside which were juice, coffee, and a brioche. "*Voilà.*"

He stared at the yolks. "Eggs Benedict?"

"I hope so. At least, that's what the recipe said."

"Looks great. How's it taste?"

"I don't know. I never made it before."

He smiled. "I'm honored. Where're you headed?"

"Work. I thought about babysitting, but I think you can manage without me. Oh, the police brought back your car. I left the keys in the kitchen. Not that I expect you to go anywhere. Just take it easy, okay? Read the *Times*, play Nintendo, take a walk. Up to you." She blew him a kiss and was gone.

After a leisurely breakfast, he had to use the bathroom. Dunston threw back the covers and winced as he got out of bed, feeling as if he'd been run over by a garbage truck. He wondered if Maks kept aspirin in the bathroom. Getting to his feet, hunched over, he hobbled, rather than walked, across the deep pile carpet. Passing a full-length mirror, he eyed his reflection. His naked body was covered with bruises and scrapes, purplish welts, and occasional sutures where small lacerations had been repaired. He cocked his head, more curious than surprised by his appearance. He felt damn lucky to be alive. Christ, did he have to take a piss.

When he was done, he absentmindedly opened the medicine chest. There wasn't much inside: an outdated bottle of Tylenol, in actual capsules; a fifteen-ounce jar of Vaseline; an antique straight razor with an ivory handle; and two amber medicine vials.

He opened one and found a handful of Motrin 800. Just the ticket, he thought. He looked at the date on the label. The prescription was two years old. He couldn't recall Motrin's shelf life. On the off chance it had lost some potency, he took two, rinsing them down with a healthy swig of tap water. He replaced the vial and idly picked up the other.

He twisted off the cap and found it empty. The label was made out to Christine Lassiter, dated the last week in March. He remembered that must have been just before she entered the hospital. The vial had contained fifty milligram Serophene capsules, and the instructions read, TAKE THREE DAILY FOR FIVE DAYS.

Dunston slowly put back the container, frowning. Serophene, Serophene . . . He vaguely recognized the name as some sort of specialty medication, but he couldn't remember for what. He was certain it wasn't an antibiotic; an antihistamine? Something puzzled him, like a memory resurfacing. He closed the cabinet and hobbled out of the bathroom.

The lush carpet felt delightfully soft underfoot. He returned to the closets, searching for something to wear. He entered a large walk-in. It contained a man's wardrobe, no doubt Mr. Lassiter's. There were several hanging suits, stacked shirts, and a rack of shoes. There should be something a little less formal in here, he thought. In weather like this, he wouldn't be needing socks or underwear.

He leafed through the clothing until he found a pair of gray sweatpants. Putting them on, he found them loose but acceptable. Then he picked out a woolen buffalo plaid shirt which came from L. L. Bean. Slipping it on, he buttoned it and judged the fit satisfactory. That left only the shoes. He instantly spotted what he wanted, a pair of fleece-lined slippers. Clothes made the man, he thought.

He returned to the bedroom, retrieved the serving tray, and carried it downstairs to the kitchen. Through the kitchen window, he looked out across the back porch. He recognized the setting at once. In the distance was the watery horizon of Oyster Bay, and before him, the well-tended expanse of grassy yard where Maks revealed herself to him. Dunston casually strolled outside.

The weather was delightful, with low humidity, blue sky, and not a cloud overhead. He felt his tension diminish. A morning couldn't be more idyllic. It was so pleasant, in fact, that his mind completely relaxed, exposing a defenseless subconscious. There occurred a sudden and jarring juxtaposition of thoughts, in which the preceding day's events resurfaced. His hands began to shake.

It *wasn't* a mistake, he thought.

He clasped his hands to stop their trembling. The nightmarish significance of what happened was inescapable. He was too familiar with the workings of the Center to reach any other conclusion. The place simply functioned too damn well. Not only was it no mistake, he realized, but the whole thing had to have been *planned*, with him in mind, as . . . what? Victim? Donor?

When had it all begun? he wondered. Could it possibly have been conceived after his admission for the surgery?

That was doubtful, for there was nothing spur-of-the-moment about what transpired. It had to have been planned long before he'd been admitted, and probably not later than when his case was booked into the OR schedule. Perhaps everything had been planned even earlier, and with him specifically in mind. And then when he'd somehow thwarted them and the godawful plan had fallen apart, they had unquestionably tried to destroy him.

But why, why?

He sat there wringing his hands, feeling chilled to the bone. Instead of answers, all he resurrected were horrible memories, little flashes of terror, mini-nightmares of partial remembrance: the drugs, his one-in-a-million escape, the filthy, tepid water. Something, or someone—an animal?—scurrying; the bizarre lab, or what he thought was a lab; the autobot tracking him, coming at him relentlessly, firing at him . . . his dash, his wild, final lunge . . .

The morning was no longer bright, for it was clouded over by his memories. He may have beaten the odds once, but what did the future hold in store? Somewhere, there were answers. There were answers to everything. And if he intended to survive, he damn well better find them.

Dunston impulsively dashed back into the house, his mind awhirl.

Two hours after he met with Cheryl and Jim, Victor Sawyer's mood was foul. Although the administrative aspects of being project director had been largely thrust upon him, until now everything had gone reasonably well, at its own pace. But he was a geneticist, accustomed to logical, scientific answers, not a detective. What they'd dropped in his lap was an unfathomable bombshell. It made no sense whatsoever.

Why would the world's most advanced hospital be interested in anything to do with the Human Genome Project? Was it even remotely possible that it was conducting its own research? If so, it was completely unauthorized. The monthly liaison reports listed everything in the field being conducted anywhere in the country, and activity at CHP showed up nowhere. But there was no denying that an enormous quantity of genome data had been siphoned off, and appeared to have been done so for a long while.

At least they'd been able to determine a time sequence for the data loss. Initially, most of the preliminary "borrowed" files pertained to STM design and construction. But more recently, especially in the past nine months, the data transmitted dealt with what were generally considered more far-out, peripheral aspects of the project—things such as cloning, and memory transfer.

"We've got to presume that the Center has its own little STM," said James.

"That's presuming too much," said Sawyer.

"Is it? It's sure got the technology to build one. Its automation techniques are light-years ahead of what we usually work with, and automation's nine-tenths of the game in using an STM for gene sequencing."

"But it doesn't have the parts."

"You're right," said Cheryl. "It didn't have those parts on its original manifest. But guess what, coach?" She was staring at a computer console. For the better part of the past hour, while they brainstormed, she'd been working at Sawyer's desktop unit, accessing networks and calling up databases. Most of what had gone into the Center's construction was confidential, but Cheryl was a pro. The directors at Langley would be mortified to know that she could even rattle off the names of case officers who ran Central American agents, if she wanted to. Her current interest, however, was in sifting through the Center's various requisitions after its initial budgetary allowance.

She tapped the monitor with a fingernail. "High resolution micro-mirrors, six of 'em. Ordered seventeen months ago." She looked up at her boss. "As far as I know, they've only got one use."

"Maybe there's some new medical application," said Jim, none too optimistically.

"Not according to the most recent catalogs," said Cheryl. "No, it's an STM, all right. But pointed inward, not at outer space. We're talking the cutting edge of nanotechnology here, folks. We've been snookered and one-upped at the same time."

"All right," a testy Sawyer conceded, "you've made your point. Let's say the Center does have an STM. How do we know what they're doing with it?"

"That's just it, we don't. It's next to impossible to get into their system to find out. But I think we can make certain assumptions."

"Like what?"

"Well, like Jim said. If *we* had an STM for genome research, we'd use it on sequencing. Now we know that in sequencing, the limiting factor's automation, which is spelled S-P-E-E-D. Don't you see? The Center's done it backwards. First they solved the automation business, which controls just about everything they do over there. And *then* they built an STM."

Sawyer had a worried look. "You're not implying . . ."

She gave a defeatist shrug. "It's a distinct possibility."

"That they've actually unraveled the human genome?" he said incredulously. "What we figured would take us fifteen years?"

"I don't know, Victor," she said, exasperated. "But it sure as hell could be."

Sawyer gave a little grunt, and a no-nonsense expression replaced his disbelief. "Okay, worst-case scenario," he said, propping his elbows onto the desk, all business now. "Let's get back to presuming. Not admitting, mind you, just presuming. Presuming that the Center's computers have mapped the genome. Obviously, we can't get them to talk to us, and their computer center's playing it very close to the vest. If you were in their shoes, what would you do with that information?"

It was Jim's turn. "Possibilities? Unlimited. Especially in light of their inquiries about cloning, and all that. Making spare body parts. Cryobiology—bringing the dead back to life. Creating a master race. And on, and on."

"But what in the world for? What good would it do them? We're not dealing with people here. We're dealing with machines."

"Not entirely," said Cheryl. "There are people who interact with the Center fairly often. Call them advisors," she said, remembering what Maks had told her about Dunston. She still hadn't met the man, and this was as good an excuse as any. Her tone turned deferential. "With your influence, maybe you could suggest a meeting with one of them?"

While Sawyer paused to consider it, she sat back smartly. She chanced a look at Jim. Her lips curled into a smile when she saw him finally staring at her breasts.

"I think I know the people you mean," said Sawyer. "I met one of them at a conference a little while back. Arthur something-or-other. It's certainly worth a call. But first I have to report this to the brass. No choice in the matter. It's part of our agreement. Of course, the Secretary's *numero uno*. My guess is he'll inform the NIH, who'll probably pass it on to Congress, maybe even the Pentagon. Christ, I hope they don't screw up what we unearthed."

*   *   *

Dunston found his keys in the kitchen. He ignored his sundry aches as he left the house and got into his Mustang. He quickly headed for Jericho Turnpike. His dashboard clock read 8:45. Traffic was heavy but beginning to lighten. With any luck, he'd reach Weiman's St. James home before the internist left to make rounds.

He knew Arthur was a night owl. It wasn't unusual to find him prowling the hospital corridors at two A.M., which made Dunston doubt the man awakened before eight. After what seemed an interminable drive, he finally pulled into Weiman's driveway at 9:25. He looked around and groaned when he didn't see his friend's car. Disheartened, he got out of his seat, walked to the house's front door, and rang the bell.

Weiman's wife Angela responded to the singsong chime almost instantly, briskly opening the door. She seemed to be expecting someone. She looked distracted, upset. But her expression turned to astonishment when she noticed Dunston's injuries.

"Hello, Ange."

"My God, Chad, what happened to you?"

"It's a long story. I'm all right. Is Arthur already gone?"

"Yes, but I don't know where he is. Do you have an idea where he might be?"

"Should I?"

"I guess not. I don't know what to do. We were supposed to leave for the airport this morning. Aruba." She looked terribly worried, running a hand distractedly through her hair. "Arthur went to the office last night, nine-ish. You know how he is. He said he had a few last-minute things to do, and then he wanted to check on his patients before signing out to whoever's covering him. I thought he'd be home by twelve." Tears welled up in her already bloodshot eyes. "Only he never came back."

"Did you try the hospital? The on-call rooms?"

"Yes, they've looked everywhere. He isn't there."

"What about the office?"

She looked exasperated. "Each time I call, I get his service. The idiots insist he's already on vacation. I know his office girls aren't coming in. He gave them the week off. I'm a wreck, Chad. I haven't slept all night, and I'm at my wit's end. Am I overreacting? Or should I call the police?"

Dunston gave it a moment's thought. "It might be a little early for them to start a missing persons thing. Look. Arthur and I have offices in the same building. I'll head over there now. If his office door's locked, I'll get the super to let me in. Nose around a while, see what's what. Then I'll give you a call, okay? Don't worry. I'm sure it's nothing. He's probably still with a sick patient somewhere."

There wasn't more anyone could ask. She forced a smile in a face still dulled by anxiety. "All right. But you'll call?"

"Whether I find anything or not." He clasped her hands in his and gave her a reassuring hug. Then he slipped away and returned to his car.

His office building was twenty minutes away, and Dunston arrived at ten A.M. sharp. He didn't bother going to his own office, because he'd cancelled hours for the week, expecting to need some sort of post-op recuperation. Instead he took the elevator directly to Weiman's third floor suite. He tried the door and found it locked. He rapped firmly on the wood paneling, waited twenty seconds, then knocked even harder. No answer.

"Son of a bitch."

He backtracked down the hall, saw by the elevator's indicator light that it was two floors below, and decided to take the stairs. He pushed open the adjacent fireproof metal door that marked the stairwell. He skipped down the steps in Lassiter's slippers, taking them two at a time, until he reached the basement level. In truth, there were quite a few things he had to discuss with Weiman. First and foremost was what he'd been avoiding for weeks, what he'd pushed into the back of his mind and tried to forget, or suppress, what he had assumed was a simple blackout after he'd donned the helmet for the alpha intercept.

Although he promised himself to speak to Arthur about it, he'd done nothing but procrastinate, out of what he presumed was simple embarrassment. He knew he was also plagued by shame. But now, more than ever, in view of what happened to him the day before, he needed answers. Had the Intercept gone smoothly? Had anything like his blackout occurred to Arthur?

And most important, the question he was loathe to ask: was his blackout somehow related to his near death in the Center?

The basement corridor was bare-bones, simple concrete walls without decoration. The super's office was at the end of the hall. Dunston heard the dull roar of the hot water boiler as he passed the utilities room. Seconds later, he approached the super's abode. The door was open. Dunston paused in the doorway and rapped on the lintel.

Elmer Creighton was sitting at his desk. A gaunt man in his late fifties, he had the still emaciated look of a recently recovered alcoholic.

"That you, Doc? Startled me." He studied Dunston's face. "Jeez, who'd you tangle with?"

"I fell out of a window."

Elmer grinned slyly. "Yeah, right. While her husband was comin' through the bedroom door."

"Seen Dr. Weiman today?"

"Nope." Elmer looked at his wall clock. "But it might be a tad early for him."

"He was supposed to go to Aruba today."

"Then for sure he ain't been here."

"Only, his wife says he never came home last night."

Elmer frowned but said nothing.

"What time do you stop working?"

"I usually knock off about six."

"His wife said he had a little extra work to do in his office last night. Around nine, say. Then he was going to drop by the hospital before heading home. Except he never made it."

"You check with Sally?" Creighton asked, referring to Weiman's office manager.

"His whole staff's off this week. Anyway, I was just up there. Door's locked. How 'bout letting me in to look around?"

"Sure." Creighton stood up and took a large key ring off a screw-in hook on a wall board. After closing the door, he led the way toward the elevator and pushed the up button. "I suppose you tried the hospital?"

"Right. He never showed."

The elevator doors opened and they got in. Creighton pressed the button for the third floor. "Dr. Weiman's not sick or nothin', is he?"

"Not as far as I know." He looked at the thin old man with newfound respect. "You mean, maybe he had a heart attack and went to another hospital?"

"Along those lines."

"I hadn't thought of that. But unless he was mugged, he'd still have his wallet and ID. The cops or hospital would have notified his wife by now."

"Here we go." Creighton finished sifting through the keys, finding both Weiman's door key and a round key for the interior alarm. The elevator doors opened, and they stepped off at the third floor. Dunston, who felt peculiarly apprehensive, now led the way and traversed the length of the hall in a few quick strides. Reaching Weiman's office, he tapped his fingers impatiently on the door until Creighton caught up.

Creighton unlocked the door, and they both stepped inside. The super found the light switch and flipped it on. Below it was a rectangular stainless alarm panel, on which a red light glowed. Creighton inserted a round key, twisted it, and the red light turned to green.

"Old system, but I like it. Some of the other office alarms work on keypads. I can never remember the damn numbers."

Dunston wasn't listening. As soon as the fluorescent lights flickered on, he was walking through the waiting room. There was no indication of vandalism. The office was spotless, with furniture carefully arranged and all the magazines back in their racks. Beyond the waiting room was the receptionist's work area. Again, nothing. He passed down a hall of examining rooms, a lab, and lavatories, poking his head in each, all of which were empty. The only room which remained was Weiman's consulting room. It bore a black plastic nameplate whose white lettering read, ARTHUR WEIMAN, MD, FACP. Although the door was closed, Dunston could see light coming through the floor-level crack between door and rug. He knocked.

"Arthur?"

He didn't hesitate when there was no reply. He turned the doorknob, praying that it wasn't locked. It wasn't. He slowly pushed the door open, listening to the faint creak of its hinges.

Inside, behind a wide walnut desk, his friend was sitting upright in a chair. His eyes were closed, and his head was tilted back against a headrest. His usually full lips were stretched thin into a tight, wide rictus. Most disturbing was Weiman's color—a waxy, gray pallor which Dunston had long since come to associate with death. He let out a low and lugubrious moan.

"Oh no."

"He okay, Doc?"

Dunston glided ghostlike across the carpet. From force of habit, he concentrated on his friend's chest and saw the absence of respiratory movements. There would be no need to check for a pulse. His practiced eyes noted that Weiman's knotted tie was perfectly in place. It wasn't loosened, nor was his shirt collar opened, as often happened to those short of breath or experiencing chest pain. Then why the grimace on Arthur's face, as if he were in agony?

He slowly walked to the rear of the chair, eyes darting furtively about for clues. Weiman had been working at his computer. His right hand was still resting on the keyboard, while his left arm was at his side, probably having fallen there.

"Doc?" the super asked nervously.

"He's dead, Elmer. Call the police."

Creighton quickly scurried away.

The computer, Dunston noted, was still on. Though the video terminal was blank, its cursor slowly blinked on and off, awaiting further instructions. Likewise, the modem, located next to the hard disk, adjacent the phone, had glowing red lights, indicating that it was operational.

So, old friend, you'd been networking. Talking with some other computer when you died. I wonder who, and where? What were you working on when this happened? Suddenly, Dunston was filled with remorse. Here, one of his closest associates lay dead in front of him, and he'd been thinking shop.

He looked at the back of Weiman's collar and shook his head. "How am I going to tell Angela?"

Yet his professionalism remained alive, refusing to succumb to sorrow. First his eyes scoured Weiman's hardwood desk adjacent the workstation. There was little on its surface except notepads. Opening the three drawers, he found only stationery, pens, and pencils—until, in the back of the lowermost drawer, he found a single floppy diskette. He picked it up, reading the handwritten label: C. LASSITER.

Christine? What in the world did Arthur know about Maks' sister? And damn it all, now he was dead! He put the floppy into one of his pockets, turning his attention to the hardware.

Dunston was intrigued by the computer layout. He hadn't been in Weiman's office in six months, so it had to have been installed not long ago. Arthur used old hardware. It bore the Apple logo and appeared to be a midrange Macintosh offering, but a lot older than Dunston's IBM. On a whim, he reached over and pressed the space bar, trying to call up whatever had been on the screen. A searing jolt raced up his arm.

"Jesus!"

He leaped back, staring at his electroshocked hand as if it were about to start smoldering. That was no mere house current, he thought. It had to be at least 220 volts. Godalmighty, he realized, looking from his hand to that of Weiman, which still lay atop the keyboard.

Arthur had been electrocuted.

Until the power was off, he didn't dare touch a thing. Not Weiman, not the keyboard, not the workstation. And then he saw the screen.

At his touch, it had reilluminated. He stared at it in fascination.

HOST NODE, it read. B.N.L. DESTINATION: CENTER FOR HUMAN POTENTIAL. AUTOMATIC LOG-ON, 21:15:05, 26 OCTOBER. USER ID: 511432, WEIMAN, ARTHUR, MD. The space for the password was blank—obviously typed in by Weiman, but not visible on the monitor, as was customary. LAST LOG-ON: 14:02:02, 24 OCTOBER.

Saturday? Dunston thought. What in the name of God was Arthur working on? Could it possibly involve Christine? He read on.

1. ENTER FILE NAME. 2. PATIENT NAME. 3. MAIN MENU.
4. HELP.

Weiman had selected number two. When Dunston saw
what was written beneath it, his whole body stiffened, cold
as frost. To his astonishment, Arthur had typed in CHRIS-
TINE LASSITE. Only the final R was missing. He glanced
back at Weiman's unmoving hand and saw that its index
finger was poised atop the R key.

Dunston shook his head in disbelief. What the devil happened here? Arthur had gotten only that far into his inquiry
when he'd been electrocuted. A short? Or . . .

He suppressed a shiver. Galvanized into action, he
dashed from the death scene, looking for something rubberized, wishing he'd worn sneakers. He heard the high-
pitched tones of Elmer Creighton at the end of the hall,
speaking into the phone. Passing the examining rooms,
Dunston pulled open a lavatory door. He flipped on a light
switch, cursing under his breath as he looked furtively
around the cramped area with mouselike glances. Then he
spotted a plunger behind the commode. He grabbed it and
ran back to the nearest examining room.

A knife, Arthur. A scalpel blade. A scissors, something
sharp. I know you were an internist, but you must have
owned something that cuts. He pulled open the storage
shelves one by one, rummaging through them, slamming
them shut when he didn't find what he wanted. Growing
increasingly frantic and annoyed, he tried to calm himself
with logic that eluded him. Finally, on the bottom shelf,
there it was: a heavy curved Mayo scissors, old enough to
bear rust stains.

In one hand, he held the plunger, rubber end up, while
whittling away with scissors in the other. Within seconds
he'd cut out a quarter-size wedge from the rubber rim.
Dropping everything but that, he hurried back to the con-
sultation room. Hovering over Weiman's waxen shoulder,

he cautiously held the chunk of rubber between thumb and forefinger.

He lowered the piece of rubber until it touched Weiman's flesh, making the lifeless finger depress the R key. The digitalized R briefly appeared on screen, completing the name LASSITER. And then the video monitor literally exploded.

A blizzard of wire, insulation, and Plexiglas shards flew through the air. The disk drive spluttered and died, sending fumes and sparks upward in ozone-scented waves. The lights momentarily flickered, then went out.

The room was cast into an ominous, oppressive darkness.

Chapter Fifteen

THE MEETING WAS turning into something of a nightmare for Victor Sawyer. No sooner had he clued his superiors into what was going on than he learned of the tragic death of Dr. Weiman, his only contact at the CHP. Before he had a chance to locate anyone else who liaised there, an emergency conference had been called for all agencies involved in the Genome Project.

Coming out of an ordinarily slow-moving governmental bureaucracy, the meeting had been arranged with astonishing speed. Within forty-eight hours, Sawyer found himself on the New York to Washington shuttle. He landed shortly after nine A.M. for a ten o'clock meeting at the Department of Energy. From the airport, Sawyer took a cab through unusually heavy midmorning traffic. Once he reached his destination, he barely had time to wind his way through the labyrinthine building when the meeting began.

It was held in a conference room outside the office of the Secretary of the Department of Energy. Sawyer had hoped for something of a private, in-house briefing. But in addition to himself, the Secretary, and two other Energy officials, there seemed to be a cast of thousands. There were representatives from the NIH, the Defense Advanced Research Projects Agency, the National Library of Medicine, the Congressional Office of Technology Assessment, Bethesda Naval Hospital, a Pentagon-based Undersecretary of the Army responsible for defense procurement, and the National Security Council, all with their aides. Sawyer took one look at the people assembled and felt his heart sink, a feeling accompanied by visions of his pet projects flying out the window.

"Good morning, Dr. Sawyer," said the Secretary. "Help yourself to a seat," he said, nodding toward a vacant chair nearby. "Coffee?"

"I've already had some, thanks."

"We were waiting for you to arrive before we began."

"Sorry to hold things up."

"You didn't. We just got here ourselves. And we're insiders," he said, referring to the Washington scene, "so we have an advantage. Still, I'm amazed that everyone showed on time. That probably speaks to the importance of your report. Everyone has a copy, so we may as well get to it." From around the room, there was the sound of papers being shuffled. "As host, I'm giving myself the dubious distinction of beginning. Dubious, I suppose, because what you've implied here is unbelievable."

"Sir, I—"

"Hold on, I'm not accusing you of anything. No one questions your integrity."

"No?" interrupted the official from NIH. "Our people have gone over this pretty closely, and we think your conclusions are a little iffy. Maybe even self-serving."

"Don't be presumptuous," countered the Secretary. "Dr. Sawyer has no personal stake in this."

"That remains to be seen."

"I resent that," shot Sawyer. "The report's no fabrication. You've got the data. Why don't you run a computer analysis before you go shooting your mouth off?"

"Calm down, Victor," said the Secretary. "This isn't a grudge match. If you're interested in a free-for-all," he said, eyeing the man from NIH, "I'll cancel the meeting right now."

"You used the word unbelievable, not me."

"True. What about that, Victor? I know the data's accurate, but even some of our people think your conclusion seems, well, farfetched."

Sawyer composed himself, pausing to think before replying. "It depends what you mean by farfetched. I guarantee you it's not 'iffy.' The data's solid, and it holds up under analysis. As for the conclusion, if you mean it sounds forced, I can't agree with that. But if you mean improbable, I couldn't agree more. If you predicted a year ago that the genetic code would be cracked within twelve months, I'd have thought you were crazy."

"That's irrelevant," said the Army Undersecretary.

"Beg your pardon?"

"It's one thing to talk about siphoning off data, building an STM, or unraveling the genome. But, Doctor, when you imply that the Center's involved in cloning and memory transfer, that's flying with one wing low."

"You didn't even read the damn report, did you?"

The Pentagon man fumed. "Look, you sonofabitch," he said, his upper lip twitching like a conga line, "if you think you're—"

"Enough!" snapped the Secretary. "What about it, Victor?"

Sawyer knew precisely what was bothering the Pentagon. For years, the military had fantasized about creating the perfect soldier. It was the stuff of their wildest dreams: a controlled android that could fight like a man, be totally dispensable, and save the lives of the boys back home. Not that they'd ever put their money where their mouth was; it seemed as if they were always waiting for someone else to do the basic research. To Sawyer's knowledge, the closest they'd come were the Army's HMMWV, the high-mobility multipurpose wheeled vehicle that replaced the jeep, and the Airborne Remotely Operating Device, or AROD, a mobile, teleoperated reconnaissance platform. But if they got wind that the Center or Energy had secretly developed more far-reaching technology, they'd scream bloody murder. No wonder there were so many defense people here. Sawyer chose his words carefully.

"The report I sent the Secretary is preliminary, but it makes only two conclusions. One, the Center has constructed its own STM. Second, that using the STM, the Center has cracked the genetic code. Period. There are no other suggestions in there. However, the final two pages, which are titled 'Theoretical Implications,' are purely speculative. They make no claims whatsoever. They simply restate *possible* uses or future scenarios that might stem from cracking the code. I emphasize the word might.

"Look, all this is old hat. When we first started the Human Genome Project, we discussed these same things—what understanding the code *might* mean, the various ways that information *might* be used fifteen or twenty years down the pike."

"So all that talk about cloning is nothing but daydreams?"

"No, it's logical speculation. Look at it this way. The reason the Genome Project was funded in the first place was because everyone understood the significance of cracking the code. We realized its primary importance was in medicine. Let me give you an example. In 1990, for instance, we had to wait for someone to get sick before we could give him drugs or chemotherapy. We figured that once we did unravel the code, say around 2005, you could make a possible genetic profile of an individual's predisposition to disease. Medicine would finally become predictive, truly preventative, and drugs and surgery would become obsolete. Maybe even doctors too.

"Press a button on your personal computer, get a readout of your own genome, and interpret your own genetic strengths and weaknesses. At the very least, that would enable someone to adopt the proper lifestyle or choose the best diet or environment to minimize his chances of getting sick.''

''That's all?''

Where'd they dig up these cretins? thought Sawyer. Can't they read plain English? He kept his cadence slow, his tone simple. ''No, there's also gene therapy. It's already being performed in both plants and animals, to a limited extent. Basically, it involves inserting good genes into a patient's cells to replace genes causing disease.''

''How would that be done?''

''With viruses, usually retroviruses. They're bioengineered to carry correctly functioning versions of a faulty gene right into the cell. Further down the road, you could theoretically bypass the virus with what you might call genetic microsurgery, where you mechanically insert genes directly into the cell nucleus.''

''With the STM?''

''It'd help.''

''So what's this got to do with memory transfer?''

Patience, thought Sawyer. He took a calming breath. ''It doesn't. That's speculation.''

''So, speculate.''

''It's all in the report.''

''Please, Victor,'' urged the Secretary.

''Okay,'' he shrugged. ''It's like this. Once you're involved in microsurgery on the cellular level, that raises the subject of cloning—you know, Adam fathering himself? You simply enucleate a human egg, fertilize it with Adam's diploid sperm, and let it grow and divide until presto, another Adam.''

The simplistic explanation was too much for the man from the Pentagon, who squinted in silent confusion. Then an NIH staffer spoke up. ''We all understand cloning. But memory transfer?''

"Again, speculation, but not total fantasy," Sawyer explained. "Right now, no one's certain how human memory works. The best guess is that the brain stores memory in some physiochemical way, a way we'll eventually discover. On the other hand, we already know how a computer stores its memory. Eventually, we might reach a point where we can read the brain's information, then use a program to write it into a computer. They you take a cloned brain and enable it to grow with the information in the computer." He paused. "That, gentlemen, is memory transfer."

For several seconds, the room was silent.

"Heavy," someone finally whispered.

"Science fiction," said another.

"Speculation," said Sawyer.

"All right, everyone," said the Secretary. "Let's leave speculation for the moment. The point is, does anyone propose doing something about the Center's unraveling the genome?"

"Who runs the place, anyway?"

"Technically," said Sawyer, "it falls under Health and Human Services. Yet on paper, it gets funding from everywhere. In reality, nobody runs it. That's the problem. It runs itself."

"So you have no idea what it's doing with all these discoveries you claim it's made?"

"Not the slightest. But I'd love to find out. Isn't that why we're here?"

The Army Undersecretary's jowls bulged. "I say shut the bastards down."

"You mean, nuke 'em back into the Stone Age?"

The Secretary spoke to the military man. "How do you suggest shutting down a medical center?"

"Well, it's nothing but machines, right? Shut off their electricity. Turn off their water. Whatever it takes."

"Do that, General, and you jeopardize the lives of hundreds of patients. You can't simply pull their plug by turning off the utilities. No one wants a siege. I suppose we could 'shut it down,' to paraphrase you, in about a month, just by no longer admitting patients. But that begs the question. The point is, what's it doing over there? I suggest we find that out first before we talk about decommissioning the place. Victor?''

"I agree, Mr. Secretary. Something of profound, fundamental importance is happening at the Center. We know what they've done, but not what they're up to. Finding that out is essential. The problem is, we don't know how.''

"Perhaps not through your computers," said the congressional delegate. "But can't you just go in and find out?"

The general's eyes gleamed. "A pre-dawn vertical insertion.''

"A what?"

"Helicopter assault. The Delta Force.''

Sawyer nearly broke out laughing but managed to stifle his smile. "This is suburban Long Island, General, not Kuwait. I'm sure you could send the SEALs in loaded for bear, but they wouldn't have the faintest idea what to look for. I doubt they'd know it if they saw it. And they'd be endangering patients in the process.''

"You got a better idea?''

"I think so," Sawyer replied evenly. "There are only a handful of people who really come close to understanding how the Center runs. People involved in its design and construction, people who've worked with its computers. I had someone in mind, but he died rather suddenly.''

The general looked skeptical. "You're talking about a one-man operation?''

"Essentially, yes," Sawyer nodded. "But nothing clandestine. Instead, someone who knows the Center, who ostensibly goes in on routine business. Once he's in, he could discreetly nose around.''

"Who have you got in mind?''

"I don't know," Sawyer conceded. "My office is conducting a search right now. But that's what we need, gentlemen: the right man."

It was raining the day Weiman was buried. It was an undignified rain, hard and dirty, without the elegant accompaniment of lightning or thunder. Dunston and Maks were among the mourners surrounding the grave. They held hands under an umbrella as Arthur's casket was lowered into the moist earth. In the background was the rabbi's subdued recitation of *El Moleh Rachamim*.

Despite his Burberry, Dunston was shivering, more from what he'd learned than from the breeze-blown droplets that dotted his face like condensation. Absorbed in his thoughts, he was barely aware of the sobbing around him. Maks silently glanced at his furrowed brow with a look of concern.

Try though he might, he couldn't dispel the horrifying thoughts that began after the police removed Arthur's body. He'd stayed in the office while the forensic team checked the circuitry in both the computer and the building. To his absolute dismay, they found no evidence of a short circuit. True, a circuit breaker had tripped after he'd pressed Arthur's finger, casting the room into darkness. The technicians postulated that its tripping caused a bizarre power surge, which subsequently made the computer explode.

Arthur's body had taken the brunt of the blast. Shielded by his friend, Dunston suffered only a small cheek laceration, which merely embellished his healing cuts and scratches. But the electricians had no rational explanation for what caused Weiman's electrocution—no loose wire, no faulty insulation. In short, no smoking gun. One technician, after inspecting some melted wiring, half jestingly remarked that it was as if a bolt of lightning had flowed in reverse, up through the keyboard. Dunston kept silent, harboring a horrifying suspicion that the observation was deadly accurate.

And that knowledge left him trembling.

At her suggestion, Dunston spent the evenings with Maks. She went home at bedtime. Ever since Weiman's death, Dunston had been uncharacteristically reticent, almost mute. When the memorial service was over, they drove to his place in virtual silence, listening to the rhythmic thunk and swish of the wipers. Maks was worried. The zest and sparkle were fading from the man she was growing to love. She hadn't wanted to press him after his release from the hospital, assuming that his lighthearted ebullience, his assertive character, would quickly resurface. But in the three days since his discharge, and two days after the Weiman tragedy, he showed no sign of returning to his former self.

Interestingly, she didn't think his depression, if that's what it was, was solely related to his friend's death. Although she couldn't put her finger on it, she had the impression his mind was on something profoundly more disturbing, something he didn't want to talk about. Caring for him as she did, she refused to let him remain like this any longer. It was time to take the bull by the horns.

She reached across the front seat and stroked his shoulder. Both her tone and her touch were gentle. "You can't keep this bottled up forever."

No answer.

"And I know it's not just Arthur's death."

"He was a damn good friend."

He took a deep breath, as if to say something, but simply sighed, a long, oppressive exhalation. He'd hidden the floppy shortly after Weiman's death, having neither the strength or mental energy to pursue it. Or was it fear? Maks grew exasperated.

"Chad, please! If you won't talk to me, talk to someone!"

He shot her a cynical glance, eyebrows raised. "Professional help?"

"Try all the sarcasm you want," she said evenly. "But dammit, I care for you! The other night, when I brought you home, I thought you were on the verge of opening up. You started to, but then you clammed up."

"I fell asleep, remember?"

"Before that. In the car." She moved closer. "Look, I know it's complicated. And I know it scares you. Well, it scares me too. But I want to know, don't you see? I need to know!"

"Why?"

She wouldn't let him goad her. "For you. For Christine. For me. Most of all, for us. I care for you far too much to let you wallow in self-pity."

"I'm not the wallowing type."

"No, you're stubborn as a mule, and when you decide to sulk, you go first class. You work it. You bronze it. You hang it from the rear-view mirror like an ornament. There's no holding you back. God, it's frustrating. What's wrong, you don't know where to start? Okay, I'll help. Remember that little bombshell about the Center trying to kill you? That was right on target, Doctor, except you wouldn't let it explode." She paused, staring at him. "You want to wait? Fine. I'll wait as long as it takes."

She was right, and he knew it. It was a worm in his gut, eating him up inside, destroying him. He'd lied to Stingley and Donohue. No, not lied; he just hadn't told the whole truth. But after what happened to Arthur, he'd become a basket case if he didn't tell someone. He wanted to omit the part about Christine, because he had no idea what it meant. Until he did, telling could only hurt Maks.

Outside, the rain became a downpour. He slowed, looking straight ahead, concentrating on his driving. All right. If that's the way she wanted it. He suddenly felt more relaxed, even relieved, knowing he'd passed the point of no return.

"How much do you know about the Center?" he said.

"More than what's in the papers, but that's not saying much."

"And teleoperators?"

"What in the world are they?"

"This may take a while."

"I've got all day."

"Okay. We'll start with the teleoperators, since that technology was the building block for VIEWS and the Interface."

He glanced at her utterly blank expression.

"Sorry. I'll backtrack. I know you're aware of virtual reality. The movies eat it up, and you'll find it in a dozen different video games at your local mall. But even before that, did you ever see those artificial claws used to handle radioactive substances?"

"Just pictures."

"That's your basic teleoperator, built in the forties. It's a machine that operates at a distance and can perform tasks in remote environments."

"Like with uranium?"

"Or plutonium, whatever. Over the decades the technology was refined, and the operating distance became greater. Underwater salvage, for example. The operator puts on all these gizmos, like helmet-mounted TV screens and gloved tactile sensors, in order to control a deep-sea manipulator. Fiberoptics made it all work. You got the job done without endangering the man.

"That was the start. About ten years ago, I got involved with the development of telesurgery. At first we used it for teaching med students. Let's say I was taking out an appendix. I'd put on a telehelmet for a phone or satellite linkup while a student in, say, Champaign-Urbana, put one on too. He'd see exactly what I was seeing. With me so far?"

"Yep."

"The real breakthrough came with the gloves. Some wizard developed these flexible tactile fibers, small enough to be built into surgeon's gloves. The students would wear similar gloves. So now they could not only see what I was doing, but feel exactly the same things I did. It was as if they were operating themselves. Same picture, same sensations, but without having to practice on a live patient. It was the ideal environment, the perfect teaching tool. The name VIEWS is an acronym for virtual environments. All the advantages without the drawbacks. Still, most of us were a little skeptical about the starry-eyed who predicted the coming of the Messiah: fully autonomous, computer-controlled robots.''

''What changed your mind?''

''AI.''

''As in . . . ?''

''Artificial intelligence.''

''Gotcha. Is there really such a thing?''

''Well, for decades, there were basically two schools of thought. One believed that by designing the right programs, you could literally create minds, computers that could think. The other school said hogwash. Computers might be able to manipulate symbols, they said, but true AI implied attaching meaning to those symbols, and only the brain could do that.''

''I suppose the Center proved the second school right.''

''In a way. For all we don't understand about it, the brain *is* a kind of computer. What the computer jocks did was to turn that concept around, and make the computer into a kind of brain. Not in the classical sense, like having conscious thoughts, but instead by mimicking how we think the brain functions. I guess you could say that it all came together in the early nineties. Parallel processing—''

''Parallel what?''

''That's where lots of smaller computers simultaneously work on the different aspects of a complex problem. Sort of like neurons in the brain. Massive parallelism provides a dramatic speed advantage. It can access and distribute information in a millisecond. When you take hundreds of computers linked in a parallel vector and hook 'em up to the Center's superconducting supercomputers wow. Now we're talking a true neural network."

"So the Center's computer system *does* think?"

He hedged. "Yes and no. The Center has an intelligence, if you will, patterned after how we think the brain works, where computer chips stand for neurons and synapses. We're still not sure how it attaches meaning to what it computes, how it interprets sensory signals, whether it's capable of learning and emotion."

"Hmmm. Where did you fit in?"

"My biggest role was when we hooked up VIEWS to the computer. At first we just wanted to see what'd happen, whether we could train the computer like we trained students." He laughed. "Man, training's not the word. It sucked our brains dry, wanted to know everything we knew. We couldn't keep up with it. But those of us who were most interested, like me and Arthur, formed the Interface Group. There were also a few peripheral characters like Stingley. Every few weeks we'd meet at the Center, put on the VIEWS helmet, and teach the computer a few new tricks." He paused. "Or so we thought."

"What does that look mean?"

"Up until last week, I'd have sworn we were in control. Now, I don't know." His expression turned downcast. "It tried to kill me, Maks. I don't know why, but I'm sure of it. And for all of my once-cocksure certainty about Christine, I now have my doubts. And Arthur's the clincher."

She was dumbfounded. "*What?*"

"He was on line with the Center's computer when he was electrocuted. Don't ask me how or why. But it's much more than a hunch.

"You mean—

"His death was no accident.

The rain grew harder, a gray and leaden torrent that matched his somber mood. It cascaded down the windshield in thick, viscous sheets that made the driving impossible. Dunston slowed, then stopped the car entirely. For a long and silent moment, they both stared straight ahead. Although their eyesight was perfect, they could see nothing but their own anger, and revenge.

When the rain slowed, he resumed driving home. Maks was tormented by too many questions to remain silent for long.

"Intelligent or not, why would the Center's computers be doing all this? Killing Arthur and trying to kill you? What's their motive?"

"I don't know. I've thought about that, but nothing comes to mind. The idea that the place is out of control scares the hell out of me. It just doesn't make any sense."

"Could there be someone behind it?"

"A person?"

"Yes, a human being with a flesh-and-blood motive."

"That's reaching, Maks. Stretching things a bit."

"Really? You think that's more farfetched than a thinking computer committing murder?"

"It is to me. What would anyone have to gain? The place is a hospital. You think someone's after a big managed care contract, or Medicare reimbursements? That's a piss-poor reason to knock somebody off."

"Well, you're raising a financial motive. Why does anyone do something rotten? Everything comes down to money or power. Maybe it's something as simple as that."

"Let me see if I've got this straight. You're suggesting there's a bad guy out there who manipulated the Center into committing murder in order to become rich or control things? Is that what you're saying?"

"What are you getting so annoyed about? I'm not suggesting anything. I'm just looking for reasons, Chad. I want explanations, just like you."

She was right. More than that, she *deserved* explanations. It was selfish of him to withhold anything from her. The time had come to be forthright with her, to share everything he knew.

He told her about the diskette he found in Weiman's office.

Maks was dumbstruck. This was simply too much. Staggered beyond comprehension, she stared blankly ahead, fighting her indignation. She was upset with Chad for trying to keep things from her. Yet, as she gazed through the windshield in stony silence, she realized that he was trying to protect her, to shield her from further turmoil. He wasn't to blame, she thought.

Yet something, or someone, was.

"What's on the diskette?"

"I honestly don't know," he admitted. "I've been too shellshocked to check it out."

"Did Arthur make it?"

"I think so, but I'm not sure."

"We should take a look at it, Chad. Soon. There's no telling what's on it. It could be something important."

"I know, I know."

"Where's the diskette now?"

"Right here." He retrieved it from his jacket pocket and handed it to her.

"Three-M, IBM-formatted." She frowned. "Didn't you say Weiman had a Macintosh?"

"That's right. An old one."

"This is formatted for IBM. It won't run on those old Macs."

"You don't think Arthur made it?"

"Not on the relic you described."

"So what was it doing in his desk drawer?"

"That's what I'd like to know. What else was in the desk?"

"Not much. A few papers."

"I realize this isn't the best time, but could I take a look at them?"

The drive to the office building took half an hour. Chad immediately led her up to Weiman's office, which was locked. It was also cordoned off by yellow police tape identifying it as a crime scene. Dunston had Maks wait while he went to the super's office. After a few persuasive words with Elmer Creighton, he returned with the key ring. Moments later, they were inside.

Somehow, he'd expected the office to be tidied up, cleansed of the reminders of Arthur's death. But it was untouched. Other than for the absence of the body, the chaos of destruction remained, with bits of wire and plastic throughout. Tight-lipped, Dunston indicated the drawer with his finger. Maks opened it and removed several envelopes.

"Bills. MasterCard, AT&T. And a Merrill Lynch statement." She studied it. "How old was he?"

"Early fifties."

"Not a very good investor. He had less than twenty thousand dollars in his retirement account." She folded the statement and bent over, peering closely into the drawer. "Chad, write this down, will you?"

"What?"

"Numbers, written in the wood. Forty-eight, 9, 23, and 17. Okay?"

"Got it. You know, this looks like a combination to a lock."

"Or a safe. Does he have one?"

"Not in here. We may as well check out the other rooms."

They found it in a closet behind the reception area. It was little more than a foot square and weighed perhaps thirty pounds. After two unsuccessful attempts, Maks opened it on the third try. There was hardly anything inside: a gold plated stethoscope; several commemorative U.S. coins; and a three-by-five index card. Maks read its single, handwritten entry.

"9649262. Does that ring a bell?"

"Let me see that." He studied the digits. "This could be from the Center, a patient admission number. They're numbered chronologically, in the order of admission. I think this is the number of a patient who came in a little after me."

"Any idea who?"

"No. We'd have to look it up. Take the card and let's get out of here."

Soon, they returned to her house. Distracted, Dunston took a seat on the porch and gazed out across the bay, deep in contemplation. Understandably, Maks went right to work on the diskette. Within several minutes, however, she too was dejected. There was hardly anything on the diskette. Other than for a cryptic reference to File C.L.4-1, there was little she didn't already know.

Maks was increasingly coming to believe that much as she wanted to rely on Chad, if she wanted more information about Christine, she was going to have to go it alone. At least temporarily. Dunston was still too caught up in the funk of post-traumatic stress to be of much use to anyone, including himself. Much as she wanted answers, she knew they were not immediately forthcoming.

Once again, she felt as if she were hitting a brick wall. The sense of helplessness was overwhelming. The list of unanswered questions was lengthening at a lightning clip. But there *were* answers, there had to be. She just didn't know where to look.

Maks studied the hospital number they'd retrieved from Weiman's safe and narrowed her eyes, brow grim, deep in thought. Perhaps Chad was temporarily immobilized, but she wasn't. At the very least, she could put in the legwork. Her steely determination grew as she formulated a plan, sculpted of intellect, and colored by rage.

Chapter Sixteen

"HERE'S YOUR MYSTERY patient."

"Thanks, Cher." Maks took the slip of paper. "Was it hard getting the information?"

"Not through the in-house network. Our mainframes are linked to the Center. Ever heard of him?"

"Allan Schmidt," she slowly said. She shook her head. "I can't say that I have. It would be nice if I had something besides a name."

"There's more." Cheryl handed her a computer printout.

"Oh, fantastic. Let's see. Fifty-six-year old white male, etcetera, etcetera. Referring physician, Dr. A. Weiman. Now that's an interesting coincidence. Admission diagnosis cirrhosis. Alcoholic, that's novel. Complications, congestive heart failure. Expired on . . . wow. This guy died."

"You see the date?"

"God, that's amazing. He died the same day he was admitted, just three days ago. This must have been some sick cookie."

"To say the least. Look, I've gotta run. Keep me posted, okay?"

Cheryl left the bar, a Stony Brook college hangout that was midway between them. Maks sipped her beer, studying the brief printout. She felt gratified that she was starting to get answers, but they made no sense. All she'd learned was that Dr. Weiman had referred a desperately ill alcoholic, who died shortly after admission, to the Center. She frowned, biting her lip. There was something else, something she couldn't put her finger on . . .

And then it hit her.

She checked the dates again, perplexed and frightened. Schmidt died on Tuesday, the same day Arthur did. And Maks had the strangest feeling it was no coincidence. She circled several entries on the printout, removed her phone card from her wallet, and looked for a pay phone. Moments later, her call went through to the funeral parlor.

"Hi, my name's Corinne Phillips. I'm with the business office at St. Charles Hospital. I'm trying to track down one of our old receivables, a self-pay who was here a year ago. I learned that he died three days ago today at the Center, and that you picked up the body. I was wondering if . . . Schmidt, Allan Schmidt. Last Tuesday. Yes, I'll hold." She drummed her fingers on the wall, turning away to avoid eye contact with a young man trying to hit on her. She was jolted by the reply. "What? Are you certain? But the face sheet says that you . . . Cancelled by whom? You didn't get a name . . . ? Yes, I understand. Thanks."

That was strange. Maks hung up, more confused than ever. On a whim, and aware that she might be prying, Maks dialed the second circled number. The next of kin was listed as Marlena Wolfe, Schmidt's sister, in Astoria, Queens.

"Hello, Miss Wolfe? This is Harriet Watkins. I'm calling about your brother, Allan Schmidt, and . . . I know he's not there, Miss Wolfe. I was wondering if . . . When? Not in a year . . . ? Yes, no problem. If I see him, I'll tell him."

She hung up, relieved that she hadn't disturbed a grieving relative. But Maks was disconcerted that Schmidt's sister not only hadn't seen him in over a year, but didn't even know he was dead.

On Friday night, Dunston decided to go back to work.

Staying with Maks, delightful though it was with her doting attention, was growing oppressive. He was normally a man of action who found a leisurely, laid back lifestyle cloying. He wasn't scheduled to operate again until Monday, but last-minute phone calls easily meshed with the desires of his more apprehensive patients. Thus he found himself back in the OR at eight A.M. on Saturday, preparing for a splenectomy.

He was scrubbed, gowned, and gloved by 7:55, and the patient was ready for surgery ten minutes later. Although trauma surgery was his bailiwick, he occasionally did elective cases. The twenty-two-year old patient had Hodgkin's disease. By the nineties, removing the spleen of a Hodgkins patient had been largely abandoned, but there were occasional exceptions. This was one of them. Dunston had performed over a hundred splenectomies in his career, and this one—not punctured by a bullet or ruptured in a car crash—should be a walk in the park.

He nonetheless felt unaccountably jittery as the case was readied. He silently stood feet from the OR table, gowned, capped, and masked, gloved hands held steeplelike before his chest, as was his custom. He listened to the glib, black humor of Lance Elliot, the anesthesiologist, who spoke to the patient while readying his medications. Lance was younger than Dunston and something of a jokester, but without malice.

"Okay, sweetie, here are those EKG leads I was telling you about." He connected the wires to pads on her chest. "Hear that beep? That's your heartbeat. If it stops, we'll start CPR."

"Why's it so fast?"

"You're a little nervous, that's all. If Chad Dunston was operating on me, I'd be nervous too."

"You won't leave me, will you?"

"Don't worry. Only if there's a fire. In which case you'll be the second one out of the room."

"Who's the first?"

"Me."

"Is Dr. Dunston here?"

"Right over there. Like a bishop at high mass." He placed an oxygen mask over her nose and mouth.

"What's that on my face?"

"Just a mask. Remember that oxygen I told you about? Take slow, deep breaths. Pretend it's fresh air from Three Mile Island."

He strapped the mask in place and lined up his endotracheal tube and medication-filled syringes. "In and out, that's right. Don't worry." To a nearby nurse, "Josie, give me some cricoid?" Then, "You might feel that pressure on your neck I mentioned. Just keep breathing." With deft movements, he injected a dose of Brevital into the IV tubing, following it with Anectine. "All right, almost ready. That stuff works pretty fast, okay? Just count backward from two million."

The patient tried to reply but was almost immediately asleep. Elliot flicked her eyelids and saw no reflex response. Her muscles began fasciculating, an involuntary response caused by the succinyl choline, which provided total paralysis. Then he bagged her, filling her lungs with oxygen through the mask, watching her chest rise and fall, an eye on the pulse oximeter, satisfied with an oxygen saturation of ninety-eight percent. When her muscles went flaccid, he removed the mask, exposed her trachea with a laryngoscope, and inserted the tube. Taping it in place, he nodded to the nurse.

"All yours."

Josie abandoned the neck and opened a prep set, a sterile pack of towels, gauze sponges, and small basins. She poured equal amounts of sterile water and povidone iodine, an antiseptic cleanser, into the basins. Then she gloved and washed the patient's exposed abdomen, from nipples to pubis. Five minutes later she was finished, patting the skin

dry before giving it a final covering spray with more antiseptic.

Meg, the scrub nurse, held out sterile drapes for Dunston
to frame the operative site. He stepped forward and took
them tentatively, without the banter to which everyone was
accustomed.

"What's wrong, Chad?" she asked. "Didn't get any
sleep last night?"

Dunston mumbled something unintelligible and handed
the paper towels to Mitch, the third-year surgery resident.
"Go ahead and drape her."

Everyone stared at him. Reticence was not Dunston's
trademark. Those who worked with him looked forward to
his often salacious badinage and the easygoing, lighthearted
attitude which made him a pleasure to assist. Puzzled, they
kept silent as Mitch draped the abdomen with Meg's help,
exposing a rectangle of skin in the left upper abdomen.
Only when everything was ready did Dunston step up to
the operating table.

"Knife."

When Meg handed him the scalpel, she saw that his
hands had an unusual tremor. Generally, Dunston was
steady as the Rock of Gibraltar. Undaunted, he went ahead
with his first incision, a bold subcostal swipe. He sliced
through skin and fat to expose the fascia, clamping off
bleeders along the way. He opened the fascia, then entered
the peritoneum obliquely, until he was in the belly.

"All yours, Mitch."

"What do you want me to do?" asked the surgical resident.

"Have you done spleens before?"

"A couple."

"Fine. Nothing fancy here. You operate, I'll assist. You
comfortable with that side?"

"I'm okay."

"Good. Meg, hold the abdominal wall out of the way

with a medium Richardson. Can you hand me that wide Deaver? Thanks. Look, Mitch: while I retract the stomach medially, just lift up the splenic flexure and clamp the ligament. Keep your eye peeled for aberrant vessels. Then go after the gastrocolics, but be careful of the pancreas. After that, the splenic artery and vein'll be staring at you. Clamp, cut, tie. Heavy sutures. Bingo, nothing to it."

Under Dunston's tutelage, it should have been a piece of cake. But Meg was concerned. Dunston's movements were strangely tentative. He spoke only when prompted, and the way he assisted the resident was mediocre, at best. Still, the case proceeded reasonably smoothly, albeit slowly. Finally, they reached the vessels that fed the spleen. The rest should have been simple. But all of a sudden, Dunston turned his back and walked away.

For several moments, there was a confused and palpable silence. Lance spoke up. "You all right, Chad?"

Facing the tiles on a nearby wall, Dunston heard the words as if through a tunnel, distant and reverberating. He clasped his gloved hands tightly to keep them from trembling. What was wrong with him? His confidence was gone. He felt alone and terrified. He wanted to run away.

"Dr. Dunston?" asked the resident.

He found his voice, which sounded forced and creaky. "Clamp, cut, and tie. Help him, Meg. Just take the damn thing out."

Totally confused, the resident looked at the scrub nurse, who glanced at the anesthesiologist, who could only shrug. With the belly open, there was no turning back now. Mitch thought it was some sort of test, a trial by fire. Cupping the spleen in both hands, he lifted it upward for Meg to hold.

Yet a splenectomy was not a simple "see one, do one, teach one" procedure. It required delicate manipulation. Relative novice that he was, Mitch lifted the spleen much too forcefully. The splenic artery immediately lacerated, loosing a stream of blood into the air.

"Jesus Christ!" said the anesthesiologist. "Give him a hand, Chad."

Dunston remained immobile by the wall, filled with uncertainty, overwhelmed by self-doubt. Did he know anything anymore? After what happened at the Center, the entire world of surgery seemed alien to him. He sensed what he should do—had to do—but his emotional turmoil left him paralyzed. He simply stood there, mute and trembling.

By now, the overhead lamp and ceiling were spray-painted scarlet. Mitch was reduced to an open-mouthed basket case who stared wide-eyed at the wildly spurting artery. Lance, worried about loss of blood volume, busied himself with his IV line, opening it all the way to give the patient more fluid. Meg was beside herself, growing more angry than puzzled.

"For God's sake, Chad, get the hell over here!"

Something in her tone shook him out of his stupor. It wasn't simply her fury. Deep within him there was a stirring, a call to arms, a reminder of an oath he had taken. He knew what must be done. He wheeled about and returned to the table.

The drapes were a soggy, saturated mess. Blood welled up from within the abdomen, nearly to the abdominal wall, obscuring everything.

"Where's the sucker?"

Meg handed him the Yankauer.

"Not that. Give me a Poole."

He immediately twisted the multi-holed suction tip onto the tubing and thrust the device into the crimson pool. The blood quickly drained away with an intermittently slurping noise. As it did, Dunston felt his self-assurance return. A ring of authority was in his voice.

"Here's a little trick," he told the resident. "You a righty?"

"Yes, sir."

"I'll retract the spleen. Take the first two fingers of your right hand. Hold them like a scissors on either side of the splenic vessels. Then just squeeze 'em together and you'll compress the artery."

"Where?"

"Right below where you see it pumping."

The resident complied, and almost magically, the bleeding stopped. "Give me a clamp," said Dunston.

"Which one?" asked Meg.

"A right angle. A tonsil, if you have one."

She slapped the clamp into his waiting palm. Dunston expertly guided it under the resident's fingers, then squeezed the clamp jaws shut. "Don't let go yet. Meg, give him another clamp."

"Another tonsil?"

"Doesn't matter. A long Kelly, whatever." She handed the resident what was available. "Now, Mitch, clamp the vessel just above your fingers, okay? Right. Now let your fingers go."

Caught between the two clamps, the lacerated artery no longer bled. The dry but ragged tear was clearly visible in its wall. There was a collective sigh of relief from everyone but Dunston, who was nagged by a lingering sense of failure.

"Walk in the park, right?" he said. "Give him a Metz."

The nurse handed the resident a pair of scissors.

"Now just cut between the clamps, suture ligate the proximal end, do the same with the vein, and we're home free."

Within five minutes, the spleen was removed, and all the stumps were dry. They lavaged the abdomen with warm saline. "I take it you know how to close?" he asked the resident, whose smile was evident even behind the mask.

"I think I can hack it."

"Then I'll be in the locker room. Any problems, just holler."

"Yes, sir. And thanks."

It had been a near disaster turned to triumph. There were kind words and congratulations all around, save from Dunston, who walked out of the OR and into the hall straight-jacketed by lingering doubt and a sense of foreboding.

The remainder of Dunston's day was emotionally brutal. His mind kept playing the masochistic game of might-have-been. He contemplated a career shift toward teaching, going into academic medicine; but the thought of inflicting his uncertainties on students left him uneasy. He also considered just packing it in, leaving private practice entirely. Yet he felt he'd be abandoning his patients. That night, he re-hashed the day's events, discussing his misgivings with Maks.

"I could've killed that patient," he said.

"But you didn't. You were there when they needed you."

"Was I? I felt like I was on a foreign planet. I didn't even belong in the same room with them."

She considered it. "You know what your problem is, Chad? You act like you're superhuman. After what happened last Monday, anyone else in your shoes would've taken off a month or two. But not you. This is some sort of perverse dedication to your job. You waltz right back into the OR like you're Albert Schweitzer emerging from the jungle."

He stared at his upraised hands with curious scrutiny, as if they were appendages from Madame Tussaud's Wax Museum. *"Manos de piedra."*

"I don't follow."

" 'Hands of stone.' It's what the boxer Roberto Duran called his fists. Unflinching, indestructible. But Jesus, look at these," he said, watching the fine tremor in his fingers. "What's happening to me? Have I lost it?"

She put her arm around him, soothing him as a mother

would a child. "You haven't lost anything. You're as good a surgeon as ever. Psychologists call it a crisis of confidence. And you know what? Like any crisis, it'll pass. It takes time, Chad. Just give it time."

"Think so?"

"I know so. Things are very confusing right now. For me as well as for you. Let me tell you what happened the other day. I had a drink after work on Thursday with Cheryl. I asked her if she could dig up anything on that hospital number we found in Arthur's safe. I tried myself, but I got nowhere on my computer. To make a long story short, Cheryl said it was no sweat accessing the admitting office data through Brookhaven's classified network."

"What did she find out?"

"The number was assigned to a man named Allan Schmidt. He's a nobody, an alcoholic Dr. Weiman admitted on Tuesday."

"Tuesday? That's the same day Arthur died."

"Precisely. Schmidt might have been the last patient he cared for. Schmidt's diagnosis was cirrhosis caused by alcoholism. Now listen to this. According to the Center's fact sheet, Schmidt died not long after he was admitted.'

"You're kidding."

"Some coincidence, huh? The guy croaks just before your friend is killed."

"What did he die from?"

"Apparently, congestive heart failure. According to a printout Cheryl got from the Center, the body was released to a local funeral parlor. So I called them. Are you ready for this? They said they never picked the body up. They were about to drive over there when a doctor called from the Center and cancelled the order."

"That's nonsense," said Dunston.

"I though so too, but I suppose it's possible. Those people get calls from doctors all the time."

"Not from the Center they don't. There aren't any doctors there."

"Oh, Christ. I forgot about that."

"He didn't say who the doctor was?"

"No, he couldn't remember."

"That figures. Well, somebody's lying," said Dunston. "Either the guy at the funeral parlor or whoever made the call. But that raises an interesting question. Where's Schmidt's body now?"

"That's what I wanted to know. So I called his sister, who Schmidt listed as next of kin. She didn't even know he was dead. She said she hadn't heard from him in over a year."

"That's not unusual in alcoholics. They have this peculiar habit of disappearing."

"Chad, if a doctor, or someone claiming to be a doctor, *did* call the funeral home, do you still think it's impossible that a real person is behind all this weirdness at the Center?"

"Jesus, Maks. You can't let that one die a natural death, can you?"

"Why can't you admit I might be right?"

"God, you're stubborn."

"Me?"

"Okay, okay, Let's think this out. We'll forget about motive for now. In the first place, any human behind these perverted stunts would need a detailed understanding of how the Center works. If someone killed Arthur, tried to kill me—"

"And maybe Chrissie."

"—disposed of Schmidt's body, and, yes, maybe killed Christine too. That person would require complete familiarity with the Center. For my money, that means someone like me who helped design the place."

"Like someone in the Interface Group?"

"Right. And there were only three of us. Besides me,

there was Arthur and Dr. Randall McKenna.''

"I guess we can rule out the first two. Who's this McKenna?''

"Randy's a neurologist. Last I heard, he was out of town. He's a pussycat. I'd have to consider him very unlikely.''

"Weren't there people who contributed to design who weren't on the Interface team?''

"A handful. I didn't meet them all that often. I can't remember most of their names.'' His eyes clouded over. "Except . . .''

"Except who?''

"Stingley. You know, that SOB is just malevolent enough to have concocted something like this.''

"Is he really the type?''

"Are you kidding? Walter Stingley is a positive misanthrope. He absolutely hates my guts. Come to think of it, there aren't many people he likes. He's got the connections, that's for sure. Rumor has it he worked for the government before he went into a hospital-based practice. And he's very sophisticated about computers. If you're looking for a prime suspect, I'd put my money on Stingley.''

"The government,'' Maks mused. "Everything that's happened is so bizarre, so secret. When I think about those two words, I think government.''

"As in conspiracy?''

"Something like that.''

"Good Lord, Maks. Your creative mind comes up with pretty improbable thoughts. Absolutely devious. But, impossible? Hell, I guess anything's possible. Why not ask your friend Cheryl? She works for Uncle Sam. Even if she's not a conspiracy freak, she might be able to come up with a government angle.''

"I already asked her. Cheryl eats that stuff up. I also gave her the Christine diskette.''

"What for?''

"It seems to me that whoever made that diskette is someone we should look at. Or at least talk to. He might turn out to be just who we're looking for. Why are you making that face?''

"I'm not. I'm thinking." Dunston paused. "Did you check out Schmidt's social security number?"

"Looking for what?"

"Everything's on computer these days, right? For identification purposes, most places use a person's social security number more often than they assign a number of their own. Insurance companies, government agencies, universities, and hospitals, to name a few. Let's say, for the sake of discussion, that Schmidt's body was released to a different funeral parlor than the one you spoke with. If they entered his number into their computer, it might be possible to access it.''

"Sort of a cross-check?"

"Exactly."

"I have a hunch Cheryl can help with that too."

"Incidentally, you didn't tell Schmidt's family he was dead, did you?"

"Of course not! That'd be cruel."

"Indeed it would." He looked into her blue eyes then, a long and searching stare that spoke to his own gratitude. For the short time he'd known her, Maks had been anything but cruel. Rather, she'd been unusually caring, understanding, and giving. He understood what she was doing: drawing him out, getting him to talk, keeping him from withdrawing into himself. He adored her for it.

And it was working. He was beginning to feel like himself again. There was a part of him that wanted her very much. Until now, theirs had been a rollercoaster relationship of emotional ups and downs, and every time he felt the tug of desire, something had always interfered. In the beginning, Maks had worn her neediness so openly that forcing his attention on her would have been unfair. Then it had been his turn, with his injury, with what happened at the Center, and with Arthur's death.

It felt strange to have spent so much time in the company of a beautiful woman without once yielding to his physical impulses. But now that his depression was lifting, Dunston's need for her was greater than ever. As she gazed back at him, he sensed a stimulating mutuality to their attraction. His longing for her was palpable and overpowering. Maks' lips parted, and her tongue grazed her lower lip. Dunston reached for her, his fingers sliding across her cheek to her neck. Eyes fixed on hers, he was slowly drawing her toward him when the phone rang.

For a long moment, they both ignored the sound. But after three rings, he pulled away.

"You expecting any calls?"

"No."

"Then let it ring."

"Could it be your service?"

He scowled. "Better not be."

After another ring, she decided. "I'll make it quick." She picked up the receiver. "Oh hi, Cher . . . As a matter of fact, I am." His touch was too distracting; she gently took his fingers in hers. "Of course with him. Who else? . . . How important?" She straightened up and listened for thirty seconds, during which her expression turned from disinterest to concern. "All right, I'll ask." She covered the mouthpiece with her hand. "It's Cheryl."

"Speak of the devil. What does she want?"

"She wants to meet you."

"How flattering."

She poked him in the ribs. "With her boss. She says it has something to do with the Center."

He stiffened. "Like what?"

"That's what they want to talk to you about."

"I'm not interested."

She looked him in the eye. "Is that what you want me to tell her?"

"Exactly. Tell her that . . ." He stopped, deep in thought, a faraway look on his face. It's got to occur eventually, he thought. It's what Maks had in mind. Sooner or later, I've got to face it. "When is she talking about?"

"She wants to bring him over tomorrow."

He slipped away from her, got up, and began pacing.

"Hang on, Cher," Maks said patiently.

He sighed deeply and stopped. "All right. Let's get it over with."

Chapter Seventeen

THE NEXT MORNING, the doorbell rang at precisely ten A.M. After showing in the guests, Maks made the introductions.

"Chad, this is Cheryl," she said, bemused by Cheryl's expression, that of a rock star groupie about to melt at the mere mention of her idol's name. She looked like she was about to drool, and she refused to let go of Dunston's hand until nudged by Maks. "Well, Cher?"

"Oh. This is Victor Sawyer," she said, with an adolescent giggle.

"Good Lord, Cher," Maks whispered. "Get a grip."

Sawyer smiled broadly and extended his hand. Dunston had seen that kind of look before. Behind the urbane facade, here was a man who was all business, the consummate professional.

"Dr. Dunston, I presume?"

Dunston returned the handshake. "Someone once told me that presumption's the mother of all screwups."

"All too true, I think." He looked at his watch. "We're just waiting for . . . ah, here he is now."

A compact sedan pulled up on the driveway. An overweight, middle-aged man got out and approached the doorway.

"Good morning, Merlin," said Sawyer. "I think you've

met Dr. Dunston,'' he indicated. ''And Miss Lassiter.''

Maks was somewhat surprised by the bespeckled, balding man with the pencil-thin mustache. ''Is Merlin your real name?''

''No, in fact it's Marlon. Like Dr. Sawyer here, I work for the DOE. In my line of work, I do a lot of tinkering with gadgets, inventions. Someone once tagged me with Merlin, and once the word got out, I couldn't shake it.''

''Spoken with undue modesty,'' said Sawyer. ''Man's a genius.''

''Come in, everyone,'' Maks prompted.

In the kitchen, they sat down to coffee and fresh croissants Cheryl had brought. At first they made small talk, exchanging bios, discussing common threads that linked their professions. Maks listened to Cheryl's peculiarly girlish chatter with growing annoyance. And then she scolded herself; there was no reason to get pissed off simply because her friend was behaving like a man-hungry twit. No one mentioned Dunston's nearly healed bruises.

''What exactly do you do at Kashiwahara, Miss Lassiter?''

''It's Maks.''

''Victor,'' he smiled.

''Well, Victor, I'm in admin. Your upper echelon, token female in a firm run by Asian men. But don't knock America, right? You want into the market, you go with the trend.''

''From what I understand, they're doing rather well.''

''Not bad. Lots of competition. Sharks in the water.''

''But no blood, I hope?''

''Not yet.''

''My son has one of your HDTVs. The picture's really exceptional.''

Cheryl's ears perked up. ''You never told me you had a son.''

''Yes, just married. It was our wedding gift.''

"Terrific," Cheryl said deflatedly, looking at Maks. "And this is the guy I've worked with for five years?"

Sawyer didn't skip a beat. "How about computers?" he ventured, testing the waters. "I heard Kashiwahara's coming out with a new line."

"Where'd you hear that?"

"Just talk."

"That's news to me. Not that we don't use computers. But I think your information's bogus. No way we're going to tackle NEC or any of the big boys."

"Yet you do work together, that's no secret," Sawyer persisted.

Maks smiled back. "Only our samurai."

"I mean in an ideological sense."

"But we don't share products."

"Oh, I think you do. In a friendly, noncompetitive sort of way. Not that America's exempt. Cray used Apple to refine its supercomputers, and Apple used Cray to design the Macintosh. And it goes beyond national boundaries. For example, at one time Cray got most of its chips from Fujitsu."

"But Fujitsu makes its own peripherals," said Cheryl.

"I'm not referring to that. I'm saying these are essentially integrated systems, each using some of the other's components. Think of it as a gigantic food chain, where one biological niche helps another survive. Don't you see?"

Maks sipped her coffee. "Somewhat. There's more cooperation, that's for sure. I think it's mostly attitudinal, a philosophical orientation. You mentioned supercomputers. From what Chad says, America's still way ahead. But the grapevine has it that the Japanese have the industry targeted. They bought more Crays for building cars than Detroit, and they'll probably dominate the field soon. They're very singleminded that way."

"Ah, constant vision. Isn't that right, Dr. Dunston?"

Dunston put down his napkin. "Okay, Victor, you've broken the ice. Breakfast was great, but you didn't come for the calories. What do you want?"

Sawyer stared back. "Your file suggested you'd be direct."

"What file?"

Sawyer opened his attache case and removed a thick manilla folder. "Everyone has a file, Doctor. Except it's usually in bits and pieces, not assembled. Now, take yours: there's information about education, your draft status, social security, IRS, credit rating, employment history, you name it—"

"My divorce?"

"Perhaps," Sawyer said smoothly. "Almost everything about you is on a computer somewhere. For the past two days I've gone from database to database compiling your dossier. Particularly as it pertains to your profession, your knowledge of computers, and your involvement with the Center for Human Potential. It makes impressive reading."

Dunston waxed sarcastic. "I'm sure it does. But you didn't answer my question. What do you want?"

"The Human Genome Project."

"What about it?"

"It's done. Finished. The entire genetic code's been cracked."

"Gimme a break."

"I'm quite serious."

"Right." He paused to stare at Sawyer, who looked back in unperturbed honesty through steely gray eyes. Slowly, Dunston's attitude changed from cynicism to amazement, and the expression on his face turned from annoyance to wonder. "You're saying you actually unraveled the genome?"

"Not we, I'm afraid. The Center has."

"*What?*"

"Pour some more coffee, Doctor. This may take a while."

Over the next half hour, Sawyer gave a verbal presentation not dissimilar to that he'd delivered earlier in the week at the Department of Energy. Dunston listened, astonished. Though more familiar with the project than the average physician, the ramifications of Sawyer's assertion were staggering. He knew something was horrifyingly wrong at the Center, but the idea that it had cracked the genetic code only added to his confusion, raising still more questions to which he had no answers. He simply couldn't fathom what the Center would want to do with such information.

"You're sure of this?"

"Positive. Checked and double-checked."

"Well, I'll be damned. Just unbelievable. Who else knows?"

"Not the press, thank God. It's pretty well contained."

"So why are you telling me?"

"Because we wanted to get some insights, some ideas, from people who had an ongoing interaction with the Center. We know the Center's up to something, but it's not telling us what. We hoped that one of you—the Interface Group, is it?—might be able to give us some clues. Yet obviously this comes as a complete surprise to you. Do you think it'd also surprise the others?"

"It'd blow Randy McKenna's socks off. Good thing he's out of town. And as for Arthur, well . . ."

"Yes, I've heard." He folded his hands atop his papers. "Nothing personal Dr. Dunston, but I'll be frank. You weren't my first choice. I was already acquainted with Dr. Weiman. I wanted to run this by him, but since his accident—"

It was suddenly sickeningly clear to Dunston, who sprang out of his chair as if shot from an ejector seat. His face was ashen. His eyes were wide, and his mouth opened and closed like a marionette searching for words. His voice was distant. "It was no accident."

The geneticist leaned forward. "Could you repeat that?"

"I said what happened to Arthur was no accident." He cleared his throat, feeling his temper rise. "He was murdered, dammit! What, is everybody blind? Whether it had to do with this genome stuff, I don't know." He began to pace, impatiently raking his fingers through his hair. "But he was on to something, I can tell you that. Something that dealt with the Center. And when the Center found out, Arthur was killed!"

It was Sawyer's turn to be dumbstruck. "Surely you're joking."

"Joking? I'm serious. *Dead* serious. Am I making myself clear?" He stopped and leaned his arms against the table. "And now that you've napalmed my village, I'm going to light a fire under yours. So strap on your seat belt," he said, returning to his chair, "because you're in for a long ride."

For the better part of the next hour, fortified by freshly brewed coffee, Sawyer, Cheryl, and Merlin listened in awe to a reenactment of Dunston's brush with death. As he spoke, his cuts and bruises seemed more prominent. When he finished, they sat there in glassy-eyed incredulity, at a loss for words. At length, Sawyer removed his spectacles. He wiped the lenses with a paper napkin before rummaging through some additional papers.

"I suppose that explains these," he said, placing several sheets on top of the table.

Dunston examined them. One was a computer printout from the Center, attesting to a satisfactory hernia repair; another, a medical report from the Brookhaven ICU, to which Stingley had appended an attestation regarding Dunston's mental instability; and the third, a police report compiled in longhand by Captain Donohue. Dunston read through them quickly, sniffing amusedly in some places, frowning in others. He slid the pages back to Sawyer.

"Interesting reading," said Dunston.

"Very."

"Judging from everything you've said, you seem as much in the dark as I've been. And now, on top of everything, unraveling the genome." He shook his head. "Nothing makes sense any more. I keep asking, why? Why was Arthur murdered, why did the Center try to kill me? And why this sudden interest in the genome?"

"At least we both agree on the questions. Do you have any answers?"

Dunston considered it. "The other day, Maks suggested something. Sort of thinking out loud. You see, the idea of motive has always been the toughest part for me to understand. It's just so hard to attribute intent to computers and robots. So Maks said, there's got to be someone behind all this. A person, with human motives."

"Sounds like you have someone in mind," said Sawyer.

"You're damn right," Dunston said, emphatically tapping one of Sawyer's papers. "*This* bastard."

Sawyer looked where Dunston pointed. "Dr. Stingley?"

"Yes, good old Stingley. He certainly had the means. The man knows almost as much as I do about the Center. And he hates my guts."

"But that doesn't explain his motive. Why would he want to murder two of his colleagues?"

Dunston shook his head. "That, I don't know."

Merlin spoke up. "It's much more likely for a group of people to be involved in a plot like that than a single individual," he said. He touched his mustache, looking around the room. "I hope you don't mind my chiming in?"

"No, please," said Sawyer.

"This is much too complicated for one person to pull off. For the Center to figure out the entire genome, to try to kill two of its benefactors, and to perform unauthorized surgery, is way beyond a lone person's capability. It requires a group of people. And when you're talking group, you're talking conspiracy.''

"Oh brother I give up." Dunston got up and walked away from the table. "I need some air."

"Chad!" Maks called, going after him. Cheryl followed her.

Alone for the moment, Sawyer turned to Merlin. "When I suggested you provoke him a little, I didn't mean make him flip a gasket."

"He's fiery, I'll grant you that. That's a plus. You're going to need someone who can handle stress, Victor. If the man went to pieces when I ratcheted up the pressure, he's not the man you want. Agreed?"

"I see. You're not really a conspiracy theorist, then?"

Merlin shrugged. "Who knows? I just knew it would make him jump."

"What's your take on him, overall?"

"Very intelligent, obviously. He's got an edge to him. It looks like he knows how to handle himself. Overall, I'd say you scored a bull's-eye."

"I think so too," said Sawyer. He turned to see Dunston returning and lowered his voice. "Now comes the hard part."

"Know what I think, Victor?" Dunston asked. "You've got a lot of guts coming here, knowing you might be dealing with some psycho."

"I admit the thought had occurred to me. But not any more." He reflected, squinting, then put his glasses back on. "Funny. In a strange way, that business about the testicular biopsy might be relevant."

"How so?"

Sawyer talked as he thought, his fertile mind roaming. "A testicular biopsy, spermatogonia. The genome, the very foundation of life, or creation of new life . . ." He shook his head. "I'm not sure. The theoretical possibilities are endless, but I can't spot the connection. Regardless, the

Center specifically has you in mind, for whatever its little project is.''

''Correction. *Had* me in mind. For all I know, it thinks I'm dead.''

''You can't be certain of that.''

''If we were wagering, I'd take the bet. The larger question is, why me?''

''Oh, that's much simpler. For one reason or another, you were the right man. To the Center's computers, you're a walking mass of cells, protoplasm, chromosomes, and genes. I guess they liked what they saw. And so do we, Doctor.''

''What do you mean 'we'?''

Sawyer spoke in a softly modulated tone. ''As of this moment, I'm speaking in an official capacity, with approval from the highest authorities.''

''What is this, spy week?''

''Everything I've said until now is confidential, and I trust you'll keep it that way.''

Dunston began to feel uneasy. ''I don't follow.''

''Based on everything we've discussed, I'm more convinced than ever that the answer lies with the Center. Something's happening over there. You know it, and I know it. Millions of man-hours, billions of dollars, and the most profound secrets depend on what that answer is. Obviously, I can't force you. The choice is yours. But there's no doubt about it. You're the right man.''

As Dunston stared at Sawyer, he was overcome with a fear more intense than he'd ever experienced. His skin turned to gooseflesh, and a chill penetrated his body. His voice grew hoarse with the question that had to be asked. ''The right man for what?''

''The Center.'' Sawyer paused, fingers intertwined, not taking his eyes from Dunston's. ''We want you to go back.''

Chapter Eighteen

AFTER CHERYL, VICTOR, and Merlin left, the remainder of the day became quiet to the point of solemnity. Dunston had a thick aura of uneasiness that was almost tangible, as if he'd cloaked himself in a mantle that read, "do not disturb." While Maks quietly read the paper, he repeatedly passed through the house and garden, pacing back and forth like an expectant father. Her heart went out to him. She longed to mother him, to cuddle, soothe, and explain. Yet she was astute enough to understand that, as the anxiety he'd experienced was uniquely his, so too did its resolution have to come from within him.

Slowly, Dunston began to lighten up as the day was winding down. Dunston sat on the couch next to Maks, sinking heavily into the cushions with the kind of deep exhalation that bespeaks finality. She put down what she'd been reading and waited for him to talk.

"What I don't understand is," he finally said, "what makes me the right man?"

"Your computer profile."

"There are lots of people who know more about computers than I do. Like you. But I didn't exactly notice you trying to dazzle Sawyer with your knowledge."

"I'm sure he already knows and isn't interested. Anyway, that's not the only thing on your profile.''

"How do you know?"

"Victor told me. While you were sulking."

"What else is in this infamous profile?"

"Demographic stuff. Place of birth, health, education." She paused, looking away. "Your marriage."

"Don't miss a trick, do they? What else?"

"Victor, or rather, your profile, makes you out to be quite the jock, your aches and pains notwithstanding. Baseball, boating, scuba diving, and something called sporting clays." She raised her eyebrows. "What in the world are sporting clays?"

"Yuppie shotgunning. You know skeet?"

"I shot trap a few times with my father."

"Well, trap and skeet rely on set positions and pretty standard trajectories. Whoever invented sporting clays wanted something more realistic, closer to what's in the field. So now they've got these clay pigeons of all different sizes, rolling, bouncing, going straight up, whatever."

"Now, there's the thinking man's sport."

"Don't knock it. It was that or computer chess. Actually, much more therapeutic," he said, waxing into a Southern drawl. "Shucks, with a chaw of Red Man in my cheek, I could blast those suckers into powder all day."

Maks cocked her head, smiling dreamily. "What a man."

She had to avoid confrontation. The order of the day was to keep him relaxed. With a cheerful smile, she leaned forward and brushed back a stray lock of his hair. "Let's go for a ride."

"Now? Where?"

"On your boat. It doesn't matter where. It's still warm out. I feel like some fresh air."

"It's a lot more work than you think. First we have to drive there. Then we have to unsnap and stow the rain cover, fill the tank—"

"Oh for God's sake," she said, getting up and pulling him to his feet. "You sound positively geriatric. Think old, feel old. At this rate, I won't see the water again until I'm in menopause."

An hour later, they were streaking through the open water of the Sound, heading east. Maks sat in the back seat of the deep-V powerboat, her blouse dampened by the salt spray. She'd been watching Dunston stand with his hands on the helm. The high-performance powerboat had a steep deadrise angle of twenty-two degrees, and at speeds of over thirty knots, with the forefoot nearly out of the water, Dunston saw the horizon best while standing. The lines of worry had left his face. Maks smiled, knowing the outing was a sound suggestion.

It had been easy, glassy riding without pounding. North of Mattituck, Dunston eased back on the throttles and began a slow U shoreward, the first leg of their return trip. Suddenly he veered right. As the boat tilted starboard, Maks heard something thud into the keel beneath them. She dug in her nails for support. The MerCruisers made a straining, grinding noise. Dunston immediately slipped the throttle into neutral, and the boat slowly idled to a stop.

"Jesus," he muttered.

"What was that?"

He walked behind her and bent over the port side, fishing in the water with his hand. Latching onto some sort of submerged line, he traced it aft, toward the engines. Then he dropped what he was holding and straightened up, hands on hips.

"This is ridiculous."

"What is?"

"The right prop's fouled. Looks like pot warp."

"What's that?"

"The rope attached to a lobster pot. Man, I'd like to get my hands on that idiot."

"Is it in the wrong place?"

"*Very* wrong place. It should be a lot further offshore. Also, the traps should be marked with a red buoy, or flag. Whatever clown laid out these pots was pulling a fast one. No flag. He's got a plastic detergent bottle for a marker, floating about a foot under water. I didn't spot it in time. That makes for problems, my dear."

"So, what now?"

"I get the prop unfouled, that's what. Try to cut the warp off the prop. Soon as I unravel this mess, we'll be on our way." He took a deep breath. "Open that storage compartment, will you?"

He was pointing to a four-by-three-foot deck trapdoor, just forward of the rear seat cushions. Maks grabbed its ring while Dunston laid anchor. When opened, the trapdoor hinges locked in place, leaving it three-quarters ajar.

Scuba paraphernalia was belowdecks. Two air tanks were strapped in place, lying on Styrofoam cradles. Beside them was a carrying bag with air hoses, along with places for fins, mask and snorkel, a folded wet suit, and other items. Rejoining her, Dunston unstrapped one of the tanks and placed it upright on deck.

"I didn't know you smoked cigars."

"Huh?"

Maks pointed at the trap door opening. "There's a cigar box down there. Monte Cristos."

As she reached for the container, it suddenly hit him.

"Don't touch it, Maks!"

He took her hand and carefully led her to the back of the boat. Then he slowly made his way back to the trapdoor and cautiously eased the box from its hiding place. A nine-volt battery was taped to its side, and two wires connected the battery to something inside.

"I'm not sure what this is, but I don't get a good feeling about it. I'd feel better if we got it the hell off the boat."

Maks swallowed nervously, her throat dry. "Is that what I think it is?"

"I'm not going to open it to find out. Help me wrap it in that plastic liner, Okay? I don't want to get the damn thing wet."

Together, they painstakingly covered the box in several layers of disposable marine liner. Satisfied that it was watertight, Dunston gingerly put it down.

"Are we going to leave it like that?" asked Maks

"No, we're going to put as much distance as we can between us and the box. Can you hand me that bag of hoses?" He smiled reassuringly. "Don't worry, I've done this a dozen times."

Dunston unzipped a handbag-size case and removed four coiled black air hoses, all joined to a bar of silvery metal. He called the apparatus a regulator. He unraveled its hosing and held it up to hang free. He bent down and removed a jacketlike item from the storage compartment.

"Life vest?

"Sort of. It's an inflatable BC, a buoyancy compensator. A fancy vest with pockets and straps." He sat beside her, with the tank between his legs. Having stripped down to a swimsuit, he slipped the BC's backpack portion over the tank, orienting the backpack so the tank valve opening faced it. Then he set about attaching the regulator to the tank.

After removing protective tape from the valve, he cracked it momentarily open. A loud hiss expelled any accumulated dirt or water. Dunston spoke as he worked. The silvery metal to which all hoses attached was the regulator's yoke, made of chromed brass. The yoke contained the regulator's first stage, the portion attached to the tank. The purpose of the first stage, he explained, was to reduce the tank's high pressure, while the second stage—the portion containing the mouthpiece—reduced it even further. As Maks watched, Dunston unscrewed a knob that secured a dust cover. Then he positioned the first stage on the tank valve so their openings matched, and the second stage hose led off to the right. After tightening the first stage screw onto the valve, he attached a hose from the regulator to a low pressure inflator on the BC. Finally, he pointed to each hose.

"Second stage, alternate air source, low pressure inflator, submersible pressure gauge. Now, let's see if this baby's got any air in it."

"I do hope you're kidding."

He cranked open the air valve and checked the pressure gauge. The dial swung from zero to 3,100. "We're in business."

"You have enough?"

"Plenty. Don't worry. I don't plan being under long. Give me a hand with this thing, okay? Just keep it from tipping over."

Maks steadied the tank assembly, keeping it from tilting as the boat gently rocked from side to side. Dunston gave a final tug to the BC's backpack cinch. After checking that all hoses were secure, he hoisted the assembled package onto the boat's side rail. Maks held it for him, surprised by its heaviness, while Dunston donned mask, weight belt, and fins. Backing up toward the tank, he squatted a bit to slip his hands through the arm holes, much like getting into a jacket. Then he tightened the works to his torso by means of a Velcro cummerbund and two plastic buckles. Satisfied, he bit into the second stage's mouthpiece and inhaled a blast of compressed air. Then he carefully lifted the cigar box and cradled it between his arm and chest. He gave Maks a thumbs-up sign, held onto his face mask, and leaned backward over the rail, tumbling into the water with a splash. When Maks peered over the side, all she saw was a trail of bubbles.

As he slowly began to sink, he jackknifed underwater and finned slowly downward, watching his pressure and depth gauges while he descended. At forty-eight feet, he reached bottom. At that depth, visibility in the Sound's temperate waters was rather dreadful, especially once he'd kicked up some silt. Nonetheless, as the fine particulate matter settled, he soon delineated the five-foot crate. Working carefully, he opened the trapdoor and freed the lobsters, some thirteen in all. He then carefully placed the wrapped cigar box in the trap. He righted himself and began a slow, upward ascent.

When he reached the surface, Dunston swam beneath the hull, backward along the keel. The visibility was fair at best, and he cursed himself for forgetting a hand-held light. With a few leg kicks, he reached the stern. The outlines of the twin props were easy to discern. He pressed his face mask nearer for a close-up inspection.

As he'd suspected, the left propeller blade was entangled with heavy-duty yellow nylon rope, one quarter inch thick. He estimated that at least two feet were ensnared in the blade. He turned and looked toward the yellow detergent bottle.

There was a sudden tugging about his face. As he eased his head forward, the mask began slipping toward the right. It felt as if some invisible force were trying to wrench his mask off. It took several seconds for him to realize what was happening. He stopped moving and hovered motionless in the water. Dunston slowly raised his left arm in an orbit above his head. An instant later, his hand encountered the monofilament line.

Jesus, Joseph, and Mary, he thought. It was heavy duty fishing line, snagged on the mask strap buckle. Some unsuspecting fisherman had lost his line to the same illegal trap which entangled the prop. But that realization was little comfort, knowing that the cigar box was only meters away. Trapped like an insect in a spider's web, he was unable to move his head in any direction. Dunston cautiously reached for the Wenoka strapped to his shin and slid it out of its sheath. Tracing the outline of his face mask frame, he located the source of his entrapment and slowly cut away the strands of tangled monofilament.

He took a deep, relaxing breath through the mouthpiece, moving his head in an arc, assuring that it was free. Satisfied, he returned his attention to the prop. He counted at least six strands of pot warp choking the blades. Using the serrated edge of the knife, he began sawing slowly. It was easier than he expected. Yielding to the force of his strokes, the rope's braided strands quickly parted. In less than five minutes, before he became arm weary, the prop was free. He swam away from the severed line. Out of the corner of his eye, he noticed the submerged yellow bottle, now unfettered, buoy itself to the surface.

It had taken much longer than he'd intended. He prayed they had enough time. he broke the surface and quickly tossed his face mask topside. Maks helped Dunston scramble up the stern ladder. Without bothering to remove his gear, he hurried to the console and throttled forward. The boat quickly sped away from the site.

As they skimmed across the wavetops, they nervously looked over their shoulders toward the package in their wake. From the corner of his eye, Dunston watched Maks, whose knuckles were white around the windshield's rim. The boat had gone five hundred yards when a watery blast erupted behind them, sending a white geyser skyward.

Wincing and stunned, Dunston throttled back. As the boat slowed, Maks leaned toward him, seeking the protective warmth of his arms. They sat there holding one another in unspoken terror, aware that someone, somewhere, was on to them.

Chapter Nineteen

AT MIDDAY MONDAY, Cheryl called Maks at work. She was in a hurry. After some meandering chitchat, she got down to business.

"Were you aware the diskette you gave me is a second?"

"Meaning what?"

"You know, seconds. Rejects, something with imperfections. There's not much of a market for seconds in the technology sector, but in this case, there were only little scratches, dings in the plastic. Those diskettes go for less than half price."

"I've never seen them advertised."

"They're not. At least, not to the general public. The market's in bulk, for commercial use. They're sold by the case."

"What does all this have to do with Christine?"

"Maybe nothing, but you wanted me to find out who made the diskette, right? Seconds are much easier to track down by their serial numbers because so few of them are sold."

"I didn't know they had serial numbers."

"Actually, they're lot numbers. Here on the Island, only one place sells them. Americorp, that technology superstore? I was able to do a little waltz through their computerized records. There were only three buyers for one-case minimums with that lot number. One was the school of communications at the University, and the second was the Board of Education.''

Maks held her breath. ''And the third?''

''The third was your good friend Dr. Stingley.''

Maks was astonished. ''*Stingley*. I don't believe this. Chad will go nuts when he hears this.''

''You don't think it could have been one of the other two?''

''An undergrad in journalism or the school board? No way.''

''I don't think so either. So I did a little checking on Stingley. You know he worked for the government?''

''So Chad said.''

''Ah, but was he aware that until ten years ago, Stingley was chief medical officer in the Defense Intelligence Agency?''

Maks' heart skipped a beat. ''I think you're serious.''

''Never more so. In a way, everything is starting to make sense. When Victor was in Washington briefing the muckymucks at the DOE, he said the people who objected the loudest were defense and Pentagon-types. They claimed his conclusions about cracking the genetic code were 'iffy,' wild speculation. It seems to me those boys have something to hide.''

Maks was staggered. Even though she'd been the one to bring it up, she'd long ago dismissed the concept of conspiracy as fanciful. The idea that Christine might have died as a result of government duplicity was incredible. Yet beyond that, what Cheryl discovered only raised more questions. Most important, if Stingley were involved in Dr. Weiman's death, could he be so careless as to leave the diskette in the desk? As usual, nothing made any sense.

''What am I supposed to do with this bombshell?''

"Let Victor handle it. The whole thing is very sticky. Politically explosive. You can't mention it to Chad either. The time's not right, and Victor would have my ass if he knew I told you. You remember how he reacted when Merlin mentioned conspiracy. And after that bomb on the boat, I bet Chad's waffling with the idea of going back to the Center. You have to promise me, Maks."

Maks nodded.

"Oh, one last thing. That patient who died, Schmidt? I cross-referenced his social security number for you. He was a Vietnam vet, in more DWIs that you can count, and in and out of detoxs for twenty years. Funny. He was transferred to the Center the day he died."

"From where?"

"The VA. He'd been a patient there for two months. His mind was gone from the booze."

"Did you come across anything at all which might explain why Dr. Weiman kept his admission number in the safe?"

"Not a thing. I can't imagine why he'd be interested in the guy, but I could be missing something. Tell you what. I'll fax over the information I have and let you check it out."

Over the next few days, Maks' aptitude for listening was largely responsible for Dunston's return to a kind of shocked normalcy. After learning what Sawyer had in mind and with the bomb still gnawing at him, he had ridden a roller coaster from terror to outrage to numbness in a series of psychological steps not dissimilar to those undergone by the terminally ill, who suddenly learned their prognosis was death. If the process went favorably, it ultimately led to acceptance of one's fate. Throughout, Maks listened to his often-rambling verbalizations with sympathy and quiet reassurance. Yet although she was instrumental in calming his state of mind, it was not that alone that won him over. Deep inside, his sense of professional obligation reemerged.

In the military, such obligation was akin to a call to arms, a reaffirmation of one's code of duty and honor. In the medical arts, it was an understanding of one's role as a healer. Dunston slowly came to appreciate what was expected of him.

Yet Dunston's greatest motivation was neither Maks' assistance, his duty as a physician, nor his realization that death might yet be in the cards for him that won him over. Rather, it was the resurgence of a profound curiosity about the goings on at the Center. Sawyer had been amply convincing, and now he had to find out for himself. He was like a larva molting, shedding layer after layer of understanding until he finally felt ready to take flight into the unknown.

It was an undertaking, Merlin hinted, replete with arcane terminology and an ample overlay of Special Forces technology. Dunston was no firearms devotee, but he knew enough about weapons to understand the implication that he return packing firepower. They had no idea who was behind the Center's strange goings on; and if the bomb on the boat proved anything, it was that he had no qualms about killing whoever got in his way. But a shootout, if it came to that, was strictly a fallback position. More important was a one-on-one linkup with, and thwarting of, the Center's computers.

"First and foremost," Sawyer said, "we have to find out what the Center's computers are up to. Second, if you get a chance, we'd love to know more about what its STM is doing."

"I thought you already knew that."

"It was all presumption. We *presumed* their STM literally read the genetic code on a molecular level, in order to map the genome. But for what? It's got to be doing something with the information."

"Those are related questions."

"Perhaps. It's certainly within the realm of possibility

that the Center's ultimate goal relates to what it's learned from the STM. In any event, we'll be grateful for anything you learn.''

''It sounds like you're being pressured.''

''That'd be putting it mildly. The military has gone bonkers over this. Conspirators in their midst and all that. Cabinet-level personnel are in a state of paranoia. The idea of waiting a month to empty out the Center is making them delusional. They see plots and counterplots. They want answers yesterday, but they might settle for tomorrow.''

''I won't be ready by tomorrow.''

''I know. But the closer you get every day, I buy time. I can stall them, but not forever. Some even agree with that idiot brigadier about storming the place with guns blazing. I need you on this, Dunston. How much longer do you think it'll take?''

''I don't plan to hang around there long, Victor,'' he lied. Time permitting, he had some very personal questions he wanted answered.

''I realize that. But give me a rough idea.''

''Well, memorizing the layout shouldn't be tough. I'll need details and specs on every bit of hardware and software that was ever delivered. The hardest part will be going over programming and computer languages. I'm a little rusty, but I think a good day's concentration should do it. A lot depends on Merlin's help.''

Sawyer smiled. ''He has some toys he wants to show you. Once you see them, I don't think you'll be sorry. And then we can talk strategy.''

''The only strategy I have is getting out of there alive.''

''Admittedly. And with good reason. Shall we say Friday afternoon, then? For an early Saturday return?''

Dunston looked away, fighting a current of uncertainty that swirled about him. Finally, he nodded his head. ''I should be ready by then.''

* * *

Dunston found the middle of the week unexpectedly difficult. He'd either repressed or forgotten the tedious nature of computer programming, especially the time-consuming aspects of the more esoteric computer languages, though not the language fundamentals themselves. On Thursday, he burned the candle from dawn to dusk, leaning over his dogeared texts like a schoolboy, fortified by cup after cup of espresso, not taking time to eat. He wasn't hungry anyway. Over the course of the day he'd grown progressively more somber and withdrawn, but not from sullenness. Rather, it was a singleminded, goal-directed intensity that left no room for distraction. Finally, shortly after seven P.M., he closed the last book and sat back to rub his eyes, admitting he could no longer ignore getting bifocals.

His few moments of solitude were shattered by the arrival of Cheryl and Victor. Cheryl, loquacious as ever, could be heard clear across the house, her voice unrestrained by Sawyer's more modulated tones. The trio snaked its way toward Dunston in the living room, where he'd secluded himself by a low and warming fire he'd kept alive by the hour. It had now turned to faintly glowing embers. He silently awaited their arrival, puzzling over Cheryl. She had the brains of an Einstein, the maturity of an adolescent, and less culture than yogurt. Yet he realized that her knowledge of computers was uncanny, and her presence was therefore indispensable for the grilling he knew Sawyer had in mind for him.

Sawyer began the conversation.

"So, Doctor. How go the preparations?"

"Not bad. Most of what I've forgotten's come back pretty fast. I still haven't figured out exactly how I'm going to get the computers to 'fess up once I'm in there. *If* I get in."

"Oh, you'll get in, all right. In fact, Miss Lassiter has that nearly worked out."

Dunston shot her a quizzical look. Maks smiled sheepishly and was on the verge of saying something when Sawyer held up a hand.

"More about that later. First, do you feel comfortable with the blueprints?"

"Upside-down and sideways," he said. "I could find my way around blindfolded."

"You may have to. Much of the Center's unlit. How about your computer language skills?"

"Got most of it down. I'll look at it again tomorrow."

"What did you originally train in?"

"C, mostly. But I once knew a lot of assembly. That's what I was brushing up on today."

"What's C?" asked Maks.

Cheryl's look dripped incredulity. "Maks, don't be such a dweeb."

"I'm serious."

"Did you ever study programming, Miss Lassiter?"

"One semester of BASIC in college."

"Have you kept up with it?"

"Not really."

"Victor," interrupted Dunston, "she has nothing—"

"On the contrary. Miss Lassiter is playing a pivotal role in the project, as you will soon learn. She has every right to grasp what you're referring to. With your permission, Doctor?"

Dunston shrugged. "Up to you."

"Thank you." He turned to Maks as Dunston motioned for coffee. "Computers, you know, communicate through numbers. Binary digits, or bits, those infamous zeroes and ones that frighten people away. Computer languages allow you to program—to give your computer a series of instructions—without ever having to utter a single zero or one. Now, programming languages have three levels of sophistication. A high-level language has a structure fairly close to English. A low-level language, like the assembly language Dr. Dunston referred to, is but a hairsbreadth away from zeroes and ones. A mid-level language is somewhere in between.

"As it implies, the BASIC you learned was intended as a teaching tool, not a serious computer language. It's a high-level language that's easy to learn and simply requires you to know programming commands and the language's syntax."

"Syntax?"

"Programming commands are called vocabulary," said Cheryl. "Language syntax is the order of the words."

"BASIC's vocabulary only has about 140 'words,' or commands," Victor continued, "which is why it's so easy to learn. Learning the syntax is a little tougher. But once you've gotten the hang of it, the rest is just practice."

"So what's C?"

"In a moment," said Sawyer. "Like you, ninety percent of all programmers began with BASIC, not only because it's easy to learn, but also because it usually comes with the computer you buy. However, BASIC isn't perfect. No language is. BASIC has, well, what we call lack of structure. A language called PASCAL, on the other hand, is very structured, but it does poor string handling."

"You've totally lost me."

"Hmmm . . . I suppose that is a tricky concept. All I'm saying is, there are different languages at different levels, all having strengths and weaknesses, better for one purpose than another. Other popular languages are named PRO-LOG, LISP, FORTRAN, and ADA. PROLOG, for instance, is best for expert systems and theorem proving, while if you want a job in missile guidance control, you'd best learn ADA."

"I'll keep that in mind."

Cheryl rolled her kohl-rimmed eyes and tapped her blackened nails while Sawyer continued his explanation.

"Now, C. C is the ultimate computer language. Unlike

BASIC, it's considered a midlevel language, and nowhere near as English-like.''

"So why use it?"

"To understand that, you have to know something about operating systems.''

"Like DOS?''

"Yes, like DOS, although DOS is mainly for personal computers. Any operating system is a series of instructions that controls the computer so that you, the programmer, can talk to it. Some operating systems, like the one at the Center, were specifically designed for larger computers that dealt with multiple users at once. This 'time-sharing' capability is something PCs can't do, so other operating systems came into vogue. The one I'll tell you about is called UNIX.

"UNIX was originally written in that tedious assembly language. Assembly uses two-to five-letter mnemonics, instead of zeroes and ones, to represent programming instructions. It's conceptually difficult because it's so unlike English.''

"And there isn't just one assembly language," said Dunston. "There are several.''

"Precisely. But let's not unnecessarily confuse the poor girl. So: here we have this new multiuser operating system that all the universities want, but it's written in obtuse assembly language. That just wouldn't do. Finally, someone came up with the bright idea of simply rewriting the operating system in a higher level language, less primitive than assembly. That language was christened B, which was later modified and upgraded to C.'' He paused. "And there you have it.''

Maks was still bewildered. "This UNIX operating system and C have something to do with the Center?''

"Exactly. The Center's computers deal with thousands of users at once—say, inquiries from the dietary department, sending out lab results, or communicating with ter-

minals off campus. It's a true multi-user system, because
the computers have multiple things to do simultaneously.
UNIX helps put it all together. As I said, most of UNIX is
written in C—"

"But some was written in ADA and LOGO," said Dunston. "Unless, somehow, it's internally rewritten itself. In
which case I'm screwed."

Maks shook her head. "That's it. Thanks for trying, but
I give up."

"No, please," Victor persisted. "This is already more
complicated than I intended. All I meant was to give you
an overview. End of lecture, deal?"

Maks sighed. "All right."

"Now, Doctor," said Sawyer, unfolding the Center's
blueprints. "You'll be entering here"—he indicated—"at
the offloading ramp. It's one floor below the lab. We have
a strong hunch, backed up by your recollections, that the
Center's shenanigans involve the lab. But since we have no
way of confirming that, it might be pointless nosing around
there."

"Not to mention lethal."

"Right. At any rate, we'll probably get what we want
from querying the computer directly. Once inside, your destination is level two, where you'll be offloaded by autobot.
From there, proceed down the stairwell to the computer
center at level three. After that, you're on your own."

"Hold on," said Dunston. "That's a quantum leap. Even
if the Center thinks I'm dead, it's sure to have my photo
and everything else about me in computer memory. You
think it's going to let me mosey on into the OK Corral
unchallenged? Those autobots have optics. It's not about to
offer me a free ride."

"And it won't. You see, you're not going in as yourself."

"I'm not?"

"You're going in as a toilet."

"Say again?"

"Miss Lassiter will explain."

Dunston narrowly looked her way with the skepticism of one practical joke too many.

"It's something I discovered just last week," said Maks. "Kashiwahara recently opened a small health care division. A trial run. About three months ago, it linked up with two other Japanese companies to develop this high-tech toilet. No joke. They think there's a market for it. They call it 'the intelligent toilet.' Apparently, it releases something like litmus paper into the bowl. Color sensors analyze levels of sugar, protein, ketones, and nitrites in the urine. And they're built in a miniature chromatograph to do a quickie stool analysis. All the results go on computer."

He clucked his tongue. "What'll they think of next."

"The Center ordered three for installation. Their shipping crates will be delivered Saturday morning. Two of them will contain just the toilets. And the third—"

"I get the picture." He turned to Sawyer. "Okay, suppose I make it to level two. The place is crawling with surveillance equipment. How am I supposed to get to the computer center undetected?"

"A fair question, and one Merlin will explain tomorrow. Quite ingenious, actually."

"I bet. Today, the intelligent toilet. Tomorrow, the world. What time tomorrow, anyway?"

"Is nine at the Upton office too early?"

"That's fine."

Sawyer rose to leave. "Incidentally, I wouldn't worry about that business with Dr. Stingley and the Christine diskette. My friends in Washington have gone over it with a fine-tooth comb. They think it's a red herring. If there is a conspiracy, he has nothing to do with it."

Dunston had a mystified expression. "What business are you talking about?"

He hesitated. Chad's cooperation had disarmed him and

now he'd opened up a whole new can of worms.

"God dammit! Are you saying he was the one who made it?"

"Yes, but it turned out to be meaningless."

"I don't believe this," Dunston said. Rolling his eyes, he looked upward. With Maks close on his heels, Dunston stormed out of the room.

Stingley's phone number and address were unlisted. It took five minutes for Dunston to coax the address out of the ward clerk on the psych unit and another thirty minutes to drive to his Belle Terre home. It was after nine when Dunston and Maks pulled up. Compared with the other houses in the neighborhood, the split-level ranch was surprisingly modest.

It was also unlit. It hadn't occurred to Dunston that the psychiatrist might not be home. He had confrontation in mind, and the obsessive aspects of his behavior blinded him to reality. Maks was close on his heels as he briskly approached the front door.

"Don't do anything stupid, Chad."

"I wouldn't think of it. Nothing more than a broken nose."

"Aren't you in enough hot water already?"

"Scalding. All I want is some answers."

He rang the doorbell; when that wasn't answered, he repeatedly worked the heavy brass knocker. After thirty seconds, a light went on inside the house. Stingley's disembodied voice called through the door.

"Yes, can I help you?"

"It's Chad Dunston. I want to talk to you."

"Have you completely lost it, Dunston? It's the middle of the night."

Dunston was infuriated. "Open the goddamn door before I break it down!"

There was the click of a latch, and the door slid ajar,

protected by a security chain. Stingley's face appeared in the opening. "You could lose your medical license over this. Now get out of here before I call the police."

"Give me five minutes of your time!"

"Don't be an idiot. Go home and sleep it off."

When Stingley tried to shut the door, Dunston rammed it with his shoulder, much as he'd slammed into the gunman in the ER. The chain exploded from its attachments in a blizzard of paint chips and splinters. His momentum carried him into Stingley. The psychiatrist's glasses went flying as he was knocked several feet backward.

"This will cost you, Dunston."

Dunston took a menacing step forward, silently balling his fist. Stingley cowered. "All right, all right," he conceded, hesitantly reaching for his glasses. "You made your point. What is it you want?"

"I want to know what you're up to. I want to know why you made a computer disk of a four-year-old girl. And I want to know what the hell's going on over at the Center!"

"I have no idea what you're referring to."

Dunston grabbed him roughly by the lapels, thought better of it, then released him, mentally counting to ten. "All right. Let's pretend for a moment you don't. There are some pretty odd things going on in that hospital, Dr. Stingley. Things involving me, Arthur Weiman, and Miss Lassiter's young sister. What I'm asking is, what do you have to do with all of this?"

"Me? You must be kidding."

Dunston studied him. "Are you part of some group that's fiddling with things over there?"

"Group, as in conspiratorial cabal?"

"Something like that."

"Why on earth would you think that?"

"Because it's more than one man alone could pull off. And because you were once highly placed in the government, in the DIA."

Stingley gave a wry smile and shook his head. "Ah, the government. I gave them nearly twenty years, you know. Twenty damn productive years, and then came the budget cuts . . . I resigned my commission before I was let go. So the long answer to your short question is, no. I wasn't part of some outside group that infiltrated the Center."

"All right, then. Were you *individually* involved in the peculiarities that went on there?"

"I don't know what you mean. Look, Arthur Weiman came to me a little before his death to get my professional opinion about what happened to him during the alpha intercept."

"You know the sequence of events?"

"I know what he claimed, that both of you had some sort of blackout during the process. He and I had a long chat, and I did a brief exam. Neurologically, he was fine. And I made no psychiatric diagnosis that could explain what occurred."

"What then?"

"I was intrigued by his story. So I returned to the Center, to query its computer in that room Weiman described off the lobby. I got some interesting data."

"You made the Christine diskette?"

"How do you know about that?"

"It was in the desk drawer in Weiman's office. I found it when I discovered his body."

"What you found, Dunston, wasn't everything I learned. His diskette was highly edited."

"What are you talking about?"

"When I told Weiman what I discovered, he insisted on getting a copy. I hadn't completely finished studying it, but he was persistent. So, I gave him an abbreviated version."

"Where's the original?"

"It's here. Upstairs."

"Get it!"

* * *

It was nearly midnight when they returned home.

Dunston gave the disk to Maks and followed her upstairs. She sat in front of her personal computer and switched on the small workstation lamp. Then she turned on the power and slipped in the diskette, with Dunston peering over her shoulder.

The data that appeared on the screen reached out to them. They both stared at the wording wide-eyed, unable to speak. In the monitor's artificial illumination, the beads of sweat that broke out on her forehead were almost immediately visible. The information streamed fast and furious from the diskette. Maks grew anxious and impatient. She feverishly went from screen to screen, trying to absorb what she was reading. But its impact was too much. She started trembling, overcome by a feeling of intense despair.

"Dear God," she said. "It can't be."

OUACHITA TECHNICAL COLLEGE

OUACHITA TECHNICAL COLLEGE

Chapter Twenty

A TORTURED CRY escaped her, calved from a sob frozen in her throat. Her face was drained and colorless, with one hand over her mouth. Behind her, Dunston silently agonized over what he saw on the monitor.

"Chrissie's alive, isn't she?" she managed.

"Maks, don't jump to—"

"She is, dammit, and you know it! The poor kid's somewhere in that damn hospital!"

"We can't be sure of that."

"Bullshit! You escaped from the OR, so why couldn't she? How much proof do you need, anyway?" She went from page to page, pointing out words on the monitor. "July thirtieth: unable to locate subject thought to be C. Lassiter . . . August nineteenth: nocturnal movements again detected on levels two and three, search unsuccessful . . . September twenty-seventh: continuation of intermittent faint sounds, pattern recognition suggests human phonation, source elusive. For God's sake, Chad, Christine's alive! Except she's no big, strong adult like you. She couldn't get out!"

All at once her fury was spent, replaced by anguish. She put her face in her hands, sobbing, shoulders quaking. "She's just a little girl, a baby. She's only four years old, and she's been trapped in that place for six months. She must be scared out of her mind! We've got to do something!''

He placed his palm on her shoulder, and her head with its golden hair came to rest against his fingers. He felt the warmth of a tear on the back of his hand.

"I don't know, Maks. But I'll do my damndest to look for her. One way or another, we'll find her.''

"When you return to the Center, I'm going with you.''

"We'll talk about it. We've got a long day tomorrow. Let's get some sleep.''

Maks arose without another word. But in her silence lay resolution, a fierce and adamant determination that would brook no interference.

The following morning, they arrived at Upton early. Absorbed in their thoughts, they'd spoken little en route. Maks' stated intention of the previous night remained unchallenged. In the lab, Merlin was already there, as was Sawyer.

"Did you find Dr. Stingley last night?'' Sawyer asked.

"It's a long story, Victor. I'd rather not go into it right now.''

"As you wish. Ready for the tour?''

"Sure,'' Dunston said. "Off to the war room.''

A queer smile spread over Merlin's face, a look Dunston had never seen.

"I call it the arcade,'' Merlin said.

He turned and led the way with childlike glee. When they passed into an ultramodern machine shop, Dunston thought Merlin could just as easily have been named Q, after the technical genius of James Bond fame who was quite possibly the inspiration for Merlin's flighty eccentricity.

The half dozen men in "the arcade'' were in various stages of activity. All wore full-length, zippered white surgical coveralls, and white surgical caps. None paid the slightest attention to Merlin and his visitors. Three of them, either indolent or bored, sat in a semicircle on folding chairs, drinking coffee and discussing the Islanders. The other three were involved in various mechanical projects, bending over instruments and apparatuses unrecognizable to Dunston. The shop was mainly silent save for a faint background whistling Dunston found distracting. Impatience accompanied his mounting curiosity.

"So, Marlon, how're you going to make me invisible?"

"Who said you'd be invisible?" Sawyer asked.

Dunston whirled, snapping at Sawyer. "Don't screw around with me, Victor."

Sawyer smiled. "Not invisible to us. To *them*. Merlin?"

"You familiar with Stealth technology, Doc?"

"Swell," said an exasperated Dunston. "Yesterday I was a toilet. Today, I'm an airplane. Tomorrow I am a fountain pen."

"Follow me," said Merlin. "I hope you're not claustrophobic."

Dunston peered ahead, mumbling to himself. "Something's not right with this picture."

"We know you're good at scuba diving."

"Oh, I get it. An *underwater* airplane."

Merlin stopped before a hanger, from which hung a loose, black body suit, thicker than a diver's wet suit, but not as bulky as EVA apparel in outer space ventures. "Beauty, isn't she?"

"Sure is. What is it?"

"We don't have a name for it yet. When you squeeze into this baby, the Center's optical sensors couldn't spot you unless you walked up and said hello. Just be sure not to trip over the floor-level laser guides. Interrupt their circuits, and they're on to you pronto."

"Comforting thought. How does the suit work?"

"Like this. The Center's optical sensors aren't your typical TV-surveillance setup, except in the ORs and the patients' rooms. Since they figured no human would be prowling the halls, the corridor and stairwell sensors rely on infrared and x-ray wavelengths. That's where this suit comes in. Move closer, feel it. Heavy?''

''Not too bad,'' said Dunston.

''Good. We started with a mil-spec, top-of-the-line Navy SEAL neoprene wet suit. Covers every square centimeter of your body, nothing exposed. Then we impregnated it with a Stealthlike coating that blocks all five radar wavelengths that could be aimed at Stealth. Take my word for it, nothing can see this baby. Not x-ray, not radar. It's deflected, or absorbed. Follow me?''

''So far.''

''Now, the infrared. Humans give away a characteristic heat signature. Dead giveaway. So what we did was to eliminate the heat by making you cold.''

''Frigid?''

''Are you trying to be funny?''

''I'm trying to stay alive.''

Merlin took in Dunston's seriousness. ''Fair enough. I don't think you'd consider it particularly frigid. The suit's lining is Gore-Tex and Thinsulate, so you'll stay comfortable. Then, we built in layers of flexible freon coils, woven through every inch of fabric. To the Center, you'll be a cold nonentity. Do your part and they won't spot a thing.''

''What about my breath? That would show up. Do you use scuba tanks?''

''Forget it, too bulky. We designed a custom air source-regulator out of titanium and ceramic. Not too big, and it's insulated. Just clench it between your teeth and no heat'll escape. Here you go,'' he said, holding up a thin cylinder. ''About the size of an extra-large Corona cigar.''

''How much air does it hold?''

''It's not air. It's oxygen. Enough for forty minutes breathing time.''

''How'd you manage that?''

"Well, it's triply compressed, about ten thousand psi. The regulator's in three stages instead of the normal two, which lets us step down gradually to breathable pressures. It's also got a diaphragm-type intake valve that mixes ambient air with the oxygen, so what you wind up with is slightly enriched room air."

"What about when I breathe out?"

"Now that's the beauty of it. Your breath goes back into the suit. Nothing's vented out. You'll probably breathe more shallowly than usual because of the pressurization. Add it all up, and you got forty minutes."

"No problem with oxygen toxicity?"

"No, that's only at depth. At sea level, the only thing you have to worry about is getting the cylinder hot. Do that and we're talking heavy-duty explosives. Just put in the mouthpiece and inhale lightly."

"Forty minutes, huh?"

"Should be plenty of time. Just remember not to spit that thing out until you're clear of the Center."

"Don't lose any sleep over that. Anything else?"

"I hope you've got nothing planned, because I'm just warming up. Come over this way."

Maks trailed the two of them, keeping silent to dispel her fears, which were considerable. Dunston and Sawyer followed Merlin to another workbench, where he dialed the combination to a drawer lock. The latch clicked open, and a horizontal compartment the shape of a safety deposit box automatically extended. Merlin lifted the lid and removed what appeared to be a keyboard. It was the size of a floor tile, but about two inches thick. He gingerly handed it to Dunston.

"Be careful with that."

Dunston looked it over. "Is this some kind of word processor?"

"Like hell, you say. This is to a word processor what the space shuttle is to a biplane. That's a laptop computer, my friend. But not just some IBM ThinkPad. This is the cutting edge, *compadre*, the technology of the year 2000.''

To Dunston, the computer was eminently nondescript. ''Could've fooled me.''

''And it might, if you're not careful. You've gotta understand this beauty. We kind of borrowed its guts from IBM-Siemens. They've been collaborating on a new generation of dynamic access memory chips, D-RAM. Most high capacity commercial chips hold four million bits of information. The Center used chips that store sixteen million bits. Don't ask me where they got 'em, because I don't know.''

''I have a fair idea,'' said Maks.

''I bet you do, little lady. And I intend on asking you about that later. Now getting back to what I was saying. A sixteen million-bit, superconducting chip makes one helluva fast processor. But take a look at this.''

Within thirty seconds, Merlin had disassembled the laptop and cautiously extracted a fingernail-size sliver of silicon. ''This is true artistry. I realize you probably can't tell the difference, but this little number is a chip containing sixty-four million bits of information, the equivalent of ten good-sized novels. There are a bunch of 'em in the circuitry. And that, Doc, is how you're going to outsmart the Center.''

''You got this from IBM?''

Merlin held a finger to his lips. ''Stop shouting, for Christ's sake. Not got. *Borrowed*. And these chips are prototypes, the only ones they have. Lose this laptop, and I'm up the creek.''

''How's this supposed to help me access the files?''

''Simple. You're gonna pull an Ali, beat 'em to the punch. Float like a butterfly, wham-bam the suckers with lightning speed before they figure out what hit 'em. See these two horizontal slots? We're sending you in with two floppies. The first is going to FUBAR their hardware—''

"FUBAR?" asked Maks.

"Fucked up beyond all recognition, pardon my French. It'll drive them crazy, while the second simultaneously accesses and records the files you want. *Capice?*"

"How long is this going to take?"

"Long? I'm talking nanoseconds here."

"And none of what I do will harm the patients?"

"Nope. Think of the Center's computers as a human brain. The brain has a cerebral cortex, which processes thoughts, and a brainstem, or autonomic nervous system, which keeps the heart pumping. All this laptop'll do is shut down the cortex—all their minis and micros linked in parallel for AI functions. But the brainstem won't be touched. The hospital and patients will be perfectly safe."

"You're sure?"

"What'm I, talkin' Greek here? Of course I'm sure. I'd go into details, but . . ." He looked distractedly about. "Where's McKitrick?"

"I expect her any moment," said Sawyer.

"I'll leave the explanations for her. I build the stuff, but she knows how to apply it."

Dunston looked around for Cheryl and wondered what bizarre getup she'd be wearing today. A stray thought nagged him. "Marlon, let's say I make it to the computer center. Where am I supposed to hook this thing up?"

"Into any port on the mainframe. There are dozens. I'll show you the schematics. They'll accept ordinary RS-232 cables, just like the wires that link the video monitor to the CPU you got at home. All that stuff's industry standard. It'd probably be easier to yank a plug out of one of their minis and put yours in, but that's the area you're going to be shutting down. Anyway, they can't see you. So what difference does it make?"

"What happens if I don't make it to the computer center?"

"Why shouldn't you?"

Dunston shrugged. "Who knows? Maybe I'll trip and break a leg. Wearing that outfit, I'm not exactly Baryshnikov."

Merlin knew what was bothering him. "Worried about the autobots?"

"The thought had occurred to me."

Merlin opened another drawer and withdrew a gadget the size of a toaster. "In that case, you resort to this. It's a portable coax H-V probe, which we can hook onto the suit. They use one like it for cable injection testing."

"For what?"

"Testing electrical conductors. Phone wires, antennas, communications equipment. And computers, of course. You see, all that stuff is very susceptible to interruption by electromagnetic pulse, EMP."

"I thought that only happened in nuclear explosions," said Maks.

"That's right. Problem is, the government can't exactly go around setting off nuclear bombs to test communications devices. So it relies on EMP simulators, of which this is one." His lips widened into a disturbingly maniacal grin. "Somewhat modified by me."

"Modified how?"

"Thought you'd never ask. You see, a simulator injects a signal, not unlike EMP, to see if the internal circuitry can withstand the energy generated. I won't bore you with the different types of simulators and their wavelengths. This wonderful device injects an oscillating decaying frequency that delivers a thousand kilowatts in a hundred megahertz bandwidth. A dose of that, and your autobot'll melt like wax."

"How does it work?"

"Like this," continued Merlin. "Ordinarily, a simulator injects pulses into individual pin connectors in the conductor they're testing. Delicate work, and cumbersome. Dials to turn, rot like that. But fire up this gizmo," he said, touch-

ing a small red button, "and you're ready for action."
When he pressed, a dual-pronged antenna projected twelve
inches out of the simulator's metallic skin. At its tips, an
inch apart, were glistening silvery knobs resembling buckshot. "The prongs are insulated, but not the tips." He hit
the button once more. "Press a second time, and you're in
business." An intense crackling noise arose from between
the metallic tips, the sound of unbridled energy. He released
the button and the sound disappeared. "Works like a stun
gun. No adaptor plates, no pin testers, no distribution cables. Just a quick zap, and this'll release a coupled surge
that'll liquefy the most hardened conductor."

"Isn't the autobot's frame protected?"

"No, just the outer walls of the Center itself. Who'd
figure on a ninja in a wet suit jousting with a roving robot?
If it doesn't get you first, the thing's no match for you."

"An encouraging thought."

"Now, let's give that suit a try. We have a couple of
sizes. Dr. Sawyer figured you for a medium large, but we
can take in or let out parts, if we have to."

Dunston peeled down to his underwear and, with Merlin's help, pulled on the suit. It felt very much like an ordinary wet suit, only bulkier. It fit like a second skin, yet
it was surprisingly flexible. It was one-piece construction,
with a neoprene-like hood and boots already attached to
allow an uninterrupted circulation of the coolant. Inside,
Dunston felt surprisingly comfortable, without the immediate sweating that befalls the out-of-water diver. The hood
covered his entire face, the only opening being for his nose.
The eye slits had lenses of insulated silicon.

"How's your vision?"

"Pretty good. No fog."

"You lose a little peripheral, but that's unavoidable.
Turn around, give it a whirl."

Dunston gave the suit a brief workout. He tried a few

jumping jacks, side flexes, and deep knee bends. The fabric hugged his every movement.

"How's the temperature?" asked Merlin.

"Cooler than I expected."

"Good. I was afraid it'd get too warm." He stepped behind a nearby panel and flicked some switches, eyeing the readings on adjacent gauges. "Perfect. The invisible man. All I can see is your mouth. I suppose you could keep it shut, but suffocation's not in the plan." He walked back to Dunston. "Let's fit that EMP simulator. You've got a lot of hardware here, so pay attention and don't get confused. Everything'll be attached with Velcro straps. The laptop's most important, so we'll hang it right in front, at waist level, even with your fingertips. With any luck, you won't be needing the simulator, but the best place for it is around your thigh. You got a preference for right or left?"

"Left, I guess. So if the autobot attacks, I just press the button twice?"

"Yep."

"And then what? Knee him to death with the box?"

"No, the antennas have an extender, remember? Before, I let it out about a foot. But keep that button pressed down, and it'll extend out to eight feet. Everything but the tips are insulated, so just grab and point the extender in your hand and twang the metal toad like you're its fairy godmother." They turned. "Ah, Miss McKitrick."

Cheryl's green eyes stared at Dunston. She cocked her head to one side, inspecting him as if he were an alien. "Positively neolithic."

"By the way, darling," she said to Maks, "did you get the documents I faxed you?"

"To my house?"

"No, to your office. Yesterday afternoon."

"I was gone, Cher."

"Oh, well. I can send it to your home. Anyway," she continued, pulling two floppy diskettes from her briefcase, "this is what's going to make the Center spill its guts."

"All that on two floppies?" said Dunston.

"Yes, Doctor. All that. One sends, one receives." She paused. "You want me to continue, or are you going to keep on playing Lloyd Bridges?"

"Merlin, are we done with this thing?"

"Until tomorrow. Let me help you."

Dunston pulled out of the suit until he'd stripped down to his underwear. He was aware of Cheryl's sidelong glances, but he was accustomed to the occasional coed changing in the OR locker rooms. He said nothing until he'd donned a pair of white coveralls. "You're on, Cheryl. This is big time, huh?"

"The biggest. I don't give a crap about the Center's superconductivity. This'll make their sixteen bitters freak. You got one of those loaner chips, Merlin?"

"Right here." He carefully handed it to her with a tweezers. She inspected it with a hand-held magnifier. "Gallium arsenide. With insulated, bipolar, field-effect transistors. Their electron velocities are five times greater than the Center's silicon chips. I know this is a little technical, Chad, but trust me. The circuitry's perfect."

"What are you going to do with this stuff?"

"Simple. We're going to change the parity."

"The sequence of zeroes and ones?"

"Right. Once we're online, with the floppies, your laptop will give warp-speed instructions to the computer center to alter its parity into, say, all odd numbers. Now, that won't make sense to them, because their computers are used to their own parity sequence. So they'll run a parity check. One of their SEC controller chips—"

"Securities and Exchange Commission?"

"Get real. Serial communications controller. It'll realize something's wrong and order an interrupt routine. When it tries to reinitialize their hardware—which doesn't take a lot of time, but it's time they ain't got—our floppy FUBAR's their packet.''

''What packet?''

''A bit stream's a packet. You know, numerical bytes. But while they're doing that, our sixty-four-bit floppy retransmits first and neutralizes them. They'll be temporarily out of commission. Not long, but enough. They'll be down. And while they're down, you activate the second floppy to access their files, the ones about the Human Genome Project and what they're doing with it. Shouldn't take long. By the time they finish reinitialization, you should have gotten everything we want.''

''That's all it takes?''

''If it works.''

''And if it doesn't?''

''Then you're on your own. But it should.''

''And after that?''

''You haul ass out of there with the floppy containing their files, and come home to momma. We'll make sense of it.''

''I don't know. This hardly sounds foolproof.''

She shrugged. ''Best we could do under the circumstances.''

Dunston's mind was already awhirl, reviewing other things on his personal agenda, things he knew would consume precious minutes. ''How much breathing time, again?''

''About forty minutes,'' said Merlin. ''If you don't push it, forty-five.''

Forty-five minutes, he thought. Enough time, he wondered, to steal down to the computer center, foul up the works, access the files, do some personal prowling around, and escape? He'd be cutting it awfully close. ''How am I supposed to get out of the place?''

''Same way you got it. Up two flights and out the service door. The doors don't lock from the inside, so you don't have to sweat it. Of course, you could probably go right out the lobby and through the front door. Who's going to see you but some freaked-out families? But we'd prefer you went out the back. We'll have a car waiting there for you."

"Okay," Dunston agreed. "From the top. Take me through this whole thing again."

It took them all day for Dunston to review the entire process, stopping only for a hurried lunch. By four P.M. he was finished, if not exhausted. They'd been through the routine a half dozen times. He figured he'd absorbed all he possibly could in the short time allotted before his return. He also knew he'd earned an evening's relaxation and a shot at a decent night's rest. Sawyer and Cheryl bid their adieus. He waved good-bye and thumbs up, staying behind with Maks to help Merlin pack up. Merlin pulled him aside.

"Just remember, you haven't got all day in there."

"Why do you keep reminding me?"

"You're planning a little side trip, aren't you?"

"What makes you say that?"

"Because I'm no dummy. And because I know everything that happened to you. And because I'd do the same thing, if I were in your shoes."

Dunston's eyebrows raise. "Like what?"

"Like taking a little walk back through the lab to see what's in there. Like getting a look at their STM. Like trying to figure out what you thought you saw moving outside the lab. You know, little stuff."

"We *know* what he saw," said Maks.

"You do? Since when?"

While Merlin stood there stunned, Maks and Dunston reviewed the previous evening's events. The recitation took them little more than ten minutes. Merlin could only shake his head.

"What about the diskette? He should have told us about that."

"Yeah, but I'm betting he didn't know what to make of

it. You'd have to be aware of what happened to Christine to come up with that kind of deduction.''

''And Christine? This isn't the sort of information you can overlook.''

''Oh, I don't plan to. Seeing if I can find her ranks right up there with locating their STM. I didn't want to tip my hand while Victor was here, because I don't know how he'd react. He might've been inclined to cancel the whole thing.''

''There's still the time factor, you know.''

''I'm aware of that. Don't worry, I know I've got a job to do. But if I can pinpoint Christine's location, it'll make getting her out of there all that much easier.''

Merlin nodded thoughtfully. ''Okay. Just so you remember the priorities.'' He changed the subject. ''Ever seen an STM?''

''No, but it must look like any other electron microscope.''

''Not at all. It's tiny, like an old, circular forty-five record player with this erector set and fly wheels on top. Not that it matters. The Center doesn't have an STM.''

''*What?*'' said Maks.

''Victor doesn't know it, but the Center has an AFM, an atomic force microscope. To be precise, an optical lever AFM.''

Dunston looked like the wind had been let out of his sails. ''Oh great.''

''Don't start having seizures on me. It's not such a big deal. They're not all that different. This is how they work: an STM uses a sharp tungsten probe to move along a surface. It keeps the electron tunneling current constant, so it can trace the hills and valleys in an atom's landscape. On the other hand, an optical lever AFM works by bouncing a laser beam off a little mirror on a diamond tip. Light reflected by the moving mirror is detected by a position sensor. The tiniest deflection is amplified, or levered, by the system's geometry to measure surface changes in the atoms, or in the interatomic forces." He looked into their faces for signs of understanding. "That's it in a nutshell. They don't look all that different."

"No more tunneling?"

"Nope. Just a thin laser beam, a mirror, a diamond tip, an optical deflector, and a round pan, which looks like something Edison invented."

"Why are you telling me all this?"

"Because I want to keep you out of trouble. And anyway, I've got a little score to settle with that place."

"That makes three of us. What's your beef?"

"Borrowing some of my research, for starters." He turned and removed a small shotgun from a recessed, pantrylike cupboard. "Take a look at this."

"I'd rather not. I've seen what those things can do."

"This just might save your life. I say that if it's good enough for the Secret Service, it's good enough for you. Just between us, it'll be a year before they get their hands on this particular model. You've shot before?"

"Some skeet, sporting clays. Never considered myself that good."

"Probably the firearm, not you. It doesn't matter. This isn't a marksman's tool. It's a modified scatter gun." The entire piece was no more than sixteen inches long, of matte-finish, glareless black. Merlin pointed out the various parts. "Twelve-inch barrel, more than sufficient at the range you might need. We're talking twenty feet, max. Magazine extender tube underneath. Holds six rounds. This is the pistol grip, which you hold in your right hand. The trigger's in front of it. Your left hand grasps the forestock. Okay?"

"So far."

"Now, this is an autoloader. You don't aim the thing. You shoot from the hip. Just point and pull the trigger. The recoil's pretty fierce, but you're a shooter. I figure you can handle it. This piece is already loaded, so be careful. See that button in front of the trigger guard?''

''Yeah, the little red thing.''

''That's your safety. Pushed in like that, it's on safe. Push it out,'' he indicated with his finger, ''and you can blast away.'' He pushed it in again and handed it barrel-first to Dunston.

Dunston hefted it up and down. ''Lighter than I thought.''

''Four and a half pounds. All plastic, Kevlar, and ceramic, except the barrel. We'll strap it to your right hip, across from the EMP simulator. It won't even reach your knee.''

''What's it loaded with?''

Merlin scratched the stubble of his chin. ''I had to give that some thought. The first two rounds are, well, little cluster bombs. Eight pellets of double-ought buck, nitrocellulose base, C-4 explosive. Blows up on contact with the target. It won't put down an autobot, but it'll blow a computer into plastic and wire fragments. The next two rounds are specially hardened number four buckshot.''

''Used for what?''

''People, mainly. Tear 'em in half.''

''You expect me to run into people?''

''I don't know what to expect, but I figure it can't hurt.''

''And the last two rounds?''

''Something we perfected from the frogs. It's a seventy millimeter-long slug they called Silverplus. Used to be made of steel. We modified it to have a uranium-carbide core. It's intended for penetration.''

''That could make quite a hole.''

''The cops used the original Silverplus for shooting through car doors and engine blocks. With this core, you can expect five inches penetration into solid iron, eighteen inches into concrete, and God knows how much anything else.''

"You really think I'm going to need this thing?"

"Boy scout motto, Doc. Be prepared."

"Fine by me. That it?"

"Not quite. Now we're all expecting you to make it to the computer center, right?"

"That's the general idea."

Merlin held up a piece of black cable. "Boy scout motto again."

"Be prepared?"

"It can't hurt. Let's say, for some crazy reason, you don't get down there. When I went over the architectural plans, I noticed that every fifty feet or so there was a wall jack. A sort of sprocket that an autobot or service robot could plug into."

"For what?"

"Maybe its floor guidance system became defective and it had to link up with the computer center, I don't know. Anyway, the plans also show connections from these jacks right to the mainframe. *Voilà.*" He held up the twenty-four-inch cable like it was a dead eel. "This is our modification of Digital's Thinwire coax. One end has an adaptor for your laptop, the other plugs into the wall jack. Any problems, plop this baby in, and you have interactive access to the computer center." He rolled up the cable and tucked it into one of the neoprene suit's zippered pockets.

Dunston smiled. "Thanks, Marlon. Could come in handy."

"You bet. Oh, one more thing." He went to a drawer and carefully removed several sheets of tissue paper. Between them was a quarter-size circle of what appeared to be clear glass. He held it up to the light, grasping it by the edges to avoid smudging. "I got this from some buddies at NASA who owed me a favor. This is a laser-polished magnifying lens, made at the Corning Glass Works around the same time they worked on the Hubble Telescope."

"Interesting. What's it for?"

"Trouble. Last resort stuff. Think back for a second to the AFM. It uses an FEL, a free electron laser. The difference between it and a gas or solid-state laser is that the FEL uses an accelerator, whose magnetic field helps it add energy to light waves. The Center has a simplified, compact accelerator with unusually low voltage requirements. But don't let its size fool you. Its power potential is enormous.

"If the AFM's in the lab, which I bet it is, and you're in a pinch, get to that AFM. Turn it on and refocus the laser beam by re-aiming it off the mirror near the diamond tip. Hold this magnifier lens in the laser stream and point it toward, well, a target."

"What'll it do?"

"I don't know. It's never been tested. But unless I miss my guess, this magnifier will produce a quantum surge of energy out of that beam. It could be dangerous, but we're talkin' crunch time. Might blow the whole place apart. But if your life's on the line, you might want to consider it. Here," he said, rewrapping it in the tissue paper. "Stick it in your pocket. With any luck, you won't have to use it, and it'll be a souvenir for your grandkids." His hands fell to his sides. "Guess that's it. No more trinkets."

Dunston shook his hand with gratitude. "You really are a wizard, Marlon. I appreciate everything you've done. I hope I never have to use this stuff. But you know what? I'm scared to death. That place terrifies me. I want a quick mission—in and out. Yet maybe something will mess things up. If I have to resort to any of your gadgets, I'll be one grateful guy." He reached out and hugged the man closely. "Thanks, pal."

Tears in his eyes, he took Maks' hand, turned, and left.

Dunston had another doctor covering for him. Ever since his misgivings during the splenectomy, he thought it best for his own welfare, and that of his patients, to postpone patient care until the present matter was resolved. Thus he left Upton with Maks and drove back to her place with mixed emotions. On one hand, he was relieved that the matter would soon be settled, one way or another. On the other, the idea of actually returning to the Center was giving him nearly hallucinogenic flashbacks. He had recurrent visions of the autobot stalking him like a pheasant trapped in a cornfield.

When they reached her place, Maks opened the door and turned on the lights. Dunston had come to realize that he loved her with a frightening intensity. Until he met her, he thought that, for devotion and loyalty, there was nothing like a small dog. But now, he was determined to have her—not just physically, or even spiritually, but in her entirety.

It was strange how their romance had blossomed without sexual intimacy. It wasn't for lack of interest. The mood had just never been quite right; and on the rare occasions that it was, one jarring development or another had posed emotional stumbling blocks. Theirs was a relationship of mutual trust and support. Dunston presumed that when the right moment came along, they would both know it. He didn't question their emotional compatibility, or that he might even ask her to marry him. Assuming he survived.

While he put away his jacket, she went into the kitchen, returning moments later holding a crystalline pitcher filled with martinis. In an era of light beer and catalog merchandising, the image was a bit dated, but Lord, a stiff drink was just what Dunston wanted. She wordlessly gave him a glass and poured. The pitcher was frosty, beaded with condensation, a stream of thin rivulets forming a jagged pattern when she filled his glass.

"Are we in the mood for a double today?"

"More like a triple." He took a deep sip. "God, that's fantastic. What's in it?"

"Just gin and vermouth, with a twist. The secret's in the refrigeration."

"You don't say?"

"You keep it in the freezer. I mixed it before we left. It beats room temperature or ice cubes. Makes it viscous, sort of oily. Can you tell?"

He emptied his glass in a long swallow and held it out for another. "I sure can."

She smiled and shook her head. "Emily Post says you're supposed to sip it."

"Screw Emily Post."

"A little late for that, unless you're into necrophilia." She took a sip of her drink. "I meant what I said last night, Chad. About going with you."

"Of course you are. In the van."

"No, I want to go *in* with you. Into the hospital itself."

"Out of the question. Maks, I'm risking my life going in there. It's dangerous enough as it is. There's no way I'd want to jeopardize you."

"But don't you see, the Center never heard of me. I think we'd stand a much better chance if there were two of us. It knows everything about you, sure. But to them, I'm a cipher, an unknown. They don't know what I look like, what I sound like, my blood type, *nada*. To the Center, I'm a complete stranger."

"Stranger or not, they'd kill you in a second."

"Not if they don't see me. Merlin's got those suits in different sizes, right? I'm sure the small one would fit me."

"Forget it. This is a one man job. What could you hope to accomplish?"

"This." Maks walked away from him, toward a closet. He watched her glide across the carpet. Before she made the martinis, she'd slipped into an oversize sweatshirt. Christ, he thought, she looked fabulous, even when dressing down. Maks vanished into the clothes closet and emerged carrying what looked like a portable typewriter.

"Merlin's got his special laptop," she said, "and I've got mine."

"That's a laptop?"

"Yes, sir. A prototype digital optical laptop. I'm sure this is what Merlin wanted to talk to me about at the shop, if we'd had time."

"It's a lot bigger than his."

She nodded. "Enough to give, him penis envy. Optics use lasers, and those beams need lenses instead of wiring. The number of lenses makes it a tad larger."

"What do you hope to accomplish with that thing?"

"This machine operates at more than a billion cycles per second. Compared to this, his laptop's speed is puny. Optics let you process an incredible amount of information simultaneously. You use the optical channels to link computers, don't you see?"

He wasn't sure he did. "Link for what?"

"Look, I'm not asking for much. I have no intention of going hand-to-hand with an autobot. All you have to do is get me near one of those wall jacks Merlin described. My laptop uses the same linkup cables as his. While you go about your business, I'll hang around the wall jack. Once you've FUBAR'd their system, I'll know. The whole place will come winding down. That'll be my signal to plug in *my* cable and do what I have to do."

"Which is?"

"Find out about Christine. It'll work, believe me."

"Why didn't you tell Merlin about this?"

She hesitated. "We haven't exactly tested it yet."

"Christ, first him, then you! I say forget it. It's too damn risky."

"Chad, please! I know you're trying to protect me, but don't you see how important this is to me?"

"I know, but—"

"No buts! Just call Merlin and ask him, okay?" She paused, a beseeching expression on her face. "I promise to go along with whatever he says."

"Even if he says no?"

"Even if."

He knew he had no choice; he couldn't deny her a simple phone call. "All right, one call."

"And you'll let me talk to him?"

"Yes, provided you agree his word is final."

"Okay."

Dunston walked to the phone, knowing this was a gamble that might be the biggest coup in his life—or his biggest mistake.

Chapter Twenty-one

MAKS' CALL TO Merlin was patched through to Victor Sawyer. Dunston stayed off the phone, pacing back and forth as he listened in the background. During the brief conference call, Maks made a convincing pitch. From the tone of her conversation, Dunston could tell that she was winning them over. Finally she hung up, a smile on her face. Merlin, she said, promised to take care of everything.

When he finished his drink, Dunston was tired. He went upstairs to take a relaxing, hot shower followed, perhaps, by a brief nap. He wanted to be well rested prior to their ordeal in the morning. After bathing, he left the bathroom with a towel wrapped around his waist. Maks was in the computer room, standing over the fax machine. Dunston walked in and peered over her shoulder. Maks looked at his damp hair.

"That's what I'd like," she said. "Maybe a bath."

"Find anything interesting?"

"No, just some loose ends on Schmidt. Cheryl faxed them over. His health history, personal data. It's not very useful now." She put down the documents. "Here, take a look."

She left the room and prepared for her shower. Feeling lightheaded from the drinks, Dunston lazily leafed through the dozen or so papers. Cheryl had made a thorough search. There were several discharge summaries from Schmidt's repeated hospitalizations, an impressive arrest record, Internal Revenue Service documents, and social security information. The final page was a copy of an old driver's license photo. Dunston picked it up, frowning. Confused, he went in search of Maks.

He heard the water already running in the shower. Dunston rapped on the door and got no answer. Easing it open, he poked his head into the room.

"Hey, Maks?"

"I'll be out in a second."

"Why did Cheryl fax you a picture of Arthur?"

"A picture of who?"

"Forget it. Finish your shower."

Dunston stared at the fax, perplexed. The man in the picture was a dead ringer for his friend. A sickening thought occurred to him. Was it possible that Arthur was still . . . No, he had *seen* the dead body. Returning downstairs, he poured a final martini from the frosty pitcher and quickly downed it, warmed by the fire in his gut. The fax didn't make any sense. He tried to figure it out, but the alcohol was making his head spin. As the thoughts went round and round in his head, he walked unsteadily to the couch. Finally he sat down and closed his eyes, forcing himself to think. But in less than a minute, he was asleep.

When Dunston awoke on the couch, he was stiff and perspiring. A nearby lamp burned brightly. He rubbed his eyes and yawned. According to his watch, it was one A.M. He switched off the light. For several moments, he sat there in the dark and tried to remember what he was doing there. Suddenly, it all came flooding back—the photo, his brief conversation with Maks, the drinks. It made no more sense to him now than it did earlier.

He recalled that they were due to leave for the Center at seven in the morning. He was ready to do battle, but it was an uneasy readiness. His thoughts crept through the darkness, like secrets.

He wondered where Maks was. He sat up slowly, hammered by a splitting headache. He carefully got to his feet and went to the bathroom for a Motrin. He found the medication vial, took one, and washed it down with tap water. As he closed the door to the medicine cabinet, he again spotted the smaller bottle with Christine's name on it. He picked it up and realized that the label's inscription was one of those loose ends that had been nagging him. Serophene . . . He returned it to the shelf.

Passing the master bedroom, he saw that Maks was curled up asleep. He didn't want to wake her. He continued slowly walking across the carpet toward Christine's room, brows knitted in the darkness, when it struck him. He suddenly remembered that Serophene was a brand name for clomiphene citrate, a drug used in reproductive endocrinology. It was usually prescribed to stimulate ovulation in certain infertility patients. He was mystified.

With renewed uneasiness, he paused before he got into bed. Christine had gone to the Center for a routine tonsillectomy, only to die from a rare cardiac disorder. Could the Serophene have contributed to her death? From what he recalled of the drug, he doubted it. More to the point, why would anyone want to make a young child ovulate? And what worried him most of all, if the vial's dates were accurate, and assuming Christine took the drug as prescribed, the medication would have made her ovulate on the exact day she entered the Center. The whole idea was sickeningly preposterous.

He felt chilled to the bone and returned to the master bedroom. Without disturbing Maks, he pulled up the covers and moved as close to her as possible, drawing what heat he could from her body. Unable to sleep, he stared into the darkness, unblinking, trying to calm the terror mounting within him. In a few hours, he was going back to the Center.

Chapter Twenty-two

DUNSTON HEARD THE crush of driveway gravel and pulled back the bedroom curtain's sash. It was 6:30. Outside, the van, the size of a UPS delivery truck, slowly pulled to a stop, omitting a horn honk of arrival. On its side was written, "H&R Plumbing and Contracting." Dunston could see the driver, dressed in beige coveralls. No doubt the others, including, at Sawyer's request, captain Donohue, were within. He heard Maks' voice behind him.

"You're up."

"Finally. The van's here. Are you ready to go?"

Maks emerged from the bathroom walking in that graceful, slinky gait he adored and entered the clothes closet. He could tell she was on edge. It didn't take her long to dress. She came out moments later, wearing an oversize pullover bigshirt, long and loose, with a drawstring tie. Below it, capri-length leggings hugged her limbs.

He went to Mr. Lassiter's closet and put on a T-shirt, sweatpants, and sneakers, knowing he'd soon be changing in the truck. "I guess we're outta here," he said. "Sooner begun, sooner done. Come on. Let's do it."

"Ready when you are." She touched his face with a trembling hand. "Worried?"

"Does it show?"

"Probably not as much as I am. But everything'll be okay. I just know it."

"Where'd you get your confidence?"

"From you."

Hand in hand, they descended the staircase, crossing into the kitchen.

There was an abbreviated honk from the van. "We better get going."

She looked at the wall clock. It was precisely seven. They left the kitchen, crossed through the foyer, and went out the back door. It was a brisk, overcast day, hinting of rain. At their approach, the van's side door slid open. Merlin's face was first to appear.

"Top of the mornin' to you, Doc. Slept well, I hope?"

"Well as can be expected."

"Good. You're going to need it. We're right on schedule. Miss Lassiter," he said, fixing Maks with a stare, "I hope your laptop's as good as you claim. Your lives depend on it."

"Don't worry. It is."

Chad followed Maks. The darkened interior was light enough to see by. In addition to the packing crates, both sides of the cab had low, bracketed metal benches. Cheryl sat on one, feigning boredom. The others present—Donohue, a technician, and Sawyer—waved or said perfunctory, nervous hellos. There was just enough bench room for the newcomers, who squeezed in beside one another. Sawyer rose to close the door, then knocked twice on the driver's partition. The van took off. Sawyer checked his watch.

"It's a forty-minute ride, barring traffic. We shouldn't run into any problems on a Saturday morning. On the way here, Merlin rounded up gear for Miss Lassiter, and I stopped by the office to have our computer touch base with the Center's receiving department. They're still expecting a shipment. No last minute changes. We're in business."

"Time to get suited up, guys," said Merlin. "Maks,

mind if I check out your hush-hush laptop while you change?''

She nodded and began to disrobe. A jealously protective part of Dunston was glad to see that she wore underwear. He stripped down to his undershorts. ''Just leave our outer stuff on the bench?''

Merlin nodded and carefully examined the laptop. ''Pretty fancy. You sure this'll work?''

''I hope so, for my sister's sake.''

''You honestly think she's still alive?''

''I do.''

On the open highway, the van picked up speed. With understandable jitteriness, everyone was silent, the only sound being the vehicle's monotonous drone. Merlin had packed everything Chad and Maks would need in a large cardboard box behind the three wooden crates. He opened it and carefully unfolded the insulated suits. He stood up and, holding one by the shoulders, helped Dunston pull on the tighter areas. Then they both assisted Maks.

The process was cumbersome, hindered by the van's motion. Dunston began to sweat. Before their hoods were applied, Merlin probed the suits' lumbar areas for switches which would activate the circulating coolant. After their hoods were on, the coolant began flowing. The immediate change in skin temperature was a welcome relief. After making final adjustments and securing the hood, Dunston turned to Maks.

''Is this right out of *GQ*, or what?''

''Which planet are we visiting today?''

''Good question.''

''Turn this way, guys.''

With exacting care, and assisted by the technician, Merlin affixed the remaining paraphernalia. The laptop computers went on first. The auxiliary cables, coiled like sunning snakes, were taped to the top in clear plastic bags, which also contained the floppies. Next, for Dunston, came the EMP simulator, followed by the hip-mounted shotgun.

"What the hell is that?" asked Donohue.

"Something your department might get in ten years. If it's lucky."

"Hope he doesn't need a permit for that thing. It'd break my heart to arrest him now."

"Never thought of that," said Merlin. "How're we doin' for time?"

"Fifteen minutes," said Sawyer.

Merlin stepped back and looked everything over. "How's it feel in there?"

Dunston carefully jogged in place, then glanced at Maks. She nodded. "We won't win any marathons, but it'll do."

"I don't give a damn about races. I want you to survive."

Chad and Maks shared a silent look.

"That little goody's in your breast pocket," Merlin said of the lens. "Just in case."

"What little goody?" Sawyer asked.

"Insurance policy," Merlin deflected. "Okay, folks. Time to turn you into cargo. Might be a little cramped, Miss Lassiter. It wasn't designed for the two of you. You'll have to sit on his lap."

"Oh, how romantic."

"What about the regulators?" asked Dunston.

"Not till we get there. Just follow his lead, Miss Lassiter. Keep it out of your mouth until you're loaded. Ready for the crate?"

Chad looked at Maks, who nodded despite the tears in her eyes. "Okay, Mr. Wizard," said Dunston. "Turn us into a toilet. Pity. Cinderella settled for a slipper."

They unroofed the thick crate with a crowbar. Dunston carefully climbed in first, with the help of a stepstool, Merlin, and the tech. A chair was in the crate, bolted to the floor. Dunston sat down and strapped himself in, impressed: they'd even provided a seatbelt. Then he helped Maks clamber over the top, swinging the laptop up to his chest so she could sit on his thighs. He put his arms around her.

"Comfy?" he asked.

She forced an upbeat tone. "Beats walking."

"Time?" Merlin said.

"Six minutes."

"Okay, Doc. Take these regulators."

He reached up. "Got 'em."

"Miss Lassiter, follow the Doc's lead. Don't panic and you'll be fine. As soon as we pull to a stop, we'll seal the crate. Any last minute questions?"

"You're not carrying a spare rosary, by any chance?"

"Sorry, plumb out." He slapped the side of the crate. "Sit tight."

Dunston strapped them both in and inspected their new surroundings, the rough-hewn walls of a wooden carrying crate. Maks' head was just below boxtop level, shielding them from the others in the van. Alone with his thoughts, Dunston mused about what he knew and didn't know.

From outside the crate came forced words of encouragement from Sawyer. Soon the van began to slow, beginning a series of easy turns that eventually led to the Center.

"Places," Merlin called. Everyone other than Merlin and the technician, who now both wore H&R Plumbing coveralls, squeezed behind a partition. From the back door, only the two men and three boxes were visible.

Merlin handed Dunston a small crowbar. "I only put in four nails, one in each corner. Once you're in place, just jimmy 'em loose. Leave the bar on the bottom of the box. And remember, no regulators until you feel the crate being lifted out of the van. Got it?"

"All set."

Merlin smiled. "Good hunting, guys." He pulled the box's square lid atop the crate and began inserting the nails.

Inside, all was darkness. Maks felt a momentary disorientation, which soon left her. She sensed the van coming to a stop, probably for the driver to show his ID, before resuming speed. A minute later, it stopped again, then backed up and halted. Maks guessed they were adjacent the offloading ramp. She was comforted by Dunston's arms.

Their crate was last, third in line. In the distance, Dunston heard a mechanized whir, a sound he'd come to associate with autobots. Despite the comfortable temperature of his suit, his skin turned to gooseflesh. The whirring noise grew louder as the autobot approached, drawing to a stop beside the van's open doors. There came another sound, electrical, this time, lower pitched, followed by a muffled thump on the van's door.

"Give me a hand getting this thing onto the fork lift," Merlin said.

Dunston whispered to Maks. "I'll give you the signal to put in the regulator. Slow, easy breaths, like I showed you. Okay?"

Her reply was a reassuring squeeze of his forearm.

One by one, the crates were removed from the van. Dunston imagined they were probably being transferred to a dolly pulled by the autobot. Finally, he felt the two metal lifts slide under the crate. In the darkness, he fought the nauseating tug of vertigo as they were pulled into the air, then slowly carried backward, out of the van. He signalled Maks. They both put in their regulators as the van's doors closed with a resounding thump.

Maks felt the forklift move them backwards, stop, then swivel to one side. She sensed the crate descending until it came to rest on the dolly's flat surface. The metal lifts slid out from under the box. They were alone.

It dawned on Dunston that he'd been holding his breath. He inhaled, and the triple-pressurized air forcibly flooded his lungs, as if he were scuba diving at a depth of ninety feet. Reminding himself that his air was limited, he inhaled slowly, evenly, avoiding the panicky impulse to hyperventilate. He listened carefully, reassured by the smooth, regular sound of Maks' inhalations. Soon his breaths were as shallow as he could comfortably manage.

They started to move. The second crate gently nudged theirs, jostled out of the grasp of inertia. Within seconds, they were moving at a steady pace. Maks sensed the drop-off of a small declivity, probably a ramp. They were descending into the Center.

Chapter Twenty-three

DUNSTON'S SKIN TINGLED with the fear of imminent discovery. Much as he wanted to believe Merlin's pretensions as to their invisibility, he inwardly expected a warning klaxon to start blaring at any moment. He nervously fingered the crowbar with one hand while touching the shotgun's pistol grip with the other. But nothing occurred. The ride was smooth and virtually soundless. They proceeded deeper into the building.

A digital watch with faint, visible numbers was built into the suit at the inner left wrist. Two minutes had elapsed. The mechanized wagon train stopped, backed up, and slowly inched forward several feet before drawing to a halt. This was followed by the sudden roller-coaster sensation of the floor dropping away, and Maks' stomach wanted to rise into her chest. She was on an elevator, descending.

An increasingly basso whir of overhead gears, followed by a gradual stop, marked the end of their plunge. If things were going according to plan, they should now be on level two. They jolted forward, the autobot pulling their wheeled platform. Dunston remained motionless, listening, sifting the silence for audible clues. He sensed Maks shiver, and he held her more tightly. They picked up speed, rounding one corner, then another. Finally, after what seemed an in-

terminable ride, they slowed to a stop. All was quiet. He
looked at his watch. Five minutes elapsed. They had to get
out of there soon.

There came the sound of uncoupling as the flatbed was
freed from the autobot. Something moved—an unloading
crane, or the arms of the autobot, Maks couldn't tell which.
Then, one by one, the crates were offloaded onto the floor.
Once accomplished, the crates were abandoned. She heard
the muffled click of the autobot linking up with the now-
empty dolly. Then came the muted, rubberized hum of autobot and dolly, growing inaudible as they receded into the
distance. She took a deep, relaxing breath and patted Chad
on the thigh. With any luck, they were truly alone.

Dunston checked his watch: seven minutes. Once satisfied that all was silent, he motioned for Maks to move sideways off his lap. He took the crowbar in both hands. He
could tell that they were sweating beneath the neoprene,
yet his grip was firm. He had a mini Mag-Lite in one of
his pockets, but he wanted to avoid unnecessary light at all
costs. Using his gloved fingers, he found the seam where
the lid mated with the crate. He wedged the crowbar into
the gap and began to pry.

He was afraid the nails would emit a rusty screech. Yet
Merlin must have lubricated them, or used ones made of
Teflon, for the lid came off without a sound. Dunston and
Maks slowly stood up, holding the lid over their heads. As
his gaze rose from within the crate, he could see light. It
was faint, a reflection from the red beams of the laser guidance system, resembling the red glow of a photographer's
darkroom, but fainter. Still, it was enough to see by. He
carefully looked around.

They were in one of the Center's labyrinthine corridors.
It was fifteen feet wide and equally as high, made of the
precast concrete typical of the Center's construction. More
important, thought Maks, it was empty. The three crates
stood squarely in the middle of the hall, at least five feet

away from the pencil-thin red beams on either wall. There
were no other boxes or cargo in sight. Maks thought she
could make out a stairwell fifty feet away.

Taking pains to remain silent, Dunston took the lid from
Maks and lowered it over the rim of the crate until it rested
on the floor, at a fifteen degree angle to the wooden box.
Merlin had left the stepstool in the crate with them. After
an apprehensive look around, Dunston motioned for Maks
to get on the stool. Once she was atop it, he made an up-
and-over gesture. Then he hoisted her by the waist until she
straddled the crate, like a balance beam. With a nod from
Dunston, she dropped silently to the floor. Following her,
he stepped onto the stool and pushed himself up with his
arms until he could swing his right thigh over the rim. After
steadying himself, he brought his left leg up and over, then
dropped the several remaining inches between his soles and
the floor. He landed without a sound. He checked his watch.
Nine minutes had gone by.

Maks' heart was pounding. So far so good, she thought.
Despite her fear, she was spurred on by the thought of
Christine, alone in the building. Her shallow respirations
were solid and reassuring. She saw Chad crook a finger at
her, motioning with his head to follow him. They started
down the hall in the direction of the stairwell, which
loomed more prominent with each passing step. The laser
beams gave her the impression of being on a runway glide
path. There was no indication of being detected. Thus far,
their suits were as good as Merlin's word.

Dunston looked overhead. Every four yards was a halogen lamp, the kind which lit his way when he and Weiman
had approached the computer center for the alpha intercept.
He recalled that they were switched on by infrared sensors.
Their continued darkness was reassuring.

So was the location of the wall jacks. Dunston found the
first one beside the stairwell and pointed it out to Maks.
He looked around, felt the cables in his pocket, and fought

an impulse to just *do* it, to plug in, link up, access the data, and get the hell out of there. But after a moment's hesitation, he knew he had to move on. Merlin *had* said hooking into the mainframe was preferable. Also, there was that other little item, the fact that the lab just happened to be down the hall from the computer center.

He made a gesture with his palms for Maks to halt and wait there. Pointing again to the jack, he helped her remove the access cable from its protective plastic bag. He watched as she attached it to her optical laptop and switched the computer to standby. Using hand signals, he indicated that she should remain there until he returned. From their previous discussions, she knew that a brownout would be the signal to plug in her computer. Dunston gave her a hug. Chancing a deep breath, he headed into the stairwell.

Watching him disappear, Maks' emotions rode a pendulum, swinging from bearable edginess to abject terror. Her heart pounded with the horrible uneasiness of being watched. Though frightened of being alone, she knew she had no choice. It was her only chance to find her sister. She knew that without her, Christine was doomed. The situation was compounded by fear about what might happen to Chad. She could feel the pulse beating in her neck, and she struggled to control her breathing. It seemed an enormous struggle to stay in place and do nothing.

In the stairwell, Dunston found the handrail and proceeded with utmost caution, for there was no laser light to guide his way. Each step, each movement, was guided by touch and feel. As he descended, an image of the Center's topography came to mind. The hospital was built into the side of a hill. On one side, at the main entrance, ground level was called level one, with the lab and computer center two flights below. However, due to a seventy-foot gradient as the hill sloped away from the Center's front to back, the rear of the lab, where he had gone crashing through the grass, was actually one flight above the ground. The architects rightly thought that construction into a hillside would save heating costs.

He was now halfway down the staircase, grim-faced, jaws firm beneath his hood, imbued with a sense of purpose. Yet another part of him wanted to be anywhere but there. Preferably, on his boat, fuel tank topped off, shooting straight across calm water. The thought was a pleasant distraction. He conjured up an image of an early morning sun breaking the horizon on Long Island Sound, at six in the morning on one of those windless days when the Sound was flat as a glistening mirror. He idled out into open water, preparing to throttle over for an awesome hell-run to Shelter Island. A gutsy sense of power stirred in his blood. He was alone on the sea, at one with the sun, the sky, the water. Reaching channel depth, he opened the throttles. The twin MerCruisers roared, and he rocketed toward the rising sun. . . .

He reached level three. Unlike his earlier visit with Weiman, the stairwell had no hidden mechanical door, only a doorframe. He paused, feeling he'd won a minor victory, for a door's opening would have been detected by the computers. He cautiously peered through the opening into the long, dark corridor. The overhead lamps remained black, unglowing. Breathing easier, Dunston stepped into the hall.

He would have been completely blind were it not for the floor lasers, similar in razor straightness to those one story above, but paler, yellower. Still, they provided enough visibility to ward off disorientation. Coupled with his knowledge of the architectural diagrams, the light was sufficient. He glanced to both sides, satisfied that the corridor was silent and empty, before proceeding with his cautious exploration.

Difficult as it was to walk on boot-clad tiptoes, Dunston managed. He knew precisely where he was and went to the right this time, rather than to the left, as he'd done with Weiman. He reached the end of the corridor, stopped, and momentarily steadied himself against the wall on an out-stretched arm and fingertips. Then he carefully patted himself down, ensuring that all equipment was secure. Satisfied, he looked around the corner and went on.

Sticking to the middle of the corridor, he strode seventeen measured paces, roughly fifty feet. He slowly stopped, feeling rather than seeing it—the tangible, perceptible aura. Even through the layers of his suit, the ambient air seemed to throb. He was surrounded by a life force. Looking to his left, Dunston made out the wide rectangle of a doorframe. He had reached the computer center.

This is what he'd come for, the very heart of it all. He took slow, deep breaths, painfully aware of the muted hiss of air that rushed through his regulator. But he doubted anyone could hear it, internally vented as it was. Fortified, he stepped inside.

He'd gone no more than three paces when he stopped again, amazed. Spread out before him were the precise, even rows of small minicomputers, tethered together with heavy coaxial cable, linked in parallel. He counted ten rows of twelve, one hundred twenty in all. Standing before them, he sensed a lifelike vibrancy, the emanations of unrestrained intelligence. The enormous room was steeped in eerie darkness. Here and there, red and green operating lights blinked on and off, like the navigation lights on a convoy of ships. As before, his vision ran up the aisles, drawn to room center.

The two supercomputers stood like rectangular monoliths, which, from his perspective, seemed taller than their fifteen-foot height. Gaze unflinching, Dunston stared at their sheer mass. He began slow, even paces in their direction, alert for any sudden sound or movement. All his senses were alive. As he approached, he was aware of their rumbling background noise, a deep, vibrating hum. They emanated sheer power with an enormity capable of inspiring terror. Yet much as he had reason to fear them—to hate

them, even, to want to destroy them as they had tried to do
to him—he was fascinated by their technological perfec-
tion.

Drawing closer still, he tried to swallow, but his throat
was too dry from the combination of anxiety and compressed air. The floor beneath his rubberized boots shook
with a tremulous unsteadiness induced by the superconduc-
tor's magnetic fields. Even through the visual distortion of
his lenses, he could see that the supercomputer mainframes
had more working lights than the myriad of smaller computers. They rose up in a resplendent panorama of light and
sound. Twinkling panel lights punctuated the dimness, and
faint sounds chirped like mechanical crickets. Creeping
closer, he heard the soft, on-again, off-again whir of winding tapes. He was dazzled by the computers' complexity
and speed.

Enough praising Caesar, he thought. Time to bury him.

The hair on his neck prickled. He suddenly had the eerie
sensation of being watched. His head whipped around, and
he scanned the room. There was no one. He looked up for
ceiling-mounted surveillance cameras, but the roof was too
dark and too high for him to see anything. None were in
the architectural plans, and yet . . . get to work, dammit!

Dunston was now sweating, despite his suit's insulation.
The adapter sprockets would be in the rear of the mainframes. He walked more quickly now. As he cautiously
skirted the large computers, he felt a sudden drop in temperature permeate the layers of insulating neoprene. It was
some escaping coolant, he recalled, the liquid nitrogen or
helium that helped the supercomputers function. Perspiring
as he was, he found the coolness soothing.

Reaching the back of the mainframes, he looked up. The
large machines towered before him. Across their rear was
a maze of wires, connectors, and circuitry. What the hell
. . . ? He checked his watch: sixteen minutes. As a result of
his sweating, his lenses had begun to fog up. He would

give anything to be able to see better. He desperately wanted to use his Mag-Lite, but he knew it would give him away.

Think, old son! Take your time and check out the paneling, like Merlin told you. You can do it. Just one row at a time.

Dunston stood there, alert eyes flicking from side to side, breathing more deeply than he knew he should. Steady, steady, he told himself. It's *got* to be here!

He finished one row of circuit panels and moved to the next, carefully side-stepping. It all seemed such a jumble. And those God-awful lenses . . . there! He moved closer, in small increments, until his hood nearly touched the computer. He peered intently, restraining an impulse to touch it with his fingers. But there was no doubt about it. It was one of the many two-and-one-half by half-inch communications ports Merlin told him to look for. Better still, the faint lettering above it was marked INPUT.

His heart beat faster, and his hand had a noticeable tremor. Daddy's coming home, he thought, reaching down for the laptop. He switched it on and carefully held it upright. He uncoiled the attached coax and held it up to the port. Despite the regulator clenched in his teeth, he felt his lips widen into a sly grin when he saw that the adapter would fit the port perfectly.

Without a wasted moment, he quickly removed Cheryl's first floppy diskette from its plastic baggie-type cover. Holding it by its corners, he inserted it into the disk drive slot on the laptop. One of the laptop's small lights went from red to green. Clutching the computer in his left hand, he lifted the adapter toward the port. Then he surprised himself by pausing for a moment.

He felt strangely apologetic, the peculiar melancholy a rancher might feel before shooting a favorite quarter horse with a broken leg. He knew it had to be done; he was merely paying homage and saying good-bye. But then he snapped out of his reverie, aided by the memory of betrayal—and revenge.

In a dark, unseen corner of the room, where the far wall met the ceiling, an optical lens moved. It housed an infrared sensor, analyzing the image of his heat emanations. Unknown to Dunston, his excitement was generating far more body heat than his protective suit was designed for. First, the sensor detected small wisps of warm breath escaping from the edges of his mouthpiece. Using that as a guide, its computer-enhanced thermal graphics began tracking him. Like the prismatic effect of oil on water, he was being perceived as moving gradations of color. In the computer's brain, the kaleidoscopic image rippled, following Dunston as he moved forward, stalking him like prey.

Just do it, he told himself. FUBAR the computer with odd-number parity. In the room's dim lights, the massive machines before him seemed to pulsate. Now or never, man. Deep within their mechanical interiors, the supercomputers throbbed with life. He raised the plug.

"Good morning, Dr. Dunston."

Dunston's fear-stricken wheeze made him spit out his regulator. The computer's odd, mechanically synthesized voice seemed to come at him from all directions at once. His thudding heart was pounding into his brain. He looked wildly about but saw nothing.

"I can't let you do that, Dr. Dunston."

Any hesitation he had was now gone. He gulped in a lungful of icy room air and thrust the adapter into the port. But just as their couplings touched, there was a dazzling pyrotechnic explosion at the end of his cord, and the adapter was ejected from the mainframe. For a few brief seconds, fumes and sparks spewed everywhere before fizzling out, leaving an ozone-scented residue. Dunston held up the cord, stunned. The adapter was melted into a sodden, grotesque shape.

Oh God oh God oh God . . . His sudden feeling of pow-

erlessness was exceeded by the stark realization of immediate danger. He ripped the melted coax out of the laptop
and furiously threw it at the mainframe. He had to get out
of there *now*.

He tore off his hood and flung it away. His chest was
heaving, and his breath made streams of frosty vapor. He
heard a sound like the pulling of levers, and the room suddenly became aglow, lit up like a stadium at night. He
looked up, temporarily blinded, shielding his eyes with his
hand. A mist of vaporized body heat swirled around his
face. When his vision returned, he spotted the nearest aisle.
He bolted for it.

He ran like a sprinter, clutching the laptop in his left
hand. There were fifty feet remaining between him and the
doorframe. His eyes fixed on it—his goal, his salvation.
But from all around him, the synthesized male voice
boomed in resonance.

"I'm glad you returned, Doctor."

He charged forward, determined.

"You understand I can't let you leave."

"Fuck you, shithead!" Ten feet.

"You will stay."

"Like hell"—Just as his outstretched knee reached the
plane of the doorframe, a searing jolt of electricity coursed
through his body. It hit him with stunning force, knocking
him off his feet and sending him backward. He was hammered to the floor, nearly losing consciousness. His mind
cleared in seconds.

Wired, he thought. A retrofit. It wasn't on the plans, but
it should have occurred to him. He shook off the cobwebs
and quickly sat up, securing the laptop below his waist. He
heard a mechanical whir and craned his neck around. One
of the alpha intercept chairs was being lifted through the
floor, rising into place.

"You cannot escape, Doctor," the voice said firmly.
"The chair, please."

Dunston was overwhelmed by fear and rage. But each emotion cancelled out the other, enabling him to think more clearly. As the chair locked in place, bathed in a strange glow from an overhead spotlight, his fingers went to work on the shotgun's restraining straps. He freed the weapon in an instant, leaping to his feet, pointing it at one of the mainframes. Thumbing off the safety, he placed his finger on the trigger when it suddenly occurred to him what he would be doing.

"The patients," he softly reminded himself.

Once the surveillance cameras focused on him, the computers reacted defensively by shutting off the lights. The room was plunged into darkness, save for the chair, captured in a tubular circle of light that rose toward the ceiling. The beam had an otherworldly, phosphorescent glow, alien and foreboding.

"The chair, Doctor," the voice commanded.

That was more than he could take. Pushed over the edge, the hatred that had been seething inside him erupted into madness.

"No!" he shrieked. He pointed the shotgun at the chair and fired.

In the darkness, the muzzle blast was blinding, a yellowish stream of fire accompanied by ferocious recoil which nearly tore the weapon from his hands. But his aim was true. The explosive roar of cluster bomblets hitting their target was almost indistinguishable from the shotgun's blast. A momentary blizzard of steel and Formica flew through the eerie bluish glow. When it cleared, nothing remained but a twisted hydraulic stump.

Dunston wasted no time. Pivoting like a second baseman, he pointed the shotgun toward the door. Aiming from the hip, he lined up the muzzle with the left side of the door frame and fired. The explosive pellets struck the junction of joist and lintel. In a thunderous shower of sparks, the ceiling rafter sagged, and the side beams were blown apart.

Dunston raced for the doorway, halting inches from what was left of the frame. He stopped, picking up a ragged piece of sheet metal torn from a support rod.

He flicked it through the opening like a Frisbee. It passed harmlessly past the plane of the door, landing in the hall with a tinny clink. Satisfied, Dunston leaped through the doorway, encountering no resistance. He had barely landed on both feet when an onrushing autobot savagely struck him from behind. The wind was knocked out of him, and he went sprawling.

He slid ten feet across the floor and struck his head on the far wall. He gasped for air, his diaphragm in excruciating spasm. A light trickle of blood clouded his right eye. Wincing, he struggled to roll to his side.

I'm going to die, he thought. He lay there helpless, awaiting the stinging shot from the autobot's pneumatic chemical gun, the shot which would undoubtedly end his life. Three seconds passed, then four. The corridor lights went on, responding to the infrared sensors which detected his body heat. Grimacing, he chanced opening his eyes.

The front wheels of the autobot made faint, grinding noises. It seemed stuck there, fifteen feet away, adjacent the laser track on the opposite wall. It moved frantically forward, then minutely backward, a jostling hesitation.

It can't turn around, he realized. And it can only fire from the front. The collision must have knocked one of its wheels out of kilter. Dunston frantically looked around for his shotgun. Finally he spotted it, directly across from him, right in the path of the laser beam behind the autobot. Blinking away the blood, he scurried on hands and knees to retrieve it.

Just as his hand closed around the pistol grip, the autobot moved. He heard an electric whine. It was like that of a golf cart but higher pitched, almost screeching. He looked up and saw the autobot accelerating in reverse, bearing down on him.

Jesus, it's trying to run me over! He held fast to the shotgun and rapidly rolled toward the center of the corridor. The autobot whizzed by, missing him by a hair's breadth. His eyes stung with blood and sweat, but his vision was good enough to see that the robot was quickly drawing to a stop eight feet away. The computer center, knowing the target had evaded it, issued unheard instructions. Then the autobot was facing him. When the little portal on its front panel slid open, Dunston's hair stood on end. Unless he acted at once, he was dead. He leveled his shotgun just as the PCG's thin barrel swiveled his way. He fired twice in rapid succession.

In the hall's narrow confines, the roar was deafening. He was bowled over by blast and concussion as ragged shards of exploding autobot flew in all directions. The air was filled with dust, gunsmoke, and debris. Dunston's ears were ringing. He coughed, choking, waving his hand to clear the air. He struggled to all fours and then fell back, sitting. It was then that he felt the stinging in his shoulder.

His eyes widened in stark, adrenaline-charged fear. His jaw went slack as he turned his head, mortified, toward his injury, expecting to find a BB-size hole in his neoprene suit, where the PCG had hit him. Instead, he saw a two-inch sliver of black plastic, protruding like a toothpick. It was a fragment of destroyed autobot.

Dunston stared at it in fascination. Tears streamed down his face, as much from joy as from the smoke, dust, and perspiration. With a dry cough, he cleared his throat and pulled out the shrapnellike fragment, oblivious to the small pool of blood that quickly filled the hole.

He hurriedly got to his feet, knowing his joy would be short-lived. Where there was one autobot, there were sure to be others. He inspected his equipment. The EMP simulator was securely strapped to his thigh, and his shotgun still held two rounds. More importantly, the laptop across his midsection appeared unscathed, its operating light in the green. He suddenly remembered why he was there. His thoughts turned from escape to his mission. There was still a chance, albeit a slim one, if he acted quickly enough. He patted a zippered pocket for the length of ThinWire-type cable Merlin had given him. Then he charged down the hall, shotgun at the ready, perspiring more profusely than ever.

The overhead halogen lamps switched on as he raced by. He found that reassuring, for although exposed, there would be no more groping about in the dark. Where had that damn wall jack been? The stairwell . . . it was around the corner, in the hall, at the base of the stairwell!

He flew around the corner, racing so fast he nearly tripped. A gunshot rang out as he bounced off the far wall, and he heard a bullet whiz by his head. His fear was surpassed by astonishment as he looked down the corridor. Approximately fifty feet away, a stationary autobot was poised beside the open stairwell, waiting for him. He'd been surprised when he first learned about the PCGs, but he was now positively dumbstruck that some, at least, were equipped with firearms. The only thing that had saved him was the mad way he careened and nearly fell as he rounded the corner, obviously throwing off the robot's aim. But he could clearly see the autobot's gunbarrel adjust itself his way, threatening to suck the life from him. He was infuriated.

"Suck on this, asshole!"

With another ear-splitting blast, he fired the shotgun's next-to-last round. The uranium-hardened slug penetrated the paneling beside the gunbarrel, destroying it, slicing through the machine's innards and blasting a gaping hole out the back. The slug had such residual energy that it struck the wall at the far end of the corridor, blasting an eighteen-inch hole through the concrete. Dunston thought he heard a scream, but his ears were ringing too much for him to be sure. He watched the wheels on one side of the autobot collapse. As if in slow motion, it toppled over into the stairwell's opening.

The bastards work fast, he thought. Knowing he hadn't a moment to spare, he ran toward the now visible jack. He pulled up in front of it, panting, fumbling with the zipper to his pocket. He pulled out the ThinWire cable, uncoiled its two-foot length, and inserted one end into the wall jack, narrowing his eyelids against possible sparks. But the adapter slid in like a hot knife through butter. He heard the laptop begin to click.

He lifted it to look at its six-inch square monitor. Lettering appeared, white on black.

SPECIAL PROGRAM X-1 CONNECTED TO CENTER FOR HUMAN POTENTIAL MAINFRAMES, it read, followed by, SENDING . . .

Dunston stared at the small screen. Each passing second seemed endless. His heart still pounded, and he breathed open-mouthed, as much from anxiety as exhaustion. Removing the hood had interrupted his suit's cooling system. He sweated profusely, and a bead of perspiration fell from his chin to the monitor.

"Come on, baby," he cajoled. Hadn't Merlin said it would take a nanosecond?

OVERRIDING SYSTEM ATTRIBUTES, the screen said. CHANGING PARITY.

"Thank God!" he said. As he watched the blinking cursor, he softly invoked, "Odd numbers, odd numbers, odd numbers," nodding his head in time to the chant, as if *davening*.

A sound was coming from around the corner at the other end of the hall. Just when he recognized the dreaded electric hum, the autobot rounded the corner and stopped, facing him. Gripped by terror, Dunston released the laptop and went for the shotgun. But suddenly, unexpectedly, the overhead lights dimmed. The autobot slowed. Then it totally lost power, coasting forward several feet before stopping entirely. Throughout the building there was a low, creaking sound, a rumbling groan, like the tortured shifting of a ship's heavy timbers in storm-tossed seas.

Chapter Twenty-four

TERRIFYINGLY ALONE IN the bowels of the Center, Maks heard the booms. The first one made her jump, and she winced when the others came moments later. They appeared to originate one floor below her, the sound reverberating up through the stairwell. They unmistakably sounded like explosions, separated from them though she was by tons of concrete and steel. She fought an impulse to run—but toward them, not away, for an instant later, she recognized them as shotgun blasts.

Chad was in trouble.

But his instructions to her had been explicit: don't budge. Any false movement would betray her presence. If she were discovered, any hope of helping Chad, and *all* hopes of discovering what happened to Christine, would be so much dust in the wind. She prayed that Chad would be able to fend for himself. In the meantime, all she could do was remain by the wall jacks, trembling in her suit.

Finally, after what seemed like ages, the signal came that she'd been waiting for. There was a perceptible decrease in the Center's power, what Chad had referred to as "winding down." Although there were no overhead lights, the floor lasers dimmed, and the Center's indefinable aura of massive strength definitely lessened. That was all she needed. She switched on her laptop and removed the cable. Inserting one end into her experimental optical computer, she placed the other end into the jack. Then she began to type.

SUBMIT WHEREABOUTS AND INTENTIONS FOR PATIENT CHRISTINE LASSITER, she wrote.

There was a brief pause, the slightest hesitation, and then her machine proved its worth. True to her expectations, information began to flow into her diskette in an unending stream. The rapid sequence of lettering was unintelligible. But unlike Chad's, her laptop had a "pause" feature, like a VCR. Every few seconds she would hit the button to read what was being sent into her floppy. Much of what she saw was medical jargon that was of little significance to her, but here and there words like "experimental," "reproductive," and "investigational" hit her like a sledgehammer. Dear God, she thought, Chrissie was being used as some sort of guinea pig!

The thought was infuriating, intolerable. She was filled with an immeasurable rage that made her want to hit, to punch, to lash out. Yet much as she recognized her own fury, she was equally cognizant that her job was only half done. She still had to learn where Christine was being held. Through sheer imposition of will, she managed to hold her anger in check. Returning to the lettering streaming into her laptop, she paused the sequence here and there to make out what she could.

She found what she was looking a few seconds later. Her eyes played over the telltale lettering: LOCATION UNCERTAIN, BUT MAJORITY OF PHONATIONS APPEAR TO EMANATE FROM LABORATORY ENVIRONS. Phonations? A voice—Chrissie's voice, somewhere near the lab! As the bit stream continued into her diskette, she furiously closed her eyes, trying to recall what Chad said about the Center's layout. She racked her brains, piecing through what she recalled from the diagrams and Chad's descriptions. Suddenly, she remembered.

No longer paying heed to the lasers, she ripped the cable from the jack and leapt into the stairwell.

Dunston stood there, gripped by fear, his whole body shaking. His quivering hands gradually lowered the shotgun and wiped away the sweat stinging his eyes. Slowly, he lifted up the laptop still attached to his waist.

PARITY CHANGE COMPLETE, the monitor flashed. INTERRUPT ROUTINE IN PROGRESS. INSERT DISKETTE X-2 INTO DRIVE B.

Thank God, he thought. His trembling fingers pushed the second diskette into the disk drive. The screen, having gone blank, lit up again with the words, FILE SEARCH UNDERWAY. To Dunston, the lightweight laptop suddenly seemed to weigh a ton. Exhausted, he let it hang from his belt. He leaned against the wall and closed his eyes in relief, breathing deeply. He wondered how long before the Center's supercomputers reinitialized the hardware and rectified the parity. During the ride in the van, he'd asked Cheryl and Merlin, but they didn't know. Their best guess was five minutes. Feeling his strength return, he checked the laptop.

FILE SEARCH COMPLETE. ACCESS UNDERWAY. COPYING . . .

The lettering was replaced by a blur of digital numbering at incredible speed, totally illegible, as each line and sector of the accessed file was copied onto the floppy. But a diskette, Dunston knew, could only contain so much information, no matter how its capacity had been expanded by Cheryl. Still, he was surprised when the process took no more than five seconds.

COPY ROUTINE COMPLETE. REMOVE DISKETTE.

He did just that, ejecting both floppies and turning off the laptop. After replacing them in their protective baggies, he unplugged the coax and stuffed it back into his pocket. He estimated he had over four minutes left. He glanced with satisfaction at the two autobots, one destroyed, the other without power. A smile spread over his face. But it was no time to gloat. Under the neoprene, he was sweating like a pig. It was time to get out of there.

As a precaution, he switched on the EMP simulator. "Boy Scout's motto," he mumbled. Checking to see that he had all his equipment, he turned to the stairwell. He drew abreast of it and halted, demoralized.

"I don't believe it," he groaned. The destroyed autobot, still smoldering, had firmly wedged itself into the doorway when it had fallen. Ordinarily, its four-foot height should have been no problem for him to clamber over. But when he tried to lift his leg, he discovered that his neoprene suit was much more rigid than before. The lack of coolant, combined with his perspiration, had interfered with its flexibility. He supposed he could take the suit off. Yet, as tight as it was before, it now stuck to him like glue and would take at least five minutes to remove. That was time he didn't have.

He touched the top of the robotic barrier, wondering if he could pull himself high enough to vault over. But the machine's shorted circuits made the paneling dangerously hot. The neoprene of his glove began to smoke, and he yanked his hand away. There had to be another way. He turned and started down the corridor in the direction of the other inactivated autobot.

"Chad!"

He whirled in his tracks. There was Maks, on the other side of the robot which blocked the stairwell. Seeing him, she spit out her mouthpiece, holding it in her hand.

"Your regulator!" she shouted. "They'll spot you!"

"They already have," he shouted back.

She looked frantic. "What are we going to do?"

"It's time we said good-bye to this place. The best way is back in your direction, but I can't get over this stupid autobot. Watch yourself. It's so hot it'll peel your skin off!"

"Chad, my computer worked! I'm sure I've found Christine! She's hiding somewhere near the lab!''

"The *lab?*" His brain spun. He cast an over-the-shoulder glance the length of the hall.

"Isn't it down your corridor? Chad, please! We've got to find her! Help me over this thing before the Center powers up again!''

Confused though he was, he began to suspect she was right. "Dammit, Maks, we've only got a couple of minutes! You've got to come over to this side! I'd use my suit as a bridge, but I can't get out of it! Can you slip yours off?''

"I think so." Unlike him, by remaining virtually motionless in her refrigerated garb, she'd perspired little. She immediately set to unzipping her suit. Within fifteen seconds, she wriggled free, pausing only to retrieve the regulator and her optical computer, with its priceless information. "Okay, what now?''

"Toss your suit and laptop over here!''

She did. Dunston ejected the diskettes and secured them in one of his pockets. Then he carefully lay the garment's fabric atop the destroyed autobot, where it began to smolder. He forced a calm, reassuring tone into his voice.

"Maks, you only get one shot at this. You can do it, trust me. Nothing more than a little high jump. Go back up the stairs until the third step from the bottom.''

She instantly complied in an unquestioning, no-nonsense manner. "All right.''

"One giant step'll do it. Just jump into the middle of the wet suit, and skip on over. Don't think about it. Just do it!''

"But—''

"Come on. Now!''

Still blindly clutching her regulator, Maks shivered with fear. It was only about four feet from her concrete perch to the autobot, yet the intervening gap seemed immense. She intuitively understood that any hesitation would be her undoing. Forcing all thought from her mind, she leapt in one graceful bound.

Despite his reassurances, Dunston's heart was in his mouth as he watched Maks' gazellelike stride through the air. Her right foot landed square in the middle of the autobot's neoprene-covered top panel, and then she was off it again, leaping toward his outstretched arms. Dunston caught her in a bear hug, clutching her tight as he lowered her to the ground.

"Is your foot okay?"

She looked at her sole, which bore a black smudge. "I think so. A little smelly, but what else is new?"

"That's what we're going to find out. Hurry, this way!"

He led her down the corridor in the direction of the inactivated autobot. Detecting a smell, he crinkled his nose at the unexpected aroma of cooking food. A vision of the hospital's layout flashed in his mind, and he suddenly realized that the hole he'd blasted in the wall was adjacent the Center's kitchen. If that were so . . . God Almighty! In the heat of combat, exacerbated by the nerve-racking computer access and the dimmed corridor, the hospital's architectural design had become a blur. He now understood that Maks *was* right, and that they must be very close to the lab. The lab, he recalled, had a wide glass window. And he still had his shotgun.

And then, suddenly, there it was, just as he remembered it from his visit with Arthur. Now, however, the door through which they'd gone lay open. Probably, Dunston guessed, from the brownout. Underpowering did strange things to sophisticated electronics. He and Maks entered without hesitation. As before, the lab was almost totally dark. For a moment, he lost his bearings as his eyes adjusted to the darkness. Where the hell was the window? To the best of his recollection, it was in the lab's rear corner. He and Weiman hadn't seen it on their joint visit, for their vision was blocked by tall rows of automated analyzers.

And then, from the depths of his subconscious, the memories resurfaced.

Walking slowly past the machines, with Maks in tow, he began to recall things he'd only vaguely remembered, or perhaps suppressed. The first memory was clearer, for he'd been alert, then: inconstant flashes or flickering, from somewhere in the back of the lab. When he'd walked toward the twinkling, he thought he'd heard the hum of something mechanical closing, only to find nothing. The second recollection was more remote, for he'd been drugged. He recalled a peculiar vapor like moonlit fog, a fragrant mist that teemed with life, rows of smooth, dew-covered receptacles . . .

He continued walking, trying to calm the pounding of his heart, frowning as he scoured his memory. He seemed to recall stumbling through some hidden door into the mist-filled chamber from . . . where? Hadn't he found himself in a sort of unused passageway beyond the lab? The room grew darker. He reached into his pocket for the Mag-Lite and switched it on. What he saw made him suck in his breath. During his visit with Arthur, an unseen door *had* closed, after all. Now lacking power, it lay open. A steamy vapor rolled toward them in undulating waves.

"Get a load of that," he whispered, awestruck. "This is it!"

"Is Christine in there?"

"Probably. We'll find her."

The flashlight's beam cut a yellow swath through the fog. Dunston hesitantly stepped into the cryptlike chamber. He couldn't understand why the room was so dark. He swung the flashlight toward the near wall on his right, expecting to find the window, covered with shades, perhaps, or blinds. Instead, he found the solid masonry of recently filled-in cinder blocks. He walked over to it and touched, sniffing. Even the damn mortar smelled fresh. So he'd been wrong after all, as had the plans. The window wasn't located in the lab proper. It was in this bizarre, hidden access.

"Can you believe that?" he mumbled. He clutched Maks' hand and checked his watch. If Cheryl and Merlin were right, they had just over two minutes before the computer center corrected its problem, two minutes in which they had to find Christine and discover the lab's secrets. After that . . . He glanced at the shotgun, which he held barrel downward. He'd seen what the slug had done to a concrete wall, and that was *after* it had passed through a mass of wire and metal. He had no doubt his last shot would create the escape passage they would need.

Chancing another look, he swung the beam back toward the room's darkest confines. What in the world . . . ? There, not more than five feet away, was a tabletop workstation, on which rested the optical lever atomic forces microscope. He quickly headed toward it, wanting at least a cursory inspection. He bathed it in the glare.

"Chad, what are you doing? We've got to find Christine!"

"Hold on a second."

It was just as Merlin described. Astonishingly simple in design, it had a haphazardly improvised appearance, resembling a Rube Goldbergian erector set on a baking pan. Dunston could clearly see the small mirror and diamond tip. Just behind it was a long, rectangular box he took to be the free electron laser.

Incredible, he thought. Merlin would be pleased to learn his hunch was correct. That still didn't answer what the Center was doing with the device, but there wasn't time to dwell on it. One hand on the shotgun, he arched his beam through the rest of the room. The light glinted off a nearby receptacle.

What he saw made his mind go numb. His eyes widened, and he stood there agape at what he could now clearly discern but once only drunkenly glimpsed. Like iron filings drawn to a magnet, he approached the receptacle in a trance.

It contained a growing, unborn baby. Behind him, Maks gasped.

The size of a bottled water dispenser, the receptacle was filled with gently swirling fluid that had the straw-yellow hue of human plasma. In the middle of the flask, a gossamer sac of amniotic membranes randomly billowed in the circulating fluid, like the gentle waving of sea anemones. Seen through the veil of the membranes, the living fetus floated in its own amniotic fluid.

His light still shining on the receptacle, Dunston swallowed, dry-mouthed, at once aghast and fascinated. The fetus appeared to be about six months old. As he watched, it did a lazy roll, unencumbered by the uterine muscle which would ordinarily surround it. Its tiny fists opened and closed, and its unborn lips pursed, a sucking movement. Dunston could make out a thin skein of tiny red capillaries stretching across nearly translucent eyelids.

And then the baby's eyes opened and stared at him.

Maks screamed, and Dunston's heart nearly erupted from his chest. She dug her nails into his arm as they both jumped back in shock. Her voice was a terrified whisper.

"Can it see us?"

"I don't think so."

Or could it? At that appalling moment, he couldn't recall a single thing about fetal physiology. He quickly walked around it, shaking his head in disbelief, keeping his beam steady. Where the placenta was attached, blood-filled tubing fed it, protruding through the receptacle's exterior. He recognized it instantly, for the tubing had the same caliber and texture as the bypass conduit used in cardiothoracic surgery, tubing that came from a heart-lung machine.

"Chad, give me the light. I've got to find her!"

He handed it to her. "Start over there. I'll look this way."

She took the light and moved away, shining it over the walls, looking for gaps, crevices. "Chrissie!" she shouted. "Chrissie, it's Maks! Where are you? Answer me!"

Her desperate pleas were met with silence. She frantically moved onward, momentarily leaving Dunston behind. As much as he was trying to help her, he was hopelessly distracted by what he'd seen. He slowly shook his head, incredulous. But the evidence was incontrovertible. The Center had perfected a technique called ectogenesis, a method of bringing babies to term outside the human uterus.

An unborn child was growing in a womb of glass.

He was aware of reports where scientists had grown rat embryos in glass dishes to the point where their hearts were beating—but to have come this far? To have adapted the methodology from lab animals to humans? To have created truly *in vitro*, totally artificial uteri, that were being used to grow a complete test tube baby? The idea was staggering!

As his mind wrestled with the impossibility of it all, his foremost question was, why? Was this the secret the Center had fought to protect, be it cloning, genetic engineering with the AFM, or whatever? Did he and Christine play a role in it, and to what end? He was glutted by fragmentary thoughts which flickered through his brain like fireflies: ovulation, sperm and egg, a testicular biopsy, the Serophene.

The Center's power was suddenly restored, jolting the room into brightness. Hidden doors crashed open, the same doors through which Dunston had dazedly stumbled after his escape from the OR. While he was still reacting to the glare, an autobot rushed toward him at top speed. Dunston reached for his shotgun, a fraction too late. Before he could level it, the robot struck him full force. The shotgun went flying, and he was savagely knocked into the wall behind him. His head struck the concrete with a heavy thud, and he slumped to the floor.

He lay there in a stupor, not quite unconscious, but much more than dazed. His mind functioned in slow motion. Although he was aware of something sliding under him and being lifted, then being carried away, his muscles could not respond. He felt a breeze rushing past his numb cheeks. But he was a rag doll, dead weight, virtually unable to move.

Walking with her back to him on the other side of the room, Maks' mind was occupied. She swung the flashlight from side to side, intent on finding Christine. The commotion behind her was muffled and distant, lost in the liquid symphony of the autoanalyzers. Reaching a dead end, she turned around.

Far behind her, she saw Chad sprawled atop an autobot, his body encircled by coils. Maks screamed. The flashlight fell from her shaking fingers, but not before she saw a hidden wall slide open. When the autobot motored beyond it, the wall immediately closed, abandoning the room to darkness.

Like a boxer reviving from a knockout, Dunston felt the gradual return of his senses. He could move his muscles, but with infinite slowness. Something was pinning him down. He felt the tug of gravity, and he thought he was ascending. Then his upward movement ceased, and sliding doors opened. He was being ferried into some sort of corridor. Suddenly there were lights overhead, and he was entering a room. He blinked his eyes, clearing the cobwebs, and gazed to one side.

And there, to his absolute amazement, stood Arthur Weiman.

His one-time friend was poised like a fashion model, arms folded, leaning back against the wall, a smile on his face. He seemed to be enjoying Dunston's captivity. As he looked on, the autobot rolled to a stop beside a long, flat table topped with a foam rubber mattress. The gleaming stainless steel had the familiar appearance of an operating table. Dunston's eyes went wide, and his mouth opened in fear and anticipation.

"Finally," said Weiman. "It took a while, but I knew you'd be back. Very predictable. As long as I've known you, you're nothing if not persistent."

"Arthur, have you gone crazy? Get this thing off me! For the love of God, what are you doing?"

Weiman shook his head. "Such blind optimism. You really are a Pollyanna. I don't suppose you'd voluntarily slide over to the operating table, would you?"

For the first time, Dunston inspected his surroundings. He was in a small, well-equipped treatment room. A bottle of IV solution hung from a pole beside the OR table, and a small, metal tray held a half-dozen surgical instruments. There was also a kidney basin filled with crushed ice, ordinarily used for preserving tissue specimens. He thought back to his escape from the Center and the planned testicular surgery. He had no doubt what Weiman now intended. He looked back at the internist, who produced a compact stun gun.

"Arthur, are you *insane?*"

"How did I know you were going to say that?" Without further explanation, he stepped forward and touched Dunston's temple with the gun. Chad shuddered, and his body again went flaccid. Weiman turned to a computer keyboard and typed instructions.

With utmost smoothness, the autobot transferred Dunston's limp form to the table's soft mattress. Weiman went to work securing Dunston's arms and legs with heavy restraints, making sure to position the left arm for venipuncture. He cut away the neoprene for access to the underlying veins, then put a tourniquet around Dunston's left biceps. He spoke as he worked.

"You're a bright guy, Chad. I know you can hear me. You've seen enough stun guns to realize its effects will wear off in a few seconds. But you make me wonder. *Am*

I insane? Quite possibly I am. Not that it'll make any difference where you're concerned.''

Dunston could indeed hear him. The paralysis that caused his immobilization had no effect on his sensorium. Soon he felt his muscle function return. His first few words were slurred.

"You're in pretty good shape for a dead man."

"So it would seem."

"What are you doing to me?"

"Oh please. Spare me. You know they didn't get the job done the last time you were here. You've got something I need."

"Like Schmidt did?"

"Don't be an idiot. When I admitted him, Schmidt and his pickled brain were barely alive. I just hurried the process along with a little voltage. Could I help it that he looked like me? He added new meaning to the term 'dead ringer.' You see, you and your bozo pals were getting a little too close for comfort. I'm not sure how you avoided my little surprise on your boat, but you have to admit the body switch threw you off for a while."

After looking over Dunston's forearm, Weiman produced an intravenous infusion catheter. He palpated the veins with his index finger, selecting a prominent one on the back of the wrist. He caught himself opening a packaged alcohol swab and hesitated. With a self-deprecating laugh, he tossed it away.

"Am I a creature of habit, or what? Here I'm trying to protect you from a few germs, when in a few minutes, they won't matter at all!"

"You are some piece of work."

"Soon to be some *rich* piece of work. Have you ever wondered what it would be like to be filthy rich, to have more money than you could possibly spend? That bitch I married always made me feel like such a pauper."

"That's what this is all about? Money?"

"Maybe you're not aware of it," Weiman continued. "There are three million infertile couples in this country." He began to open the catheter's sterile packaging. "What do you think they'd pay for a healthy baby? And not just *any* baby. But one that's beyond disease, genetically perfect?"

"I give up. You tell me."

"My research says a hundred K. Now, out of that three million, say there are about ten thousand who have the means and who want the product. Do the math. We're talking a billion dollars."

"Charming. How are you going to come up with ten thousand perfect babies?"

"From *you*, my friend. And young Miss Lassiter, of course. I know the little shit is around here somewhere. When I want her, I'll get her back."

"Why us?"

"Because the bottled fetuses you saw were just a trial run. The ova came from the kid, sure. But the donor semen I used left something to be desired. That's where you came in.

"You know the best thing about you, Chad? It's not your surgical skill, or your rapier wit, oh no. It's your genes. You and the kid both have fabulous DNA. The way your body seemed to hold so much promise during the alpha intercept, I just had to have more."

While Weiman spoke, Dunston's mind was working furiously. His gaze flickered around the room, searching for weapons or a means of escape. Without being obvious, he painstakingly began to wriggle his right hand beneath the strap, trying to loosen it. If Weiman were allowed to continue uninterrupted, Dunston knew he'd be dead within minutes. The yellowish solution in the IV solution bore a strong resemblance to the anesthetic Pentothal. Somehow, he had to throw the older man off. He watched Weiman tear thin strips of adhesive tape.

Suddenly his eyes fixed on the IV catheter. It was one of the longer sizes, a three-inch, sixteen-gauge plastic tube over a surgical metal stylet. The stainless inner needle's tip was razor sharp. With virtually no other options, Dunston immediately understood what had to be done.

"Why are you doing this, Arthur?"

"Don't waste your time. If you have to talk, why don't you say your prayers?"

"You're such a . . . pathetic little man."

Weiman's nostrils flared. "Pathetic *fat* little man? Isn't that what you meant to say? I'll be thrilled to get rid of your juvenile sarcasm! 'Skipped the weigh-in, Arthur?' That's what you said at the Intercept. Comments like that made me hate your guts!"

As Weiman examined the exposed veins, Dunston completely relaxed and let his eyes roll backward beneath his lids. He felt his limbs grow heavy, and there was a peculiar tingling in his abdomen he'd come to associate with bio-feedback. He imagined himself scuba diving, totally at ease, barely having to breathe at all. He knew his blood pressure was falling. And without enough pressure, his veins would collapse.

"Christ, your veins suck."

Weiman leaned closer, peering at a spot where the veins had flattened to nothingness. He slapped Dunston's skin with his palm, hoping that the minor trauma would make the vessels expand. But it didn't. Choosing what he thought would be a likely spot, he hovered over Dunston's arm and worked the catheter's tip beneath the skin.

It was just what Dunston had been waiting for. He peered out of the corner of his eye. With Weiman as close as possible and the catheter momentarily trapped in his flesh, he wrenched his upper torso violently sideways, throwing his head at Weiman. His forehead struck the internist's nose with the nauseating crunch of shattered cartilage. Weiman screamed and straightened up, releasing the catheter. His hands flew to his flattened nose in a protective reflex, and a torrent of blood seeped through his fingers.

Dunston wasted no time. With all the strength he could muster, he tore his right hand from its restraint and reached for the IV catheter. He seized it by its hub just as a bellowing Weiman lowered his hands. Blinded by rage and blood, the internist reached for Dunston's neck. Spotting an opening, Dunston lunged.

Wielding the pointed catheter like a dagger, he put all he had into the thrust. Its stiletto-sharp tip punctured Weiman's chest, just below the sternum. A muffled cry rose and died in Weiman's throat. For the briefest moment, his body went rigid. Then, he collapsed to the floor with a shudder.

Dunston lay back, gasping. He was relieved and sickened at the same time. He could still hear Arthur's voice. Everything Weiman said was going around in his head, like a squirrel in a cage. But his thoughts quickly returned to Maks. When the fire in his lungs diminished, he loosened all the restraints and bolted from the room.

His neoprene suit was in tatters, but he still wore the EMP simulator. He retreated through the now-darkened corridors, finding his way as much by touch as by sight. He finally stumbled into the waiting elevator and leaned back as its door automatically closed behind him.

Maks clenched the shotgun in both hands. The safety was off, and her finger rested outside the trigger guard. Just aim and shoot, Merlin had said. Lost and alone, she was beyond terror, driven by a fierce will to survive. She would kill if she had to. Directly in front of her, the hidden wall began to open again. Growing tense, she took a deep breath and put her finger on the trigger guard.

"Chad!"

Like an embattled warrior, Dunston stumbled toward her. She lowered the weapon and stepped into his warm embrace. They clung together shaking, bound by love and joined in gratitude. But their privacy was transient. Dunston heard the dreaded motorized whir and jerked his head around. An autobot hovered not ten feet away, its menacing portal open and ready, preparing for the kill.

Maks shrieked and jumped back. Dunston cursed the stupidity of his distraction and frantically reached for the shotgun. He was lifting it up when the autobot fired.

The sibilant hiss of the PCG was followed by his own weapon's loud report. In the fraction of a second that followed, time warped into a frighteningly expanded moment, during which his mind was assaulted by a rush of jumbled thoughts. He was surprised and angered by the stinging bite of the air-driven drug, and equally astonished that, after five successive hits, his own gun missed. Lacking time for accurate aim, the heavy slug went several inches wide of the mark. His painfully expanded vision watched it plow harmlessly through the air and strike a pipe on the wall behind the doors. And then all hell broke loose.

There was a deafening explosion, followed by a rolling wave of orange fire that hurled Maks backward, into the nearest receptacle. Her head struck it with a loud crack, and she slumped to the ground.

The area had become an inferno. From the hole in the pipe, the yellowish-blue stream of fire issued upward, as if gushing from a torched Kuwaiti oil well. The blaze intensified, hiding her from sight. "Maks!" he shouted again, to no avail.

Alarms began to sound, followed almost immediately by a spray of water as the overhead sprinkler system was activated. Dunston again shielded his eyes and checked the nearby floor. The explosion had knocked the attacking autobot on its side. Nonetheless, its portal was still open in his direction. All at once, the PCG's strawlike barrel began to move, seeking him out. Sickened and in fear, Dunston's stomach wanted to heave.

He steadied the shotgun one final time and pulled the trigger. There was the deadened, metallic click of a striker falling on an unloaded chamber. Jesus, it was empty! He threw the weapon down and leapt aside, out of the robot's field of fire. Scurrying back into the lab, his eyes searched everywhere for Maks, but the blaze obscured his vision. He held a protective hand at eyebrow level as he continued retreating from the autobot. Nearing the area of the sealed-up window, he sensed that, without his shotgun, their only escape might be a hasty retreat through the walls of the hospital's main entrance. But even if he could find Maks, what about Christine? Undoubtedly, other autobots were now searching for them. He reached toward his left thigh and pressed the button that powered up the EMP simulator.

He blinked, wondering when the drug would take effect. When it did, he wanted them to be long gone. He took another rearward step when he heard a scream.

The cacophony of sounds made the cry indistinct. Was it Maks, he wondered, or Christine? He looked wildly about, barely able to see because of the fire. Where the hell *was* she? Had Maks awakened and gone off after her sister? He stopped, eyes wide and searching, glancing from hall to lab and back again. Then he heard it once more, short but unmistakable, a high-pitched wail of terror. Dear God, he thought, was it a patient? The first few molecules of tranquilizer reached his brain, and he felt a wave of vertigo. He was momentarily torn, desperately wanting for all of them to flee, but sickened by the thought that he might have injured a patient. *Primum non nocere*, went the physician's credo. Above all, do no harm. His indecision was temporary, for he knew what he had to do: his duty. Before the drug could accumulate in his tissues, he had to get around the autobot, whose wheels spun and swiveled like an up-ended tortoise trying to right itself. Dunston held the simulator in one hand, aiming its dual-pronged antenna toward the robot. He worked the extender, and six feet of twin

antennas sprung out like a switchblade knife. He quickly
touched their metallic tips to the autobot's shell and hit the
button again.

The coupled electric surge was greater than he thought
imaginable. The unbridled energy coursed through the
stricken machine, wreathing it in an electric light show that
glittered like dancing neon. But when he was preparing to
retract the antennas, there was an unexpected, intense
crackling noise, and a jolt seared up his arm. It was a peculiar feeling, electrocution. Just before he lost consciousness, he thought the top of his head would explode. He fell
sideways, passing harmlessly through the horizontal sheet
of flame, unaware that his toppling body had landed right
next to Maks.

His thudding shoulder jarred her awake. Maks lifted her
head and shook it, trying to clear the cobwebs. When her
vision returned, she saw the outline of Dunston's still face,
profiled in the beam of the Mag-Lite.

She shouted his name and slid next to him, cupping his
face in her hands, fighting back tears. There was a roaring
overhead, and she looked up into bright, licking flames,
coming from God-knew-where. She held her breath and
lowered her head to his chest, listening. Then, ever so
slowly, she exhaled, smiling. The thump of his heart was
clear and steady, and he was taking slow, easy breaths.
Speed was clearly of the essence. On knees and elbows,
she quickly clambered over his upper torso like a spider,
careful not to move him for fear of worsening some unknown injury. She retrieved the flashlight and, next to it,
her regulator, having forgotten that she'd blindly hung on
to it in the confusion. Then she carefully retreated back
over him. She was in the process of swinging the flashlight's beam around when she was buffeted by an ear-
splitting explosion.

The concussion knocked her to her side. The flames
above her intensified, and their glare made her lids narrow.

A weakened section of pipe beneath Dunston's errant shot had given way, emitting a surge of pressurized gas that blew apart an enormous chunk of the wall behind it. Maks rolled onto her chest and squirmed forward beneath the flames, wriggling like an infantryman, shining the light into the semidarkness at floor level. And then the scream reached her.

It was short and strident, a high-pitched wail of terror. And she knew, without a moment's hesitation, that it was her sister's voice.

"Christine!" she shouted. "Chrissie, I'm coming!"

The scream seemed to come from the direction of the explosion. Fighting panic, Maks shined the light ahead and crawled forward on her knees. Fire and smoke were everywhere, and the light's beam cut a lazy swath through the choking fumes. Christine was nowhere to be seen. Dear God, was she okay? She shrieked the child's name again but heard only the flames' incessant roar. Her light played over the mechanical hulk toppled onto the floor. It was the autobot, smoking and destroyed, parts of it actually melting. She hurriedly skirted it, desperate to find Christine.

The unending jet of gas-fed flame streaked up and over her head, spreading horizontal wavelets of fire above her, rising at an angle toward the ceiling. The heat was intense. As she crawled beneath the flaming geyser, Maks felt her topmost hairs singe, followed by the streaming of liquid down her face. She hesitantly dabbed at it, almost certain it was blood. But it was clear, and delightfully cool. Shortly her whole body was soaked, and it finally occurred to her that it had to be water coming from an automated sprinkler system. The sprinkler was working full force, dousing her and everything in sight, though not sufficiently to quickly quell the flames.

Maks crawled furiously ahead, her vision hampered by the torrent of spray which rained down. She blinked her eyes and squinted, trying to see more clearly. She screamed

Christine's name again but still heard nothing, perhaps because her ears still rung from the explosions. The blazing propane had a thunderous roar all its own. She halted for a second, soaked, deafened, and woozy, contemplating her next move. She realized there was nowhere she could go but forward.

Her arms began to ache, and her elbows were scraped and raw. But after a few maddening minutes she was finally out of the lab, into the hall beyond. She lifted her beam, shining it at the wall below the punctured pipe. Three feet off the ground, the second propane explosion had blown a two-foot-wide hole in the wall. Beyond it was a blanket of darkness. Could it be some sort of testing area or an unlit patient's room? She doubted it. Such places would now be illuminated. She was desperate.

"Christine!" she shouted. But as before, there was no return voice. She bent past the jagged hole and carefully inserted her beam into the dust-filled blackness. She was peering into a five-foot-wide passageway, and she experienced an eerie, gooseflesh *frisson,* suspecting she was looking into the hidden, unused area from which Dunston made his first escape. She prayed it would not be his last. She swung the light to the right, then trained the beam toward the center, seeing nothing but shattered concrete and debris. And then she swung the beam to the left. What she saw made her gasp.

She was staring into the face of a terrified child.

Maks felt as if she were paralyzed. She squinted through double vision, knowing full well who the youngster was, but she was suddenly too numb, too overcome with emotion to voice the name. Above a tattered gown, the child's hair was matted. Her face was covered with dirt and grime, and tears coursed down her cheeks. She seemed mute, but her earlier screams proved that to be untrue. She was just scared out of her mind. She averted her eyes from the light's bright glare, revealing her profile.

Maks, still silent, felt the tears well up. She was absolutely familiar with that profile—the gently upturned nose; the fine, blond, almost white hair; the clear blue eyes: the eyes of her sister.

Maks' journey had come to an end. Her heart began to pound with the recognition of discovery. She felt jubilant, wanting to shout. But she knew the first order of business was to keep her sister calm. If frightened anew, there was no telling where the child might bolt.

Christine moved minimally sideways, out of the flashlight's glare. Maks immediately averted the beam. Not only was a blinding light uncomfortable, but there was also no way her sister could see her. The light fell on the child's surroundings: a bunched-up blanket, empty food containers, drinking straws, a roll of toilet tissue. Finally, it was time. Maks carefully controlled her voice. "Christine," she called.

Christine seemed not to hear. She kept her eyes lowered and away, saying nothing, tucking her head into her chest in fear and solemnity.

"It's okay," Maks urged. She spoke in calm, reassuring tones. After all these months, did Christine even recognize her voice? My God, how had she escaped? How had she *survived?* The air-driven scent of food from the nearby kitchen reached her, and she realized the answer to that enigma.

Child though she was, her sister had always been bright. She must have stayed alive by using her wits and her intelligence—scurrying, scampering, remaining unseen, pilfering whatever was necessary to survive. Maks was overcome with compassion. She realized that, over the months, her sister must have heard the autobots passing beyond the wall. They'd probably scared her to death. Christ, what gumption! Maks would be damned if she'd let anything more happen to her sister. She had to get them out of there!

"Chrissie? Chrissie, it's me, Maks."

The child looked back at her, but her eyes were filled with suspicion and disbelief, perhaps because her older sister was still bathed on shadow. Maks moved cautiously forward, trying to minimize what she knew must be terror. She swung her beam from side to side, inspecting the narrow confines of the concealed retreat. The passageway had about eighty feet in which one could move about. It appeared sealed at both ends, like some sort of air lock. But undoubtedly there were little openings she was capable of slipping through, for food, to relieve herself, or simply to move about. Lord, what love and admiration she felt for her sister, a gutsy little girl who managed to survive by sheer determination.

Another sheet of fire erupted with a boom that quickly receded. Christine screamed, her terror mounting. Maks felt a tug of desperation.

"Chrissie, Chrissie. It's me, Maks. Come here, honey." She inched ahead, but the terrified child, still not convinced, continued to inch backwards. "Easy, easy," she said. "I'm not going to hurt you, you know that. It'll be all right. I'm going to take you home, Chrissie. You remember home, right?"

Christine paused, a hint of recognition beginning to glow in her eyes. Her den was a squalid lean-to of makeshift cardboard and soiled blankets covered with scraps of moldy food. Maks toyed with the idea of making a lunge, but she decided on a different tack. As she neared her sister, she turned the flashlight over. With the beam now pointing at her, she held it out like an offering.

"Chrissie, shine the light at me."

Christine hesitated, then took the handle ever so slowly. She momentarily weighed it in her hand, as if it were a foreign object. Then she raised the beam until Maks was captured in its light. Maks bit her lip. For a moment, they were both silent. Finally, Christine spoke.

"Maks, you're all wet. Why aren't you wearing any clothes?"

Maks gave a little cry and leaned forward, jubilant, tears of joy streaming down her cheeks. She lifted her sister up under the arms. Christine dropped the light, recoiling slightly.

"Honey, what's wrong? It's okay, it's all right."

And then Maks realized that, after months of stealth and evasion, the child's reaction was more symbolic than real. Finally, Christine's token resistance disappeared, and her small arms reached up toward her older sister's neck. Maks drew her toward her naked breast, hugging her tight, soothing her with kisses until they were both weeping. But there was work to be done. Now that they were reunited, it was time to locate Chad. Their departure from this hellhole was long overdue.

Back in the lab, the intensified sprinkling splattered water on Dunston's face. He groggily opened his eyes, not sure where he was until the roaring fire overhead reminded him. Even thought it had only been a short time since he was shot, the drug was rapidly accumulating in his tissues, assaulting his brain, making him woozy. He propped himself up with difficulty.

"Maks, Maks, where are you?" he shouted. His voice sounded weak and lifeless.

In the distance, Dunston thought he heard his voice being called. He struggled to get up, away from the flame, listening intently.

"Chad, we're coming! I've got Christine!"

Where the hell was she? His legs felt rubbery, and his vision was just beginning to blur. Yet now out of reach of the fire, his own surging adrenalin counteracted the drug, stimulant overriding depressant. Her voice seemed to come from within the hall, or somewhere beyond. Now standing, he stumbled in her direction with the broad-based gait of a drunk.

Inside the passageway, Maks held Christine's small frame against her chest. Cradling her in tight satisfaction, she began backing out through the opening of the hellish environment of the corridor, hoping against hope that Chad was still safe in the lab.

Roaring fire was everywhere, and they were drenched in the sprinkler's stinging spray. Christine tucked her head. Maks sensed the sudden rigidity of her sister's body, and she held her in firm, reassuring closeness.

"Easy, Chrissie, easy. I won't let go for anything."

Christine felt pitifully frail in Maks' arms, but otherwise she appeared physically okay. A little malnutrition, perhaps, but nothing that seemed like permanent damage. At least nothing visible. In the hall, Maks skirted a wall of fire. Suddenly, something whizzed behind her, scraping her thigh as it burst through the blaze, speeding down the corridor. Maks watched the autobot slow to a stop. Then it began maneuvering her way.

Maks glared at the machine. It's nothing more than a black box on wheels, she realized. But her emotions refused to accept that intellectualization. In her mind, she anthropomorphised the robot into something humanly sinister. The mechanical rectangle was the embodiment of evil to her, a malevolent incarnation intent on destroying her and those she loved. She felt imbued with a rage more intense than she'd ever known. She despised the machine and everything it stood for. She spoke through bared teeth, her voice akin to a snarl.

"You bastard," she hissed. "You're dead. I'm going to blow you to Kingdom Come!"

But with what? Maks looked wildly about her, at the flames which licked at the ceiling and walls. Bits of debris were everywhere—pipes, concrete, and beams, some of them ablaze. But nowhere was there a weapon. Unless . . . She glanced at the regulator, which she'd been mindlessly

clutching ever since she joined up with Chad. She recalled
Merlin's caution against overheating the regulator. Something about oxygen under pressure. As her head whirled,
the autobot continued stalking them, twisting and swiveling
in response to the laser guidance system. Holding Christine
tight, Maks jumped to the side, skittering out of the autobot's line of fire. Curiously, she felt no fear. Instead, she
was incensed, furious. She wanted to kill.

There! She spotted a foot-long section of two-by-four
lying in the corner, shattered and ablaze. Could she reach
it in time? Crouching against the wall, under the undulating
veil of flame, she glanced at the autobot, whose front portal
was sliding open. As she watched, a small hollow tube
began to protrude. She sprang.

Keeping low, virtually crushing Christine against her,
Maks traversed the ten feet separating her from the burning
piece of wood. She tucked the regulator in her underwear
as she hurriedly stooped to seize the piece of lumber.

With a whooshing sound, a blast of high-powered air
whizzed by her head, an inch from her face. She straightened up, throwing herself against the wall, out of the autobot's sights.

She seethed with rage. "Try to get me, you son of a
bitch!"

Holding the blazing wood like a torch, she sprinted toward the autobot. Its swiveling PCG tried to track her, but
she zigzagged like an open-field runner. Dodging and dancing, she heard another sibilant hiss as the air-driven drug
shot past her. She skidded to a sliding halt just beside the
open portal. As the PCG turned her way, she swung the
fiery two-by-four in an underhand arc. She was furious.

"Want a hot lunch, Tin Man?"

With all her might, Maks thrust the piece of wood
through the portal. It wedged tight, burning end inward,
forcing the PCG off to one side. Her fumbling fingers, now

free, tore the regulator from her waist. She was still seething.

"How about some fresh air with your meal?"

She quickly but carefully placed the regulator atop the glowing embers in the portal. Then she danced off again, toward the lab. Behind her, the autobot's mechanized whir became a high-pitched screech. It seemed to have gone berserk, turning this way and that, still trying to line up its target.

When she was inches away from the lab, Maks tripped on a chunk of dislodged masonry and tumbled onto her outstretched arm. Try though she did to keep hold of Christine, her sister rolled out of her grasp. The child whimpered, and Maks reached for her, pausing only to glance at the autobot. Her heart sank.

The PCG was aimed directly at her.

She pulled Christine under her and closed her eyes, using her body as a shield. But before the drug could hammer her, Merlin's pressurized cylinder erupted. Christine screamed when the autobot exploded, spraying torn bits of plastic and metal over their heads like shrapnel. Maks sagged, catching her breath. But there was no time to celebrate. Her first priority was Christine, then Chad. Scooping her sister into her arms, she found the entrance to the lab. Choking at the heavy smoke, she climbed inside.

"Maks!"

A clearly dazed Dunston propped himself up on a wall. Tears streaming anew, Maks quickly reached him, then held the trio in a three-way embrace. Dunston's eyes focused on the child. At the sight of the stranger, Christine closed her eyes and tightened her grip in her sister. Droplets of water bathed her face, washing away the grime. Dunston reached out to rub her cheeks.

"Incredible," he murmured to Maks. "You found her, huh? Hard to believe," he said soothingly.

"Chad, we've got to get out of here! One of those autobots nearly flattened me, and I'm sure another one's going to show up any minute!"

"What about going back down the hall?"

"No good. It's all blocked off, and the place is a firetrap! Isn't there another way?"

Through increasingly woozy vision, he looked through the lab, toward the bricked-up window. "Well . . ."

"What about your shotgun?"

"Out of shells."

"Oh Christ!"

"Just a minute." He tried to keep from reeling as he stared back across the lab. Then he plunged ahead, his right hip thudding into something, making him wince. He squinted, concentrating. Good Lord, it was the workstation for the free electron laser! He held on with both hands, fearing that if he let go, he'd collapse and never get up again. It *had* to have an on-off switch somewhere. His numb and trembling fingers finally found it and turned it on. The laser emitted a high, turbinelike whine.

"What are you *doing?*"

"Our ticket out, babe. I—"

The chemical gun's snakelike hiss seemed louder than ever. Dunston shouted and clutched his shoulder blade, simultaneously turning to look behind him. Through the hole in the lab's wall, another autobot had silently positioned itself. The PCG slowly moved, trying to line him up again.

"Bloody pig!" Maks said. She hurriedly put her sister down. A three-foot length of one-inch diameter pipe lay at her feet, torn free by one of the blasts. She lifted it in both hands and charged the autobot like a woman possessed, shrieking in hate and vengeance. She wielded the pipe like a baseball bat, head and shoulders down, leaning into the swing with a fierce rip that made Dunston envious. Her first swing shattered the optics, sending a shower of glass across the room. Her backswing took out the stem of the PCG and then she lifted the pipe over her head, bringing it down like an axe in a vicious, floorward arc.

"Filthy, rotten bastard!" she raged. "I'll turn you into scrap metal!"

She swung the pipe again and again, pulverizing the autobot into unrecognizable slivers and fragments. Dunston, meanwhile, found the strength to pick up Christine, who whimpered softly against his shoulder. Maks finally paused, out of breath. Beads of perspiration coursed down her neck into the cleft between her breasts. The results of her wrath lay about her feet in pieces.

"I think it got the message," Dunston managed.

Maks nodded, lungs heaving, her breath in spasm. The pipe fell to the floor with a clang as she plodded heavily their way. She held out her arms for Christine, eyeing Dunston with concern.

"How're you doing?"

"Been better. Listenta me . . . You gotta do it, Maks. I'll keep holda Christine."

"Do what?"

"The laser. Gimme a hand." His drugged mind frantically tried to recall what Merlin had said. "My breast pocket . . . Get it. *Hurry.*"

"What are you talking about?"

"Maks, *pleuse!*"

The fire was roaring about them. She quickly rummaged through one pocket, then another, her trembling fingers searching for the polished magnifying lens. With his remaining strength, Dunston hugged Christine, keeping a brooding guard over her. Her tattered hospital gown, speckled with food droppings, had risen up to her chest when he'd lifted her. She was naked underneath, her abdomen exposed. Something about her umbilicus caught his trained eye, and he looked closer. In the lower half of her belly button was a healed semicircular incision which, to a surgeon, meant only one thing: laparoscopy.

His brain screamed. Not a tonsillectomy, dammit, but a laparoscopy! That's how Arthur had done it! A gynecologic procedure, the "belly button" operation, intended to view the female reproductive organs, such as fallopian tubes and ovaries. Ovaries which, if properly premedicated with Serophene, could release multiple ova, eggs capable of being fertilized. *Her* ova, God in Heaven, *his* testis. Test-tube babies. It was positively monstrous!

His knees felt like buckling, but he wouldn't allow it. Hold on, for Christ's sake! Another autobot could arrive at any moment! His breathing grew labored as Maks still fumbled from one pocket to another.

Dunston's peripheral vision was almost completely gone. "Know what's waiting at home for you, Christine?" he asked. "Your own bed. You'd like that, wouldn't you?"

"I want to sleep with Maks." She slowly lifted her face and stared at him. "What's your name?"

Christ, he thought, what spunk! Here, the world was on the verge of collapsing around them, and she was carrying on polite conversation! "Chad. You're one helluva brave kid, Christine. Don't worry, you're safe with me," he said, as much for his own reassurance as hers. God, where *was* everything? What was taking Maks so long? "It's okay, I'll protect you." He wondered if he was up to it.

"That's all right. They come mostly in the dark."

"Who?" he wheezed.

"The black things on wheels."

He was fading fast. He prayed Maks could locate the lens.

"But you fooled them, didn't you?"

She beamed. "Yeah. I can hide real fast."

"Chad! Is this it?" She held up a tissue paper-covered oval.

"Yeah . . . Take the paper off. Don't smudge it." He shook his head, his vision gone completely diplopic.

"Chad," whispered Christine, clutching his neck. "I'm scared."

"Me too, kid."

"I knew you'd come."

"That so?"

She nodded. "I dreamed someone would rescue me."

As he hugged her, he felt an overwhelming compassion, and a love almost as great as he felt for her sister.

"Hold tight, sweetheart. Whatever happens, stick with me." His double vision made eyesight almost impossible. Fortunately, the laser beam was a bright, sapphire blue.

"Chad, please!" Maks pleaded. "What do I do now?"

"I . . . Help me with this."

As his lightheadedness grew more profound, he pressed against the workstation with all his might, directing Maks to help him. Under their combined efforts, it grudgingly gave way, sliding in the direction he indicated. With the little strength he had left, he helped her line it up with the resurfaced window.

He desperately needed time, but he doubted if he had thirty seconds. His memory had grown as fuzzy as his vision. He was a marathon runner, hitting the wall. Exhausted and panting, he struggled to recall what Merlin had told him. He sensed Maks growing frantic.

"Chad, hang on! What're we going to do next?"

"We're gonna blast a hole through that wall, that's what. Soon as it goes, we haul ass outa here. Not high . . . Jus' jump."

"Are you crazy? What about Christine?"

"Dammit, do what I tell you! She's safe with me! You're gonna work the lens. Just get ready." His vision was blackening as he turned to the child. "Chrissie, I'm countin' on you. Don't let go, okay?"

She gave a fearful nod.

Consciousness dwindling, he finally remembered what

Merlin said. "The lens, Maks. Hold it in fronta the laser beam!"

Uncertain, she looked at the lens, then at him. "How far in front? At what *angle?*" she said, nearing panic.

"Lemme have it . . . Stand outta the way, near the wall."

"But—"

"Move it!"

Maks was torn, wanting to comply, but terrified for Christine. Biting her lip in fear and trepidation, she finally moved back. Clutching Christine firmly, Dunston leaned across the table, knocking over God-knew-what—hopefully, not the mirror or diamond tip. Through the mantle of descending darkness, he could scarcely see, and what little he did make out rippled like a mirage. Christine's firm hug spurred him on. With adrenalin-stimulated clarity he concentrated on the laser beam, which now resembled an undulating wave. He held the lens as steadily as possible in his fingertips. The whole room was spinning. He concentrated, placing the lens in the laser's stream.

The intensely magnified beam bounced off the mirror, sending a colossal surge of energy toward the wall. Dunston was far too gone to see it, but not unaware of the sound. The entire wall next to Maks exploded with a horrific roar, sending pulverized cinder block and ash outward, creating an enormous opening toward the world beyond. Rocked by the blast, Christine screamed, but Dunston could scarcely hear her. All he could see was light, shadow, and smoke. Maks—where was Maks? He prayed she hadn't waited for him.

On the verge of unconsciousness, racked by pain and exhaustion, he summoned up his last ounce of strength to crush Christine to his chest. Holding her for dear life, he desperately staggered toward the light, praying his rubbery legs wouldn't give way. One final lunge carried him through the gap, into the brightness beyond. His last conscious thought was to protect Christine. Swiveling in midair, he held her atop him as he plummeted downward, back first.

Then the outdoor brightness turned to starry twinkling, flashbulbs popping against his retina, before darkness overtook him entirely.

Chapter Twenty-five

OUTSIDE THE CENTER, Sawyer's van had returned for the rendezvous fifteen minutes early, parking in an inconspicuous spot in the back. At the muffled sound of the first propane explosion, Donohue drew his gun and leapt from the van's front seat.

"What the hell was that?"

"Can't tell," said the driver, a man of few words. "It came from over there." He pointed in the direction of the blocked-over lab window a hundred yards away.

"Move it!"

The driver hit the gas, with Donohue furiously jogging alongside. The van swerved onto the service road and screeched to a halt below the lab. Its rear doors burst open, and everyone jumped out.

"Any idea where we are?" asked Donohue.

Sawyer pointed toward the cinder blocks. "That's where the lab window used to be. Why's it bricked over?"

"You expect me to know?"

"Isn't that smoke over there?"

"Screw the smoke!" Donohue shouted. "I'm going in!"

"In where?"

"Back through the service entrance."

Sawyer grabbed his arm. "Are you nuts? That's sui-
cidal!"

"I got a death wish, so what? They could use a hand!"

Just then, the lab wall erupted. Fragments of block and
concrete whizzed outward, several pinging off the van,
causing minor dents. The air was filled with dust and choking ash, quickly swept away by the wind. Everyone looked
up toward the huge opening where the glass window had
once been.

As the smoke was clearing, a nearly naked woman tumbled from the opening. She landed heavily on the grass one
story below but almost immediately jumped up, obviously
unhurt. It was Maks. For a moment she worriedly stared
up at the smoking hole, then began to scream unintelligibly
in the direction of the damage. Everyone gaped. From her
frantic mannerisms, the worst seemed to have happened.
As they continued to collectively gape in dumbstruck helplessness, another body literally hurtled through the opening.
Donohue's jaw dropped as his mind searched for appropriate words, finally settling on "holy shit." The figure was
falling right toward them. Before anyone had a chance to
scatter, the body slammed back-first onto the top of the van
with a loud, metal-bending thud.

Donohue, trained for chaos, was the first to react. He
clambered onto the front fender, peered over the top, and
found himself staring into the closed eyes of an unconscious Dunston.

"Jesus Christ," he said, holstering his gun. "It's déjà vu
all over."

"Who is it?" asked Merlin.

"It's him—Dunston."

"Miss Lassiter?" considerably shaken but uninjured, ran
toward them at a furious clip. "For God's sake, help him!"

Concentrating as he was on the physician's face, Donohue hadn't noticed what Dunston was clutching. At the
sound of her sister's voice, Christine stirred. Seeing a flash

of movement, Donohue jumped off the fender in fright, not knowing if that unkempt . . . *thing* . . . were animal or extraterrestrial.

Christine, who'd been whimpering softly, stopped sobbing long enough to find her voice. "Maks?"

Maks went agog. Dear God, she thought. She stopped running, feeling limp. She so profoundly wanted to believe that Chad succeeded, that she was unable to. While nearly everyone was staring dumbly at Maks, as if the action had been freeze-framed, Cheryl found a smock and tied it around her friend's shoulders, like a cape. Maks' lips visibly trembled. Paralyzed by joy and disbelief, she tried to speak but couldn't.

"Miss Lassiter?" Sawyer said.

Thus prompted, the name Maks never truly thought she'd say again softly ushered from her throat. "Chrissie?"

"Up here," came the tiny reply.

"Christine!" Maks shrieked.

Momentarily forgetting about Dunston, she ran to the van's opened rear doors and vaulted over the fender onto the cargo floor. She put both hands on the roof and tried to pull herself up, but she didn't have the strength. In ashen panic, she looked around for something to stand on.

"Gimme a hand, Victor," said Merlin.

They interlaced fingers and palms, creating a step for her. Nearing hysteria, Maks trilled something incomprehensible as she stepped onto their joined hands. She regrasped the van's top, and they carefully hoisted her up until, her waist coming level with the roof, she was able to swing her legs up and over. Going onto all fours, her eyes linked with those of her sister.

Still nestled in Dunston's protective grasp, Christine was looking back over her shoulder. His body had taken the full impact, protecting her from injury. For a moment, the two sisters simply gazed at one another with nearly identical expressions of longing, grief, and torment. The full light of day only enhanced the emotions they'd barely savored in the Center. The reality of reunion was too much for a still incredulous Maks. Overwhelmed, the dam broke. The tears she'd tried to hold back now liberally gushed forth. Sobbing uncontrollably, she crawled forward on hands and knees.

"Who the hell is Christine?" asked Donohue.

"Her dead younger sister," said Cheryl.

Donohue contemplated the reply, then shook his head. "You broads are all alike. I need a decoder ring to understand what you're saying."

Maks pried her sister free from Dunston's encircling arms, still oblivious to his presence. Christine, now crying in earnest, threw her arms around Maks' neck. They hugged each other tight in tearful, joyous reunion. They rocked ever so slightly from side to side, and Maks caressed her sister's damp and matted hair. "Oh baby, baby, baby."

Meanwhile, Merlin had managed to scale the van's roof by climbing up the front. He reached for Dunston's neck and was almost immediately reassured by the steady throb of a carotid pulse. Despite the massive dent in the sheet metal roof, Merlin spotted no blood or obviously broken bones.

"Radio for an ambulance," he called.

"How's he look?" asked Sawyer.

"Like Tyson worked him over. But he's breathing." He looked at Dunston and shook his head. "Luckiest sonofabitch I ever knew. Twice in three weeks, who'd a guessed it? Must be trying for some sort of record."

Her sobs reduced to sniffles, Maks eased out of her elated embrace and gazed adoringly at her sister. Christine still wept. But soon, drinking in the warm, affectionate look on her sister's face, Christine's crying lessened to a throaty, spasmodic quake. Maks lovingly wiped away the tear-stained grime and smiled, shaking her head from side to side, not knowing what to say. There were so many questions, she didn't know where to begin. She thought back to that awful day she'd brought Christine to the Center. She tried that as a conversational starting point, but she could get only as far as, "How . . . ?"

Mind elsewhere, Christine looked over her shoulder. "Chad saved me."

Chad . . . Dear God, Chad! She'd been so consumed by the realization Christine was alive that she'd been incapable of another thought. Panic returned when her gaze ran the length of Dunston's prostrate form. Overcome by fear and guilt, she held her sister by the waist and quickly crawled to Dunston's side.

"Somebody call an ambulance!" she screamed.

"On its way, Miss Lassiter."

"Is Chad dead?" asked Christine.

The tears flowed again, and Maks' hand flew to her mouth. Trembling, she reached out to touch his cheek.

"He's alive," Merlin told her. "Just down for the count. Took some wallop."

"Can't we get him off of here?"

"Better wait for the EMTs. He could've fractured something."

"Oh no," she said, her voice a quavering whisper.

Merlin carefully patted Dunston's pockets. Unzipping one, he found the protective baggies. He lifted them up and closely inspected the floppies. "What'dya know, McKitrick. I think he hit paydirt." He handed the diskettes to her. "How's that grab you?"

"Could be," she said. "We won't know until we get back to Upton."

"Do you know Chad, Maks?" asked Christine.

She pulled her sister into another embrace, as much to hold her again as to dispel her mounting emotions chill. "Yes, baby, I do."

Christine watched the flow of her sister's tears. "I bet you love him."

"Very, very much."

There was the wail of a siren in the distance. It started to rain.

Epilogue

IN A CORNER of the ICU, the small group kept a vigil at Dunston's bedside. Christine was in the bed next to him, holding her sister's hand atop the side rail. Since arriving at the hospital, she'd been bathed, fed, and examined, both physically and psychiatrically. A staff gynecologist confirmed that she had, indeed, undergone a laparoscopy. But a pelvic ultrasound revealed that her internal organs were intact and sonographically quite normal. After spending more than an hour with Christine, a child psychologist told Maks that her sister would likely have night terrors, but they'd eventually pass. Ongoing play-type psychotherapy was advisable for the immediate future. Everything considered, however, she pronounced Christine an astonishingly resilient, resourceful child who should suffer no indelible emotional scars.

After her testing was over, Christine, who'd said virtually nothing for half a year, kept up a cheerful, non-stop banter. Maks absorbed every word, saying little, relishing the sounds she thought had been denied her forever. Every few moments she cast a fretful glance at an unconscious Dunston. She was amazed that Christine looked so robust and had even grown a half inch in height. No one was entirely clear how the drugged child had escaped her captors after surgery, but it was apparent that the hidden lair she'd managed to construct was a base for nocturnal forays into the nearby kitchen, which she'd skillfully, liberally looted.

Dunston, similarly, appeared to have come through well. Donohue insisted he must have had training as an acrobat. There were no broken bones, no internal bleeding; only a nasty concussion and the after-effects of the as-yet unidentified drug. They could only speculate how long it would take to completely wear off.

At the Center, the fire had been completely extinguished. A SWAT team, which had rushed in poorly prepared and with a rather cavalier attitude, had disabled the remaining autobots, but suffered two casualties in the process. Weiman's severely burned body was found at the foot of a scorched operating table. In the lab, shattered glass receptacles and unrecognizable fetal tissue were all that remained of the only life Weiman had ever been able to conceive.

Once the Center was secured, Cheryl divided her time between its computer center and her own computers at Upton, enjoying the luxury of a government car and driver. The process had consumed her entire day, but the information she gleaned was invaluable, telling all. She reviewed her findings with Sawyer, who in turn informed his own boss and all those on the "need to know" list.

Precisely at seven, Dunston groaned. Everyone got up at once and hovered over the bedrails. But he didn't budge, and his stentorous breathing resumed. A tan though aged nurse, looking like a sun-dried tomato in a white pants suit, lazily took his pulse and walked away.

"He'll come around," said Merlin. "Guy's hard as nails."

Maks simply stared at him, smiling good naturedly.

Dunston's lids flickered. He tried to raise his head, but it fell back heavily against the pillow. He grimaced, caught his breath, and slowly opened his eyes. He blinked, trying to focus. "Maks?" he rasped. "You okay?"

She sought his hand and squeezed. "Yep. A little high jump, just like you said. But how do *you* feel?"

"Like I got hit by a truck."

Those standing nearby shared a heartfelt laugh.

"I say something funny?"

"You *were* hit by a truck. Actually, it was the other way around."

"What're you talking about?"

Merlin and Maks shared the explanation. Dunston's face had a no-way expression, believing he was being put on, until he noticed everyone nodding in unison.

"Unreal," he said. "First a patrol car, then a van. Maybe I went into the wrong field. How was my form?"

"Considering the degree of difficulty, the judges awarded it nine-sevens across the board."

"Room for improvement, huh?" The flood of memories returned in a mental rush. "Jesus, what about—"

"Hi, Chad."

He turned to his right, squinting through the side rails. Then he beamed. "Christine! How're you feeling, kid?"

"Good."

He looked at Maks, lowering his voice. "Is she all right?"

"Perfect. Who wouldn't be, after riding the world's only human airbag?"

He felt immense relief and chest-swelling pride. "We actually pulled it off, huh?"

Tears welled up in Maks' eyes. She leaned over and hugged him. "There are no words, Chad. You have no idea. To have you both back, at the same time? This is the happiest day in my life. I can't possibly thank you enough for—"

"Oh," Cheryl interrupted, "I'm sure you'll think of something."

Maks looked at her and grinned. "I can't imagine what you're thinking."

"Wait, *wait*," said Dunston. "What about the fire? The patients? *Jesus*, if I caused—"

"Ease up, Doc," said Merlin. "The fire's out, all the patients are fine. We know all about Dr. Weiman. And *we* control the Center now."

His look of incredulity faded. "This is really hard to digest." He put his hands behind his head and looked upward in reflection. "You know, there were moments when I thought I screwed up the whole thing. And destroyed myself in the process. But for us to actually get out of there alive," he said, turning to gaze at Christine, "with this gorgeous kid as a perk? Unbelievable." He paused and looked at Maks.

"Yeah," Maks smiled. "Unbelievable."